THE
TRACKING
HEART

MELISSA CROGHAN

Grateful acknowledgement is made for permission to reprint excerpts from *Bears, a Brief History*, by Bernd Brunner.
Published by Yale University Press, New Haven and London

Book cover oil painting by Melissa Croghan, Book cover design and photo by Robert Kalmbach

The Nepaug Press
Contact publisher at negaugpress@comcast.net
www.trackingheart.com

Printed in the United States of America
ISBN 978-0-9847497-0-6 (trade paperback)
ISBN-10: 0984749705

Library of Congress Cataloguing-in-Publication Data 2010910429

West Simsbury, CT

1.mystery –fiction 2. Bears – fiction 3. State parks – fiction 4. Thriller – fiction 5. Classic love story – fiction 6. Nature – fiction 7. Wilderness – fiction 8. Suspense – fiction 9. Brothers – fiction 10. Small town - fiction

Praise for The Tracking Heart

A many-layered story of lost loves and covered-up crimes…. Park ranger Callie Major doesn't expect to encounter someone from her past when she comes across an illicit campsite, but the camp's resident is Newton Denman, Callie's one-time best friend.

As the narrative moves between the two characters, more is revealed about why Newton is on the run—he's the primary suspect in a murder he had nothing to do with—and why Callie returned to the mountain where she lived as a young child. The book moves back and forth between the characters in the park and those in Callie and Newton's former hometown, including Newton's mother and brothers, and Pete Myrick, the police officer investigating the murder, who has his own history with Callie. Multiple plotlines converge in this complex, satisfying nature story.

– The Kirkus Review

Melissa Croghan writes with grace and ease about her vivid cast of complicated characters and the result is a morally complex and deeply suspenseful novel. My first impulse on finishing The Tracking Heart was to set out in search of Callie and Newton and especially the bear. A splendid debut.

– Margot Livesey, bestselling New York Times novelist of Eva Moves the Furniture and The Flight of Gemma Hardy

The Tracking Heart draws you in with its unanswered questions, its aura of mystery and danger and threat, not to mention its straightforward narrative verve. What keeps the reader turning the pages, though, are the layered relationships, the love and longing, reversal and betrayal, all writ large against the backdrop of Pennsylvania's mountain wilderness. It's a story of family and community and the strains we often unthinkingly place upon them both, and it's also a love story that manages to be both contemporary and timeless.

– David Maine, bestselling New York Times novelist of
The Preservationist and *Fallen*

For John, my father, in dedication to his work at the CCC creating America's first National Parks, and for Eileen, my mother, for making me tramp into the wilderness, instilling in me first knowledge of and love for the great outdoors

Acknowledgements

I give great thanks to the patient early readers of this book Michael Malone, Andy Levy, and Wendy Vardaman. I also appreciate the sharp eyes of Ann Greene and Kate Rizzo, my middle draft readers. I am deeply thankful to my editor and many other readers and copy editors, including Julie Rodriguez and especially Heather Kalmbach, for her thoroughness.

I am forever in debt to the article about the mammoth black bear in *The Philadelphia Inquirer* that sent me on this great adventure, and to Shoes from Unionville, whose generous spirit and distinctive name provided me with the inspiration for old Spoons, not to mention his love of fly fishing that would turn up in Newton. As for the content on feldspar mines and other features of the Pennsylvania mountains, any errors beyond fictional liberties taken in some parts of the novel are all mine.

I would not have been able to write this book without having dozens of conversations beforehand and along the way with Hubert and many other remarkable hunters from Pennsylvania and Michigan. I heartily thank the Armory at the University of Arizona for giving me, an unlikely candidate, special permission to learn how to handle a rifle and pistol, and to prove myself a capable markswoman.

I must thank the English Department at the University of Pennsylvania for allowing me to get down a first draft of this book when I was supposed to be writing a doctoral thesis. I will not forget a boy named Nature, a young hunter who was the first incarnation of Newton. I cannot thank Rob enough for his invaluable support, and Anthea who gave me distraction from the struggles of birthing this book.

I am profoundly grateful to Tim for his belief in this book, not to mention the unforgettable camping trip with Newtonesque car breakdowns and bear scat sightings in the Grand Canyon of Pennsylvania.

THE
TRACKING HEART

Part One

Unlike other animals the bear does not gather and store food but rather enigmatically disappears for a time – rather like a tree that sheds its leaves and seems to die, only to flourish again in the spring.

from <u>Bears</u>, *a brief history*, Bernd Brunner

Chapter ONE

She parked her Jeep and started up the old cart road. Her coat was thin, but Callie Major didn't mind the cold. She preferred it, really. It was a very pretty thrift shop coat, long and green. The sweep of it comforted her. Out from under a lambswool hat her dark hair fell loose down her back. It was early evening, the sky glimmered briefly, and in what must have been a trick of light her hair gave off sparks as she walked.

Less than an hour later, she left the cart road and took a trail up the mountain. Callie found what she was looking for, a circle of pitch pines that locked arms. She studied each tree, then chose one. She came to this place when she needed most to forget the things that had happened before she took this job at the State Park.

A pitch pine is not an easy tree to climb but Callie knew how to get good hand and footholds. It would have surprised her if someone pointed out that it was odd behavior to climb trees at night, in the dead of winter. There was no moon on the rise, no horizon line. The sky had turned a clotted white. Callie found herself a seat in a v-wedge of branches, and was scanning the woods as if someone might appear any second. She had a good lookout.

Chapter TWO

Three days on Grandmother Mountain and Newton Denman had lost the bear's tracks. This was August in the Pennsylvania Alleghenies, the third hot day in a row. Staring down at the soil, Newton noticed some moss pink and maidenhead fern. A greener area ahead, he thought. This cheered him, and he followed the trail of ancient ferns up a steep bend, pausing once to take off his red t-shirt and wrap it around his head to catch the sweat.

Around the bend where the trail stopped was a huge quarry unlike any he had seen. It was serpentine, its far boundaries curving to the right and behind where he stood. The mountain pool had walls of solid white rock and was filled with silver water, a tarnished silver in spots where the sun missed. He was standing near a bushy hemlock, about to sink down and rest when he heard a splash, something in the water coming from the right where the quarry turned. Now he could see. It was a woman swimming.

Newton stepped backwards, concealing himself in the hemlock fronds. He gasped, and caught himself before crying out. She had heavy black hair that hung over one shoulder. She raised her arms, about to surface-dive, and he saw her back arching forward, beautifully muscled, long and slender; then the flash of her bottom, the backs of her calves before she went under. She came up a good distance from where she dived. Newton scrambled out from under the hemlock boughs, the shirt around his head catching in the branches. He left it there and spread his fingers through his damp curly hair. She dove again, and then once more, each time staying under the water a little longer, like a dolphin sporting, or maybe a nymph who loved to play outdoors. When she floated on her back for a minute, kicking high with her toes, seeming to positively revel in the silver spray, he was sure who she was. The sun was shining right on her face, and although he was a hundred feet above, there was no mistaking the shape and action of Callie Major.

He grabbed the hemlock branch that overhung the quarry, and swung heavily down to a rocky ledge closer to the water. He tried to call out but his voice failed him. He could not form her name. Finally, in a hoarse cry: "Hey! Hello!" He snatched his shirt from the hemlock and waved it. She stopped splashing and seemed to be treading water, staring at him. Then she turned on her stomach and swam clean, long strokes away from him to the opposite side of the quarry. Newton couldn't decide whether to head around the huge perimeter which had no path that he could see, or to jump in the water with his clothes on and try to meet her on the other side. It hardly seemed possible it was Callie, not unless this was that mountain she used to talk about, the one where her great aunt lived, that old Indian lady she was going to visit one day. But if it was she, on this very mountain, he couldn't bear for her to vanish again, not after her disappearing act twenty years ago.

She was climbing ledges that went up like steps at the far side. "Wait! Please, please don't go!" Newton's shirt was clenched in his hand. He strained forward, toes at cliff's edge, his barrel-like torso nearly parallel to the water. "Callie!" He watched her, turning slowly to look at him a second time. It occurred to him that she might not recognize him, and even if she did would she want to see him? Newton was paralyzed with fear and longing as he saw her standing naked, waist thicker than he remembered, peach-hued breasts that he had never seen – did she sun herself all over in the privacy of this mountain quarry – collar bones that stood out, shoulders as straight as a clothes hanger.

On the other side of the quarry stood Callie. She was looking him over, now shaking her hair with a hand, wringing the water out, still staring as she stepped backwards, bare feet sure of every rock and pine needle cluster that lay on the ground. She had been here before; she knew the ground. She didn't take her eyes off of him until the pitch pine forest enclosed her.

Had it really been Callie? Maybe being charged with crimes you didn't commit makes a person delusional, Newton thought. Maybe he had imagined her splashing in this quarry. Newton began setting up camp at the edge of the quarry. For a moment the tree the bear had marked came back to him, the eerie, light shivering gash on the linden, and the way it smiled seductively but sharp toothed at the same time. It made him shiver to think of it. Miles from here, that tree was where he had started after the bear. But the tracks that led him up this mountain had vanished, and on top of that he had lost the woman he thought was Callie Major swimming in these waters.

He moved mechanically to prepare a fire and get something to eat. If he stopped moving, even for a second, he was convinced he would sit there, immobilized, staring out at the water, as he had most of the day. Oh he had tried to find her, spent three hours combing the scrubby vegetation and dwarfed forests nearby. Then sapped, he collapsed on a blanket at the edge of the pool. But night was coming, and he knew better than to set up camp in the dark. The temperature dropped quick in the mountains after the sun left, even in late August. Had to stay warm, had to eat. He would cook up the squirrel he took in an easy shot that afternoon.

He moved his gear away from the cleared area for a fire. Bait bag, knapsack, flashlight, sleeping bag, a few books spilling out of the knapsack. He was the only reader in his family and had not considered leaving home without a single paperback. Of the ones he'd brought, a slim volume on bears intrigued him most. He pulled it off the shelves of the Littlecomb Library and checked it out a couple of weeks earlier, a lifetime away it felt like. He stood reading for a few moments, and reluctantly set it down inside his tent and went to work gathering tinder.

"Newton?" He dropped the bundle of fire starters in his hands. Twigs, knots, dead pine branches scattered at his feet. The dark-haired woman picked up one of the pine boughs he had dropped, and handed it to him.

And was this Callie? For a minute, although they stood just two or three feet apart, Newton thought her less like herself than when he saw her hours earlier, kicking in the water. She was wearing a forest green uniform. A bunch of keys and a plastic card dangled from the metal buckle on her brown leather belt. Sticking out of the pocket on her breast was a small radio.

"You don't know me?" Her smile was guarded.

Nervously, he gathered up the fire starters. Newton felt that she was somehow disguised now, her hair bound up tightly at the back of her head, her round forearms just peeping out from the crisp, long sleeved shirt tucked into broad cuffed trousers. He liked the way she looked so important and proper in this uniform, but the insignia on her shoulder and the badge above her shirt pocket made him shift uncomfortably.

She put her hand to her belt and lifted the plastic card for him to see. "Want to read my identification?"

Newton pursed his lips, his mouth was dry. He stepped forward, his fingers touching hers for a second as he held the card and read: Callie Major, Preservation Ranger, Pitch Pine State Park, Nottingham County Parks and Recreation Department. He raised his eyes to hers.

She was no longer bold, her eyes shifted away, shy and unsure. She's jittery too, Newton realized. I bet she's happy to see me. He reached for her, pine branches falling from his arms and scraping past his face as he grabbed her by the shoulders.

"I know you. How couldn't I? Me, your old best, best friend."

Callie was stunned as he held her shoulders and exalted at their reunion. She wanted to cry with joy, for she never expected to see Newton Denman again. She was dissolving. I am weak as water, she thought, inhaling the waft of pine mingled with his sweat and sweet breath. But water is non-resistant, she reminded herself. And I need to resist. She felt herself stiffen.

"If you're done shaking me, I have a question. Newton, what are you doing here?"

This was not a query he could afford to answer. Two sticks of tinder spiked him in the neck as he released her. "How about you?" He dropped the branches all at once, and began to lay the fire. "Why are you on this mountain, you a cop or something?" He moved to reset the kindling he had stacked earlier. "Are you one of those guards who patrols the woods, arrests people for picking berries, feeding the bears –" He bit the inside of his cheek. Wrong subject.

He reached for a couple of small logs and leaned them tepee style over the kindling. Newton crouched, and lit the tinder. He stared at the first thin flame race along the back of a pine branch.

There was a furious crackling as the bony pine pieces burned, and then the sound of Callie's boot kicking dully at the ground. She was standing several feet off from him. Newton watched sparks fly up from the fire, get lost in the sky. He glanced over at her legs, the small calves slightly apart, their outline showing in the straight legged pants. He looked up at her. "Jesus Callie, *why* did you leave Littlecomb that way? Not a word to me; you and your aunt Teeny just up and left."

Callie stepped back from the fire.

Newton noticed she was trembling.

"We were not best, best friends at the time my aunt and I moved out of Littlecomb. We were not special to each other, we were not – anything," she trailed off.

To steady her emotions, Callie looked out over the quarry. With her eyes glued there, she asked, "Do you know where you are?"

"Outside of the State Park, right?"

"Sure, but still you're on state forest land. There's no long term camping here, not anywhere near the Pine Barrens. It's an old forest, not meant to be violated," Callie said with a touch of righteousness.

He was staring at her ankles again. She wondered if he simply couldn't look her in the face. "It's a wilderness area, I can see that," he muttered, shifting his gaze to the down timber at the woodedge.

"Yeah, it is," she said, referring to a standard Park policy that storm damage was not formally cleared away by the Forest Service. It was left to take care of itself.

"Guess I figured it was all right to do a little hunting in untended ground like this," Newton whispered.

Was that guilt she heard in his voice? Her skin prickled and she made an effort to shrug off that extra antennae she carried around, that pain in the butt sensitivity she often chose to ignore.

"Not through here." She waved her hand. "State Game lands are farther west."

"Right." His chest sagged and he shrugged his shoulders. "I thought I knew where I was, that is until I hit these twisted pine trees. No state park marked on my map." He rubbed the side of his mouth, not quite hiding the smile. "Of course I never carry a map. Just follow my nose, keep the stars in line. You should remember that. You were the one with the almanac."

She lifted her chin, a flicker of a grin. She had watched him bend over, enjoying the way his backside rose suddenly. He wore thin baggy pants, and she even noted his big knobby knees, the rounded bones swirling together like ampersands.

Still crouching, one knee on the ground in front of the fire, he said, "Yeah, I know I'm a good ways from Littlecomb." He got up and rummaged through his supply bags until he found the squirrel he'd shot earlier. "So what town are we near?"

"Closest place is Tuscatanning, down in the valley," she paused. "You're sitting on the northern peak of Grandmother Mountain. It used to be the site of feldspar and chrome mines. See this quarry," she nodded at the rock formations shouldering the bank to her right. "There must be fifteen more of these in the region. But none so nice as Blue Quarry." She nodded at the water before them. "Lots of quarries around here. Mine openings, too."

"Gottcha." Newton smiled. He was getting ready to skin the squirrel. "So I'm near Tuscatanning. Damn, I knew this mountain was familiar." He flashed a sideways glance, mischief in his eyes. "Birthplace of Callie Major, and home that Aunt Teeny hated and hauled her away from."

Callie had a flash of herself panting after her cousin Mary down the steep switchbacks of Grandmother Mountain and coming out on the fire road that led home. The two girls had been camping on the mountain top and though it was a mere overnight it was lovely to be coming home. The stacked stone chimney dwarfed the cabin, smoke touched the sky in wispy cutouts, and above all there was the smell of Winoshca's fresh preserves filling the air. The sharp, rich smell of blackberries gave way to a darker odor, one that Callie inhaled hungrily. It was the breath of a large animal she could not place and yet she identified with it, sensed it was there at the cabin – in spirit if nothing else – to warn her.

She and Mary put down their packs. There was a strange car parked out front.

"Don't go in," Mary said, her fear unmistakable. But it was too late. Callie ignored all warnings and ran for the cabin. She could not wait to try the blackberry jam, she could not wait to see Winoshca.

The ranger watched Newton handle the squirrel. She was touched by his frank memory of things she had told him twenty years ago. Had to be in the late seventies, she figured. It struck Callie that one kept friendships with a history the way a tree does the rings in its deepest center. No matter what new growth takes place the core ring, the old friendship persisted. It was an inner sanctum to be respected.

And did she respect what they had been through together? She wondered. Truth be told, she had tried to forget.

The squirrel was large with a soft white belly. Newton stretched the animal full length on a flat slab of rock and pierced the skin, blade up, careful not to damage the meat. Callie looked away. He's forgotten, she thought. Doesn't remember how I hate to see animals ripped into. She lowered her chin to her chest and stared out at the water's shifting colors.

The sun lowered behind the far pines. The pool was a deep silver, some blue threads.

Newton bustled around the fire, setting a cast iron pan over the makeshift grill. She heard the squirrel drop into the pan.

"Hungry?" Newton joined her, looking out over the water.

"Ummmm-no." She shaded her eyes against the brightening sun. Ten minutes, and it would be a stream of red across the water. "I have to get back. Got to check in before evening shift."

"You're not going to leave? You just got here."

"Oh Newton, one million years have passed since we saw each other. We can't act as if it's all the same as when we were twelve and thirteen. You have no idea what's going on now, with me." Callie heard her voice quaver. Two minutes with this near stranger and she was losing it. How pathetic was that? She did not want to look at him. Oh yes, he did have charming ways. Sure he used to say he wasn't like his brothers, the lady-killers, and it was true he wasn't just like them, but didn't he have those carnivorous eyes? Denman eyes.

The beeper on her radio went off. Callie walked to the edge of the woods to answer it. Newton went over to the fire and shook the squirrel in the pan.

When she came back to the fire, radio still in her hand, Callie fired some questions at him. Why was he here? How long did he think he could camp out in a State Park and get away with it? How was he going to survive; did he plan to live off dead squirrels?

He answered her last query. "I'm a fair woodsman, I doubt I'll starve."

She smiled.

"Okay, I'm not surviving entirely on game I get myself. I stop off pretty regular at wayside stores to pick up the stuff I need."

Callie cast her eye over the campsite. "You're pretty civilized, I'll give you that."

"What do you mean?"

"Those." She walked over to the books lying next to his sleeping roll. Ignoring *The Deerslayer* by James Fenimore Cooper, she opened an anthology of American poetry. "Anne Bradstreet; Philip Freneu," she read. "I never heard of them." Callie picked up where she left off in her survey of his camp. "What a mess of stuff you have. Looks like you plan on staying a year."

He didn't answer.

"Why don't you move your gear to the State Game lands? Plenty of legal fishing there."

Staying a year, he thought. Lord, I hope not. He swallowed hard, hating himself for covering up the real reasons for this hunting holiday. Newton forced a smile. "I haven't fished much in a long time."

"You used to carve your own fishing rods."

"I used to like to carve."

"You were always catching those Rainbow Trout."

"The rivers in these parts are so full of them they might as well be native trout," Newton said. "Strong teeth, those fish have, and their scales are so fine, smooth to the touch."

Newton noticed that Callie had lost interest.

She crossed her arms. "Tuscatanning is your closest place to get provisions. If a park official should see you, I don't know; anyone I work with could tell in a shot that you were up mountain, hunting. That's for sure. You ought to clear out."

He nodded complacently, and saw that she took this as an encouraging sign.

"Good thing, too. Around here, fall doesn't stick long. It's nice one day – like now – and next thing you know winter jumps on your back." Callie snapped her fingers. "I wouldn't try testing your endurance skills against Old Grandmother's winters."

"I've got snowshoes," he said lightly, wondering if she meant to further insult his abilities to survive in a wilderness.

"You're going to stay?"

Newton studied her closely. "Are you going to let on about me to your work buddies?"

She had turned to the quarry, on their left. "It's hard living on the mountain in winter. Even in town. The snow covers everything, a body can get lost. The roadmaster can't keep up. He tries, though. He always talks about how he's going to keep Route 32 clean, the one that runs out of town, past the park campgrounds."

Newton thought of his yellow truck hidden in the deer thicket just off the interstate, probably not much farther than these campgrounds she was talking about. Maybe he should move it deeper into the woods.

Callie glanced around for her radio. She must have put it down somewhere.

"Check out the mist." He pointed at the quarry.

"The sun's giving up her best, right this second," she said. Again, the two of them gravitated to the cliff edge. She was exuberant. Newton watched her shoulders lift in the light.

The air was cooler than the water, and there was a fine vapor at the quarry surface, now rising slowly in slender pillars. Had she pointed to a Roman hill fort Newton would be no less enthralled than he was now, drawn into her excitement over this phenomenon of the mist at Blue Quarry.

"There!" She said triumphantly. "Here comes the red heat." The columns of mist trembled into myriad crimson dimensions. Callie exhaled loudly. "I bet the Greeks played their first Olympic games near a pool of water like this, and they danced at the end of the day – they weren't so spartan as some people think – they danced, or leapt into the water, into a red mist just like this one."

"We could do that, me and you," Newton said, without thinking. "Dance. Dive in the water, I'll be Greek, and you –" He flushed. What in the world had induced him to suggest play-acting; this wasn't him, was it?

When he looked at Callie he saw she was shaken.

Across the quarry, the prisms began to shatter one by one as the sun moved westward and then vanished into a dark mass of pines.

They stood in the gray light until a lift of wind sent a mild chill down their backs. Callie spoke. "Your food's probably burnt."

Newton jumped to the fire. He held out the pan. "Done to perfection. Kind of crispy, but it'll be delicious."

"Looks awful," Callie teased. She reached for her backpack.

Newton found a knife to ply the squirrel from the pan. "It'll taste better than spring lamb. That's what all the old hunters say about fried squirrel."

"That's what your daddy says about it, I bet. Or your brothers. All your teachers." She was not teasing now.

It struck Newton that she didn't know his father was dead. Neither of them had broken into talk of past times, or of their lives in between then and now.

"I'm heading off. My Jeep's down this way," she gestured to an impossible looking pass in the woods behind Newton's camp. He set the frying pan down at the edge of the fire and went for her radio lying on top of his books.

"You might need this." As he held it up they both smiled, he remembering her forgetfulness, and she remembering that he knew.

Newton handed her the radio. "It wasn't just nothing between us, Callie. It wasn't."

She fumbled for her wide brimmed Ranger's hat, jerking it out of her pack so violently that a few items fell out, a collapsible metal cup, a plastic bag of herbs, and a soprano recorder. She gathered up the bag and the cup, and he the instrument. When she reached for it Newton held it at bay.

"You used to play this at our treefort." Playfully, he fretted the recorder, his lips not touching the mouthpiece but singing instead: Green grow the rushes O."

Feeling foolish and wrong Newton dropped his head, and handed her the wooden instrument.

He walked after her as she stepped into the grove beyond the clearing. She turned, putting on her hat. "I used to think I hated you."

Newton felt dizzy. He started walking sideways into the grove, not sure of his footing.

"Newton!"

He swung around.

"You're about to walk into a mine shaft." She was a few steps ahead of him.

He jumped back, feeling alert again. "Where are you?" he called, watching her disappear into a thicket.

"Watch where you walk at night." Her voice sounded yards off, somewhere down the steep hill.

"You didn't let me fall into the pit, did you? You couldn't do it!" he bellowed.

Chapter THREE

To be inside the Big Springs Lounge was like being inside a great bear's stomach. This was the observation of Spoons Denman, a regular at the bar. The air was close and the inmates in the Lounge sometimes complained about this. Still, you could take your ease. It was dark and warm, and it felt safe. Spoons didn't mind having been swallowed. Just like him, the other fellows there were a little chewed up.

Outside the Lounge it was a bright September afternoon. The sky wore a coat of cobalt blue. In the parking lot Trooper Pete Myrick sat in his car thoughtfully eating a corn muffin he had stashed in the glove compartment the day before. He made a decision to leave his gun behind when he opened the door of his Crown Imperial. All he wanted to do was talk to old Mr. Denman. Leaving the weapon or bringing it along, it hardly mattered to the people of Littlecomb, Pennsylvania. Either way, Pete was not viewed fondly by them. He had left town years ago, and after his return even the guys he grew up with felt oddly uncomfortable around him. It wasn't just that he had become a state trooper. There was a sadness to Pete, an inwardness that invited people to turn away.

The men of the Lounge in Littlecomb sat on their stools with feet tucked this way, legs wrapped so, as if each of them was homesteading a beloved site. Closest to the fireplace sat George and at his elbow was his brother Nat who spoke up when he saw Trooper Pete Myrick walking over.

"Is this the day we can expect an arrest?"

"Sorry to disappoint," said George, "but Pete is, how did you say: still building your case?"

Ignoring them, Pete pulled a stool up next to Spoons Denman, grandfather to the missing, accused man, Newton Denman.

"You seen the Gazette?" Nat said to the men at the bar. "The story says Newton is hiding out somewhere up the Seven Sisters." This was a mountain range east of Littlecomb. Pete edged over to the older Mr. Denman, who turned all of a piece to greet the police officer. Spoons' back had calcified, and this stiff as a broomstick motion was the best he could do.

"This new dog I got doesn't race off and leave me. He holds to a trail, too."

"I heard you were trying a slow-track dog these days."

"Did you know that big blond man Myrick is after my grandson?"

"That's me, Spoons." Pete had to smile. "I'd like to talk with you about the night the school burned down, and Theresa Waters died."

The old man tipped his torso away from the bar. "Newton is a good boy, but he's a hunter gone wrong."

"Tell me."

"He loved her, and that's when he started lying to himself."

"Her?" Pete tried to remain calm. He had an awful feeling he knew who the loved one was, but he wanted to hear it from Spoons."

"In the name of the Lord in this fall of – what the blame year is this anyway?"

"It's moving along towards the millennium, Spoons. This is 1996."

"In the year of the Lord, I do mean *her*. That Seneca lady. Irish, too. Beautiful lady." His small mouth which resembled a pale daisy several times crushed, puckered and then closed up. Pete waited.

A moment passed and Pete got up. Spoons was dozing off at the bar. He began to snore, his chin sinking into his hand and his white hair blowing straight up.

Six days earlier, George and Nat were in their regular seats at the Lounge. It was nowhere near closing but already Natty knew he and George had overdone it. He hauled his older brother out of conversation with Gib Setter, who kept right on talking just as if George were still sitting next to him at the bar. The two Denmans swung out of the Lounge, climbed into George's Ford pick-up and started for home to grab their hunting gear and head for Roundtop Pike. Pulling into the side yard, George said, "Now wait a minute, there, Natty. I think we forgot something."

"What's that?" Nat, who had gotten out of the car, rocked forward on the lawn.

George laughed. "We forgot the road beers."

Nat turned in a half-circle, as if pondering this. "We could pick 'em up on our way out of town. Let's get the gear in the car first."

Inside the house Newton had crawled under the covers. He knew it was early to turn in, but he was always tired lately. He was almost asleep when he heard his older brothers bang in the door. They were back outside in a short time. Newton rolled over once and opened the window at his bedside. Two tall forms weaved down the front walk, packs and sleeping bags slung over their shoulders. There was Nat, the brim of his hunting cap touching his nose. Wiry, and fidgeting as usual, he was shorter than George only by an inch or two, but he looked much smaller. It was hard to miss George's big chest and curly hair, even in the dark. Newton sighed when he saw, too, that his brother had taken his jacket. He pulled his head in the window. All drunked up, he thought absently. He dropped off to sleep.

George started to put the key in the ignition. It wouldn't fit. Nat was clutching his sides it was so funny. "You know what we done here, big brother? We climbed into the wrong truck."

George was slow to grasp their mistake. "How'd we get here?"

"It was parked right out front. Close to the house. We climbed in, that's all. I never saw anything so funny as that fool look on your face just now. Key wouldn't fit, hunnhh?" Natty's eyes watered. "Hey, what are you doing? Ol' Newt won't like this one bit, George. We better take the Ford."

George had jumped out of the truck and was rummaging through a pile of rusted traps behind the wooden slats under the house. He returned, keys in hand. "I've seen Newt hide it there." As he started the engine, he said, "Don't get riled, we aren't gonna steal his truck for the weekend, just use it for a quick run up to the Lounge to get beer. I always did like riding in Newton's yellow Chevy." He grinned at Nat, and turned onto High Street.

"Your mind's made up I see," said Nat. He shrugged. "Guess the good boy's home keeping Ma company. Say, was Ma home? I didn't see Spoons either."

"Gran'pa's asleep by now," George said. "I don't think Ma was home."

"It doesn't matter. Newt doesn't need the truck. He's such a sit-at-home these days."

"He's a good brother," said George, waxing melodramatic. "He's about the sweetest kid."

"He's thirty-five," Nat reminded him.

"Sweetest kid brother a man could have."

"I'm your brother, too."

George snorted and reached over to slap Nat on the back. The truck veered off onto the shoulder, and a little ways into the ditch in front of the Littlecomb Elementary School. It stuttered to a halt. George tried to start it ferociously. After four failed attempts Nat shouted at him, "Hey, quit. I think you flooded it."

George glared at the ignition.

Nat opened the door. "Give it ten."

George followed Nat into the schoolyard. Walking a little unsteadily, he pointed at the window of a classroom a few yards off. "That's Miss Block's first grade room. Bitchety Block, that's what she was, wish I'd said it to her face when I was just a pup." He pursed his lips.

Nat was laughing. "She wasn't a soft teacher, but I learned my numbers good in that class. Sometimes she was nice."

"That so?" George was leaning forward, straining to see in the classroom window. "She had me by the collar so many times I couldn't count."

"One, two, three, teacher and me," sang Nat in a low, comic voice. "She liked me. She did. We learned our numbers good."

George was sweating and took off Newton's jacket. He kicked at one of the rocks that lined the myrtle under the window. "She pinched me too." He was getting mad, but Nat didn't notice. "One day she came over to me so close I could smell her face powder, an inch thick it was. She pinched both my cheeks together and lifted me clear off the floor.

"'Featherhead, featherhead!' that's what she yelled in front of the whole class, my legs dangling off the floor." George stroked his cheek as if it still hurt.

Nat smiled, and picked up Newton's jacket off the ground. "You're pretty funny tonight, George. One and one is two," he started to do a little dance. "This is what she taught my class. She did! I remember it to this day. She took an umbrella and used it like, you know, a prop."

"Off the floor, I say." George's face was red. "Pinched my cheeks and picked me up right off the floor. Everyone laughed."

Nat whirled lightly in a circle. "And then, Miss Block, she tapped it in front of her and did some kind of jig thing," He waved an imaginary umbrella and did a sidestep, "One and one is two. Two and two is four –"

Nat stopped dancing. His brother was at one of the windows in the old building. The weights and pulleys groaned as George raised the unlocked window. "I always wanted to do this," he said. "Didn't know before I wanted to do it, but I know it now." His palms were on the window sill. He hoisted up on his arms.

"George?" Nat watched his brother disappearing inside the building. As he pulled himself through, the window slammed down on his sturdy hunting boot.

George howled. "Goddam school. Still biting me!"

"Say Georgie, are you okay?" Nat raised the window, glad to see it stick above his arms. "Now you come out. This is trouble. Let's get out of here. What's happened to Georgie?" He stopped mumbling as a car passed by on the road. Nat ducked. "Someone's going to see us here," he yelled hoarsely. "I'm not feeling too good. Hurry up."

Inside, George was whirling papers and sweeping books off of the teacher's desk. A few minutes later, and he had ripped every student exercise and poster from the walls, kicked half the desks over, and heaved several more across the room.

Across the street from the schoolhouse, Theresa Waters, who was walking Honey, her cockerpoo, heard the commotion. Honey heard it too. Her silky ears flew up and she yapped mightily.

Theresa stared at the truck and the figure in front of Littlecomb Elementary. It was dark, but she could make out a white and maybe navy or black striped jacket. "Why Honey, that's one of my former students. Newton Denman's been wearing that jacket around town since high school. And there's his truck. Now what on earth?" The sight of one of her students was of special interest to her for she had only just retired from teaching, and was apt to feel nostalgic lately.

For forty years she was the art teacher at the school, giving the Littlecomb boys and girls their only education in the laying down of tempera paints, the thick glue of it – great for painting the green haze of maples that hung on close to the town – and watercolors, too, perfect for the winter studies of blackened corn stalks against the faintly purple snow. Mrs. Waters was proud of her ability to share the subtleties of the Alleghenies with those untrained youthful eyes.

"Is that you, Newton?" she called, waving a stout arm.

Nat turned, realizing that a woman was calling out. He didn't want to appear suspicious. After all, his fool older brother had broken and entered a public institution. He waved, then felt his stomach surge in sickness. Those Steel Pike Slingers at the bar tonight were starting to hit him hard.

Theresa Waters picked up her dog. "Come on Honey, let's go over and see if everything's okay." Tall, moon faced, lithic in stature, Theresa held herself proudly despite her failing health. They say the diabetes is spreading, she thought, that my heart is freezing up on me. I don't believe it. I know for a fact my heart has always held me strong.

The diabetic neuropathy had affected her feet, she admitted that much. As she walked haltingly across the street – the dog licking her ear – Theresa smiled at the memory of her former student. Newton and that bright, lonely girl, Callie Major. He was wild about her. Why, she gave the boy artistic inspiration, she drew picture after picture of bears, and Newton, he drew picture after picture of Callie drawing the bears.

Honey wriggled out of her arms. Theresa was thrown off balance but this was nothing new to her. Small steps, she told herself. Take small steps, Theresa, and keep your eye on the road.

She'd already had two falls this year and was determined not to have it happen again. The recovery time had been slow, and she felt it was time she couldn't afford. Her young granddaughter whom she adored had come to live with her. Something else that made Theresa happy was that she had recently begun to paint in oils again. She had worked long hours all these years as a teacher, and it was time for her to return to her art. Her dream was to paint nursery rhymes, to illustrate in oils a beautifully bound, hand-stitched book.

If only she had some of those drawings she did five summers ago. It would have been great resource material for her nursery rhymes. She had drawn or painted every single day that summer, and even turned the sunroom upstairs into her personal studio. Too bad that hadn't worked out. Nearly every one of those paintings destroyed. She let herself mourn them for the briefest moment. She would make up for it though. Theresa had resolve.

When she got to the school building there was no one to be seen. "Yoo-hoo, Newton. Anybody home?" As she rounded the corner of the cafeteria, Theresa was struck on the head.

It happened too fast for her to see. Not a forceful blow, but it was enough to topple the art teacher. She became aware of Honey barking at her side. Stunned but not seriously injured, Theresa climbed to her feet. She was upset at the turn of events. Most horrible of all, she realized she was being followed.

A racket coming from the nearby classroom caught her attention. Theresa hobbled towards the commotion, with Honey at her heels. She murmured to her dog, then stuck her head in the open window.

"Help me. Someone please! What on earth?" Theresa blinked at the destruction wrought by George, whose back was turned to her as he ducked behind the coat closet. Later George would remember thinking: it is herself, Miss Block. Bitchety Block has come to get me in her classroom. He was so convinced it was she, that he called her by name. "Miss Block!"

But he would not show his face. Then he got confused. Was Miss Block still alive? He couldn't remember whether maybe she had died some five years back. Had she risen from the dead, or maybe just driven over from the Dewey Garden Retirement Home outside Littlecomb?

He looked down at his boots and wondered at the clammy, cold hate he felt.

A minute later a loud boom sounded in his ears, and he thought that there must have been an explosion down at the steel mill where he worked. He turned to the window. The ghost of Miss Block, or whoever it was, had disappeared.

The rage was gone. But he was more clammy than ever. From outside came the sound of a dog barking. It was an odd, almost whispering voice.

There were footsteps out the window. George listened.

"Sweetheart, come here."

George froze at the voice. Was someone calling a dog or a person?

"Come here sweetheart," said the bassoon deep voice. "Don't run. You've fallen once already."

George stayed hidden behind the coat closet. Outside there was a scuffle, and another boom, or was it a bang? All was quiet. Long minutes passed before he moved. There was not a sound. Whoever it was had gone away. George stepped between the overturned desks, heaps of torn school papers, primers, and alphabet posters. He leaned against Miss Block's somber brown desk. "Moldy old twit," he said, fishing in his pocket for a match. His hand shook as he lit the cigarette. He inhaled deeply, lost his balance and dropped the match. George caught himself on the ledge at the front of the big desk. He turned dizzily to see a small flame starting up where the match had fallen. His reactions were slow. For a half-minute he simply stared at the crinkling papers and shrinking primers. Huge magic-markered numbers glittered on the math posters, 1, 2, 3 coming alive in the flame. They danced like the cartoon numbers on Sesame Street.

George steadied himself and then jumped at the fire to stomp it out. But the flame leapt at his pant leg and he had to beat it out with the small woven rug in front of the teacher's desk. The fire spread fast. Now a quarter of the room was in flames. George leapt across the room, fumbled several seconds with the window sash and dove out the window.

He ran to the truck, finding Nat head down between his legs on the passenger side of the front seat. He was retching what must have been the accumulation of beer and Steel Pike Slingers, a drink that was five parts liquor to one part fruit juice.

"Oh for God's sake," George said. He handed his brother a plastic grocery bag from under the seat.

Parking in front of his mother's house, George half-hauled Nat out of Newton's truck and across the yard. "Hold on. I have to put Newton's key back."

"Whazzit?" Nat felt awful. He looked at the house, and thought he saw someone staring out the window at them.

His older brother slapped him on the back. "Let's move it. It's time to go hunting."

Callie

Callie Major sat up with a start. She was at home in her apartment in Tuscatanning with her cat, Iris, in her lap. What was she doing up so late? She must have dozed off. No, not quite, she realized. She stroked Iris' cool fur. *I wasn't dreaming, but reliving something familiar.* The cat jumped down, and Callie sat very still with the image of herself crunching through snowfall and then climbing a pitch pine. She navigated the close sharp branches and managed to find herself a seat high up in the tree. After a while it dawned on her that she had been sitting somewhat squashed in a v-wedge of branches, waiting for someone or something. And there it was, a shaggy creature, a bear walking towards her on those very humanlike feet it has, walking on its metatarsals just as we do, Callie noted. The bear from "Rose Red and Snow White," the bear from "Beauty and the Beast." *Downright juvenile of me,* she thought, but just the same she felt pure excitement leap up in her bones.

The bear stopped a few yards short of the tree and dropped down on all fours. Almost at once, the snow shower ended and a pale moon shone down on its glossy fur. Its coat rippled once and Callie had a sense of the animal's skin underneath, skin that most deemed thick, but Callie knew otherwise. She knew instinctively that the living skin of a bear was every bit as sensitive as her own eyes. At that moment, the moonlight caught the bear's great head and fur-lined eye and snout. Callie was frightened, remembering that black bears climb trees easily.

Oh dear God, don't climb, she thought. Then, with unwarranted boldness: *don't raise your hackles at me, don't harm me.* Then Callie's own skin began to prickle with the knowledge that the bear heard her, and would not climb up and maul her. Callie's own skin was on fire as she understood that the bear's skin was like a thousand human eyes, and that these eyes held the ranger's future.

And most disturbing of all to Callie was that she knew she was configuring that which had not yet happened.

Chapter FOUR

Two hours after Nat and George left the house, State Trooper Pete Myrick knocked at Betty Denman's door. It was half past one in the morning.

"Theresa Waters is dead," he told her.

Betty Denman stared, disbelieving. "I heard fire engines."

"Yes. There's also been a fire. The Elementary School was burnt to the ground."

Betty motioned him inside. Pete nodded and took off his hat.

He had splendid hair, a high yellow color that complemented his face. People said his complexion resembled nothing so much as a newborn with mottling and skin as smooth as porcelain.

Pete bore an air of looking hopeful, yet conflicted. He wanted to feel compassion in his job but years on the force had taught him otherwise. He was conflicted over being in charge, though he had no choice since he was the only police officer assigned to Littlecomb, conflicted over having left Arizona in a hurry a very long time ago. Pete felt the conflicts started when he said goodbye to Littlecomb at age nineteen, and tried on a life out west in Arizona. He should have stayed there. He knew this now. He hated the damp, close hills of Littlecomb. Some days he felt as though there was mold growing right up his trunk. He remembered the light out west, the way the sand poured out of your shoes like gold. He still dreamed of standing on top of impossible mesas, arms uplifted as shooting stars wreathed the skies. Not that this had happened, but in Arizona, he felt, there was always the sense of the possible.

"Sorry to catch you all up in the middle of the night." His thumbs disappeared under his belly as he hooked them into his uniform belt.

"Sit down, Pete," said Betty, staring for a second at his hands.

"Flames licking at the windows, first one, then another window'd get lit, until every bit of that schoolhouse was in full blast color. That's what Mr. Waters said. He was over to the school looking for his wife. Said she'd been gone an awful long time walking their dog."

"Theresa gone?" Betty sucked in her breath sharply and reached for her cigarettes. "What is the meaning of this visit anyhow?"

Pete sat down at the kitchen table and spread his hands across his thighs. He glanced at Betty Denman's worried face, and now Newton, who had just come down the back stairs from his bedroom.

"The fire department did their doggonest to put it out, but it was out of hand by the time they got there. Oh they tried," Myrick shook his head. "They had to rotate the fire fighters in and out of that smoky building, so hot the men were getting their blood pressure checked by the ambulance crew."

Betty turned to Newton. "Pull up a chair, sweetie. Pete here, has come to talk to us." She paused, the color starting up in her face. "For the life of me I can't see why! Coming to my door at one in the morning. As if one of us Denmans had something to do with this awful death."

What did Ma mean, Newton wondered. He sat down, still half-asleep. What was going on, anyway?

"Hullo Pete," he said. He and Pete had gone to school together, same grade for a few years until seventh, when Newton's advisor pushed him ahead a year. Pete was a moody but likeable guy and Newton respected him for taking off out west the way he did back when they were all fresh out of high school. Pete had lost his right forefinger to a rattlesnake (it was a horse wrangling situation), had prospected for gold – he kept a vial of gold nuggets – worked as a ranch hand up near Navajo country, and returned to Littlecomb when he was twenty-five, never to leave again.

Sometimes Newton wondered what had brought Pete back to Pennsylvania. He turned to the police officer. "So what's going on?"

Betty spoke up. "Mrs. Waters died in a fire tonight."

"Oh my Lord," Newton said softly.

"She didn't die in the fire," Pete amended. "She was walking her dog as she does every night, according to her husband Ralph. It was about ten twenty when she left her house. Twenty minutes later Mr. Waters goes to look for her because she and the pup are always back in fifteen minutes."

"It's a cockerpoo," said Newton, who had often spoken kindly to the dog, mostly because he saw it pleased her owner, Mrs. Waters. "I used to see them on their way to the butcher. She went every so often to pick up a bone for Honey."

Pete nodded, surprised at how well Newton knew Mrs. Waters' schedule. "Mr. Waters saw her walking home on the sidewalk near the cafeteria end of the school. He knew something was wrong because Theresa was careful about keeping Honey tight in hand, and there was the dog running circles around her, its leash dragging on the ground. Then he realizes that she's walking unsteadily."

The chair Pete sat in creaked side to side. He looked at Newton. "It was right there on the corner of High and Vine that she told her husband she saw you at the school."

"What?" Newton swung around in his chair.

"When Mr. Waters pressed her for details, she explained that she had heard your voice, too. This was after she went over to Littlecomb Elementary to see what was the matter. Next thing she knew she was struck on the head."

Newton jumped up, all six foot one of him ablaze with indignation. His mother placed a restraining hand on his arm.

"I'm sorry Newton. Let me get through this. I'm not accusing you. Ralph Waters walked his wife down the street another half block to the street lamp, and that's where I met them. By then, the school was in flames, and the fire department had been alerted.

Pete rubbed his thighs where the blue pants had a dull shine. "Right away I saw that Theresa Waters had a blown pupil. I knew it was bad."

"Her pupil?" Betty's voice cracked.

"Head injury. One pupil dilates, gets bigger than the other after a blow to the head. Mrs. Waters was still in shock, and so wasn't in terrible pain then. But Ralph Waters was beside himself, saying maybe it was her diabetes, that it can cause changes in the retina.

"The ambulance got there, and those guys could tell by her eyes that there was probably internal bleeding. We got her to Wellsboro as quick as we could. No helicopter available, so we had to drive. Soon the pain started to hit her. They gave her something."

Newton was having a hard time focusing on the rundown of events. He cared for Mrs. Waters. Of course he did. Only right this second he could not move his own brain beyond the idea of a looming warrant for his arrest.

"Once we got to the hospital," said Pete, "the doctors saw the hemorrhaging. They rushed to operate. It was too late. She died of internal bleeding. It'll be a while before the autopsy comes in, but I'll bet anything it tells us what Theresa said herself. She got whacked on the head."

Newton and his mother exchanged glances. He pulled his chair closer to Pete's and enunciated his words as though each was a rivet he was driving home. "I did not kill Theresa Waters."

"Were you at the school earlier tonight?"

"No. I was in bed asleep."

"Any witnesses to attest to that? Betty, were you home then?"

"No," said Betty. "Two hours ago I was cleaning up after Bingo down at the community hall."

"What about your brothers? Some of them around?" Pete rolled his shoulders back and sat up tall.

Newton paused. "George and Nat came in the house once. I was going to bed early. They didn't come upstairs to tuck me into bed, if you know what I'm saying."

"What time?" asked Pete.

"I wasn't paying attention. I didn't check."

"It would have been pretty early, maybe nine o'clock," offered Betty. "Those boys were eager to leave on their hunting trip. They like to go at night, get up in the hills, and be ready to get to their blinds early the next day."

"Ask Spoons," said Newton. "He's always home."

"Hey Spoons," yelled Betty. His bedroom was right off the kitchen.

"Not here."

"Do you know what time the boys left hunting?"

"Don't know. Been asleep," returned the raspy voice.

Pete tapped the tablecloth with his pen. "Leave the old man be. Nat and George don't concern me right now." His smile shortened into a taut string. "Newton, there is a witness, besides the deceased, who saw you tonight. At ten to eleven, Gib drove by the school on his way home. He spotted your yellow truck with the wire siding parked right out front of the school."

Newton tensed. "My truck?"

"Gib also saw someone wearing a blue and white striped jacket. You know the jacket."

"Mine," Newton whispered, feeling in the pit of his stomach that it was certainly George in that jacket. For a second he felt an enormous wave of pity for him. What if he and Nat had hurt this woman? What then? His pity turned to fear. Suppose it was his brothers and they didn't speak up.

"Listen, Newt, I know you've been through a lot, what with your daddy dying and all," Pete swallowed, making a conscious attempt to take the offensive. "But there are some people who will say you've been closing off like a regular turtle lately. They say you don't act friendly."

"And who would that be, our nosy neighbor Elijah Jones?"

"I'm trying to help you," said Pete.

Newton looked at him sharply.

"If you were there, if you know something, now's the time to talk up. Between friends." Pete meant it. He had always liked Newton. In their teenage years he was one of the more intelligent boys, and thoughtful too. He attracted friends, boys as well as the girls, who were drawn to his intense brown eyes that held so many feelings. The truth was those girls would have been disappointed, thought Pete. The feelings were there, sure, but there they stayed locked under his brow.

"Between friends?" Newton's voice rose half an octave.

Now the officer remembered that Newton did not spend much time with the kids who considered him their friend, or wished he would become so. He was never standoffish. Newton was a softie, too kind by far to hurt people, but he seemed to have set his limits as to how much time he would spend hanging out with the other guys. Until Callie Major moved to town, Newton's family claimed most of his time.

"I think you better go on home, Pete Myrick," Betty said, lighting another cigarette. She was in a bad temper. Newton could tell by the way she closed one eye when she took a puff.

"Sorry about this, Mrs. Denman." He studied Newton. "So far, people are focused on the fire at the school, and on caring for Mrs. Waters' family. But I'm afraid for you. Afraid I'll be back in the morning with a warrant. He paused. Betty and Newton had nothing to say. "I'll just go out the kitchen door," Pete said. He stuck his hand out to say goodbye. Reluctantly, Newton took it.

Before Pete could look for a sign from his friend, anything to explain the tragic events rationally, Newton turned away. The state trooper shook his head and sketched in a few mental notes of the kitchen. It was a spare room brightened by two colorful baskets of laundry. One was stacked so high the clothes looked like they might topple over. A torn white undershirt hung down one side of the basket, and folded neatly on top of that was a pair of green boxers.

Pete stole a glimpse of mother and son, then took his leave.

Callie

Newton Denman, *here* on the mountain, it hardly seems possible. Did he take the old cart road up, did he notice the fig trees at the first turn? As it happens, figs are his namesake. I asked him about his name once. We were sitting cross-legged between the work shed and Betty Denman's flower garden. It was high summer, the daylilies waved in the breeze.

"My mom quit smoking once for about two months," Newton said. "That's what my daddy told me. It was when she was pregnant with me." He frowned. "Fig Newtons were her favorite cookies. She ate so many of them when she was carrying me that it got to be a joke between her and Dad. That's how they came up with my name."

"I thought you were named after the scientist," I blurted. I had imagined Newton growing up to be like Isaac Newton.

Newton was disappointed at my reaction. I smiled brightly. "Look, so long as you have to be a fruit cookie, why not figs?"

We sat a good while, not talking. Then I jumped up to take a whiff of the curving yellow lilies. They were thin as paper, with bright red spots in their throats.

"My mom, she has such troubles," Newton said, fingering the front of his t-shirt.

I wanted to say something to cheer him up. "She grows beautiful flowers."

He grinned nervously. I thought he was happy until I saw the way he contorted his shirt into a twister.

We had fig trees when I lived on Grandmother Mountain, and there is a whole line of them along that first turn coming up the mountain. I don't know who planted those, but Winoshca, my great aunt tended to the ones at our cabin. We had lots of fruit trees, pear and apple trees, grape vines and raspberry bushes too. It was 1958 that year and I had been with Winoshca and her daughter Mary since I was born. Or around that time. To be precise, I was a month old baby with a father who had disappeared, and my mother dead. My next closest relative who volunteered to take me in was my mother's only aunt, Winoshca. She rescued me. She was good to me.

Winoshca could trace our ancestors back to the Susquehannocks, a size-able tribe back when part of the Iroquois confederation lived in Pennsylvania, and also to the Senecas who came down from New York. Winoshca made sure Mary and I knew that we were directly descended from Chief Cornplanter's tribe in the Alleghenies. Most people don't know that there are Indians left in Pennsylvania. All the reservations are empty, but we are here, a number of Senecas who know better than to leave our home mountain ground.

Of course I'm a paella, a mix, an omelet. My mother was not one hundred percent Seneca herself, and my father was a jockey, from where I don't know, a loner who never settled in any one place, or with one woman. I guess he was sure of only one thing. He didn't want to be a father. Aunt Teeny used to say he was a no good, a race track junkie. That's all I knew about him. All I want to know, thank you very much. Only decent thing my parents did was to leave me some porcupine quill earrings – they were my mother's – and my father, he left behind a history of steeplechase winners and a book on Greek mythology. I would read the myths at bedtime and had my favorites. The ones about Artemis the huntress I liked best of all. There were her grace and dancing pow-ers at great gatherings in the temple where she and her brother Apollo stood out from the crowd, and her communion with the trees and animals. Her solitude. She hunted too. It wasn't that I approved of her hunting animals – I didn't – what I liked were the tales that showed her passion to go after, track down the things she wanted most.

I half-believed in all those goddesses and gods on Mount Olympus when I was a kid. I said to Newton, "Artemis talks to me in my dreams. Maybe she sends her spirit powers to guide us in the same way wild animals do for Winoshca in her dreams, or like Jesus does for the congregation in our church."

I had been to Sunday school for the first time and was loving Jesus wildly the fall that my maiden aunt, Teeny Wick, came up Grandmother Mountain to take me away. My father was her only brother and when he married May, Teeny was furious. May was Winoshca's niece, and Teeny wanted nothing to do with Indians. She told her brother not to marry May, but he went ahead anyway. Teeny didn't approve or forgive. She came to the mountain that fall to show us all, to shame us.

It happened this way. It was a strangely hot October. Everything that breathed on the mountain got fooled into thinking it was still summer. Not one frost so far, and the month was almost gone. Early Friday evening my older cousin, Mary, and I got together our bed rolls, sterno cans, and flashlights. The two of us were going off on an overnight in the Great Meadow. I was excited about going to the top of the mountain. We'd see old Grandmother's crown of pitch pines from where we planned to sleep.

All packed up, we clattered down the cabin steps following Winoshca to the wing of wild fern that edged her herb garden. For such a tall, big boned woman she was surprisingly quick at bending so far down to those plants. Pruning a yarrow root with her fingers, she said to us, "Don't forget, no fire tonight. The woods are too dry. Now come hug me goodbye."

Winoshca, that lovely haptic woman, embraced us warmly. Turning to Mary, she said, "You watch out for her."

"Yeah, she's special and I'm not."

The bite of jealousy in Mary's voice made Winoshca wince, and me, cringe. It was not my young age that prompted my great aunt to make sure Mary kept an eye on me. There was more, and I didn't like it. Winoshca sometimes treated me as if I was *different-special*, which is not the same as being just regular-special-because-your-family-loves-you. Worse, when I was young I had no idea what it was about me that was different.

She checked through our provisions and then waved us off. We hung back longingly in her tall green shadow.

"I wish we had two-way radios," Mary said anxiously, pulling at her strong chin. Twelve years older than me, Mary was wiry all over. Even her dark hair was thin and springy. "Suppose Callie gets hurt, or something else happens in the woods, or – " Embarrassed, she stopped. Even at her most helpless, I had never heard Mary admit she couldn't do something entirely on her own.

"You'll be fine, the both of you. I will know where you are." Winoshca brushed her fingertips across her temple, and stepped over to the thicket near the trail.

There was no technology to speak of at the cabin, not even a phone, and yet once we heard the conviction in her voice Mary and I had absolute faith in her ability to watch over us from afar. Mary strapped on the knapsack. "Come on Callie. We'll take the logging road and from there get on the trail that runs next to Black Run Creek.

Still, I hung back at the thicket, near Winoshca. I heard the possums scratching through the vines. Along the tangled edge were the rock doves. I listened. When they are in a group they will heave their wings like a flap of angels.

Chapter FIVE

Betty listened until she no longer heard Pete's car down the road. Then, turning to Newton. "It's got to be a terrible mistake." She stared at her cigarette. It had a two inch line of ash. Newton got up. "Going to bed," he said, opening the door to the back stairs.

She gazed after her son, then turned to the business of making bologna and American cheese sandwiches for the both of them to take to their respective offices the next day. She measured out the coffee into the percolator, gave the counter one last swipe with the sponge, and turned off the kitchen light.

Betty was lying in bed wide awake when she heard the commotion. She knew her house and all its sounds. There went the creaky floorboards, the ones in Newton's bedroom that sloped downhill to his bureau. And now his drawers opening, the clink of something like metal rings. His duffel, she guessed.

Betty was in his bedroom in a shot. Newton looked up, dressed and surrounded by his backpack, sleeping bag, and plenty of other camping gear. "Going hunting, Ma. Maybe, I'll run into George and Natty."

"Now?" she said, consternation in her voice. For a second time that night she held his arm. "You've got to stay so as to show how you're innocent. Pete, he won't take this right. He'll say you're running, that you have something to hide."

Newton smiled helplessly. "I'm sorry Ma."

Oh she thought he was handsome standing there in his soft brown wool shirt, those high color cheekbones and dark eyes. He was her most cherished son, her best looking and best acting boy. Why was this happening – and why didn't he need her anymore, confide in her like he used to?

How could Betty know that while Newton loved her deeply he had never confided in her so fully as she imagined. Certainly he could go to her with a problem. "Ma, I am deadly sick to my stomach," got her attention at once. Betty was a compassionate mother when it came to ailments or concrete complaints such as one's terrible teacher, broken bike, or lost library book. But there was only so much she could take. She was fragile. Newton could not have gone to her and said that he was feeling defeated, that it was one of those winter days where everything you think about doing is an overwhelming prospect. And worse, he would not have shared what he had done about it, that he had set out across a snowy field and was cheered by the cold beauty of the night, by the way two fir trees formed a loom, their branches scraping, lowering under the weight of snow. He was mesmerized by the snow falling and weaving a mysterious pattern in the trees.

And that's when something in him lifted. His head was clear.

Betty watched her son rummage in the corner of his room.

"Don't ask me to help."

"I didn't."

"You know I don't like dealing with closets."

Newton sorted through his belongings for thermal blankets, ropes, twine, lanterns and flashlights. Bending over the heap that overflowed from his closet, he pulled out two mess-kits and a fly rod he had made himself. He studied the rod a minute before putting it back. He was a packrat, just like the rest of the family. Next, he dug for cooking utensils he hardly ever took camping.

"I washed some of your underpants and jeans," Betty said. "Want me to get them?"

He swiveled, half in the closet and half out. "I already grabbed what I need. Would you give a call to work for me?" He came out of the closet. "Tell them I'll be back in four or five days." Newton stuffed three books into his duffel. "Tell them I'm taking Christmas leave early, or something like that."

"Doesn't look to me like you're going out for any short trip."

"I might be gone a week. No more than that." He took her hands and pulled her over to his bed. They sat at the edge. "They can't arrest me, not yet."

"You say you want to catch up to your brothers?"

Newton hedged. "Well, maybe. I'm not sure yet."

"They never consoled you much before," she said, with a bite to her voice. She stood up. "You boys are like bear cubs, sweet and cuddly as kids. But you keep a cub a few years and what does he do but turn on you."

"I'm sorry, Ma," Newton said gently. "But I have a right to go hunting if I want."

It was just past three a.m. when he drove out of Littlecomb, his thoughts tripping over each other with what to do next. He tried to sort things out. George and Natty wouldn't burn down a school. And they surely wouldn't murder Mrs. Waters. No way. Besides, they didn't know where the truck key was. Or did they? Newton went over last night. He hadn't been asleep yet, not when Natty and George came in. His older brother had been a terrible student, but as far as Newton knew he didn't have a bone to pick with the art teacher. I was the only one had anything to do with Mrs. Waters, he thought. He had no idea where his brothers had set camp, not even the direction they were headed. They never went back to old stands the way he did. Besides, he didn't want to see them. Not now. The traitors; run off to leave him with the rap. *If* that's what had happened.

But he didn't know, not for sure. No matter how mad he got he couldn't rat on them. For as long as he could remember Newton wanted his brothers' approval. He was unlike them and had not measured up. In moments of clarity Newton could look at the two men and know full well that he was glad he was different. Still, his desire as a child to be accepted by them had been set in permanent glue, and he could not seem to unstick himself.

That he was actually more skilled than they in a number of ways meant little to him in the face of their older brother status. He felt quieter, smaller than Nat and George. He needed to go off on his own to recharge his faculties, where they throve on other people, and were gregarious and well-liked, especially George. Never mind that by their middle twenties Natty and George had made very little of their lives. Newton refused to notice how their charms had begun to tarnish.

The Denman men stick together, he reasoned. If George and Natty had anything to do with Mrs. Water's death, they'll own up to it. He gripped the wheel hard. His eyes were wet, and he reached over to the passenger side for his all-purpose bandana. Newton caught a whiff from under the other seat. The smell of vomit nearly made him sick.

Nervous energy drove him into the Allegheny region above Littlecomb. For five days Newton shot in all the closes he knew best, and tried to think of nothing but hunting and where to set up camp for the night. He did not stop to check the anger that steeped in him like poisonous phlegm. Get on with it, he commanded himself one morning. Take a look at what you've bagged so far. Ringneck pheasant, quail, chukar partridge. Give me one of Natty's good bird dogs and I might become a regular wing shot.

Just when Newton believed he had succeeded in smoothing his own feathers, out came an involuntary sputter. "Drop dead Pete Myrick," he said, stalking his campsite and staring through the trees at an open field. "And I used to figure you for an okay – hell, should of known better." And Mrs. Waters, dead. Newton shook his head in wonder. There was a period in his school years when she had been the only one who believed in him. She was his advisor and thought he was so smart he should move ahead a year after seventh grade. Newton was bored, it was true. And didn't she get him in that special class on American literature? He still read those books. Mrs. Waters had also sent letters home urging Mr. and Mrs. Denman to consider preparing Newton for college. There had been her mistake. His parents, especially his father, didn't like the high minded thoughts she was instilling in his boy. In the end, Mrs. Waters – for all her interest in him – had made that piece of his adolescence miserable. Newton let her know just how miserable, but he had handled it badly. Oh he had hated himself for that one.

In hindsight, though, Newton recognized she had done some good. It was her incentive that later inspired him to go to college, after all. He had managed to hold down a full time job, and get to classes at night.

He was still upset that she was gone, but gradually anger was replacing shock. How could Mrs. Waters think he was skulking around Littlecomb

Elementary at night, and that he meant her harm? Was it George and Nat at the school, and if so, Mrs. Waters must have lousy night vision if she thought he looked one iota like his brothers.

That was a lie, he realized. If the three Denman boys lined up side-by-side, he and George did look most alike. Newton did not question his plan to remain loyal, but like any self deceptions, the truth will out. He spat on the ground, and could not help but fume.

"George and Natty, you ain't worth two dead bugs." This had been one of his father's expressions, and it pleased Newton to use it.

He was making his way home slowly, turning every so often off the interstate to go fishing or to bring in something easy, a possum or woodchuck, anything to delay his return to Littlecomb. It was in the late afternoon, some fifty miles from home, that Newton found a signature that turned his life around.

Had his grandpa Spoons been there, he might have confirmed then what would happen, what he saw as Newton's inevitable path towards the strangest black bear known to man.

Newton would not have stopped but for his truck. At first he hoped that the off balance feel as he drove was his imagination, but then there was that familiar, awful kachung, kachung noise that told of a flat tire.

He bounced the spare out of the truck and quickly changed the tire. Lingering for a minute in the cool woods at the edge of the highway, Newton's eye fell on a tree with a huge claw slash. The late daylight was throwing down its best glances, breathing life into the gash in the tree. Newton saw a gargantuan, toothy smile. As the light bent away, the gash shivered.

Newton had stumbled upon a bear tree, a mysterious marking on tree bark that is rarely seen, even by hunters. Bears mark their territories on such trees and it is thought they may be doing more than that. They're sending messages, Spoons used to say, messages that humans fail to understand.

This animal had chosen a tall, medium-width linden. Newton studied the uneven blazes. Then he measured the claw slash. The rift of bark was enormous but it was the precise claw and teeth marks that made Newton uneasy. He gauged the recess where teeth had ripped a tunnel, now filling with ants. He checked the size of the claw gash again. This beast must be at least nine feet long, Newton thought. His heart pounded. Unheard of. Goliath for a black bear.

There were tracks, too. A double set of them around the base of the tree. Two bears, but one was smaller, had to be a cub about a year old. A goliath female, Newton amended. He stared at the human-like, five-toed mark of the larger black bear, and then at the smaller tracks. He leaned back hard against the linden, mopped his neck and face and slid down against the tree in a sitting position. Seeing the cub tracks brought to mind an old issue.

That nightmare. His frame shook, an unpleasant cold sensation from head to toe. *The thing that has stood in the way of me hunting bear. Almost as if a law had been set down telling me not to.*

Then Newton, who was good at switching gears, counseled himself. *Don't get spooked. Don't be stupid. Why should I ignore the chance to go after this remarkable creature?*

All at once it was clear to him that he'd be foolish to return to Littlecomb with the slim hope that the real murderer and arsonist would be turned up. *Stay here*, he told himself. *Find the bear.*

The first important business was to get more provisions. Newton drove into Lick Creek, where no one knew him. In town, it was Sunday, he double-checked his measurements with a few men at the local bar who hunted bear. No one believed the claw size he described, and then after a few drinks two of the guys admitted they were shook by what Newton had seen. They had heard rumors of such a bear over near Tuscatanning, a bear who grew as big as a house before your very eyes. The hunter pressed them, but the men got defensive and said maybe it was all tall tales. That night Newton paced his motel room in the clothes he had worn for days. At last he collapsed into bed with his book about bears. He fell asleep with it on his chest and dreamt of Callie, who seemed to be in the deepest kind of sleep, and so far away that he could not reach her.

The next evening, it was a cool night in late August, Newton set out for the bear tree. He had more hunting equipment than he needed, and in his exhilaration he had also bought a spare sleeping bag, more ammo, a mess kit, coffee pot, a few extra cooking utensils, bacon, potatoes, and much dehydrated food.

As he approached the tree, his step slowed. Here is where he would begin tracking. All at once he was filled with dread. Newton was loath to look again into the face of the bear tree. Of their own accord and much against his will, he felt, his eyes dragged over to the linden and its monster markings, a hieroglyphic configuration that shifted in the dying light. Something about the gash frightened him, and it was not the mere size of it. It glittered in the sunlight, inviting him to go to an unknown distance.

In the following week and a half Newton learned where the creature hunted and fished, where it lapped up ants and fed off berry bushes. He followed the down timber that marked its sometimes clumsy trail, and he tracked upwind as he had been taught. No matter what tactic he used or how well he thought he had judged the bear's landmarks, he could not get close, the trail would go cold. And yet the more Newton sank his teeth into the challenge, the keener he felt. He had a sense of purposeful action. He felt revived, no longer sunk in worry over what had happened in Littlecomb.

Newton went for three days without once thinking about his family, his long standing job as an environmental chemist at Barnes Utility Plant, or even the criminal charges he sensed were imminent. He never got tired, not even under the weight of his rifle, sling, and Leupold scope. Sure he slipped a thumb under the gun strap to give his shoulders a break, but he had fashioned his sling so that it supported his rifle. He moved with his Remington at the ready.

He had been gone from Littlecomb for two weeks when he finally got himself to a telephone.

"Is that you? Listen Ma – oh it's good to hear you – I meant to call days ago."

"Where are you? Are you all right?"

"Sure, I'm fine. This thing started as a little vacation hunting, but you know what, I believe I'm going to bring in something big."

"Newton, you have to come home."

"I was planning on it, but – " He pressed his cheek against the receiver and listened to her suck on a cigarette at the other end. "Did Myrick and the boys up at barracks, did they find out who did it?"

"Not exactly. Pete came over again. Oh Newton I'm scared for you. Your brothers are too."

"Ma, they must have known where I hid my truck key."

Betty was silent for a minute. Newton wished he could read more clearly what it was that had her breath coming in knots over the line. "No, they haven't talked much about that night, except once to Pete," she said finally. "But we are worried – I just know you didn't do such a thing, not one of my sons."

"That's right, Ma," Newton said dully. "Don't you worry on that score." But he had panicked the second he heard that his brothers had not owned up to the crime. "There's a warrant out for your arrest." Betty's voice was toneless. "They want to bring you in for questioning. People are talking. Pete tried to get me to tell him about your bad relationship with Mrs. Waters."

"I liked Mrs. Waters."

"Not always, you didn't."

Newton felt himself receding. He had gone off to find a hiding place. It was a game of hide and seek, and he didn't want her to tag him. He would not let her call him *it*, and bring him home. The only thing that made sense right this second was his plan to go after the black bear. "Ma, I can't come home just yet. Soon though, real soon. I'll be there and we'll straighten all this out. Right now I'm going after a bear like nothing you could ever picture. I'm onto something. You'll see. You'll be proud," he said, forgetting that his hunting skills had never been his mother's measure of his worth.

"Sweetheart, you aren't thinking straight," Betty said. "It doesn't look good that you've run off. And what about your job?

Newton thought about this. He used to enjoy testing the water coming out of the Barnes Utility Plant, making sure it was safe. But after twelve years he was plain bored with the sameness of his work, and for some time now it had been a chore to face another day inside the environmental control lab.

"I've called over there at the plant and made up so many excuses for your extended vacation that they're fed up. Larry Orkel has been covering for you. You don't get home, they'll lay you off for good."

"Larry Orkel is a good man. He's been wanting my job."

"What are you talking about?"

What good is a job if I have to go to jail, Newton thought. "Tell them I quit," he said to his ma. "I got better things to do now, anyway."

Callie

We were fired up. Winoshca had quelled our fears, and we set off that October afternoon on our adventure to the Great Meadow.

"Let's take the shortcut," Mary said, swinging ahead of me.

"Where?" My eye was on her rhythmic walk, thinking how funny it would be if she broke into one of her nutty dances. Lately she played the "Purple People Eater" on her record player. Whenever Winoshca was out in the woods Mary cranked the volume and sprang wildly around the kitchen.

"Right there," my cousin said, pointing at a pasture bounded by post and rail. Attached to the fence was a glistening barbed wire, the only electric one on the mountain. The pasture was owned by a tenant farmer who rented from the State Park.

"How do we get over? It might be on."

"We can do it." Mary sized up the fence, then shoved her pant cuffs securely inside her cracked, leather boots. "Grab the outside wooden post and make sure only the bottom of your shoe touches the wire. You won't feel the shock," she glanced at my feet. "The soles of your shoes are probably thick enough, but we'll test it." She spat at the wire. It spat back at her, hissing and crackling. Agile as a monkey, she climbed over.

I shrank back.

"Don't be a little fart. Look, you can do it."

I nodded, following her example, first spitting, then climbing.

"Don't let your arm or leg touch anything," Mary yelled, as I wobbled and teetered at the top, trying to swing one short leg at a time over the hot wire. I did it though, landing with a flump in a pile of walnuts.

I was fine, not one bruise. All of October's fruits were hanging on way past their due, and those walnuts were soft as cooked squash. Mary picked up a stick and waved off the black and white cows that had surrounded us, and we walked along the pasture edge on a path of fallen walnuts. Their sharp tang filled the air, and I stopped to pick one up, crumple it through my fingers and breathe in the black silt. Everywhere, we saw summer's leftovers.

As the sun drooped low in the sky we got back on the logging road. We walked down between the burly honeysuckle. Their thick sweetness told on them, not to mention the bees that drummed in the vines. Above the bee hum was a louder music. It was the crickets scattered on the road, all of them dying. Bellies up, they were on their backs, their poor tube bottoms waggling pathetically. Rubbing their wings, but too weak to walk, these crickets.

They should have been long gone, right along with the honeysuckle, but it was seventy-five degrees out and they didn't know to do anything else except keep on singing.

We had to watch where we stepped so as not to crunch them. Then I got an idea. At every cricket we met I raced to the nearest hump of grass and plucked two long green blades.

"Not again," Mary howled, as I knelt by yet another buggy creature and placed the grass by its head, slapping one blade down perpendicular to the other.

"May you rest in peace," I said seriously to the insect decorated with a grass cross. "You are a cricket in Christ."

"You got to be putting me on," Mary said. She had not been attending Sunday School with me, she was too old by then, but in minutes she was gathering the flattest, longest blades of grass for me.

"Let there be light," I added, having noticed the fireflies also resting in the grass, their flickerings a good dimension to this liturgy. Their frail light switched on and off slowly. They too were weary of the trickster Fall and his heat spell.

Later I would look back and be amazed at the effortless faith I had. On this night Mary and I stooped to pray for each minute creature we encountered on our way to Great Meadow. We took the trail up the creek and I was more excited every step of the way. After the steepest bend around Black Run, Mary said it wasn't likely we'd get a glimpse of the meadow for a while yet. I guessed she was right, what with the crescent moon skulking under a couple of busy clouds, but then I peered through a clearing in the forest on the far side of the creek, and there she was, the shining grassy breast of Great Meadow. Winoshca had told us that this was the place where animal spirits came to graze at midnight.

I stood dead still. Even as Mary hiked on ahead I looked into the opening of the meadow and knew that something was coming, not here, but at home. I must warn Winoshca. "I want to go back to the cabin," I called out to Mary. She turned slowly around, and gazed at me.

"Please," I said.

Briefly, Mary considered my request. "No way. We've gone this far."

"I mean it. I think we should."

"Don't be a little fart." She turned back to the trail.

I was squeezing my eyes shut, as if that might help me to see clearly ahead. But the light in my head was faint. I opened them, and the sky had dimmed. The thin moon, all she gave me was a furtive light.

Once, my aunt Winoshca told me that I was deeply connected to nature. She acted as if it was a mysterious gift, something more than the ordinary. She said I had a knowing sense of things. Here it was and I did not know what to do next. Now the crickets started up in full force. For being so close to death, they sure could sing. In the grass, the fireflies panted for air. The crickets clapped their wings. I imagined cymbals.

Early in October Newton found neighboring retreats, all belonging to the black bear. There was a line of dented shrubbery, a large hollow log, and one low cave that showed years of habitation. These discoveries did not help him close in on the bear. Six and seven times he saw her tracks mark a trail, and then disappear, mid-path. When this happened he would stand stock still, confounded. Suddenly uneasy, he'd spin around, certain something or somebody was watching him.

Mid-day in late October, overcome by his failure to follow the bear's tracks for any length of time, he decided to give it up, forget this hunt and go home to the horrors that awaited him there. As he trudged down the mountain pass it crossed his mind that he was running away from the bear, and from Callie. "Nah, crazy thinking," he said aloud. The word coward was not in his vocabulary. He pushed on, guided by clear days and bright evenings. Some nights the stars stood shoulder to shoulder.

He had been taking his time, driving short distances and stopping frequently to trap and hunt. Better game up here than I've seen in a long time, he thought. Bust brush down home a month and I'd be lucky to come up with a total of two birds.

Then the damp weather came. Huddled in his pup tent one night under a steady rain, he felt an intense loneliness, and had a sudden image of this loneliness rushing ahead of him, and waiting, magnified, in Littlecomb when he got there. He thought about how he would love to see his mother, and how she always foresaw the storms that came to Littlecomb. First came her prediction, and then she'd leap up from her kitchen chair to check the barometer, just to make sure she was right. Out of everything in that town, he missed her alone; and yet he had to consider the danger he'd risk by returning. Danger nothing, he'd be a downright fool to go back.

It was a soggy night. Newton was bone cold. The Remington hung over his back. He checked its position and felt better. He was using a .22 when taking out small game, but it was his thirty caliber rifle, the Remington 700 that he counted on to bring down the bear. He thought for a minute about his position in Littlecomb. Before this crime he was fleeing, he knew that he had garnered a reputation as both marksman and persistent hunter who made durable stands in the woods, and sometimes returned to an old stand to track a prey that had eluded him the year before. On and off he had overheard snatches of praise, his brothers, neighbors, and even Spoons and the old men he played checkers with had talked up Newton's hunting prowess, how he would study an animal's habits and range and then go tirelessly after it until it was his. And so what? Newton thought. Is that it then; me, a patient woodsman who lands his kill?

"God only knows," he said loudly. "And you're not telling."

He stared off at a glimmer of the stream showing through the trees. The light was dappled, so bright and quivering that he found he could not look away. The stream was fast running, owing to the rains. For a second it made him think of where he used to fish in the Pennwood River. The brook trout were plentiful there. He used to squat on a shouldered bank and identify the large and small forms even as they huddled dead still in the pole weeds. For a second he entertained the thought that fishing in the wilds was more honest than hunting game. Perplexed as to why this should be so, he went forward towards the rippling light, a good, free running stream. No dams and very clear water.

Newton decided to travel back to the bear and whatever it was about her that teased him with the promise of his triumph over her. He sloshed through the mud, breaking camp. Once, as he dragged the tarp over a bunch of winter rue he thought of Callie on a summer night when he meant to console her. They were only friends, mere kids, and yet that moment was electric; Callie

Major's waist length hair under his touch, its silkiness, one hundred sensations at once. His hand shook.

He remembered how he and Callie walked to school together, him waiting each morning for her near the pale bloom of fall roses mid-way between their houses. He sucked in his breath when he saw her, that never cut waist length hair, black as onyx and glossier, in the morning sun, and her skinny self bounding towards him. Newton used to raise his brows in wonder. She always looked the same, intense, straightforward, strong, but each time he saw these qualities it amazed him.

She must have been twelve, and he about thirteen when they met. He knew a little about where and who she came from, but now he wished he had listened more closely. Tuscatanning, Winoshca. These were names often on her tongue.

Callie

After sleeping like dead people in Great Meadow, Mary and I woke early, packed up our sleeping rolls and hiked back towards the cabin. Coming up on the last stretch home we saw signs of visitors. Mary and I exchanged glances. Winoshca rarely had guests over. Ignoring Mary's warning yell, I scampered ahead, anxious to see my great aunt. Inside, there was an unpleasant surprise. My aunt Teeny Wick and a large man with a balled up handkerchief held over his nose were standing in our parlor.

"So this is the young lady in question," the man said, the handkerchief expanding as he spoke. He coughed and turned to Winoshca: "We are deeply regretful at having to prowl through your house. It's really not necessary that we do," he added, raising a brow at Teeny.

She had not greeted me, and was busy marching around the room, sticking her nose into every cubby hole she could find. "Winoshca," she said, "you keep the sorriest house I have ever seen. Dirt in the corners. Downright messy."

The man, who introduced himself as Mr. Backer, smoothed his creaseless blue, polyester suit. He coughed two more times and blew his nose. I don't know what it was that got to him, the good strong smell of earth and mold from the back room, or the ripe tomatoes and raspberries side by side, up for canning.

"You are not welcome here, Teeny," Winoshca said, in that voice with the high, sweet hitch to it. I don't think she owned a menacing bone.

"I cannot understand you, aunt," said Teeny, "especially as I've come way up this mountain to do you a favor. Not only will I take Callie off your hands, but I will spare her *this* uncertain future." She swept her eyes up to the nice wood hewn rafters, took a melodramatic breath and inclined her head towards the heavy man who had taken a seat at the kitchen table. He spread out a bunch of papers and looked up expectantly at Winoshca.

"If you think for one minute I will put my name down on anything that signs Callie over to you and Mr. Adoption Man here, you're off your rocker." I was secretly thrilled. If, on my behalf, Winoshca turned into a menacing figure that was a-okay with me.

Mr. Backer was nonplussed. "We don't need your signature. I thought I would show you the papers, a common courtesy Miss Wick wanted to extend to you."

"I wish I had never left Great Meadow," I burst out, forgetting my instinct to come home the night before, and to warn Winoshca. Everyone looked at me. I glanced nervously from face to face, then settled on the big sugar bags and pectin set out on the counter. On the stove the glass jam jars clanked against each other in the boiling vat of water. Aunt Teeny's lips were set together, taut as the ends of iron pokers. She reached out and grabbed my hand, pinching my fingers so that they were crammed on top of one another.

That was it for me. I wrenched out of her grasp. Mr. Backer went for me, but I ducked his flabby arm. I slammed out the door. Aunt Teeny came after me. Despite her small stature she had muscle. She was a fast waddling duck, short legs, and bill to the ground.

It was raining leaves. The air was thick and grainy. Not a peep of sun. I tore down the logging road, certain I could outrun Teeny. It made me furious that she had said our house was filthy. True, we had one dirt floor and Winoshca was not one to always be scrubbing, but things were clean enough and I liked it the way it was. Our bathroom was twenty yards behind the cabin, as nice an outhouse as you will see any place. I'll vouch for it, and I should know since it was my regular job to keep it clean, and plenty of toilet paper. Toilet paper. Adoption papers. There was a night when Winoshca and my uncles were in the cabin chuckling and stewing at the same time. The talk was about how the white man had cozened so many Indians into signing away their land, way back when. Winoshca ran off to the outhouse and came back in holding up a roll of toilet paper that had evidently gotten wet at one corner and dried in warped waves. By way of explanation, she waved the roll under my nose: "Around here, this is what we call *Treaty Paper.*"

I should get riled about things like that, but I loved her, maybe especially in those righteous moments. But she was no neatnik, that's for sure. One morning Mary made her look inside the icebox at one of the shelves.

"What?" protested Winoshca. "All I see is milk, chicken breasts marinating in my spices and mushrooms, rice in a bowl, and those cut peppers I'm going to use in the chicken tonight."

"Mama, you are staring right at a shelf coated in raw egg and cracked shell bits, a mess of it there for a week."

Why Mary didn't bother to clean this up herself is anybody's guess, but Winoshca laughed and went to work getting rid of the hard as a rock mess. She did not notice such things like the breadcrumbs from her sandwich sprinkling the seat of her chair, or the dust bunnies curling in the cracks of the window-sills. What a useful talent, when you think about it, this not-seeing the casual dirt in life.

She did notice the spider webs in our house. Winoshca would not let us go at them with a broom or any other implement. Spiders lived in all the ceiling corners. The web right over her bed was cone shaped, a perfect white cave that ate all the evil bugs. "Spiders are nearly as sacred as bears," she said. "Spiders keep down the mosquitoes and flies. They keep all things in balance."

I don't know how it happened, but Aunt Teeny was gaining on me. Should I keep running? I got the sinking feeling that it was too late for Winoshca to hide or rescue me. I looked around for signs of help, but it was daytime and my pals, the fireflies, were on low light. No word from the crickets, either, but straight ahead the electric fence beckoned. Mary's shortcut. Here was my getaway to Great Meadow.

Aunt Teeny would never be able to climb the forbidding, barbed fence. I felt good about that, and then I got another idea. I eyed a deep cow pie and when she was not ten feet behind me, splat, I jumped in, angling my heels to dig in at the far side and shoot the goods out behind. I did a half turn to see if I hit my mark.

Teeny yelped as the rank and viscous stuff hit her full in the chest and splattered her cheeks.

I was up over the fence. Nothing to it. Then, to my surprise, I stood still on the other side. I waited, curious to see how my aunt would react to the electric jolt. Not enough to kill her, I reasoned coldly. She was the fool all right, had no idea the fence was electrified, and I watched as she laid a bare palm right down on the wire that was fixed on the top post. This time she did not yelp.

More curious than ever, I came a step closer and saw she had fallen back. She clutched her hand, and her face was wet with tears and muck. I climbed very carefully back over the fence, just the way Mary taught me, and walked up to Aunt Teeny.

"I'm sorry." Her sticky, poop reeking face was close to mine.

She laughed like a madman and snatched me by the back of the neck. "That's all you have to say, you're sorry?" She shoved me forward, and we plodded solemnly single file down the trail towards the cabin.

I went to live with Teeny Wick in Chambersburg. From there she packed us up and we moved to Carlisle for a year, and then north to Wellsboro for six months, and after that back south to Harrisburg. Finally we settled in Littlecomb, which sits in the foothills of the Alleghenies, not far below Grandmother Mountain, the place that was the beginning of my journey.

During those years that Teeny took me from town to town she forbade me to write letters or call Winoshca and Mary. I dreamed of them often. The three of us were in the kitchen canning one thing in one dream, another in the next. Sometimes it was our tomatoes, then the pickles, but most of all, the jams. The cabin was hot and steamy, we sterilized the glass jam jars in the boiling kettle, and I myself bubbled with self importance because Winsohca had picked me to be the chief jam taster-tester. I had a long wooden spoon ready in my hand.

I dreamed too of the Great Meadow, the white field through the trees and above the creek bed, and in the field there was something louder, greater than the crickets who emerged in the grass. It was behind, above, and below the cricket song. The roaring was real enough, and it was there the night Aunt Teeny took me from the mountain.

Chapter SIX

In Littlecomb, Pete was on his way to Betty Denman's house for the third time since the death of Theresa Waters. He wondered if it wasn't a mistake to have gone over right after the crimes were committed. All I did was to alert Newton that he could be a serious suspect, and then he took off to God knows where, Pete thought. I harbored a foolish idea, Newton. I thought we were friends, and that you might talk to me that night.

As he swung the nineteen-ninety unmarked police car around the bend of High and Vine, Pete took in the scorched schoolyard. He was sad to see those dull, comforting brick walls of Littlecomb Elementary diminished and burnt, even its insides where the scary big lunch ladies served children mystery meat in the cafeteria, the claustrophobic sweet dank classrooms, and of course, the haven, Mrs. Waters' high ceiling art room. All burnt up. He couldn't drive by without feeling horrified by this malicious act. And he was not alone. Pete's superior officer had made this clear yesterday.

"Let me remind you of the sort of headlines that the *Littlecomb Gazette* is running," Detective Hal Rendell said as they stood at the Coca Cola machine outside the barracks. He snapped open the paper: "Get this one: 'Still No Word on The Terrible Torch Who Took Our School.'"

"Yes Sir. I read my local paper."

"Myrick, this isn't one of those file and forget reports. And while I'm on the subject of reports, did I tell you I'm going to outfit all the men on the force with laptops." He checked Pete's face as if he might not understand current computer lingo. "We're moving towards the millennium, man! We can't afford to be slowed down by police reports laboriously, and need I say – illegibly scrawled in notebooks."

Pete sighed. The detective Sergeant was new to the county, and just brimming with ideas, very few of which sounded useful to Pete. "These new laptops aren't exactly light. You let me know if someone ever invents one of those machines in compact form. But I can't even picture that, and all I know is it's easier to slip a small notebook into my pocket. I hate to say it, sir, but we cops are not especially lily-fingered around expensive gadgets. Before you know it someone will spill a cup of coffee right on the keyboard."

"They're water resistant, man!" Rendell had looked at Pete with great discouragement. "Listen, I was told that you're the officer to handle this case, and Myrick, I want you to use all the tools we have available. This town is not going to dismiss what happened that night. If you think Newton Denman killed the Waters woman and burnt down the school, then go find him."

"I am not one hundred percent certain he did it. But if he did, I need to put everything together carefully. I want to be prepared."

"That's your motto, isn't it?" said Hal. "You must have been a Boy Scout."

"I was an Eagle Scout, but that's not what taught me to be prepared."

Pete glanced in the rear view mirror, glad the schoolyard was out of sight. He went over in his head what Mrs. Waters had told him the night she died. She saw Newton's truck. She thought she recognized his jacket, and she thought she heard his voice. Then she was struck on the head, and in a daze she escaped her aggressor and got out of the schoolyard before the building burst into flames. It seemed to Pete that the fire had vanquished all evidence of her murder. There was no murder weapon, all finger and footprints were burnt up, and Pete had to acknowledge that with the very scene of the crime destroyed, he had little to go on.

The dead body is the best evidence I have, he thought. That autopsy better turn up something useful.

Owing to the confusion over how she died, it had been a time consuming neuropathology. Pete felt he hadn't been quick enough to detect her skull fracture on the night of the crime. It was several minutes before the pupils of her eyes alerted him to trouble. Then came the fluid dripping from one ear. He was not a trained paramedic (Pete had no stomach for that sort of thing) but he had done his best, trying to mop her up with gauze he kept in the car. Pete winced, remembering another occasion in his life where he had no stomach to handle the emergency. He had learned then, a long time ago when he was out west, that he had to be prepared.

As to the business at hand, how to prepare for the arrest of Newton Denman when all the facts were not in, and why would this guy who never had an angle or a manipulative bone that Pete knew about, set fire to the school? He had done enough checking up on the Denman brothers to know that none of them stood to gain from insurance fraud, extortion, or any other financial gambit. What other motive then, except the personal. The motive for burning down the school could have been revenge or murder. Pete had not hung out with the brothers in years. Any one of the three might have a personal life he knew nothing about.

Going with the idea that someone needed to burn all evidence of murder, the slip-up, optimistically, was that Theresa had escaped to tell the tale. Pete wished it was that simple. It was discouraging to consider her foggy perception of Newton that night.

The old police car lurched as he parked in front of the Denman place. Pete smiled at how eager his new superior was to update the force with cop laptops, when no one made a move to give the force police cars that would go fast enough to keep the moonshiners in sight.

The car gave a second lurch and Pete felt it might as well have been himself giving an involuntary shudder. He did not relish this part of his job. Betty was a tough egg. When he came by the morning after the double crime and handed her the capeas for Newton's arrest, she was outraged.

Behind the anger, though, it wasn't hard to see the fear in her eyes. With too little patience (he now realized) and too much guilt at the thought of how much he was upsetting Betty, Pete had explained why he had to go to the district judge and get a bench warrant. Standing in her kitchen that day, he noticed the clothes basket. There was something blue and white resting on top of the t-shirts. "That's not a jacket is it?" he had inquired, almost absently.

Betty hopped up from her chair. "Jackets in this warm weather?" she said, scooping up the basket and carrying it into the adjoining mud room. "Forgive the mess of clean underwear. I'm always doing wash for the boys."

"Big boys," Pete muttered, thinking that surely Nat and George should be doing their own laundry.

The state trooper frowned as he walked up the Denman drive. This third attempt at reason with Mrs. Denman found Pete once again seated at the black and white checkered tablecloth in the kitchen.

"I am not saying it was Newton, okay," said Pete tracing a finger over a square of tablecloth, "but I do need to ask you a couple more questions.

"Is there anything else you can tell me about Newton's relationship with Mrs. Waters?"

"She was a meddlesome advisor to my boy. She upset him, always pushing him to do better. I told you this."

"She thought he should take college prep courses. Wasn't that right?"

"All that idea did was upset him. He started doing badly in school. She pressured him. He was only in sixth grade. My poor boy."

"And he stopped seeing her, didn't you say? Newton wouldn't show up for his scheduled advising appointments with her."

"Who would blame him," Betty said.

Pete nodded. "Recently, was he keeping to himself more than usual?"

"What if he was?"

Pete paused, the red practically rising from his face. "People sometimes, well you've heard how people can – Newton keeping so isolated, well he simply could have gone off the deep end."

Betty eyed him curiously. She reached for her cigarettes. "You do recall, perhaps, that his father died not six months ago."

"Yes, I am sorry. Of course that would make anyone withdraw. But what about this," Pete motioned to the cloth on the table. "We have this situation where – if it wasn't Newton who drove that truck – who was it? At the Big Springs Lounge there are plenty of witnesses who say George and Nat set off for their hunting trip at nine sharp. You also said that was the time they planned to leave.

"Course it does seem unlikely that Nat and George took Newton's truck, especially since I remember clearly a little conversation I had with Newton himself. It was all about his truck key."

"What do you mean?" Betty said shortly.

"I was giving him a lift to pick up his truck. The vehicle was over at Ray's getting its annual inspection, and on the way there Newton told me that he didn't like anyone but himself driving his truck, and that he didn't even let on to his brothers where he hid the key. Funny, he was adamant on that point."

Betty tamped the cigarette pack on the table.

Pete felt that odd shudder cross his chest again. "I'm sorry, Mrs. Denman, but I want you to think about this. Wouldn't Newton or Spoons wake up if some stranger came along and jump-started the yellow truck in order to steal it. Isn't it possible Newton wasn't asleep at all? Isn't it likely he was the only one who could turn on the ignition in his beloved truck?"

"So you're convinced Newton drove the yellow Chevy that night? Get out of here, Trooper. I don't want to see you again. Unless you have to search the house once more because maybe I'm hiding him in my oven?"

Pete felt horrible. "I have to ask you another question. Where is Newton? You must know where he's run to."

Betty looked at him dispassionately. "He's gone hunting, Mr. Trooper. I believe he's in the state of Pennsylvania, and that is all I know."

In the hallway, Pete stopped. He realized he was looking around for that basket of clothes he'd seen last time he was here. "Say, I'm sorry, Mrs. Denman, but do you remember me saying something about a jacket when I was here before?"

"Can't say I do."

"Perhaps Newton took his blue and white jacket with him on this extended hunting trip?"

"I don't remember any such jacket. Good bye, Mr. Myrick." She closed the door in Pete's face.

He did not leave immediately. Pete stood listening. Inside somebody was moving quickly, almost scurrying. A door opened and closed. On the night of the murder and the arson, Pete had noted the colorful array of clothes piled up in the kitchen. The second time he visited Betty, Newton was gone, the older brothers were living at home, and the laundry basket was in the kitchen full of freshly washed items, t-shirts, jeans and boxers. Nothing out of the ordinary except that flash of blue and white stripes, possibly the jacket Newton was sighted in the night of the crimes. But why didn't Newton take the jacket with him when he ran off? Presumably he would want to bury the evidence. Unless someone else had that evidence? Someone else had worn the jacket in the first place.

Chapter SEVEN

Ten miles below the Pine Barrens sat Tuscatanning, weathered, hunched, and squeezed into a stream valley. It was a small town in the saddle of the twin peaks of Grandmother Mountain. The buildings on Main Street were set too close together, perhaps with the idea that an arm of houses would create warmth and protection against the snowstorms Old Grandmother hurled off her twin peaks in winter.

The thing that baffled census takers and government employment bureaus, passers through and the occasional tourists was how Tuscatanning survived. The soil was too thin for successful farming. There was no longer a market for the feldspar and chrome whose alchemy made such mysterious colors in the mountain quarries. Logging, once a reasonable means of getting a living, had been banned by the State Forest Service in favor of a wilderness management program. Today, industry scarcely touched Tuscatanning. One small family-run cheese factory and a struggling textile mill gave some jobs to the in-town natives, mostly third and fourth generation Irish who had migrated up mountain, out from under the tyranny of the steel mills and cost of living in the changed, expensive Pittsburgh.

Within the state forest land was a large park that ran up the north peak of Old Grandmother, as the mountain was sometimes called. Pitch Pine State Park was staffed by rangers, many of them recent transfers in the mobile hierarchy of the park system. Working alongside the rangers was the valuable outdoor crew who repaired the Park washouts, planted trees, fought forest fires, trimmed brush and repaired trails. The crew was mostly Senecas, ousted from their land in northeastern Pennsylvania where the Kinzua Dam was built. Some of them had ancestors in the Pitch Pine region of Grandmother Mountain, and so here they had come. A tattered autonomous people, not even a tribe of them, but still they knew who they were and how important it was to find a place connected to the history of their dead, many of whom were buried on Old Grandmother. The Indians who worked for the Park answered officially to its superintendent, Bud Mason. Unofficially they listened most to the direction given them by one of Pitch Pine's Preservation Guide rangers, Callie Major.

Tuscatanning was a depressed area, more people on welfare than not. There was one bar in town and two eating establishments. The most popular place was The Jolly Logger Inn, containing the one bar and hotel, plus palatable food. Although food was served at Spence's Grill and Grocery, few people other than Callie Major went there to eat.

The companies that came to town rarely survived, and people were used to being laid off when a business folded. Maybe it was the long unworkable winters, the difficult terrain and distance over which materials had to come that promoted business failures. The small Native American population claimed that the twin peaks held a mountain spirit that damned most commercial developments. This spirit, they said, sent out a bucking wind that threw off all encroachments on the land. People joked that it was the wind that blew the bookkeeper's papers willy-nilly at Shield Construction, that the air spirits were the real culprits behind that company's eventual bankruptcy.

The mixed people of Tuscatanning lived outdoors as much as possible, in winter snowmobiling, hunting, trapping, skating if Black Run Creek froze. And they were event- minded folk, social events, that is, and in the warm weather there were two county fairs, church picnics, and softball games.

Despite the changing companies, the erratic work situation, the Tuscatanners, as they called themselves, scraped along, clanning together and living as if they thought themselves lucky.

Playing the daily numbers was a popular pastime in town. Ranger Jack Marsh had just stopped in at Spence's Grill and Grocery to put down five dollars for a lotto ticket.

As he and his buddy, Vernon Vale, were turning from the cash register Jack spotted Mary Cowell. "Hey Mary, seen your cousin around?"

Mary was a wiry woman with slouched shoulders and beautiful olive skin, ruined Jack thought by her phony, metallic red hair. He remembered when she had dark hair, almost as pretty as Callie Major's. Mary turned to him, "Yeah I saw her. Just a minute ago on her way to Tusca's." She smiled slyly, and whispered something to Vernon.

"What was she laughing about?" Jack wanted to know when he and Vernon stepped outside.

Vernon sniggered. "Something about how pretty boys never know when to quit."

Ignoring the slight, he squinted across the street at a long haired woman with a sure, easy gait, heading towards Tusca Drugs. It was Callie.

"Go for it," Vernon said. "Thought you wanted to make up with her?"

Jack smiled indulgently at Vernon. He was crass, there was no doubt about it, but Vern was so eager to put you down and build you up at the same time that it was kind of intriguing to be around this oddball taxidermist.

"I've changed my mind, I'm not chasing after her. At least not today." The bells on the door front at Tusca's jangled as Callie stepped into the store. Jack shook his head defiantly. She would come around to his way of thinking, he was sure of it. He tipped his hat back and slid his hands into his uniform pockets. Unlike the cheery, leaf green that the Preservation rangers wore at the State Park, Jack Marsh's uniform was drab and brown. But the color suited Jack's style; he was, in a word, *bright* looking. His light hair, blue eyes, and kinetic, well formed body needed some toning down. If the uniform restrained him, so much the better.

Jack was hardly twenty when he became a ranger, just like his father, Al Marsh, and his grandfather, Miles Marsh. The son of Scottish immigrants, Miles was one of the first lot of forest rangers in the country, working for the old Department of Agriculture on which the park service was modeled.

It was in the nineteen-forties that Jack's father, Al, got work as a ranger at the then new Pitch Pine State Park. He and his wife Esther had one child, Jack, and it might be said that they always let their son know he was everything to them. But there the good part ended. When Jack showed a smidgeon of fear over anything as a child, his father said, "Don't be a sissy." When the boy was sad and there were tears, Al chastised, "Don't be a crybaby."

His father and mother, who cannot be blamed in full for their ways, also passed on to young Jack the idea that men quite naturally had a roving eye, whereas women did not. Or, more truthfully put, Miles felt women should not. Why it was practically Jack's duty as a man to sow his wild oats. This had dire consequences. After roving and roaming to his heart's content, Jack was confounded when he fell in love with Callie.

He had no training, no preparation whatsoever for such an area as love and equality. Parity between men and women, what did it mean? And with no understanding comes the easy way out; pay lip service, and practice not.

By the time he was twenty Jack felt the weight of family tradition. Follow suit, he thought. Be a forest ranger. Marsh had been back in town for six months now, having returned from a five year ramble as a seasonal ranger that took him to parks in the four corners, mostly Colorado and New Mexico. He had gone off to see the world outside Tuscatanning, and returned no wiser for his travels. Jack had developed a heart that mistook contest for romance.

Since his homecoming he had romanticized, not only Callie, but all of the Alleghenies. Today he looked on the face of Grandmother Mountain, and as was his habit, he blinked several times until he produced a tear or two that blurred the mountain into a soft roundness, a wobbly, yielding view Jack thought very like a woman's breasts.

The rangers at Pitch Pine where Jack worked with Callie were divided into two categories, the Protectives and the Preservation rangers. There was some blurring of the lines, but strictly speaking, the latter were the educators, and the Protectives acted as campground patrols. Jack was a thirty-year old Protective with two advancements from different parks. Together, he and Callie Major were second in the park hierarchy under Pitch Pine's superintendent, Bud Mason. Bud valued Jack's energy and commitment to park rules. The superintendent could depend on him to offer campers vigorous, assured advice on how and where to camp. Jack was a little weak on technical information, such as the geology or ecology of the park lands, but he was gregarious with the campers. He never panicked in a park crisis; in fact he loved to take charge, set things right. Bud Mason worried over this last habit of Jack's. When the young man hatched a new idea on park maintenance or patrol he could be downright bullheaded. His boss had a hunch that Jack, like half of the patrol rangers who carried guns, hunted on occasion. Bud, not a sportsman himself, did not want to know the specifics. Let them hunt, he thought. So long as they do it off park property.

Standing outside Spence's Grill, Jack and Vernon compared numbers bets and talked about the relative merits of the newest semi-auto .357 pistols. Then Vernon said he had to get back to Newberry, the taxidermy shop he managed.

"I'm going that way, I'm parked near the store," Jack said, glancing one last time across the street at Tusca Drugs. The two men walked leisurely, Vernon tapping the thin cigarette he'd just rolled, and Jack with his hat off, running the flat of his hand across his short white-blond hair he meant to have trimmed in a fashionable cut. Under the razor of the Tuscatanning barber he had ended up with a buzz.

Jack honked good bye to Vernon and headed out of town towards the park, thinking that he had not once told his friend how uncertain he was of Callie's love for him, how in fact, just a few months back she had crushed him. As was his ritual while he drove, he shifted his driving eye from road to mountain, framing the peak, holding it in his field of vision as if it were his.

In Tuscatanning, secrets covered the mountain region the way snowstorms did in winter, all surfaces brilliant, inviolate. The town council had a roadmaster and crew, but Jack and others in town had little faith in them. They got out there after a storm, but how much could you do when a new snow blast covered things up before you got clear the first time?

In the largely glass constructed Nature Center of Pitch Pine State Park there were few places to hide. But this morning Callie was flattened against the wall, vainly attempting to make herself small. Please don't see me. Go away, Eddie Egret, Callie thought, reverting to her code name for Jack Marsh.

For once it worked. Moving into overdrive, Jack Marsh sped down the halls of the Nature Center without spotting her. She felt huge relief. He reminded her of the cattle egrets in the fields outside Littlecomb, those dashing white birds who rode on top of cattle, posturing and pestering, waiting to pick through cow manure for food. Jack was Eddie Egret, so desperate for her he would pick through her life, ride her back, and never fly away.

No time to ponder Jack. She had a class to teach.

The narrow classroom with tall windows was full of students, most of them in their early twenties. They were studying at Pitch Pine State Park to get their licenses to become rangers. One of the students, a tanned young woman, was staring out the window at a birch tree, its thin branches interlacing in the wind. It was mid-November, and the first day of winter classes. The ranger program at Pitch Pine was designed to follow the change of seasons, matching class material with field work that fitted the environment and weather.

Looking directly at the young woman, Callie explained the details of their syllabus, exam information, and field assignments. She wrapped up her introductory lecture. "You should know this. I wouldn't be here teaching you, if I didn't love to daydream, stare out windows at birch trees."

The woman blinked, and smiled shyly at Callie, who was saying, "It's possible I've spent too much time gazing at the beauty of Pitch Pine. The state park gives me this job of teaching the basics because I haven't moved on, haven't taken promotions, as most of you will. I am what the park euphemistically calls a homesteader, I'm one of the permanent rangers." Callie's hand went to her hair. She had a habit of lifting it off her shoulder. Sometimes she felt the heft of it weigh her down. Homesteaders are the only ones who know their way around the park, she thought, dropping her hand to her side. People change positions too damn quick. Besides I've turned down those offers to go to the Great Smokies and to Glacier Park for a reason. I've done my stint out west and God willing, I'll never to go back. She shuddered at the memory of insufferable heat, and the blare of sunshine everywhere she turned.

To the class she said, "My first lesson to you is that for your own good, for better pay: stay mobile, take the promotions. They'll lead to administrative positions, even directorships."

For ten years now, Callie had worked as a Preservation Ranger at Pitch Pine. She began training the year she was reunited with her great aunt Winoshca Cowell. Aunt Teeny had for years discouraged such a meeting between her ward and the Indian woman. She wagged a finger in the air when she spoke of Winoshca's refusal to adapt to the modern world. She *would* persist in living in what Teeny saw as unsanitary conditions, the cabin without wooden floor-boards, no shower, the bathroom outside in some sort of makeshift latrine. And Winoshca would not give up her root and herb gathering habits, a time consuming, useless occupation, Teeny felt, especially when there were super-markets that sold nice plastic bags of anything from basil to marjoram.

Chapter EIGHT

Callie

My sense of place (I never want to leave Grandmother Mountain) couldn't be more opposite than that of my peripatetic adopted aunt. Teeny Wick quit so many jobs and hauled me from one town to another enough times to make my head swim. When I turned twelve she finally moved us to a town I liked. One week in our new neighborhood in Littlecomb, and I was in awe of Betty Denman. She was beautiful, spunky, and clearly she loved all her sons. The first time I saw her she didn't even notice I was there. Newton and I were crossing the backyard after my first climb up the treefort when we heard his mother.

Her voice was muffled under a bed sheet that had flopped down over her head from the clothesline above. A pearly line of smoke swirled out of the tent covering Betty Denman. She emerged from under the yellow flannel sheet.

"Jiminy Christmas! Damn, Damn, Jiminy Christmas!"

"What happened?" Newton raced over to her, me at his heels.

"Burned a hole in our good double bed sheet, that's what."

The smell of singed cotton drifted past my nose. "Damn wind blowing in just as I light up." She sighed and reached out to touch Newton's hair.

"You gonna quit again?" he said, hunching towards her. Newton was pitifully skinny, I could see every vertebrae through his t-shirt. But he had sparkly black eyes and eyebrows like no others I've seen, thin in the middle and then thick and curving around at the temples. They looked like big question marks that got knocked down.

She didn't look at him, just clamped down on the cigarette between her lips and went on getting a sheet on the line. She plastered her elbow against one drooping corner and clothespinned the other side nice and neat.

"Come on Ma, you did it before," Newton pleaded.

"Not me!" Betty said in a bright, fake way. Then she slumped a little, studied her son, and gave me a quick once over before turning back to her laundry. When I pulled my eyes away from her fine chestnut hair and full purple skirt that blew every which way as she attended to the clothes, I realized that Newton had run on ahead. I was daydreaming again, just staring at her and wishing that her family would adopt me.

On my twenty-first birthday I told Aunt Teeny I was going to get to know my Seneca relatives. There was nothing she could do to stop me. "Go on to Tuscatanning," my aunt said smugly. "Go and see if I care. You'll see that mountain life isn't for you."

In the summer after my last year of college (long after Teeny had uprooted us from Littlecomb) I set off, driving a second-hand Volvo with a creaky clutch out of Harrisburg and up the winding roads that led to the chain of peaks that had at its feet, the town of Littlecomb. As I drove into the hills and past the exit to Littlecomb I gripped that steering wheel hard, not permitting Newton to slip into my head. I ascended the mountain. Soon I was staring at the pitch pines on either side of me. The memory of these remarkable trees took me over, and I rejoiced in them, their needles clustered in starry balls that hung from dwarfed finger-like branches. So this was the way to my great aunt's place. It was a strange mountain pass; everywhere I looked were these curling trees with stately gray-brown bark cut into large oblong panels.

At least Aunt Teeny had given me directions to my aunt's place. I stuck to the hand-drawn map and found the cabin at the edge of a meadow on the mountain top. Winoshca greeted me skeptically. Less ample than I remembered, she had deep eye sockets and thin, muscled arms.

"And are you really, Callie?"

"I am, I swear I am."

"Well of course you are, but I wanted to hear it from your own lips," she said with a hearty laugh.

And most likely she did know me. I noticed that I had her same bones and thick hair. Winoshca drew back a second time, stern reserve in her voice. She told me that it was not right that Teeny Wick had kept me from my real family all these years.

"Why haven't you found your way home before now?"

"I don't know," I said, feeling confusion and remorse.

My aunt softened, perhaps because my grief over this long postponed visit was transparent. She invited me to stay the night.

Later, after a dinner of barley soup, fried zucchini with tomatoes, and home made bread, we sat talking. A light rain had started up, and a heavy wind followed, knocking the window pane and making it rattle. I shivered in pleasure, remembering the safety I had felt as a child inside that cabin.

"So many people have left," Winoshca said, stirring several heaping spoonfuls of honey into her tea. "Forced off the land when the government built the Kinzua Dam. Tried to drown our spirit, that's what they did. Think of the sacred graves that were drowned by the dam. The very last tribe in Pennsylvania was evacuated from the Cornplanter Reserve. Named for Chief Cornplanter, himself. Did you know what a great man he was? After he and his half-brother, Handsome Lake, gave up drink, they began having profound visions. They counseled their people to give up the destructive behaviors they had learned from the settlers." Winoshca sighed. "Most of our people are scattered to the winds. But not everyone. As you can see," she gestured to the cabin door.

It swung open – I had not even heard anyone drive up – and there was Mary, sauntering into the room. My cousin! I recalled that she was about a decade older than I was, and had been born to Winoshca on the far side of forty.

Mary ignored me and went directly to her mother. "Your long anticipated reunion with our lost orphan," she said, throwing her arm around Winoshca and squeezing the old lady as though she were a puppy. At last Mary looked me. "Mother thinks you have special powers," she said lightly.

"You'll like it on the mountain," Winoshca smiled. "It will come back to you, all the ways we honor ourselves, we honor the guardian spirit."

I stayed another night, and that evening there were more guests, people coming and going, mostly long lost cousins I had no memory of. Outside, the sky was threatening rain again. Nonetheless, we set up dinner at a long pine table in the yard. A huge woman incongruously named Willow Woman, and her husband, Joseph, flanked Winoshca. I was just sitting down to join everyone when I had to gasp. Jumping back from the table I looked instinctively for my cousin, Mary.

"What is that?" I tugged on her arm.

Mary didn't seem to understand.

I pointed up at six dead and bloodied sheep, hanging feet first from different limbs on the tall shade tree over our table.

"Sheep dog went mad," Mary said in a matter-of-fact voice. She glanced at the carcasses. "Killed those six ewes, ravaged five more."

Before I could ask, Mary added, "We don't know what got into him." I nodded uncertainly. The rain clouds had wandered away, and the pitch pines cast long shadows that reached into the enclosure. The sheep carcasses darkened. Suddenly, a crack of gunfire sounded from behind the cabin. "That'll be Joe," Mary said. "Had to put the dog down." I shuddered. Above, the sky was dimming, taking on the reflection of the trees. The clouds were a chalky ice-green. I glanced at the row of matted, mangled sheep.

"Hey, don't get shook." Mary was concerned.

"I prayed to the bear," Winoshca murmured. "It will be all right."

"What?" I looked at her as if she was crazy. I must have misunderstood.

"I asked her permission. The bear's. We wouldn't take an animal's life – not even that snarly dog's – any other way."

"Oh." I felt sharp darts of pain behind my eyes. Something here was uncomfortably familiar. What had I lost by living all those years with Aunt Teeny?

Six months after my visit with Winoshca, Aunt Teeny died from a blood clot that traveled to her heart. Perhaps callous, or maybe wise, I wasted little time mourning my false guardian. I was at loose ends, though, when I wrote to the superintendent at Pitch Pine State Park for late enrollment to the ranger training program. It was an impassioned, badly composed letter. I can't think of why

Bud Mason admitted me to the student program, unless it was that I told the truth about the beauty of the pine barrens.

I had planned on living with or near Winoshca, if she would have me. This was not to be, for my great aunt followed Teeny's footsteps toward serious illness. For weeks she had congested lungs, and then after complications from a bout with pneumonia, she died in her sleep.

In our several talks together Winoshca had unearthed the stratum in my heart that yearned for the natural world. I decided to become a steward of the forest, and only wish that my great aunt were alive to see that I had chosen to follow her path. I also regret that my great aunt got sick before she and I had a chance to talk more about this great bear, the spirit guide she used to speak of reverentially. It was what she did not say about the bear, in the end, that troubled me. Perhaps she no longer thought me worthy of her confidence.

As time went on I tried not to think of Winoshca, for every thought of her brought to mind her talk of the bear spirit on Grandmother Mountain. I had reason to feel uneasy, too, especially once I realized that I was pregnant. I grew uneasy, not only because of who the father was – and I will get to that – but because of the strange features of my pregnancy. I am more knowledgeable than you would think, about what goes on there. Here are the facts: I spent one night with a ranger named Jack Marsh, and that had to be the night I got pregnant.

Here is the kicker. My pregnancy did not show up for several months and believe me, I had pregnancy tests right away. The only person I had sex with was Jack, just once, and I did not, have not had any kind of artificial insemination. It was as if the egg and seed were firmly in me, but not activated for nearly three months.

Impossible.

I am, interestingly, curious rather than fearful about the bizarre developments in my womb. I seem to be remarkably healthy and feel superstitious, if you will, about getting too upset. That could affect my unborn infant.

I need to look back, and try to see what led me to this moment.

My first job as a ranger took me far away from Pennsylvania, and I have to say I hated it. Not at first, but there were things that happened that I have had to forget. Whenever a memory from that time seeps up through my pores, as it will do, I've learned how to drop quickly into hibernation. I call it that because outwardly I am able to function – much as bears breathe and even give birth in hibernation – but my feelings are cancelled, I knock them dead to sleep.

My second job brought me home to Grandmother Mountain where Bud Mason had offered me a position at Pitch Pine State Park.

It was not until this, my thirty-fourth year, that Jack came along, and *Newton* returned to my life. I have surprised myself. For many years now I've had the same job, kept to myself, and been wary of love relationships. In short, I am a cautious person, and it is shocking to witness my new desires to love a man fully. Why though, has this sweet longing come, and been so long in coming? This is no parable of leaving the overgrown forest, parting the branches to the open field beyond. On the contrary, I still walk through thickets deep with pine needles and pricking things. I have known the stab and prick of one man, but not the other, not the man I sealed my childhood with. I am pregnant, and have no desire to see or be with the baby's father.

Jack Marsh wasn't wired at the beginning. Maybe a little headstrong, but easy to talk to. It was a freak moment in my life when I said yes to this man who worked with me. Blue-eyed, boyish, and tight muscled in the shoulders and legs, Jack had the proportions to make the Protective ranger's dull, standard cut uniform seem almost jaunty.

We were rangers up at Pitch Pine. The management at the State Park gave us both plenty to gripe about, and so we had dinner together one night at the Jolly Logger Inn. When I laughed at one of his jokes, touching his arm as I did, Jack said, "I never figured you to be so friendly." Then, as if suspicious, he asked. "How come? I didn't think you liked me."

"Changed my mind, I guess."

"You could have your pick. Any of the rangers on board, I bet."

I shrugged, then caught the waitress' eye. "I'd like some coffee." And to Jack, "Want a cup?"

It seemed uncomplicated at the time. I was both passive and direct. I wanted to erase once and for all my last big relationship with a man. It had been a full five years since I had a lover. Of course I forgot that I had tried this erasure method two other times, hopping in bed with a man, thinking it would undo, cover over the bad in my life. But memory is short, and as I said, it had been a long time.

That night with Jack, we arranged for a room at the inn. I was nervous, and went over my reasons for doing this. Simple desire. Check. Long time no sex. Check. A hint of mystery. Check. Jack did not strike me as an especially happy man, but his intensity and bravado were intriguing, or perhaps amusing to me. I hadn't decided which.

I followed him toward the back stairs in the tavern.

"You know Junior?" Jack asked, bounding up the steps, two at a time.

"Sure." Junior Keeping's family had owned the Logger forever.

Jack jingled the room key. "I heard that his family buries their dead in the front yard of the inn."

"You're kidding!" I stood stock still, watching him unlock the bedroom door. Then, recovering, "No limit to family love, I guess."

I almost changed my mind about going to bed with Jack Marsh then and there.

It could have been the bed that threw things off. It had a too-small box spring and an old mattress that dripped over the edges. I could not get myself so that I was on one even plane. That's what I remember. The floppy mattress, my legs or head hanging over the edge. Myself uneven.

Chapter NINE

Pete sighted Ralph Waters in the side yard of his house.

"I'm glad you stopped by." Ralph took the police officer's extended hand in his two palms. "I hope you don't mind if we stand outside. I'm watching my granddaughter."

"Not at all," said Pete, glad to see Mr. Waters so vibrant, given the circumstances of his wife's death. He was a large man in his sixties, with plenty of smooth gray hair, and pouched eyes. The object of his happy attention was a thin child wearing overalls and a Pooh Bear baseball cap, sideways. She was swinging on the monkey bar of a jungle gym.

Pete turned to Mr. Waters. "We have the results of your wife's autopsy."

Ralph Waters seemed not to have heard Pete. "Come meet Allison, Theresa's and my reason for living." The corners of his mouth jumped, registering pain. "I'm sorry, I keep forgetting. It's so natural to think *we.*"

"This must be a hard time for you," Pete said, "and for Allison." He glanced at the elfin form.

"Theresa and I were looking forward to Allison's stay with us. Her mother is in the Air Force. She's a video photographer who got sent to Sarajevo for a couple of years. She'll be there for the next few months until her new orders come in.

Pete didn't ask about the child's father. He had heard that Wendy Waters was divorced soon after the birth of her little girl. He watched Allison hanging on her knees, and called out, "You are quite the gymnast. Very nimble."

She jumped down and came over to where the two men stood.

"I can read," she said.

"That's impressive." He noticed her staring at his missing finger. "It was a rattlesnake," he told her. "It got me good."

"Oh." She switched her baseball cap to the other side of her head. "My nickname is Allie."

"I knew a little girl who lived near here, and her name rhymed with yours." Pete was thinking of Callie.

"Did you know her when you were my age? I bet she was your girlfriend!"

This threw Pete off, but Allison hadn't noticed. "I can read nursery rhymes. You want to see? I have a big book of them." Allie ran into the house.

Ralph Waters walked over to an oak hewn picnic table on a gravelly patio near the driveway. "It's a nice table, isn't it? Got it in Lancaster. Made by an Amish man named Abner. I do like the odd homemade thing, don't you? Let's sit down. I want to know about Theresa."

Apparently Ralph was done with being chatty. "It was a complicated autopsy," Pete said. "There were a number of possibilities and little to go on. You had asked me about her diabetes. Well, the coroner ruled out death by diabetic coma. They did find a trace of carbon monoxide in her lungs but it was such a small amount that they ruled out smoke inhalation."

"Get to the point," said Ralph, no longer expansive and smiling. "Who or what killed my wife?"

Pete studied Mr. Waters. "I'm trying to be thorough. The autopsy opinion is death by homicide. She died of internal bleeding which compressed the brain. Subdural Hematoma, they call it."

"She was murdered?"

"The coroner's opinion is homicide through fatal violence, which means that at this point we don't know the whys, the intent behind the violence. She appears to have fallen and hit her forehead." Pete stared evenly at Waters. "Then she was struck by a blunt wooden object at the back of the head, from above. By who, we don't know yet."

"Are you saying someone came at her with a baseball bat?" Ralph's face registered disbelief.

"Two times she was struck. That's what's interesting," Pete mulled, reading over the report in his hands. "The weapon hasn't been identified, sir, but the coroner's x-ray found paint chips buried in her scalp. It doesn't look like your wife was involved in a struggle. There was no sign of skin fibers from someone else under her fingernails or on her clothing."

"Thank God for that," said Mr. Waters quietly. "What about this Newton Denman? Theresa said it was him."

"Circumstantial evidence, Mr. Waters. She thought she saw him, but it was dark out, and she was some distance from whoever it was."

"My wife wouldn't make up these things." He got up abruptly. "I'll be right back."

Pete wasn't surprised to see Ralph upset. If anything, he had expected more emotion from the man.

Waters returned with a large, mildewed cardboard box of papers in his arms. "I've been meaning to give these to you. They're school papers from the years Theresa was an academic advisor at Littlecomb Elementary. She did that in addition to teaching art. She was Newton Denman's advisor for a few years. She used to complain about his attitude. You probably know that he hated my wife." He dropped the box at Pete's feet. "Frankly, I'm not up to going through them."

"Thanks, they might be useful." He got up from the picnic table. "Where's Allie? I thought she was going to show me how she could read."

"She must have forgotten. Probably has her nose in a book," Ralph said, heading up his front walk, obviously intent on ending the conversation.

The police officer had other ideas. Now that he knew the child would not pop into sight any second, Pete picked up the cardboard box and caught up with Mr. Waters. "I need to know – for the record, you understand – where you were at the time of your wife's evening walk with her dog?"

Waters hesitated, perhaps in silent memory of those awful moments before his wife's death. "I was in our library. Theresa and I had put Allison to bed right before she went out on her walk with Honey."

"What time did you leave the house, to go looking for your wife?"

"It was ten forty-five."

"Any witnesses?"

"I was on the phone with my daughter Wendy before I went out. That's how I remember the time."

Pete nodded. "Fine. Thanks so much. I'll let you know if I turn up anything useful in the box." Pete readjusted the weight of the once sodden load. "Say, would you happen to have your daughter's phone number? I'd like to be able to talk to her."

Mr. Waters laughed. "Not while she's in Sarajevo, you won't. Hardly anyone can get hold of her."

Driving home, Pete had the uneasy feeling that Ralph had been lying about the cardboard box of papers, and that the man knew exactly what the contents were. And it was not as if he was helpful about how to get hold of his daughter to verify the phone call to her the night of the arson and the death of Mrs. Waters.

The trooper realized he had scarcely considered the possibility that Ralph Waters had dealt the fatal blow that ultimately killed his wife. Suppose he zipped over to the school soon after Theresa herself left, struck her, but something goes wrong and she's still walking. Then he runs into me, thought Pete. And the arsenal of fire fighters.

Yet the man's sorrow over his wife was no pretense. How to sort this death out? For starters, who was to say that the same person who attacked Theresa also set the school on fire?

Pete arrived home, picked up his paper, and then his cat, Pandora, who had punished him for forgetting to change her kitty litter by throwing the contents of the litter box all over the laundry room, where he unwisely kept the box. He swept it up, and thought about getting out the mop.

Do I have any proof that the Waters' marriage was strong? And why can't you clean up your own messes? Pete waved the dust pan at Pandora, who, feeling not the least bit threatened, rubbed contentedly against his ankles.

That night Pete dreamed he was standing on top of a mesa waving a banner. The truth of Theresa Water's death was spelled out on the banner. Pete held it up for all the world to see, only the light was painfully bright and he could not read it himself. Any number of folks from Phoenix will tell you that from May to October the sun is the enemy. This is the time when temperatures will climb to one hundred and twenty degrees. Pete could not hide from the sun.

That day it was a laser searing his eyes, and there was something else. He was aware of a slithering motion, and then he knew. He heard the awful whirring of diamondback rattlesnakes.

"Sorry to bust in like this, Sir." Pete stood in the open doorway of his superior, Detective Hal Rendell's office. "Come in quick," said the small, angular man. "Look at this, Myrick, five spanking new computers for when you boys work the rural areas."

Pete stared at his boss a moment, tempted to point out that it was nothing but rural in this county. A waste of time, he decided. "Sir, I need to talk about the Waters case."

"Got a break in it? What about the three of them, Newton and his brothers all in on the murder together?"

"Nothing points that way. As for the older brothers, they're more or less in the clear. I spoke at length with Elijah Jones, proprietor of the Lounge. He remembers how eager Nat and George were to start off and get their hunting camp set up, even if it was after dark. Jones figures they were long gone from Littlecomb by nine fifteen. They were so excited to get going they even forgot the case of beer they bought. He and four other witnesses at the bar are convinced Nat and George were in great spirits. No signs of furtive or angry behavior. But sir, there's a key point I need to discuss with you. It's this autopsy."

He unfolded the coroner's report. "It states that Theresa Waters had a blow to her head in two places."

"I saw it. Take a look at these babies." Hal ran his fingers along the space bar of the nearest smooth gray keyboard. "Each of you officers will have one while on patrol. Report writing time will be cut in half."

"Sir, about the coroner's report. It doesn't seem right."

"How so?" Hal was surprised. He had been promoted and transferred to Black Creek County from Pittsburgh where the coroners were known for their perfectionism.

"I am almost sure that Theresa was struck in three places, not two. Each one a blow to the head. You see, I was playing medic. Hate that stuff, but I was the first one to find her walking with Mr. Waters. When I examined her I remember there was that blow at the back, the front, and then, yes absolutely there was blood coming from a third wound."

Reluctantly, Hal took his eyes off the new compact computers and rested them on Pete's worried face. "This is the first I'm hearing of this? Where was the third wound?"

"Sorry sir. I'm only just confirming this myself. The blood came from her head. But as I said, no mention from the coroner. He really botched this one."

"The medical examiner not doing his job?" Hal was surprised.

"Over in Black Creek we have a coroner, sure, but he's not a qualified pathologist."

"He did the autopsy and he's not a forensic pathologist?"

"Doesn't have to be out here," said Pete. "We're such small potatoes most of our deaths only require a blood test for alcohol and drugs. The basics."

"You are *almost* sure you remember a third wound. Myrick, I want you to be damn sure before you go hire in an expensive examiner."

"Yes Sir."

Hal blocked the door that Pete seemed anxious to exit. "You can't leave," he said, smiling. "Not without your brand new waterproof Panasonic."

It seemed like Callie had been teaching these winter session courses at Pitch Pine State Park forever. At the end of that first day of class in November, she gathered everyone's registrations and social security numbers, and flew out the door. She had to deliver the class list to the park secretary's office and then hurry to meet her three o'clock schedule to guide a band of school children through the nature dioramas. She rushed down the main hall of the Nature Center.

"Hey Callie, wait up. You dropped a paper." It was Jack Marsh. He looked at the form and turned it over in his hand. "Looks pri-teeee important. Don't want to lose those student social security numbers!"

She snatched the paper from him, and felt guilty immediately for overreacting.

"Just kidding around," Jack said, smiling tenderly at her. "Why don't we go some place for a bite to eat after work, talk this thing out?"

"Again?"

He reached out to touch her arm. She flinched, her long ponytail swinging crazily from side to side. It dawned on him that she had recoiled. It wasn't as if he was hard to look at – so what made her act like he was an embarrassing mistake, something she had spilled on herself while eating. He grew incensed. He was nothing more to Callie than Jell-O in her lap. Maybe he was less than Jell-O to her. "You're not yourself," Jack said testily. "Don't see why you don't go for that operation."

Callie took a deep breath, then drew herself up, tough as nails. "Now what do you think?" She patted her four month pregnant belly which protruded slightly under the coarse thread, uniform shirt tucked neatly into her trousers. She had begun to show soon after the tests finally revealed a developing fetus.

Though Callie had decided to have natural childbirth at a birthing center she went at first for regular visits with an obstetrician. Doc Sandy, as Callie thought of Sandra Mite, her doctor, was worried about Callie, and then simply fascinated. "It would appear," she told the ranger, "you have had a delayed implantation of the egg. It was fertilized but then did not develop for three months. Amazing, really. It looks like it was simply free floating."

She stared at Callie as if she were some kind of monster.

"Okay, now you've got me nervous."

"Me too. I'll give it to you straight. This kind of thing does not happen in normal humans. I've been following you so carefully, all the negative tests, and now this – *Bing*, you're four months pregnant. It's as if you, the host, were deciding to wait until your body was really sure you had enough fuel and energy to proceed. There's only one other mammal that comes to mind, who is known for this miracle."

Callie waited patiently, though she was not surprised to hear the answer.

"Bears," Doctor Mite said, laughing. "Isn't that ridiculous? I'd better go over your files again. Something's not right here. No doubt, my mistake."

"Yeah, pretty ridiculous," Callie said, nodding vigorously and knowing that she would not be returning to this doctor. She decided she did not want to become a freak science show for the medical world. Callie's hand went reflexively to her swollen belly. The news that her pregnancy resembled that of a bear was too weird. She wanted the life of this child to proceed naturally, she wanted it,

her or him to be normal. Dismiss this nonsense, she told herself. You're good
at that. Shut it down.

"I don't know what to think any more," Jack was saying. "I swear Callie, the
way you play games with me." As he spoke she walked swiftly, passing the glass
exhibits of stuffed ospreys and golden eagles. Jack ran alongside her. "What are
you going to do, never talk to me again?"

Callie stopped outside the secretary's office. "I won't dignify those cracks
with an answer. I'm not playing games though." This was not what Jack wanted
to hear. He wanted her to confess that she loved him. She had never actually
said she didn't, he thought with a jet of hope. He leaned over her shoulder, his
palm flat against the door behind her. "It was kinda nice. In bed together, I
mean. You gotta admit that. You gotta admit it was good."

"Was it?"

Jack felt as if he had been slapped. He was close at her side, hissing, *"Indian
princess, Nature lover,* you hadn't done it in years. How would you know a good
lover from a bobcat?"

Callie opened the door, but before she went in she squinted at Jack for a
few protracted seconds. Then in a low voice, she said, "No, I definitely think a
bobcat would have more agility than you."

This stopped him short, but not for long. Loud and bluff, he laughed at
her bestial comparison, and strolled off. As for Callie, the jibe about the nature
lover burned in her ears. The Preventive rangers looked down at the Naturalists
for being sissies. Fern fondlers, they liked to quip.

The school children were wild. They weren't interested in the fungi or ferns
at the Nature Center, or the molds their teacher wanted Callie to point out to
them in the glass displays.

I should get out of this place, Callie thought distractedly. Go have my baby
somewhere else. These run-ins with Jack are bad news. Don't want to leave,
though. She gazed at the school children, suddenly recognizing one as part of
the family whose cabin stove didn't work right last summer. Callie relaxed. Bud
Mason called on me, she remembered. That's what comes from staying in one
place a long time. You get called on to tend to things that none of the newer

rangers know. If I left, who would know how to fix the stove in cabin 40, track down the woolly aphid infestations, shoo off the band of robber raccoons who ate through the rubber window linings on five Winnebagos last summer; who else around here can gauge a bear's mood when it comes poking too close to the campground?

The singular fact of Callie's relationship with Jack was that he hadn't seemed quite right for her. She sensed this and yet made an ungainly leap to ignore her feelings. He was, after all, handsome, forthright, amusing in a headstrong sort of way, and a colleague. It was natural they would get together and it had surprised no one at Pitch Pine. What did amaze people was that Callie got pregnant. Later she would realize that her great desire to have that child had guided her to intentionally forget her diaphragm. Certainly it was not ignorance of birth control methods.

Almost nightly in the months before she and Jack got together Callie dreamed of babies. She would wake up smelling the sweet scalp of an infant. She had been around infants just enough to have witnessed the ridiculous power of the baby powder, milk burp, sweet breath, and new skin perfume. It began to permeate her thoughts. This is idiotic, she scolded herself. I am the last person I know to have a tide of maternal desire.

Then one day Callie stopped resisting. She simply stepped aside. Let me be honest, she thought. Let me be flooded.

After Jack learned she was pregnant he encouraged her to abort. She said no, and when he grudgingly asked her to marry him it looked as if he was on the verge of accepting the idea of a baby. She hardly knew what to do. Didn't the child to come need a father? Of course it would, but then again Jack had told her after she was pregnant that he had never wanted any children.

Then she tried mightily to love Jack. Too bad about the intrigue she thought she saw in him on the night they decided to make love. There was no mystery to Jack, after all. He was all theater and his quasi-sad surface was just that. If by chance, there was more to him lurking below, it was a great pity, for it had been covered over with an outstanding lacquer job.

Still, she must do her best and learn to love him. She had read somewhere that this was possible. Perhaps, in time, he would learn to love children. They must marry. He was wild about her, that part she knew.

"Maybe we could be a family," she said hesitantly to Jack.

"Callie, you need to get rid of the baby. I have no interest in raising a child, never have. I don't like kids."

"Go away then. I don't need you," she told him.

After this he turned on her.

Once she made these decisions, yes to have the baby, no to marry Jack, new worries assailed her. Suppose her instincts for wanting this child were wrong. Suppose she suffered the pain of childbirth, there was the baby, and those stray pieces of herself she was looking for, eluded her still? That knowing sense of things I had at age ten and twelve, Callie thought. Almost molecular, solid, a kind of earth logic that Newton used to marvel at when we were kids, even though he tried not to let on that he was marveling.

Jack Marsh had unsettled her. For one thing she had not been entirely honest with him, had not told him plainly that she didn't love him, though it seemed to her this must be obvious.

She saw her relationship with him as yet another example of how she had lost the knowing, and acted now on misdirected impulse. Callie often felt she let the people in her life, and even the animals, or the weather flow in and out of her as though she were a shape-shifting sponge. Hardly a good way to be, in this entropic world. She had an uncanny feeling that she was more than one entity, nothing large and universal, but more a porous, too porous kind of creature.

Part Two

Despite Von Schrenck's extensive observation and detailed records, all of which point to the intimate spiritual bond the people felt toward the bears... some aspects about this peculiar relationship (were kept) to themselves.

from <u>Bears</u>, *a brief history*, Bernd Brunner

Chapter TEN

Nat Denman felt it was his duty to provide a running commentary on Newton. He was defending his little brother, he told himself. In the Big Springs Lounge Nat sat at the bar rolling a closed pen knife between his fingers. Twelve weeks had passed since Newton fled Littlecomb.

"Do you think Newt is going to catch up to this big bruin he's after? There's been talk about a monster size bear up in the mountains." Elijah gave the counter a swipe and tossed the cloth onto his shoulder.

"Newt ain't necessarily the best hunter or the worst hunter." Nat was enjoying the attention he got by talking about his brother. Betty had explained to her older boys that Newton was on a hunting trip. He was after a black bear. The brothers had let the word leak out at the bar. The regulars didn't know the whereabouts of Newton, but they understood he was hiding out, and biding his time in the most honorable way, that is to say, he was hunting bear.

"Yeah I took Newton on his first hunting trip. Taught him most of what he knows," said Nat.

"And I taught Superman what he knows," George said with a laugh, from the other end of the bar. There was no malice in his generous velvet voice.

But Nat took it wrong. Who was George to be making fun of him? Especially after what happened to Mrs. Waters, not to mention the school. He yanked on the bill of his navy blue hunting cap. He wore the cap low over his brow. Nat was going to retort, tell his brother what for, but he didn't want to start a fight right there in the bar. He was also just a shade afraid of his larger, older brother. "Give me a another beer," he said to Elijah, and then feeling bolstered, he reminded himself that he had no reason to fear George. Not any more, not since he knew some things George had missed entirely on that night at the Elementary school.

This cheered him up. What Nat didn't like to think about was how much he resented his two brothers. He could not understand why Newt, a pipsqueak bookworm when he was little, and George a drunk who all but killed himself more than once got more attention from Ma than he did. Ma called Newton her sensitive one, and George, her big, charming boy.

Nat turned to the bar. Someone was talking.

"I want you boys to hear this. I've been playing checkers with your grandpa for near half a century." It was Gib Setter, whining in his insinuating way. "I wouldn't say anything to upset you Denmans, but I've got to ask you this. Did Newton hunt down that lady art teacher? Did he do it to her?"

"That's enough." George jumped to his feet. "Come on Natty, we're out of here."

"Wait a minute," the younger brother protested, surprised and a little resentful at the way George was taking charge. It was usually Nat who told George when to leave. "You can't talk to us that way," Nat said to Gib and Elijah. "Let me set you straight. Course my brother didn't do any such thing. Didn't I tell you I taught Newt how to hold a rifle?"

"Nat," came George's warning voice.

"Sure I did, and you know what? My baby brother couldn't hurt a fly. Teaching Newton how to get a sighting on his rifle was nothing compared to how I tried to teach that boy to be kind to others."

"Cut the bull." George's voice, ever warm, had taken on a ferocious edge.

"Excuse me?" Nat yanked at his hat defensively.

"Give it up, brother. We're going home."

Nat stared at him, his face clenched. In that hot ferocious voice Nat heard George the night of the arson: "I got you Bitchety Block." And yet, Nat knew George was not the only one involved that night. For now though, it was best to keep big brother feeling guilty.

Callie cupped her hands to receive the communion wafer. It was the morning after her confrontation with Jack, and she was in Tuscatanning for the Sunday church service. When she was in church she most frequently prayed to God, who wore a formal robe during service. When she was in the woods looking at the stars she spoke to the Great Spirit because the earth and sky asked it of her. Callie exchanged these names freely, although her God and Great Spirit were one and the same.

After the Eucharist, she knelt in the balcony pew where she always sat and tried to pray that she learn to forgive. Forgive who and what – her enemies? Strictly speaking, Jack Marsh was not her enemy. Sometimes she wanted to classify her father as an enemy but then again she had never known him. He left her mother when she was six months pregnant with Callie. And besides, Callie thought, it's hardest to deal with an unknown enemy. Chin resting on her clasped hands, and knees lowered on the petit point kneeler, she wondered at the possibility of fetal knowledge, of her having known her father, after all, his hands pressed up warm against the round cave that was her mother's stomach as it held Callie and grew with her, large and hard. But shortly before she was born her father was gone. Callie grit her teeth. She could not even pray for her mother who had betrayed her, almost the same as her father – maybe worse, for her mother had chosen foolishly. She had orphaned Callie in an act that could so easily have been avoided. She imagined her mother at the site where she worked, and the place on the unwieldy scaffold where she took a wrong step. Callie could not bear to picture her mother plummeting to the ground.

The daughter judged the act bitterly. Had she been thinking, Callie decided, she would never have taken such a job when I was an infant. Had she been a *responsible* mother I would have had a parent to raise me. Callie shuddered. What she feared most was that she herself would be an irresponsible mother. Another side of her understood this was unlikely, and yet the worry was there. There were things that had happened, things she hid from in her own cave.

She switched gears and concentrated on those she felt more benign towards: her boss Bud Mason, recently widowed; Spence and his wife, the owners of the Grocery in town; her sitting-up-on-the-mountain Great Aunt Winoshca; cousin Mary; Mrs. Pope with the puffy legs who lived downstairs in her apartment building; even petty old Aunt Teeny Wick found a place in Callie's prayers. She prayed for and to these people fervently, both the live and the dead ones. Even Newton crept into her worship.

Callie prayed that Newton had left the park, for his own safety, and more honestly, for her protection against what would happen between them should they meet again. Callie crushed her eyes against her knuckles when she begged the Holy Ghost to let her know if this dear old friend turned hunter was someone to watch out for, to be cautious with. Newton's face swam before her. She prayed it away.

His eyes and smile returned. She prayed more ferociously but he remained. This time she simply stared at his face which was speaking to her out of that lovely mouth cut high and certain as the rim of a cup bending to you.

Shaken, she fixed her eyes on the pew in front of her. A little girl with a pixie haircut sat next to her brother playing rock, paper, and scissors. A good church game, quiet enough so they won't get caught, Callie thought, looking over her folded hands at the children nodding one, two, three. The boy waved two fingers (scissors) which cut the girl's flat palm (paper). In the next round the girl made a fist (rock) which could smash the scissors he produced a second time. Dear God, Callie whispered, help me not to limit my child, don't let this baby in my belly be a boy who is sharp as scissors, or a girl who is hard as a rock. Make him or her contain all your earthly elements. Sapling and flint together, that's what my child needs to be, she thought, drawing on the creation legends from the Seneca tribe.

At the altar, Cameron Shawl folded the white cloth and handed it to the minister. He passed the chalice to her, the two of them finishing off the wine from the Eucharist sacrament. Cameron Shawl was a strong presence in their church, her small shouldered, broad-hipped stance now invoking everyone to stand. When looking at her Callie thought of the letter A. Her face with its narrow temple and broad cheekbones, and the A shaped body in its flowing robes was animated and collected. How does she do it, wondered Callie. One of the Tuscatanning Police officers, part-time Deacon, mother of six, all this in one.

Deacon Shawl faced the congregation, the minister having retired to his uncomfortable high backed chair to the left of the choir loft. Swaying, as though she knew this was a ceremony and self-consciousness had no part in it, she raised her white bell sleeves. Usually she wore black, but because she gave the sermon today the priest conferred on her the honor of full ministerly vestments. "Praise God from whom all blessings flow," Shawl sang, beginning the doxology. Callie basked in the familiar words recited by the Deacon, and wished for a second that she could sit and listen to chants and hymns all day.

After the service, she went to Spence's Grill and Grocery. Spence greeted her the usual way.

"Going to forget something today?"

"Not me," she grinned.

"Rats. I was thinking I could use a few blank checks."

Every time she came into the store, for years now, he made some reference to the time she had left her checkbook behind, sitting right out on the counter. Callie was thinking that maybe she ought to leave some other item for him to turn up. His story could use a new angle.

Spence had canned food that could not pretend for the dust that layered it to be less than six months old. The produce was dubious, the bread usually hard, and the candy, stale. Still, Callie was loyal to Spence, who made her wonderful cheese and pepper omelets on his grill. He was her friend, and besides, shopping at Spence's was better than making the hour drive down the mountain to the nearest supersized grocery. She was altogether uncomfortable anywhere near that area with its huge, warehouse of food, dizzying rate of construction, encroaching executive residence developments, and general suburban congestion that wouldn't be curbed.

Today she took her time shopping. Starting tomorrow she had two days in a row off work, and she meant to enjoy every inch of it. As she picked through the bread for a loaf without traces of mold, and the produce for one firm lemon she heard a familiar voice in the next aisle over. It was Jack Marsh.

"Oh he was after something all right," Marsh was saying. "I could tell by the two month beard, the vest with all the pockets, a knife bulging in one of them; bullets probably, in another. Real tall man, dark eyes, or was it the eyebrows that were so black? Had to be a hunter." He paused thoughtfully. "Can't believe the clothes he was wearing in this heat."

"Practically a heat wave for November," said a second voice. "My guess," Jack said, "is that he doesn't know that hunting is against the law in Pitch Pine."

The second voice followed him, laughing in low tones. "I guess you would know."

Callie recognized the eager to please Vernon. The two men had moved to the back of the store. Callie squeezed one lemon and picked up a second. She slipped noiselessly to the end of the aisle so that she could hear them clearly.

"What are you talking about?" Jack crowed to Vernon. "I don't know a thing about hunting, except that it is a pri-teee serious crime in this State Park. Would you believe it, that redneck was chowing down at the bar a few minutes ago – Millie's cooking too. The only bar in town, and cooking isn't one of her talents." Both men sounded distinctly sorrowful. "But there's that raggedy S.O.B. gobbling up her greasy burgers and fries like it was his first real meal in a long time. Anybody could see he's been tracking up on the mountain."

Vernon was beginning to get excited. "I wonder if that wasn't his yellow Chevy? It's parked outside the Logger."

"You get an eyeful of that, too? It's gotta be his truck, only strange one around."

"Maybe he's after somethin' good," Vernon said. "Dog to the bone."

Callie heard Jack mutter incomprehensibly, and then loud enough for her to hear. "If he is, it's my job to nail him. Bet he's still having a few at the Logger. Think I'll just happen on over there, one more time. Go see what's what."

Callie moved swiftly to the front counter of the store. "Thought you were going to buy a lemon?" Spence called to her as she swung out the door. She stuck her head back in. "Here, catch" She pitched first one lemon, then a second at him. "I'll pick them up tomorrow, and remember – this time you and Jessie are going to try some of my lemon and dill soup." Spence shook his head and slapped his hands on his non-existent hips, snake hips, Jessie, his wife, called them.

"Laughing at your own jokes?" Vernon said, dropping a granola bar and a bottle of Yoo Hoo on the counter. Jack joined them. He stared curiously over his friend's lank brown hair, at the door slowly closing. Who had just gone out?

Her entire frame shook, including the gentle arc of the four month pregnancy, when she recognized through the front window at the Jolly Logger Tavern, Newton's dark shaggy hair and long back leaning forward over the bar. She waited a minute before going in. The bartender was busy with another customer.

She slipped into the tavern. Newton turned instantly at the sound of someone coming up behind him.

"Callie!" He had one foot on the bar stool, the other on the floor. He noticed the color in her face first. The high forehead was shiny, and her hair streaming like banners in a dropping wind.

"I had to find you," she puffed.

Newton stood up. "I almost left the mountain for good," he said, excited to see her. "But I had to come back." He paused, his thoughts coming in a jumble. He couldn't mention the bear – what about his loneliness and longing to see Callie again? That was real, that was true, but no, suppose she laughed at his romantic notions. Newton's eye traveled over her face, the cupid's bow lips, small fine chin, and straight shoulders; he stopped at the bow of her belly, and sucked in his breath.

Callie spoke quickly. "I need to talk to you. Not here. Come outside to my Jeep. It's around the corner in the church parking lot." Newton blinked hard, as if that would clarify what was going on.

"We have to go now," she urged. "No, not that way," she said as he loped towards the front door. She motioned toward the exit at the back of the bar.

He sighed, tightened his grip on his backpack and followed her out. Hadn't he often followed her to uncertain places when they were kids together? He felt for a minute the delicious sensation that she was taking his hand and hoisting him upward, like the time she got him to climb that sycamore in Littlecomb. She had urged him on, said he would see the whole Milky Way if he ventured higher. The leg up into a Callie-refracted view of the world, he thought. Let her lead me. We'll see.

She steered out of town, her foot to the floorboard as they drove. "It's not a real speedy car, especially not up a hill like this," she said, exhaling. The Jeep juddered and roared as if asked to go eighty miles an hour. The speedometer read twenty-five. Callie downshifted, the accelerator still on the floor.

"Where are we going?" Newton yelled out over the noisy motor. No answer. "Hey, what about my truck?" He had completely forgotten that it was parked near the Jolly Logger.

"We'll get it soon," Callie said cheerfully.

"Where are you taking me?" Like a man who had been drugged and was finally coming to, he demanded some answers. "Who the hell do you think you are to, to –," he took a deep breath. "First I'm glad to see you, then I see you close, and you're different. You've got a child on the way. Been married long?" His hair, badly in need of a trim, whipped against his face. He clutched his pack to his chest. "And next you just about kidnap me. Jesus, Callie –"

"One of the patrol rangers at Pitch Pine, a guy named Jack Marsh, saw you in the bar. He thinks you're hunting on park property," she said evenly. "He was on his way over to the Logger to get a closer look, maybe trail you to your camp, and then who knows what he'd do next? You know why I say that? Because, Newton Denman, I don't think hunting is the only reason you're hiding out up Grandmother Mountain. There's something else. I can smell it."

"I'm an outsider here. You're determined to smell something."

"You'd think you were the only outsider in the world."

"No I don't. And they're not necessarily noble types, believe me. Take Pete Myrick –" Newton cut himself off. What was he thinking of?

"Pete? Where is he? What's he got to do with you being here?"

"Nothing. You said something about outsiders. He's one, that's all."

"What do you mean?"

"He left Pennsylvania a long time ago. When he came back it wasn't the same. He wasn't the same. People don't seem to warm up to him. You know how small towns are. They don't appreciate their own going off, acting like Littlecomb isn't good enough for them."

Callie made no answer. Newton may have been glad she dropped the subject of why he was here, but as for Callie the news of Pete had made her sad. Finally she said, "Is your campsite still at Blue Quarry?"

Newton nodded, and she screeched to a stop. They were about a mile from town. "Keys?" She held out her hand expectantly, and jingled her own car key. "Here, you take mine."

Leaving Newton in the Jeep, almost in a ditch at the side of the road, she walked back to Tuscatanning. She found his Chevy, and unseen, she devoutly hoped, Callie drove the truck to where Newton was waiting.

"Follow me!" she called, leaning out of the driver side of the yellow Chevy. He followed in her Jeep until she stopped again some four miles from his campsite. Callie got out of the truck. "This is a better place for you to stash it," she said, signaling a tall deer thicket, "that is, if you want to keep a low profile. We can ride the next mile or so in my Cherokee."

The sun threw light on her hair which flew up with each jounce of the Jeep. The dark strands changed color as they drove, navy blue or black when the wind lifted it, and then settling, chameleon-like, it turned as violet as her shiny parka. Newton noticed the hem of her corduroy jumper showing out below the big parka, and her long legs planted firmly under the steering wheel. He couldn't look at her legs without thinking of them running, climbing, swimming. Short-waisted but legs that are miles long. Smooth, faster running legs than anybody I know, he thought with admiration. His eyebrows quivered into steep slants. Short-waisted, nothing. She hasn't even got a waist now.

Newton tried to piece together what was happening here. Into Tuscatanning for provisions; he knew it would be risky but he'd run out of staples. Had to do it, he thought. And then I was starved, that saloon just screaming at me to come in. A couple of burgers, two beers, and now this. Newton fidgeted. His ma had been right. He was on the run. Only she had misjudged him, she had gotten the story wrong, and how could he set things straight? He remembered telling her that he couldn't come home to Littlecomb because he had better things to do. At this moment, with Callie pounding up the mountain to God knows where, he had to question what sort of better things he was actually up to.

The Jeep groaned as Callie cut to the right, now on a smaller road. Still going up. A line of stunted pines showed at the road's edge. They had entered the Pitch Pine forest. Newton's legs were wedged under the dashboard. At each jolt his shins scraped the bottom of the glove compartment. He glanced at Callie. Fear was stalking his heart. What if she's setting me up? This rescuing me from the clutches of Marsh, what's in it for her?

Callie turned the Jeep off the road and into a field of shrub grass. They bumped along. Then she swung onto an unpaved road. "No one in the park travels on this old cart road, at least I don't think so. And I've been working here a pretty good while."

"I can tell. You've got this country all figured out. Listen," he said grudgingly, "thanks for getting me out of town so fast." He ran a hand through his hair. "It sure beats tangling with that cop, Marsh."

"Ranger, he's a patrol ranger." She landed hard on the brake pedal. "We walk from here."

Two miles farther, they stopped to rest on some humpback rocks at the lip of a mining shaft. They were high on a ridge and could see a thin white cloud cover breaking up below. "Where are we?" Newton asked.

"Holler Lookout. Tuscatanning is down there," Callie said. She turned to Newton, "It'd be bad news if Marsh found you. Once he gets on the trail of something he doesn't stop until it's his, one way or another." She checked herself, realizing she wasn't just talking about Marsh's gun.

Callie flushed. "I'm just trying to warn you. He shot a poacher last month, then gave some story to the Park Super about defending himself in the line of duty." She shrugged. "Poacher only got nicked in the arm, so I'm exaggerating. Maybe he wouldn't shoot you dead."

Newton hunched his shoulders and lowered his chin. "Personally, I think that guy would have a hard time dealing with *me*, if he tried to start something." He scrutinized Callie. "But what about you, why are you doing this for me? Warning me like this. You're a ranger, too."

Callie lifted the massy hair off her neck. "I don't know exactly." She leapt down from the rock. "Maybe I don't want you to get caught." Standing in front of him, close to the cliff edge, she picked up a fallen branch the length of a riding crop. Leaning forward, she pointed the tip end of it to the ground and drew a large circle, and within that, another circle. She scratched a hole at the center. "This is a sign my great aunt showed me. Aunt Winoshca," she nodded proudly. "Her tribe taught that this outer circle is the earth. We, you and me, are the inner circle. We live within the world. And that hole at the center? That's our emptiness. Deep as a pit, it's inside all of us." Her arm went limp. "We have to learn all over again how to join one another to be whole, just as this circle says, just as the earth is."

Newton took the stick from her and knelt over the circles in the soil. He traced over the earth, then moved the stick downward, making a tail. He left a space between his mark and the hole. Callie stared at the drawing made over into a large question mark. He looked up at her, and she felt his bewilderment. In answer, she said, "I've known you too long, Newton. I couldn't hurt you." Her voice dropped. "I won't try to find out what it is you're doing here."

The next thing she knew his arms were around her, his face buried in the crook of her neck. Callie hugged him back.

Chapter ELEVEN

"I'll show you what I'm talking about," George Denman said, putting out his cigarette. The Big Springs Lounge was the kind of place that still permitted smoking.

"I have my hunting license right here," George said to the woman next to him at the bar. He had every intention of impressing her with his knowledge of the requirements for the license, but when he went for his wallet in his jacket pocket his expression changed. Holy shit. He had forgotten that he lost it, or, more truthfully, he had been trying to forget that it disappeared on the night of the death of Theresa Waters.

"Hey George, that's your name isn't it? You were talking to me." The woman had just met him at the bar.

"Sure," George said, half-heartedly. "God, it's dark in here. Hey Elijah, don't you ever open the blinds?"

Elijah ignored him, but the broad faced woman looked admiringly at George, noting his expansive chest, especially the curly hairs poking out above the yellow t-shirt he wore under a rugged union suit. She wanted to joke about how he could go stand under the light. She wouldn't mind a brighter look at this man with the velvet voice.

"That's it," said George.

"What's it?" asked the woman.

Yippee, Denman crowed silently. My wallet is in Newton's blue and white striped jacket. I stashed it there that night. Then what? Natty threw on the jacket, but what happened to it after that?

"Hey honey, you there? I should say, are you *all* there. You look kind of funny."

George swiveled on the bar stool, his gaze landing on the scavenger dog trophy. He was locked into the dog's gaze and was aware that this made no sense because the canine had empty eye sockets.

"Don't stare too hard. Those trophies, they'll give you the willies," Elijah muttered, from behind the bar.

"I already got the willies," George said.

The woman next to him tried again to engage him.

"Go away." George was panicked. Have to get my hands on that jacket. Can't have it turn up with my wallet in the pocket. My prints, and probably Natty's too, on the jacket. Gib Setter was driving by that night, and the old woman who got killed, both of them saw someone at the school in the blue and white jacket. Evidence that I was there at Littlecomb Elementary.

He chugged his beer and hurried out the door. It's at home. I remember seeing it there. We were back from that joke of a hunting trip. I was unloading my gear near the hall closet. That's when Nat took off the jacket. He was standing right beside me.

Driving over to his mother's, a dog so scrawny and tall-eared it must have had coyote blood, ran out in front of George's truck. He screeched to a halt. The dog yelped. Did he hit it? No, there was the animal trotting away down the street. "Oh God," George cried. He was hunched over the wheel like a crab. "Did I kill Theresa Waters?"

He didn't have anything against her. Why would he have hurt her? Still, one time he was so drunk he had hurt someone. He was in a blackout and had leveled a punch to his brother Nat that had knocked the poor kid out. Later, George remembered nothing of that incident. So he was capable. What was that awful case he heard about on T.V., the one where a guy went into an alcoholic blackout and murdered his own parents.

George moaned out loud. He tried to switch gears, think of something pleasant. What about the good old days? He and his brothers did have some fine times together. We were the Denman boys, he thought proudly. We were the best lookin', best shootin', smartest boys in town. Nat was sharper than me. Coyote sly he was, still is. Course Newton was the only one with real school smarts. Who am I kidding, he was the best shot, too.

George was glad he wasn't jealous of Newton the way brother Nat was. Nat could be petty and small-minded. He liked the kind of mean pranks that hurt people. But then again, George reminded himself, Nat is no turncoat. Newton was.

George could never quite put behind him the day Newton ratted on him to their mother when he was sixteen. She lost it, he remembered. Told me I was dead drunk and would turn out like her daddy. It was bad. Things would have been fine if Newton hadn't run off to find her just because, big fuckin deal, he was out drinking behind the work shed. That day his ma had a dreadful look in her eye.

He realized he had been sitting in the car at his mother's house, lost to these teenage memories. Betty opened the car door before he could touch the handle. She was glad to see him.

After the woodshed incident his ma got used to seeing him lit. She got so she hardly seemed to mind it. George would say he was sorry and fling his arms around her. He was glad he could comfort her. She always looked happy then.

Tonight, though, he scarcely acknowledged her once they were inside.

"What are you needing?"

"Nothing." George was rummaging through the hall closet.

"That's a mighty determined *nothing* you're searching for."

"There's something I have to find," he mumbled, starting up the stairs.

A few minutes later he came down to the kitchen, having ransacked the bedrooms and linen closet. "Ma, where else do you store our coats and stuff?"

"If you would tell me honey," she said, walking over to him. "I might be able to put my hands on it in a second." She stroked his dark hair. "My handsomest boy," she murmured.

George smiled forlornly.

"I'm looking for a jacket," he said in a rush. "Just Newton's old blue and white jacket."

"You want Newton's jacket?" She stared at him, but would not permit herself to say what she was suddenly thinking. Instead Betty stroked her son's hair again. "I'll find it," she said. Then she dropped her arm as a deep exhaustion settled over her limbs. She gazed at George sleepily, and all she could say was, "My boys, my boys."

"It's boiling over." Languidly, Newton took his stick poker and lifted the coffee pot off the fire. He and Callie were sitting on a log at his campsite in front of Blue Quarry. It was dusk. The feldspar pool had turned a chalky white.

"Stay and eat something with me," Newton said, pouring the boiled coffee into a thermos cup. She shook her head.

"You're leaving me again?"

Callie laughed. "I'm not going anywhere. I just don't want coffee." She unzipped her parka and lifted a beaded leather pouch over her head. Taking a pinch of the contents, she held it over the flame so Newton could see. "Purple root," she said. "It burns going down, makes you feel warm inside.

Newton got her a kettle, and soon she had made the tea. "Do you want some?" she asked. Newton rubbed his neck and smiled up at her. "No, I'm pretty warm already. But thanks," he said more formally. She sat down next to him, and cradled her tea, not drinking it, but inhaling the steam. She shifted uncomfortably on the log. "You were right about something you said when we were driving in the Jeep. I am going to have a baby."

Newton nodded. "I figured."

"I'm not married."

"At first I thought you might have a husband," he said slowly. "Then, when we were on the ledge near the mining shaft, I knew you didn't." He stared at the metal lace hooks on his boots. "You didn't hug me like a married lady."

Callie looked at his round chin that the beard did not disguise. What old fashioned talk, she thought. But how sweet, how sweet Newton is; really not at all like his brothers. She started at this revelation. Maybe he never was like them, she pondered. Still, he trapped and hunted, and worse – she took a long drink of tea and made a conscious effort to redouble her efforts to dislike him. Wait a minute, she wondered. Her face heated up. How did I hug him?

She put her tea down, wedging the mug between a rock and her boot. "It was a mistake," she said quickly. "The guy I was involved with," she explained. "I shouldn't have gone to bed with him." Then, more embarrassed, "On the other hand, I think I needed to have this baby." Callie swung around, searching Newton's face for traces of ridicule or disbelief. He was not laughing.

He leaned towards her suddenly, almost sending her backwards off the log. He caught her under the elbow. "I want to think that you were waiting for me. That's why you put off marrying all this time." His voice grew thin. "But I know better than that. You told me once that your daddy left your Ma before you were even born." He looked at her keenly. "Maybe you never trusted men."

"Stop!" The tea sloshed up one side of her cup. She set it down against the log. "I'm sorry, I don't want to hear about my father." Callie pulled at her hair, twining a lock of it round and round. "Okay, I suppose what you're saying makes me wonder about what I do and do not trust." She nodded at a group of dark pines jutting out from the cliff, persevering even at their awkward angle. "I have faith in them," she said.

Newton straightened his long legs. "What about some supper. Can you trust me to make that for you?"

"Okay. I'll eat dinner on the mountain."

A half hour later, Callie was watching him prepare the food. "Last time I was here it was squirrel you were cooking. I thought that looked bad enough, but this; I can't believe you think I'm going to touch that inedible looking porcupine." She squatted beside Newton. "Couldn't we heat up some beans instead?"

"Sorry, but this is the best I can do. Nothing in the woods this morning except this old porky grousing around." He brightened. "You'll love it, I guarantee. Now watch this." Newton turned the animal over. "See, no quills on the belly. The skin peels as freely as rabbit. We'll roast him so he's nice and brown and juicy. He'll taste like spring lamb, only better."

Callie laughed. "That's what you said about the burnt squirrel."

She ate two helpings of the meat.

Invigorated by this new meal, Callie went off to the woods, returning with an armload of dry branches. "More fuel." She tossed a large piece on the fire, and then hunched forward near the flame.

"Here," he said, handing her his pronged, beech wood poker. "You do the honors."

They watched the flame separate into hot leaping fingers. "What about a cover for us to sit on?" Callie asked. Together they spread a soft red, cotton blanket which Newton took from his sleeping bag. Tentatively, he sat down on his heels, close to Callie. She was facing the fire, knees bent and arms stretched out behind her in locked position.

She turned to him. "You know what this feels like? Us together at the tree-fort. Not that we had a fire going, but it always felt good to be there."

"And it feels like that now?"

"Maybe better," she said lightly. "At the fort, we never could get that door right."

Newton was animated. "We were building that thing forever. We tried to put one at the top of the fort, bottom of the fort, every place possible. We must have moved the door ten times."

"Twenty times!" Callie smiled and leaned back so she could see the stars. Her shoulders were swaying slightly, side to side. Newton reached out to touch her hair as it brushed his shoulder. "It is a good fort we have here," she said, turning so that her hair slid through his fingers, and her lips were on his fingertips.

"Would you kiss me just once?" she said.

At first he thought he hadn't heard right. And then she amplified, "Like this." Her lips traveled lightly to the center of his palm.

Newton held her face and kissed her on the mouth, and then on each cheek.

She smiled and closed her eyes. "Kiss me everywhere."

"Just once?" he teased. Newton shifted his weight and leaned over her. He kissed her in the crook of her neck, was moving downward to the arc of her breast when she lifted up on one side and swung her legs over top his. "I can't lie under you," she said. "You'll squash me." Her parka was still zipped up and her skirt spread across his thighs.

Newton had actually forgotten that she was pregnant. His heart sank to his feet. He was concerned. "Are you sure this is okay?" In answer, she put her arms around his neck. Newton thought her face smelled like a pine forest, her hair was cold ursine fur and her mouth, as it sealed his, was a smooth piece of fire lit wood, crackling and lighting him with its flame.

Overhead it was snowing lightly, and this was odd because it had been a very mild November, fifty degrees most days. Callie sat up and looked for the sun. Newton was not beside her in the blankets where they had fallen asleep together last night. Her breasts were sore. They had grown larger and harder since the beginning of her pregnancy. When she and Newton made love the sensitivity in her nipples had been a wonderful thing, but now they ached. She massaged them some, removed a long strand of hair that had in sleep lodged itself at the corner of her mouth, and then she wriggled under the blankets for warmth. Most of the snow melted as it touched the earth, and there was only a faint white dusting that overlay the ground. Callie turned on her side, facing the fire. Through the blue smoke and the fog that was creeping up mountain from warmer regions below, she saw Newton's blue-jeaned pant legs. She was flooded with relief. He was here.

Of course he's here, she thought sensibly. We spent the night together. No big deal, she shook her head perversely, trying to reason away the airy joy that filled her head. She watched fragments of him appear and disappear in the wet snow and fog. She let the gorgeous feel of last night's lovemaking seep over her.

"You're awake." Newton was at her side. He knelt down and pulled the blanket up around her shoulder, then shifted away, suddenly shy. "Crazy weather," he gestured at the sky.

Sitting up, she caught a snowflake on her tongue. "Up here, it happens only in November. The cold air from the northern ridge crashes into the warm from the valley." She hugged her knees. The snow was turning to hoarfrost. Newton sprang to his feet. "Be right back."

"What's this?" Callie squinted at an oblong muslin bag with sprays of green poking out one end. Newton held it up for her. "It's a present. A pillow," he said. Her first thought was, oh my god, one of Newton's presents. I can't forget or forgive – oh hell, don't think of it now, she told herself. She took the pillow, and as she examined it Newton elaborated on his early morning surprise for her. "It was easy, really. Just felled a heavy topped hemlock. Real bushy, but I got the fine stuff from it." Callie tested it, resting her cheek against one side of the bag.

"It's not scratchy at all," she said, truly surprised. "I'll use it." She broke into a wide smile. "I will."

Newton grinned. "Just some thread, cloth, and whatever was soft enough in the woods, that's all it took."

Her eye went from object to object in the crowded campsite, the carefully set wall of back logs that framed the campfire, shiny black coffeepot, cast iron skillet – oil coated so it wouldn't rust, wooden poker, the cross-thatched grill of green sticks, and the broom, something else Newton had made from hemlock. The broom head was flat and bushy with twig ends wound around a stick handle and secured with twine. "You're amazing," she said earnestly. "You are positively domestic."

The snow froze as it met the vapor rising from the south valley. Encased in opaque ice, the large white flakes rattled against branch and ground as Callie and Newton walked down a trail she wanted to show him. Two yards ahead of him, and sliding down the ice-crusted trail, she called out, "This leads to a circular clearing. It's one of my favorite places."

Newton slipped and slid downhill, running right into Callie. He steadied himself and caught her with his arms from behind. "Just saying hello," he panted.

They crunched forward, not breaking the ice but cracking it into myriad origami designs. All twigs and logs glittered like jewels under glass. The sun was somewhere behind the fog, trying to break through. The pine trees glowed in the misty light, now one green limb, then another.

They rounded a bend and came out on a section of the trail that had been broadened by snowmobiles. Callie stopped in her tracks. A stand of pines shook. Two trees bowed apart as an enormous black bear with a cub at her heels emerged.

Callie looked sharply. It's her! The ranger felt her skin crawl. All her bones locked in animal tenseness. Every noise sounded far away, even the bear's low growl. A sense of wonder pervaded Callie, starting with a ping that went off in her head, as if her ears were popping, and traveling down to her chest which grew constricted as she stared at the she-bear pointing her muzzle straight at the sky.

The ranger jumped. It was only Newton's shoulder bumping her head as he leaned over to see through a spiral of fog. She reached back, clutching him with one hand. Callie knew this bear. She was the only park employee who knew that the animal, though in transit during its feeding months, made her home in these pitch pines. Years ago, her bear, as Callie liked to think of the great animal, had been a trouble maker at the park.

The she-bear used to break into campers' sedans, Jeeps and vans, presumably looking for food. Her unnatural size had terrified the tourists who glimpsed her. Most of whom backpedaled later, deciding they had to have exaggerated her great size. She seemed to choose the hardest vehicles to get into, and then as if they were playthings she had peeled off door frames with ease.

The strange part was that the food, even steaks and hotdogs in coolers, was left untouched. There were incidents when garbage cans were overturned and yet the contents, the leftover food that would have been delicious to any other bear, was also untouched. Callie and the other rangers made light of this behavior, but privately felt alarmed. Why had the bear invaded if not for food?

Callie volunteered to shoot the animal with anesthesia and cart it to the outer limits of the State Park, where she would be released. But before the ranger had a chance to carry out this mission, the bear seemed to vanish. It was almost as if she had undergone a change of heart. While other car clouting bears returned to the parking lots to repeat their crimes, this one had decided on a new life, away from the crowds and cars. As it turned out she had taken herself to the limits of the State Park. The only person she tolerated, but at a distance, was Callie. This made the ranger happy; it made her feel as though she was meeting a hitherto unknowable relative.

It had been months since the forest ranger had seen her, and she hoped that the smell of Newton and her was not a threat. The bear wrinkled her nose and sniffed. Now she cuffed her cub gently, rebuking it for nipping at her teat.

Callie's breath came quick and short and she felt an echo in her breathing. She became aware of Newton again. He's in a daze too, she surmised. He's marveling at her beauty. The cub sat behind his mother, cocking his head. The big bear sat back on her haunches. Her long black coat moved in waves and settled in short ripples as she grew still.

The strange lightness Callie felt in her chest did not go away. She felt connected to this creature, its very presence speaking to her as from a shadow realm. And yet that could hardly be possible. This bear looked absolutely real. Callie noticed her chestnut eyes, expansive ruff, her round ears, forward and alert. Turning to Newton to share the sight and the warmth that spread through her limbs, Callie got a surprise. Her lover had another sort of look in his eyes, one long familiar to her from living near hunters in Littlecomb.

The bear raised her eyes. She stared at Callie and Newton, and then with the purity of a bass cello she bellowed, she rose on her back two column legs and started towards them. Newton yanked her arm. "Come on, god dammit."

Callie shook him off.

"Callie!" Newton half-dragged her off the trail. She broke from him and ran ahead a little ways, then stopped and collapsed onto her heels. The woods were fogged over. Newton took her hands. "You're shaking all over. I don't blame you. She's the largest. She's it." His eyes lit up.

"What do you mean, she's it?" Callie asked.

Newton shook his head. "Nothing." He sank his hands into his pockets. "That was the biggest black bear you'll ever see." For a moment he was unnerved. "Her size is unbelievable. I must have misjudged. Must be the fog." He turned to Callie. "She could have ripped into us. Weren't you scared?"

She made no answer. He squinted into the woods. In the high altitude his breath vaporized before him. Everywhere he looked, the air danced in strange scraps of shifting water vapor.

Close to noon, back at Newton's camp, Callie made them both yellow root tea. Until now, she believed that the bear's whereabouts was her secret. She had even been deliberately vague with her colleagues when they asked if she had any idea as to what had happened to that rogue, monster bear who was turning campsites upside down. Callie played dumb. She was not about to jeopardize its freedom.

She looked at Newton; he seemed far away. It had altered them, their coming together into that animal presence. Callie wasn't sure exactly how it had affected what they meant to each other, but a change was in the air.

"What did you think of her?" she began. Newton made a groove in the hard ground and set his tea in it. "Big bear," he said with a grin. She noticed his face had turned a bright rose. Was it embarrassment? Excitement?

"Is that all, just big bear?" she prompted.

He was uneasy. "Listen, in all the years I've hunted I never went after bear. Even though every one of the men in my family have done it." His brows twitched with uncertainty. "I didn't think I would be interested, not for a long time I didn't, and that was mostly because of you. I remembered how much you loved those bruins."

Callie waited for him to mention what held them both apart all these years, the mangled beauty they had both witnessed. She saw his stubbornness. He would not come out and say it, but she had guessed. "You've come to Pitch Pine to hunt the bear we saw today." She stood up. "I know I said I wouldn't ask, I thought you had some other awful secret. But it's the bear. Tell me it isn't. I saw it in your face! You wanted to kill her, but I wouldn't let myself believe it."

"I'm not going to say I'm sorry because it won't fix anything." Newton looked at her. "It's taken me a long time to get here. Don't you see? It's what I came for." He paused, confused. "I think that maybe I also came to find you, although I didn't plan it."

She frowned, and hoisted her shoulder pack over her arm.

"When will you be back?" His voice broke. "I can't stand you vanishing again. Besides, you might need my help." His arms slid down her sides and rested on her belly. "I'd like to help with the baby." He held her gently by the hips. "I have some money saved. I could use it to help you. Help us."

Newton grew energetic. "It's been growing, this savings account I have."

There was no hiding her skepticism. "And what were you planning to do with it before this magnanimous gesture?"

"Oh. I thought I could start some little business of my own one day. It's just an idea." He was embarrassed. "I don't want to talk about it. Listen Callie, we could even get married."

She looked at his wide black eyes, the brows that rose in comical blots at each side of his temple, the muscle in his jaw that jumped when he was agitated. He was very beautiful, she decided. But too perplexing. The idea of him suggesting marriage, it was absurd. And yet? She felt herself relenting just a little, enjoying the notion of it. Then, shocked at how quick she softened towards him, Callie faced Newton squarely. "It's a bad idea. Unthinkable," she said, laughing much too heartily. She turned from him, blinking at the sky. "Clouds are breaking up. No more hail today."

From halfway down the trail, above which Newton was craning his neck to see every inch of her possible, Callie called out, "Why do you do it?"

"What's that?"

"Why do you hunt?" Callie shouted, already close to the pass that led to her Jeep.

"What did you say?"

"You won't do it. I know you won't!"

"What? Fall down a mine shaft?" he bellowed.

"The bear! You won't shoot her," her voice grew faint, and he guessed she had almost reached the pass that led to her Jeep.

Chapter TWELVE

"So boy scout, what did the *real* coroner turn up?"

Pete tried to smile at the jibe from Detective Rendell. "First off, they learned that the scrape on her forehead was not due to a fall, but to a blow with a blunt wooden object, possibly a two-by-four."

"She was struck on the front of the head, too?"

"Yes sir. They found bits of wood chips with markings embedded in her forehead. Now for the big news, the third injury that I made so much noise about. They found a head wound that was a graze from a bullet. A .22."

"Go on." The Detective leaned forward in his office chair. So Pete's hunch had been right,

"Looks like it was an old gun. Even the bullet was old. There was no tattooing. Coroner judges it was shot from about twenty-one inches."

"What do you figure?"

"That the guy who fired at her was a pretty bad shot."

"Uh-oh. That rules out the Denman boys."

"Yeah, you would think. Only the two older ones had been at the bar. They could have been off their mark. But you have a point. Sir, I'm going to pay the bereaved husband another call. Just an idea I have."

"Sure, do that. And Myrick, I nearly forgot. One of the brothers has come forward with more information on Newton."

"Which one?"

"It's brother Nat. Says he remembers Newton being something of a pyromaniac."

"That's a serious charge." Especially, Pete thought, when the arson of the school is in question. For a moment he forgot entirely about his prospective visit to see Ralph Waters.

"You bet. It gets worse. Not only Nat, but his neighbor Elijah Jones remembers an incident when young Newton nearly burnt down his family's work shed and a stand of pines in their yard."

Pete sighed heavily. "More homework. Newton is no way in the clear yet."

"I never thought he was," said Hal. "You say you're on your way to the Waters' place? Good enough, but don't forget your artillery."

"Right sir. I've got the laptop."

Pete was invited indoors this visit. He followed Ralph Waters into a cheerful living room with tiffany lamps and a high back sofa with a dark pink floral slipcover. There were two graceful, claw-footed Victorian chairs and one oversized recliner.

"I insisted on the leisure chair," said Ralph firmly. "Theresa just about took over the house with her paints and her Victorian furniture. I used to remind her that I had a say, too. Didn't I build this house myself?"

"Did you?"

"Sure I did. Had my own construction company for years. So I know who to go to, and how to get good materials cheap. I did most everything myself, from the dry wall to laying down the floors," he said proudly.

Near the sofa and the fireplace were several stacks of driftwood. Pete touched a piece of the gnarled wood.

"I wanted to get rid of that mess of sticks, but Theresa said no. She liked having what she called raw nature in her living room." Ralph sat down in his own chair.

"Isn't your granddaughter here?" Pete walked up to a painting, half hidden behind a tall paneled screen.

"Allison's at school until three. I see you admiring one of Theresa's oils."

"It's unusual," said Pete, enjoying the bright colors depicting the familiar narrative of 'Hey diddle diddle, the cat and the fiddle.'

A softness crept into Ralph's voice. "She was going to illustrate at least fifty more nursery rhymes. She didn't get very far, did she? This was the only one she completed."

"I like that part," said Pete, admiring a purple cow floating over the moon.

"Me, I like the little dog who laughed," said Ralph.

Pete glanced at the cockerpoo, Honey, asleep on the floor, to see if she might have served as Theresa's model. His eye swept over the flowery sofa and two chairs with embroidered needle point seats. It was hard to imagine big Ralph Waters, rationalist and engineer, sitting comfortably in one of those fancy Victorian seats. No wonder he had bought in his own chair.

"I'm planning to change the decor," said Ralph, watching Pete's eyes whisk about the room.

"Really?"

"Too many sad memories."

"Of course." Pete nodded respectfully. "Normal to have such sadness." Pete turned to face him. "And what about anger, Mr. Waters; maybe you harbored some of that towards your wife when she was alive?

"What is this about?" Ralph said. "If I wasn't angry before, I am now."

"Let's go at this another way," Pete said. "How about we go over that time period you were with your wife at the fire."

Waters dropped down onto one of the straight back needle point chairs, which groaned in proper response to the two hundred plus pound man. "Those moments at the fire were a nightmare for me. There's nothing I haven't told you already. I went to find Theresa because I was worried she was gone too long. When I got to her I saw that she was hurt badly, and all I could think of was getting her to a hospital. Maybe I was in shock, but truthfully that's all I remember."

Pete studied Ralph. "Do you own a gun?"

"No, I never have. Since when is it a state trooper's job to play detective?"

"Since every day I've been at work," Pete said, smiling. "We're too small in Littlecomb to hire outside help."

"Trooper," Waters said calmly, "You are looking in the wrong direction."

Ralph walked Pete down the front hall towards the door, and the officer thanked him for his help. "I should be able to give you some news soon on the contents of those boxes." Pete was thinking that he might as well go through them one more time, even though it was apparent that most everything was damaged by water and mold, damaged beyond readability. "Oh one last thing," he said to the older man. "Could you give me your daughter's phone number for corroboration of the time you were at home that night?"

"I told you before," said Waters, "Wendy and her camera have been out in front action in Bosnia, and she is absolutely inaccessible. She can call me, but I can't dial her. I don't even have her number." He made an effort to smile at Pete. "Speaking of phones, there's mine now. Good bye Myrick. You'll find your way out, I'm sure."

Pete took one last look down the hall, admiring again the painting of the purple cow that jumped over the moon. Then his eye rested on a stack of photos on the table under the painting. In three quick steps he was at the table sifting through the photographs for anything that might be helpful. He smiled at a close up of Honey, her pink tongue and ears quirked brightly. He was putting the pictures back down on the table when he noticed a yellow pad of reminder notes. There in black marker was a phone number that started with the access code for international long distance lines. Pete bet to himself that the next two numbers would be the code for Bosnia. He had it memorized before he left.

Callie thumbed through last week's Tuscatanning Weekly. She was at the Grill and Grocery, standing under a sign over the newspaper rack that said YOU READ IT, YOU BOUGHT IT. Everyone ignored Spence's signs. TRY THE LOTTO, WIN BIG urged another. Many people in Tuscatanning bet on the daily numbers, but only Vernon Vale had won once. VERNON VALE GOT LUCKY, $400 WINNER read the four year old sign that hung over the meat counter.

His back to the slabs of chicken, wild turkey, and pig joints, Spence stood at the grill deftly sliding his spatula under two cheese steaks. He called over to her. "Coming tonight to the Christmas Eve service?"

He flipped the steaks high in the air, as if he were making hotcakes.

"Oh probably," Callie said, placing the newspaper back on the rack. "I'll take six sassafras sticks and a pack of double-bubble, that new kind, the chocolate checkermint." Spence didn't trust the kids in town not to steal candy and gum, and kept as many small articles as he could fit on a shelf behind the cash register. He made a face as he handed her the double-bubble. "Getting the sweet-tooth by now I guess." He eyed her belly.

"I guess," she said, feeling embarrassed.

He rang her up, then handed her the goods. "Don't forget your checkbook this time!" he called as she stepped out the door onto the snow covered sidewalk.

Privately, Callie loved her big belly. Big and proud of it, she told herself, imitating the commercials on T.V. for queen-sized, Big Mama pantyhose. In fact, at five and a half months, she was still slim except where her stomach popped to hold the twelve inch fetus. She had felt the quickening early. Before she switched to the Birth Center the obstetrician down at Eastern Medical had told her this was impossible; women don't feel the baby move until four months or so, but she had said no, she felt it in its tenth week, and had felt her muscles changing daily, crampy and stabbing sometimes, all the ligaments stretching to support the uterus.

Tonight she was out of sorts as she climbed the stairs to her second floor apartment at the end of Main Street. First, Spence's curious eye; he probably wondered who the father of her baby was. Well, she could forgive him that. Tuscatanning was a small town. She knew people would be noticing her burgeoning form, and that they knew she wasn't married. Also, she was an outsider, although strictly speaking she wasn't, for her people had been on Grandmother Mountain for centuries. But Aunt Teeny had taken her away and, she, like Pete Myrick, had acquired outsider status by virtue of having left home too long.

Now what on earth made her think of Pete? Oh right, Newton brought up his name and even talked a little about him. Enough, she thought, scraping the snow off her boots. She set them out to dry in the kitchen.

It was Spence's comment on the checkbook that rankled. She had never minded his teasing before, not really. And it was true she was absent-minded. She left things everywhere; her lecture notes in the Nature Center's bathroom today, her keys in the car last week, and so on. But tonight the checkbook business made her feel unorganized and shapeless. Again, she was a quivering mass of emotion, a mutated sea sponge absorbing every feeling that swam by.

She switched on the light in the living room which was also her dining room and sleeping area. The one room apartment was not claustrophobic. You came into a narrow hall, with the bathroom and kitchen to the right, and then the living room which was large, with high ceilings and angular walls. The best part was the three paneled window with a turnlatch that opened the outside panes. The triptych opened to a stand of pitch pines across the street, behind which stood Grandmother Mountain, one of her twin peaks rising behind town, not quite three miles from where the apartment stood.

Callie had hodgepodge furniture, two outdoor canvas chairs, one fairly good reproduction early American armchair, a cedar chest and a long comfy, slipcovered sofa that folded out into a bed. The slipcover was a faded eggshell blue. All these pieces receded in the background when you walked into the room. What stood out were the five batique wall hangings, and on a low non-descript table near the window, a pair of tall glass candlesticks with bubbles caught in the glass. Each candlestick had a broad lip that curved upward like a wave.

Callie got out of her State Park clothes. In a white oversized t-shirt she had worn under the stiff uniform, she made herself a cup of tea and fed her cat, Iris. Maybe the landlord had jacked up the heat – or was it just her; her body temperature was up since the beginning of the pregnancy.

Outside, a half moon skimmed the rounded mountain peak. Callie cranked the window wide and stuck her head out. She was thinking that she was oversensitive and reacted too quickly to peoples' harmless remarks. Breathing in what others say and do, getting hurt too easily, and then letting it blow out again before I've understood it. A state of furious flux, that's me; I've been this way too long.

The fight between Newton and me over that terrible death when we were young, she thought. Is that where things started to go wrong? That was the beginning. And the other man who came along years later, my part in that nightmare. Since then it's been easy to choose the company of stunted pines over people. How good to be playful and solitary, how easy to slip into hibernation. Sleep away the bad parts of one's life.

Only problem is that I know better. A bear recreates herself in those dark hours of winter sleep. Even her waste that she cannot pass is magically transformed into powerful proteins. Powerful natural magic, that. How many creatures can claim such a feat? Wish I could get rid of the garbage in my life that way.

Callie shivered, and for ten minutes she sat inert, not quite asleep or awake. She had no desire to revisit the bizarre death that she was thinking about now. Had it been less bizarre, would that have made a difference? "Callie, let me hold you," he had said afterwards. But he was shaking her, his calloused, silt covered fingers digging into her arms. She had not been afraid of this man before, but now he was demanding. He would not leave her alone and his voice had gone shrill the way her wooden, honey toned recorder sounded when she blew too hard. Why couldn't he see that a rich tune comes by breathing softly into your instrument?

Callie noticed that it had started to snow. A quick snow shower, the weather station said. She dragged the armchair to the window and turned off the overhead light. One bright domed flake caught on the window latch. Callie sat there watching the snow come in the window. She let it melt on her face and with its touch she began to feel as if she was not such a mass of unsteady randomness after all. The snow that dissolved under her feet, the snowflakes in the night that no one could count, even these thousands of perfect ice crystals were each particular unto themselves. She thought of how she was doubly connected, to the earth, surely, and to the wall of her womb. She loved to listen to it, to breathe deeply in and out with the fetal inner sanctum.

A two-week-old snowdrift blocked the door to the highway phone booth. Newton had to dig a path so that he could call his mother this Christmas Eve. Once inside the booth, a snow shower just blown up an hour ago beat against the heavy glass panes. It had been a slow hike from camp, hard to see his way to the truck hidden in the deer thicket. Newton wondered if the roadmaster would get his equipment out this way. Didn't Callie say so? Sure would help in conditions like this.

"Hi Ma."

"Newton! I'm so glad – " she stopped short. "Where are you?"

"Still here in the mountains," Newton said lightly. Then, "I love you, Ma." He had an idea that if he told his mother exactly where he was, she'd leak it to his brothers. Who could say what they would do with that kind of information? Even Trooper Pete Myrick would pry his whereabouts out of Betty. Newton winced. It hurt to have his old schoolmate turn on him.

"You have to come home, Newton. It's no good hiding. The police, they're going to catch up to you."

"I'm not hiding," he said, locking his teeth together. "I told you before, it's this bear I'm after. Can't come home until I find her."

"You chasing her in the dead of winter?" his mother said dryly.

"You're right, she's laying low for now. I'll catch her, though; she'll show herself soon as it gets warm."

"Spring." His mother heaved; Newton thought she would cry. "You're running, son. I don't know about this bear. It could be important to you, but I think you're out there because you're scared to come home."

"Ma, I called to say I was all right, and to wish you Merry Christmas."

Betty was quiet.

Bitterly he said, "That last night I was home, you defended me, said you knew I couldn't burn down our school or murder Mrs. Waters." He closed his eyes. "Ma, you know I didn't do it."

"What then? Why can't you come home and say so to the police?"

"They've got evidence, even if it is dead wrong. I'm thinking that maybe the police will use me as a scapegoat, use me to solve the crimes. Don't you know that?"

It could be painful to listen to her, but Newton loved the familiar husky tongue, the clicks and catches in Betty's voice when she was worried. He needed to hear her talk.

She heaved. "I don't know anything these days."

Newton held the mouthpiece up in the air. He was crying. He heard her suck in her breath, and then those pucker noises she made as she dragged on a cigarette. Little smackings, almost like small kisses.

"If you didn't burn down that building, then – and your yellow truck, right outside our house that night. Never mind, that can't be right." There was a space, and in that lapse Newton was thinking about how his mother had softened towards George, ever since their daddy had died. Newton felt suddenly sick inside. He fell silent. Mother and son had little more to say to each other.

The phone hung in his hand. He was wishing there was someone else he could call at home in Littlecomb. It was Christmas, for God's sake. He began running phone numbers through his head, work numbers, neighbor numbers, and all those friends you haven't seen since school days but their numbers stay lodged in the memory bank. Pete Myrick's number came up. He was a regular in the small group Newton and Natty sometimes hung out with when they were eleven and twelve.

Before he could change his mind, Newton, emboldened by anger and a desire for justice, dialed Pete at home. It was the same house Mr. and Mrs. Myrick had died in, and passed on to their only son. "Hello Pete. I didn't call to say Merry Christmas."

"Newton Denman?"

"You said if I ever wanted to talk we could. Between friends, you said."

"Of course." Pete leapt off the couch, causing Pandora to dig her claws in before flying off his lap. "Where are you?"

"Pete, listen to me. I didn't do it."

Pete wrung his hand where the cat had taken a square of skin. He was moving to his desk where he could trace Newton's phone call. "Tell me," he urged.

"Find my blue and white jacket, and you'll find your murderer."

"Go on." Pete was hooking up the tracer.

"You know why I'm talking to you at all?"

"Because we're friends," said Pete.

"No. Probably not. It's because I know you're on the run, same as me."

Newton hung up. He stood outside the phone booth. The snow seemed to be whirling upward. Newton thought the separate flakes were joining, moving toward some far off point, maybe a distant vertex of snow. And behind the snowy mountain was town, and above him hidden by the snowfall, there had to be a moon, rising. He felt small and lost. He wondered at his words to Pete. Newton had no idea what it was Pete might be running from, but he had a sense that it was so.

He squinted, tried to see the road that led right into Valley Street. I'm not far, he thought. Ten miles or so, not far at all from where Callie must live. Said she was right at the end of the street. He yanked at the phone booth door, and was back inside thumbing through a dated telephone book that was on the shelf. His hand rested on the page that read: Major C. 509 Valley Street.

He started up his truck and inched forward in the direction of town. Visibility was bad, snow every which way, but mostly blowing up in front of the windshield. Newton clicked on the radio and through the static learned that a flash storm had hit the mountain hard. The highway was icing over and Newton's Chevy with its bald tires skidded across the surface. Where was the roadmaster when you needed him? A quarter mile or so, and he slowed to a stop.

Easier to go back to my tent, Newton decided. Turn around, stash the truck back into its snowdrift, and hike up to camp. He couldn't see the road at all. He drummed his fingers on the steering wheel, wishing he could see his way to Callie.

The flash storm in Tuscatanning was over and the sky had cleared. Callie went to her bureau drawer, found her candles she had wrapped in foil, and placed them in the glass candlesticks. Gently she shook Iris off the Mackinaw blanket on the sofa, and wrapped it around her shoulders. She lit the candles and glanced out the window. The moon had reappeared, and the icy street shivered in its light.

Callie went again to the bureau, this time for a recorder she kept in a soft velvet casing. Sitting in the armchair, feet propped up against the windowsill she began to play some scales. Outside, a small circle of green girded the moon, now sailing high above the mountain and showing like an apple cut in half; just half, Callie thought, putting down the recorder. A pale green apple.

The apple floated up, brightening the mountain peak. One sharp crenellation, as if it were a castle top. She thought of Newton up there, somewhere.

Down the street the muffled echo of church bells rang. Her church had no bells; someone must be playing a tape. It was nice though, hearing bells tonight. She had missed the service; too much puttering, or maybe? She didn't answer her rationalizations, but went instead to the kitchen to get something to eat. Iris, a scrawny calico who wouldn't put on weight, padded after her and rubbed up against Callie's leg as she fixed herself a chicken salad sandwich. She shared some of the chicken with the cat, and poured out a saucer of half-and-half.

It was almost midnight. Callie was sitting in front of the window, the Mackinaw wrapped around her like a cowl. She picked up the recorder, and played "Bach Jesu" very slowly, then speeded it up so that it was joyful and lively. Then, letting the blanket slide off her shoulders, she leaned out the window and played the ballad of "Annie Laurie." "That's for you, Newton. Merry Christmas." She stood up. Her skin was hot; maybe some hand lotion would help.

She couldn't find any lotion. First-aid cream would do. Callie squirted out a capful for each arm and her face, and rubbed it in. She sat back in the chair, her knees open to the cold air. In her breasts there was a twinging, itching, an almost pleasant ache, a little like when she was twelve and they were first forming. The cold air touched her chest, arms, toes, her neck, and blew a strand of hair off her face. She ran her fingertips across her nipples, they were sore, they were changed; their darkened areolas showed through the white t-shirt. The last bit of cream in the tube she rubbed into her enlarged nipples. Callie was still feeling the music she had played, the way both pieces had a quickening pace, one slower to get there than the other, but the two of them did the same thing, raised you up. She closed her eyes and shivered, a pleasant shiver. Soon the green moon seemed to fill the room.

Chapter THIRTEEN

Newton sprung the trap and inspected the soggy, scrawny possum. He raised a critical brow at the carcass, then looked off across the bare field. Leap year, he thought, raising his face to the come-and-go drizzle, large silver teaspoons of it brightening the earth. Just a few days ago, February had skipped over itself in its rush to get to March. Maybe that's why the hunting's bad, Newton brooded. And the bear invisible – seems like all these months have been bounding away, and me just chasing after them.

Newton was farther down the mountain than he liked to be, though as far as he knew the rangers didn't patrol these hollows on old Grandmother. Still, he preferred the higher parts of the mountain where he had his camp. Up there he could roam more freely. Only a few trails cut into the woods and meadows, and he was glad of that fact. Woods, he felt, thrive best in their own rambling configurations. Sitting on his pack at the edge of the wood, he was raking clean the possum fur with his fingers when he heard voices a little ways off, beyond a stand of pines and aspens. Newton grabbed his trapbag and was about to clear out fast when he picked up something anxious in one of the two voices. "I'll have a look-see, just that," he said nodding down at the dead possum.

He buckled the trapbag that had once been his father's small worn army bag around his waist, and walked into the woods. Slipping sideways between the trees, Newton watched where he stepped so as not to be heard.

He looked through a pair of stripling aspens into the clearing where a couple stood. The distressed voice belonged to a woman with shoulder-length hair the color of white cake icing. He couldn't make out her expression; the hair was frizzed and in a steep side part that hung over most of her face. With her was a man in a shiny blue jacket with red arms. Both wore dark sports glasses – despite the drizzle – and on their feet what looked like sneakers gone wrong. The shoes were tall like boots, with plastic bubbles protruding from the uplifted toes. They had big wavy rubber heels and seemed to unbalance their owners.

Newton shook his head in disbelief for the pair had gathered enough wood for a funeral pyre. As the man shook a bag of sawdust-chip, instant fire starter on the wood, the woman said, "Hurry up. Gawd Bobby, it's almost night, oh Gawd, we'll freeze."

Newton glanced at the sky peeking through the branches. It was mid-morning.

"It's your fault we got lost," the man named Bobby said, hotly. "Oh let's just try that trail off the nature path," he mimicked her.

"You seemed to think it was a great idea at first," she retorted. "Anyway, you're the one who wanted to go camping in the wilds."

Lost. It figures, Newton thought. Let 'em get eaten by the bear. He dropped back a step.

Then the woman said, "All your talk about Jack London; why you had to read me that story out loud – just great, the guy dies because he can't get a fire started." She frowned at the woodpile. "It better work this time."

They can't be serious, Newton decided. Nobody in their right mind would light that bonfire.

"Use it all, use every last stick of those fire starter things," she urged.

"Margaret, don't tell me what to do." He emptied the large bag over the wood. "Where are the matches?"

"I meant to put them some place dry." Margaret rustled through the pile of gear behind her, flinging out a Walk-man, a digital pedometer, and an elaborate Japanese grill. She held up a spray container. "My conditioner, I've been wondering where this went." She gave her hair a shot, and plumped it up. Newton took in the site, marveling at the energy and insanity that prompted these two to haul all this junk up the mountain.

Almost flush against the firewood was a heap of plastic tarp with thin tubular poles sewn into it, and next to this, a pair of inflatable air mattresses, and a lightweight metal chair with spikes on the bottom to stick in the ground.

"I found them! In my pocket the whole time." Margaret handed Bobby a book of matches.

"And here's what really counts." He held out a twenty ounce can of lighter fluid.

Newton took in the situation, trying not focus on his sudden recall of a fire he had started once a long time ago.

"Use the whole thing," Margaret commanded. Newton noticed that the intended fire was set at the edge of the clearing, not a foot away from a dead pitch pine.

Bobby tipped the can over the firewood.

"Hey, hold up there!" Newton parted the saplings and in two quick leaps he had snatched the lighter fluid from Bobby's hand. "Don't shoot!" Bobby fell back. He ran behind Margaret. The sight of Newton, standing over six feet tall in his boots, rifle in his hand, and chest bulging bigger than it was – what with his shell vest inside the worn, heavy hunting parka – was a terrifying sight. Newton glowered, the criss-cross brows cutting into his dark eyes.

Margaret looked hard at Newton and decided he wasn't going to shoot anyone. She was a woman who got right to the point. "We came up from the Pitch Pine Park campground. We're lost," she wailed.

"Yeah? You'd be lost all right, if you folks set fire to these woods. Put a match to these logs and that dead tree will go up like newspaper, not to mention the whole pine stand behind it." He kicked the woodpile dead center so that the side logs loosened. The pyramid toppled.

"We thought, well you know, fires don't get out of hand in the rain," Bobby said, not moving an inch from his cover behind Margaret.

"Nothing but rain since we got to this mountain yesterday." Margaret touched her limp frizzled hair.

"Raining?" Newton held out a hand in the thin misting vapor. "Pffff ..." He shook his head. "You two shouldn't be up here trying to camp, not if you don't know what you're doing."

Bobby grew bolder. "We have the best possible equipment." He stepped forward. "You name it, we got it."

Newton walked around their campsite. "Must have had a hell of a time carrying all this."

"Not at all," Bobby said, and then Margaret, almost simultaneously, "It *was* hell lugging it all." She ended with a shrug, "Even with those big old, supposedly lightweight metal, tubed backpacks."

"What's this thingamajig?" Newton picked up the digital pedometer.

"Measures how many miles we walk." Bobby had relaxed. "It's state of the art accurate." Newton laughed. "Won't get you back home, will it?" Now he had his eye on a beet-red zippered bag streamlined in the shape of a gun. "And that?"

"A holster camera bag," Bobby said. "Holds my Nikon." With a touch of pride, he added, "It's a Zoom Touch 500. We don't like to use it in the rain, though."

"No tent?" Newton asked.

"We have one, only it collapsed on us," Margaret pointed to the heap of tarp and poles in a tangle.

"It's a dome tent with excellent ventilation," Bobby put in. "It has built-in poles," Margaret explained, "in case you're not too practiced at pitching tents."

Newton turned to her. "Where's your compass? Guess I can head you back in the right direction." There was a silence. "We don't happen to have a compass," Bobby said.

"A watch will work." Newton was trying to be patient. "Have you got one?"

"Of course." Bobby sounded relieved.

"Put it down. That log will do," Newton directed. "Sun-up in the east," he gestured. "So what you want to do is use three o'clock as east, nine o'clock as west. Six is south. Go towards three o'clock. That's town. East."

Margaret thanked him profusely. Bobby looked perplexed. Then he said, "Say listen, you've been so helpful I hate to ask for anything else, but could you maybe walk us a ways out of here. Really, we'd appreciate it."

Newton smiled at their state. "I can do that. What about your stuff here? Let me give you a hand," he said, heading towards the collapsed tent. "And I thought I was a packrat."

Newton waved them off at the cart road that led to the highway, then ducked into the woods.

The couple, exceedingly grateful to him on the hike down, had a change of heart after his departure. "Nasty sort of woodsman type, wasn't he?" Bobby said when they reached the highway.

"I thought he was, you know, kind of virile looking," Margaret said. "Needed a shave, though. I'm not into the bearded look." She winked at Bobby. "Anyway, I bet we could have found our way out on our own if we had to." She turned up the volume on her Walkman.

Bobby walked behind her, muttering, "Damn sneaker boots are soaked through. A fucking gyp is what they are."

Finally back in town, they went to their rooms at the Jolly Logger Inn. And showered at once. Dressed in fresh jeans and their Macy's his-and-her matching lumberjack shirts, Margaret and Bobby toyed with what to do next. "I just want to go home," Margaret said. "I've had enough of this camping crap."

Bobby slid over to where she was sprawled in the middle of the bed. He held her face with his two hands. "You know babe, it's almost zen-like the way we read each other's minds. I am totally in your head." They cooed for a minute or two. Then Bobby said, "All we have to do is turn in our camping permits and pay up over at the State Park office."

Ranger Sorrento was on duty. A thin-faced man with worry lines creasing his cheeks, he was trying to get rid of the permit paperwork and the couple as quickly as possible so he could get home. His wife, Doreen, was due to have their baby any time now. He was recording their fees. "Not too nice out for camping this weekend."

Margaret was pivoting in the swivel chair next to Sorrento's desk. "Oh the weather wasn't so bad," she said. "You could hardly call it rain." Bobby shot her a look of incredulity. "The more I think about it," she went on, "it was bee-yoo-tiful up there at the lookout where you can see all the way down to some quaint little village."

"That would be *here*, Tuscatanning, ma'am. We're not so small, in fact our population...did you say, lookout? You must have been up by the gap near Holler Lookout." Sorrento sucked in his breath. "You people aren't supposed to hike there. No permits allowed for camping." He tried to remember the area.

125

"Above the lookout the trails begin to disappear, practically no trails up that way."

Ranger Jack Marsh stuck his head in the door. "I'm out of here; five o'clock, isn't it?" he said to Sorrento. "Just thought I better see what's going on, make sure everything's cool."

Sorrento hated it when Jack Marsh acted as if he were in charge. "No big deal here. Just a small permit problem."

Marsh was curious, and hung in the doorway.

Sorrento turned to Bobby and Margaret. "Didn't you know that visitors can't set up sleep sites outside the designated campgrounds? And no hikes beyond the lower grounds, not without a forest guide."

"We were lost," Margaret said. "It was so scary. Didn't think we'd ever get back." She looked to Bobby for help. "But luckily there was this man, you know, must have been a hermit or something – "

"We didn't actually camp up there," Bobby said.

"What kind of man?" Marsh asked, stepping into the office.

"I don't know. Tall. Shaggy." Margaret noticed Jack's blue eyes. She smiled.

Marsh half sat on the edge of his partner's desk, blocking his view of Margaret. Sorrento frowned at Jack. "Now what are we talking about here?" he said, wheeling his chair over so he could see the campers. "First delinquent camping, now some man you saw up at Holler Lookout?"

"A hermit, I think," Margaret pondered. "A nice looking one, thirtyish."

"He was a hunter," Bobby said. "Rough, real rough looking."

"A little shaggy, that's all," Margaret amended.

"About you two hiking without permits," Sorrento began.

"Hey, lay off that a minute," Marsh said to Sorrento. "These two, they're on to something else. Sounds like a poacher to me. Listen mister," he said to Bobby, "what were the circumstances? Did this guy have a gun on him?"

"Had a rifle. We were quietly enjoying the woods and suddenly there he was. He sprang out of some tall bushes. I don't mind telling you he surprised the hell out of me."

Jack Marsh stood up. "Let's approach this the right way. We've got a book that might help us out." He pulled a hardbound notebook from off the wall shelf behind Sorrento. He began thumbing through the photo copies. "These are shots of criminals on the run. Usually poachers, but sometimes we get thieves, sex offenders and perverts, embezzlers hiding out in the woods, you name it." His voice had taken on self-important gravity.

"Embezzlers?" Sorrento quirked a brow at him.

"Not yet, we haven't. But it could happen."

Margaret came over to look at the notebook Marsh opened on the desk. "Well, he was, you know, dangerous-like, the way some good-looking men are." She winked at Marsh.

Sorrento sighed. "Listen Jack; I kinda doubt this is going to come to anything. But if you want to go ahead and show these folks the pictures, be my guest. I'd like to get home. Doreen, she's getting close to her time. The baby, I mean." His furrows had deepened into crevices.

"Baby?" Jack looked up from the photo copies of photographs and stared at Sorrento for a minute. "Oh sure. Go ahead on home." The ranger was thinking about his own future child, or rather, Callie's and his. He wanted nothing to do with it, at least not so long as Callie was excluding him from her life. He'd show her. She'd come around. She'd beg him to help with the baby.

After Sorrento left, Margaret sat down in Sorrento's chair, flipping pages. Bobby leaned over the desk, shaking his head. "We don't want to get involved or anything, just came up for a weekend away." Margaret was making little shrieks and exaggerated gasps when she eyed a particularly wild face in the notebook. "Wait a minute!" She turned back several pages. Then, clapping a hand over her mouth, she let out a small "Oh." She turned to Jack. "That's him."

Marsh let this register for a moment. He hadn't really expected them to single out anyone. He looked at Bobby who nodded yes. "Oh definitely," Margaret reiterated. "Same dark eyes, those brows, nice nose, good coloring – "

"Coloring? It's a black and white," Marsh said.

"She gets carried away," Bobby said. But Jack was not listening. He scrutinized the face under the plastic cover, holding the notebook under the desk lamp. He turned to Margaret and Bobby.

"You sure this is the guy you saw in the woods today?"

The couple agreed, no question but that this was the hunter who jumped out at them.

"I know him," Marsh said. "Don't exactly *know him*, know him." He smiled, expanding his brown-shirted chest so that the buttons strained. "But I've seen him. Oh yeah, he's been around." His fist was suspended in the air, going no place. The guy who eats Millie's bad burgers, the guy Callie's covering for, he thought. Goddam, I figured he'd left Pitch Pine back in November. That scabby, no-count hunter.

To the couple he said, "You people see what it says here. This is Newton Denman and there's a warrant out for his arrest. It's for criminal vandalism and arson down state. The report says he is suspected of burning down a school."

"You know, he really was a smart ass," Margaret said, as if the episode up at Holler Gap had suddenly come clear to her. "Kind of superior acting when he saw we didn't have the compass."

Jack glanced once more at the report on Newton. "There's more here. It says he's wanted for questioning in the homicide of Theresa Waters. My God, it looks like this jerk Denman killed someone."

"We really don't want to get involved," Bobby said, putting an arm around Margaret and pulling her a little ways towards the door. She nodded, now looking coolly at Jack. "Bobby's right."

Jack leapt up. "Wait a minute. You already are involved. We need you as witnesses, to testify that you saw him on park land with a gun."

"A rifle," Margaret corrected him, as Bobby steered her out of the room.

"I'm afraid you have no choice," Jack said, coming to the door. "You have to stay and file reports of having seen this Newton Denman."

Margaret paused. "I am about to keel over from exhaustion." She leaned a little on Bobby's shoulder. "Mr. Marsh, this has been a harrowing experience. Don't you think Bobby and I can drop by in the morning? We'll do all we can to help."

"You'll be here first thing in the morning?"

"You bet we will," Bobby said, smiling sympathetically. "Nine o'clock sharp."

The next day the couple didn't show at the State Park office. Marsh waited until ten a.m. and then checked the Pitch Pine register, which told him nothing useful. Apparently Margaret and Bobby had not set up a base camp on the grounds at all, but probably stayed in town, coming out to the park for a day's hike, or maybe one night over, the record wasn't clear. Finally he traced them to the

Jolly Logger. It wasn't hard to figure. The inn and one small motel at the edge of town were the only places where tourists could get a room.

"They checked out last night," Harvey, the tavern manager, told him.

"Nuts." Jack hung up the phone. He crossed his arms and stared out the window at the swollen mountain peak.

Chapter FOURTEEN

Callie felt a courtesy towards all manner of life: the aspen's right to shake its limbs and shed its leaves on the sidewalk in front of her apartment; her cat Iris' need to roam at night; or Mrs. Pope's desire to be left alone most of the time.

It was late Sunday afternoon and Callie had stopped by with her rent check and ended up visiting Mrs. Pope. She hardly ever left their boarding house and Callie was one of the few people she tolerated. Actually, there were no boarders other than Callie. It was a medium-sized house with just the two inhabitants, Mrs. Pope who owned the place, on the first level, and Callie on the second floor. She walked slowly to the sidewalk outside the building, debating whether she ought to dash back and see if there wasn't something she could pick up at the store for the old lady before she drove out of town. No, Callie felt. She does not want to be bothered again today.

"Hey, watch where you're going!" she yelled to Vernon Vale who sped by so fast he nearly sent her crashing to the sidewalk.

"Sorry," Vernon said, backing up and extending an arm to steady her. "Something's up over at the Park Office. Jack tell you about it?"

"Jack and I don't talk much. You probably know that."

Vernon shifted his glance to the apartment wall, brown brick, cracked in places with ivy sneaking in. "It was yesterday; Jack got a lead on a murderer and arsonist, says he's on all the wanted lists."

"Mmmnn-hmmnn. Is this Jack's newest thing, playing policeman?" Callie had been in a lousy mood all afternoon. She buttoned up her long green coat. It was cold, the temperature dropping.

"It's not like that," Vernon said. "Hey, you might know the guy. Name Newton Denman ring a bell?"

Callie stared at him incredulously.

"He's the one Jack says you met while patrolling the mountain. Say, you ought to go see Jack and tell him exactly what you know about this guy."

"I didn't say I knew him." Callie tried to make her voice neutral.

"Turns out this Denman murdered a school teacher by the name of Theresa Waters. Burnt down a school, too." Vernon paused to enjoy her reaction. "Jack lost his two witnesses, but he's going to find some more. I don't have all the details yet."

"Good. I'm not much interested in the nitty gritty of Jack's tracking tactics."

"Callie?" Vernon was sure she knew more than she was letting on.

She was halfway down the block. He watched her go, dazzled as were others by her presence. She cut a striking figure in her green coat, high boots, and silver lambs wool hat.

She drove up mountain as fast as her Cherokee would permit. The Jeep wasn't old, but it had led a hard life. Plain and simple, Callie was hell on cars. She wanted to respect them as she did a tree, but it just didn't work. She was hopelessly disinterested in machines of almost any kind.

She glanced at the sky. March had come to the mountains and the hard ground was beginning to give. Even so, the Pennsylvania Alleghenies hated to give up winter and this afternoon snow clouds rowed up like fat, iced milk bottles. It looked like a steady blow; no spring shower this. Callie wasn't fussed. She liked the idea of the earth kept under a cold white cover.

It was evening by the time she pulled up near the thicket where Newton's yellow truck was hidden. Then she walked, not in the direction of his campsite at the quarry, but up an old cart road. Her extra cargo had her huffing and panting slightly, but there were some redeeming features. Her body temperature was up, and in the silence of the snowfall the second heartbeat that she felt rather than heard kept her company. She stamped along at a good pace, stopping now and then to shake the snow off her long overcoat.

Callie entered a clearing on the south side of the quarry, across from Newton's camp. As she crunched over the snow towards one particular tree, the tallest in the circle, she noticed the light and space between the tree flanks.

She was bent on pursuing a ritual she had come to rely on for about a year now. She started to climb up this tallest tree. When her belly got in the way, she had to climb more slowly, feeling carefully for hand and footholds.

The snow had stopped, and it was getting colder. Ice seemed to form in front of Callie's eyes. Staring at the frozen amber colored sacs, she sat for several minutes, swinging her legs, then drawing them up, and now dangling them again, anything to keep her circulation strong. Callie was gingerly feeling for a better handhold when she heard the rumbling, soft growl below. How did I miss her coming into the clearing, Callie wondered. How long has she been here?

It was the bear she and Newton had seen. This was the bear, Callie was beginning to believe, that Winoshca had spoken of as her tribe's Protector and Spirit guide, the bear who licks all creatures, man, woman, and beast, into their rightful shape.

Callie had to laugh at herself for confusing the bear's gender the first time they met. Reading fairy tales, and automatically thinking you, bear, were like the beast from 'Beauty and the Beast.' You were never a guy bear. I clean forgot Winoshca's words. My mistake.

Callie could almost hear Winoshca speaking. "She is the bear whose tongue reshapes and heals the world." It had seemed that Winoshca muttered something more, as well, something that indicated the bear's darker nature, or possibly a warning. But Callie had paid no heed.

On this night, high in a tree in the early spring freeze, Callie had to ask herself, 'What is wrong with me, am I crazy?' She leaned up against the trunk, looking deliberately away from the bear who was wracking at a snow-covered log. What's normal anyway, she decided, except as it's perceived from any one creature, any one heart? And bear, it is not exactly you I worship, but something in you that allows me to speak freely. And that is why I'm here, because I need to speak to you, or the woods, the snow, some part of the mountain that listens.

Callie

Almost spring now, though you'd hardly know it by tonight's icy branches. Maybe you've sent your cub off on its own. As for me, I've shown my baby a bit of climbing just now; high time, don't you think, that she or he experiences what it's like to swing up onto a branch.

Bear. I've been thinking about hibernating again. It's your fault. You do it so perfectly it makes me want to slip away for a while, the same as you do. And sometimes in these last months I get so sleepy I think I just might sleep away the rest of this pregnancy, might sleep right through the moment I give birth. Wouldn't that be nice, to hibernate the way you do when giving birth.

Bear. I wish I had a better name for you. If my tongue could only form the word that begins to fit your power and beauty. I haven't admitted this before, but the last time I was in church my tongue went numb at all the wrong times. My lips would begin to form the rote, Father, Son, and Holy Ghost, but then my tongue long trained to pray to the Father, would suddenly rebel. And then I tried to find the right words, not Father, Mother, Son, but something wholly different, outside the circumference of human names. Nothing right came to my lips, and I blame my brain for that. A large chunk of it operates on learned rules.

I can't figure out what is happening to me, this loss of faith, and sense of being altogether lost. Why is God putting me through these paces? There's too much to deal with, Newton, the baby, Jack Marsh, and now murder and arson. It might be that I have left the church for good. This makes me sad; I love the community of it, the helping others when the helping works. Last week I saw members of the congregation gathering for the crop walk to raise money for the farmers' seed for this year's planting. Yesterday, Spence and Jessie were taking flowers to the housebound folks, and food to those out of work. They asked me to help out, but I couldn't. I no longer go to services. And yet, perhaps Spirit has not left me. Maybe it lives in you. I see you watching me now.

I have come to warn you. Newton Denman means to hunt you down. Oh yes, he has designs on you. Hear me, bear? Cock your strange furred ears and cinnamon snout in my direction.

He's not only a hunter coming after you, but a hunter of humans, as well. I have learned that he may have killed someone I knew.

Is it possible, bear? Could he have done this thing? I am sick with shock and confusion. There was a night not many months back when Newton's hand spread across my thigh and as he touched me I felt the same kind of warmth that the sun sometimes shocks me with as I stand in my apartment at the open window. Only on the sunny mornings, mind you, the looking out over town to the mountain – it lasts five minutes or so – that slow in-burning, the soaking up of sun that touches the Pitch Pine Barrens.

And whatever it is in the sunlight that heals and makes me strong I felt in the union of Newton and me. Was that wrong of me, bear, to gather strength from this man? When I learned that he is after you I felt for a minute uncertain of my loyalty to you. My head was full of his touch.

Bear? You're not indifferent, are you? You are rummaging, always rummaging when I come here. Now again at the stump, flaking away a bit of it, sucking over the texture and sharp tastes of the grubs under bark. It's my greatest fear; your indifference.

Hear me, *please*. You can't ignore the facts about Newton, and it has me so mixed up, this obsession of his to find you. He is a hunter, I can't forget that. My father too, a hunter of sorts, tracking down my naive mother same as if she was a fragile creature – and she was – when he found her, out of her element at the race track where he worked. And out of her league too, with my worldly, smooth father who left her, left me before I could even see his face. Sometimes at night I have imagined his face and thought it beautiful. This terrifies me. I do not want to think him beautiful.

Guns terrify me, too, even though I learned to use one years ago. Strange that Newton, who hunts with a gun, does not terrify me. How do I make sense of this? Once the two of us were hunters of sorts. As children, we prowled Littlecomb like a pair of owls, swooping down to see what was what in those backyards, who-whoooing to each other to sound out our knowledge. He is the one who shared that suspended time with me, that piece of life when you give yourself utterly to play. Some nights we'd be utterly exhausted and yet we would not give up our game together. We couldn't stand to miss out on life.

That lasted until the end of eighth grade. Then Newton became another kind of hunter, not after the joy and pulse of the woods, but against it.

Designer guns for ladies. Yup, that's what Jack Marsh showed me in a glossy advertisement during our brief courtship, if you could call it that. He loved to pore over his hunting magazines, although he claims he doesn't hunt, just interested in the woodsmen features. *Defend yourselves, ladies*, the ad said.

Defend myself against who, men like Marsh?

I did my stint with guns, and I feel no compulsion to improve my aim. It was Newton who taught me how to fire a handgun.

"Hold your hand down so as not to get your flesh ripped out," he told me as I was getting ready to click the magazine into the bottom of the gun. I remember closing up the slideback, enjoying how proud it made Newton feel to explain the basics to me.

"Don't just point and fire," he instructed. "You have to get your sighting first."

After firing one round at the target, he put his hand over mine to show me how to lower my sighting, find my own zero. He was sweet, very patient. We were using target paper that said National Board for the Promotion of Rifle Practice. Newton was absolutely floored that I was a good shot, almost right from the start.

It meant nothing to me. Newton made a big deal of how some people don't even hit the target paper at all on their first time out, and there I was racking up a bulls eye my last three shots in a row.

A month or two later, he asked me to go out hunting in the woods with him, and I said no thank you. Mind you, I'm not especially high minded about it, but the truth is simple to tell. I am incapable of firing and taking the life of another living creature.

There you go, nudging that log back in its place. I've seen you do it before. I bet those grubs love to have the log flush up against them, so they can burrow into it as if it was the good hand of darkness. I want to be touched like that, touched hard, crushed up against the weight of something dark and brilliant.

When I was a little girl I longed to be held. Hugged. Aunt Teeny was not exactly an affectionate sort, but I discovered something else. That the earth itself could caress me, and from that came what Newton called my knowing sense of things. I'm here tonight in the snow – I see it spinning a tent in the branches overhead – I am here to ask for help.

Defend myself against whom? Men like Newton?

Are you listening to me? You, bear, I've seen the way you manage: grazing like a cow, eating anything from mushrooms, crawdads, snakes, salamanders, larger mammals, vegetable matter – bee grubs as well as the honey – any protein to mix with the vegetable. Doesn't that make you both vegetable matter and mammal? I've seen when you were upset. That time with Newton, and then afterwards. Popping your lips and groaning as if deeply concerned about something, maybe us, or the state of the earth.

You are listening. Oh please. Why is your head up, staring, perfectly still, staring, examining me? Hey beast, you are making me nervous…but wait, there is an odd numbness in my brain, a rustling now, almost as if I am breaking free of tangled briars, breaking out into the open. I have the deepest impression that you are speaking to me. What? I am having this baby, or a baby with a woodsman, a little girl? You say it will be a girl with the strength of a bear and human combined – how amazing, but Bear, yes I am having a child, a baby girl – how would you know that? But Jack, I can't say I've ever thought of him as a true woodsman.

My head hurts, my very limbs are tingling with your presence and thought planting. Enough. I am not going to give in to your animal presence any longer.

Do you hear me? No answer? Good, your impressions are melting away. Thank God for that. I don't want a total meltdown right here in this tree. Okay, I'm sorry. Forgive me for tuning out. Look, I'm still here, and I do give you credit, old beast. You are a wisdom eater, your heart is larger than anything we can imagine, ubiquitous old bear. Look at your name-shapes, bear, right in this county: Bearwallow Marsh, Bear Pass, Bear Hollow, Big Bear Gap, all of them sing your name. There are traces of you everywhere, names like that all over the world. Wait, don't leave the woods. Nothing is answered. What am I to do about Newton? He's false, he's a double-crosser. Please come back. I want you to tell me one thing. Is he a murderer?

Chapter FIFTEEN

Beyond the circle of snowy pines that held Callie, and across the quarry, Newton paced his campsite. That bumbling couple, he agitated. Not going to let them ruin another night's sleep.

He leaned over the fire to warm his hands. He had tried to put the incident with Bobby and Margaret behind him. They were not the type, he mulled, to stick around a town like Tuscatanning and report his whereabouts to a state park official. Newton went to take care of the edibles that had to be stored out of reach from animals at night. Circling a rope above his head, he aimed for a high branch on the tree. He missed, then spun the rope again, this time singing to take his mind off an uneasiness that was creeping over him:

On a summer day in the month of May, a cowboy
came a hiking, down a shady lane through the sugar cane
he was looking for his liking. As he roamed along
he sang a song of the land of milk and honey
where a man can stay for many a day
and he won't need any money.

Newton stopped short, and laughed. Poet Philip Freneu it was not. Newton shook his head. The hiking cowboy was a song Pete Myrick used to sing. Soft, and then softer, Newton sang: *Where a man can stay for many a day and he won't need any money.*

The rope caught, and he attached the cloth bag of food. As he hauled the vittles to a safe distance in mid-air, a dull explosion sounded across the quarry. A dead tree coming down? Sure, got to be a hollow pine.

He glanced at his closest gun, the thirty-five caliber Remington near the campfire, and then to the pot of honey and liquid smoke on the grate over the fire. The explosion! Suppose the bait was working, and this very instant the bear crashing around the icy perimeter of the quarry, her nostrils flaring at his enticing concoction?

Until yesterday, Newton had resisted using this kind of lure. Not even honey mixed with liquid smoke guaranteed victory. There were no surefire ways to bag a bear like this. Besides, Newton felt guilty at using the bait pot. It was cheating. The real hunter does not take his bear like a sitting duck in a pond, or in this case, with the pretence of honey at campsite. No, Newton wanted to go after the animal just as if he were an animal himself. No gimmicks. The gun, his one instrument of prey, would not give him the advantage so much as make him the bear's equal when their moment of confrontation arrived.

No bear in these parts tonight, Newton resolved. Time to turn in, put an end to this squirreliness. He stood listening, though, just to make sure. The fir trees hissed and whistled, the taller pitch pines rocked, their flat bristles lifting to the wind. He knelt over the fire, carefully spreading dirt from a tin can over the cinders so that they would burn down but not out. He wondered for a minute at his methods of tracking. Lately he didn't feel quite so single minded as the menfolk in his family. Callie had taught him other ways of thinking, and then too, maybe it was living in these woods that had taught him a thing or two. Funny how the forest, even the animals, came into his head whenever he was thinking of Callie.

Face bent over the flames, the smoky odor of bait assailed his eyes and nose. He coughed, then chuckled, thinking of George's bear trap tactics. At least I don't add steak sauce to this mess like he does. This is it for me; I'm going to get rid of this lousy bait first thing tomorrow. Newton frowned at the thought of his brother, and then cocked his ear. There it was, a second hard crunch through the thin frozen snow. Off to the left, somewhere down Hairpin trail behind his camp. Very slowly Newton half-stood up, knees bent and tipping forward on his toes like a runner at the starting line.

At the trail's edge, out tottered a tall buck, his chest glistening white on white with snow crystals. Newton's fingers slid around the rifle barrel at his side. He did this without making a sound. The deer seemed dazed by the heavy honey smoke that wavered in the air. Newton stared for a minute at the dull eyes and roughened coat, the mumpy jaws that told of hunger. Newton waved his rifle. "Aw, get out of here, before I bring that flag tail down." The deer jumped, his nose quivering at the odor as he turned and then flashed down the steep woods. All was still again. Newton strained and listened as if there was something his ears had missed. He rubbed his eyes too, thinking this would help him see more clearly in the moonless night. He peered through a cluster of walnut saplings. Newton could not shake the feeling that there was another presence in the forest with him tonight.

The saplings, bowed in spiky ice casings, obstructed his view of the quarry. He was squinting, his eyes watery because the wind was up, when a shriek ripped through the distant pitch pines and down into the canyons of the quarry. It was a full round cry, part scream and then dying into a sad, reverberating *Ahhhh-oooooooo*. The pulse in Newton's neck pounded. The cry shocked him, putting to mind the way Spoons' hounds used to give full cry. Himself about twelve, Newton might have been in the woodshed cleaning and dressing a rabbit, eager for the dollar he would get for the pelt from a bounty hunter when all at once the hounds out back would cry out, sending a thrill up the boy's back.

Yet this howl was nothing he recognized, not hound, wind, owl, bear, or fox. Behind him, something cracked, and he jerked his head around. Inches away from his cheek, Newton saw a knife suspended.

He stood paralyzed, the blood in his face frozen. The white knife came forward. "Is it you?" Newton cried.

Then a jangle, and splintered ice. Newton saw the moving blade was only an icicle, now fallen from one of the dark walnut spokes. It lay fractured across his boot.

"Hooooo!" Newton slapped his leg and forced a short laugh. What the hell did I figure I was talking to? Nerves. Too much by myself.

And then aloud, "I'm turning spooky, that's what. Those goddam city campers showing out of nowhere, they're what set me off." He trudged over to the sealed fire. Except for the spit and hum of warm cinders the campsite was perfectly still. Newton tried to gather his wits.

Got to see somebody. Can't stand this. Callie, I'll go talk to her – if she'll see me. Newton leapt up. The snow was not deep, but he fastened on his snowshoes for the slippery expedition down Hairpin trail.

It was so cold that Newton raced to climb into the cab of his truck. As he moved the Chevy into reverse something rammed its lower body. He crawled under the engine but found no problem. He started again, backing out of the thicket and onto the trail that led to the cart road.

A short distance down the highway, and the truck overheated. His gauge was in the red. He pulled over and turned the engine off. Out of the car, he swung his arms through the enveloping steam. "Shit. Don't think I can take another night of luxury in the hot springs of Tuscatanning."

Newton opened the hood to have a look at the radiator. Too hot to touch. He climbed back in the truck and waited fifteen minutes. Then he remembered he had a gallon jug of water in the box. If it was a slow leak and he turned the engine off, the water might hold out until he got to town.

Now he had a good excuse. Callie couldn't turn him away, not if she knew he had to get his truck fixed. He felt almost giddy coasting down mountain with the engine turned off. A bit of luck that it's downhill, he thought. Stay cool, truck, stay cool. He was nervous and excited. The strange shriek at the quarry had unsettled him, and he longed to see Callie, be near her for a while and talk.

Maybe she doesn't hate me so much, he thought. Does she hate me? He let her smooth rounded fingertips into the car, reaching for him, the length of him given to her touch – and then, boom, he saw her withdraw the touch, he remembered her face when she had learned he was hunting the bear. He blinked, and checked the temperature on the heat gauge.

In Tuscatanning, up two flights of stairs and suddenly exhausted, Newton leaned a shoulder heavily on her apartment door, his cheek resting against number five hundred and nine, which he had memorized months earlier, on

Christmas eve. He knocked once, then hesitated, realizing it was late. Maybe she was asleep.

"Who is it?"

He answered with her name, his voice muffled because his lips were pressed up against the oak door.

When she let him in he was surprised to see her twice as numb and tired as he. He straightened up and truly forgot his exhaustion. She motioned him to her sofa, her face pale, eyes wary but just a little bit avid, *possibly* glad to see him. She sat down at the other end of the sofa and reached forward with some difficulty to unlace the top of her boots. A long green coat, damp in spots, hung over the kitchen table behind the sofa.

"You've been out tonight?" Newton asked tentatively. "Lord, I thought I was frozen." He smiled, making a joke of it. "You look ten times worse!"

She bent over her hard belly, fumbling at her boot, fingers stiff and white, her hair, one wet mass.

Standing up and slapping his arms nervously, he said, "Let me help." Callie had scarcely looked at him since he set foot in the door, and now with a nudge of her chin which he took to mean yes, she sank back on the sofa and half-closed her eyes. Bending on one knee, Newton finished unlacing her boot. He was tenderly easing it off her foot when Callie sat bolt upright, her boot glancing him in the mouth. "Why are you here? Come to hide out from the police?"

He couldn't find his tongue.

"I know what's going on. You've been accused of murder. Our Mrs. Waters. Our old art teacher."

"Callie, stop. It's not true. I hurt no one." He rubbed the place on his mouth where her boot had struck. "I take that back. I know that I've hurt you."

They stared at one another, Newton meeting her gaze with his own level, inquiring face. "I didn't do it," he repeated.

"You weren't exactly forthright with me about hunting the bear. How do I know you're telling the truth now?"

She folded her legs, sitting on her knees in a watchful forward pose. "You march over in the middle of the night. We haven't seen each other but that one time months ago when I had to rescue you."

"Two times, we've seen each other twice in the last four months," Newton supplied. "I count that afternoon you were swimming so free – and all, in the quarry."

"All right, twice!" She rolled her eyes in despair. "What are we going to do with each other?" Callie sat back on the sofa, exasperated. She looked away, tugging on her wet hair so that it squeaked. "Oh hell," she said finally. "I believe you."

Newton rocked forward, his forehead collapsing against her calves, his entire body heaving, not in tears but convulsions of gratitude and release.

"Come on," Callie pulled lightly on his arm. "Take your parka off?"

Newton tossed his coat on top of her green one on the kitchen table, and sat down next to her. "I want to tell you what's going on. I've wanted to for a long time." He clasped his hands together for courage. "You know about my camping, my living quarters I guess you could say."

"Your illegal living quarters," she amended.

"Right." Newton squirmed. He took in the angular walls and high ceiling, the pair of wavy, glass candlesticks on the low table in front of the windows. "They're nice," he said, acknowledging the candlesticks.

"Mornings, they come alive. Bands of light playing through them." Callie glanced at the candlesticks and the four wall hangings in that part of the room. Her face softened as though some unplanned joy had stepped in. "Sorry, you were saying?"

Suddenly she was accessible to him and Newton gazed at her unabashedly, bewildered by her emotional lurches. He loved the way they took her over. She yanked off her other boot and laughed at the water sloshing out. Callie pointed a wet toe at him, her arms motioning. All of her seemed to kindle with purpose. She was magnificent and full there in the belly, and then her legs, so lithe and strong. She was pulling off her damp socks.

"Hey, could we make some coffee?" Newton asked. He felt dazed.

In the kitchen Callie filled the kettle and handed Newton the coffee and filters. He marveled at her drip coffee maker in the shape of an oversized hour glass. She got the mugs from a cabinet, and a surprise from the freezer. Back on the sofa, the two drank the hot liquid and ate a bowl each of blackberries she had frozen the summer before. Newton rolled each berry on his tongue. They were sweet and icy, and not quite thawed.

He told her about the night of the arson, how he had gone to bed early, and knew nothing other than the fact of his brothers' appearance at the house before they left on a hunting trip. "Then at about one in the morning, Trooper Myrick barges into our house. You remember him."

"Trooper?"

"Yeah, Pete's a cop now. You probably haven't seen him since you left Littlecomb."

"I did see him once."

"Then you heard how he went out to Arizona for a few years. Lost his finger to a rattlesnake while he was there, and God knows what else he lost.

"That's impossible. A rattlesnake doesn't bite off an entire finger."

"Okay then. It bit him. I guess the venom got into his forefinger and the doctor had to amputate."

"How is Pete doing these days?" she asked.

Newton's eyebrows made a tortured sign. "Well you knew him when we were kids. Shy, blond, big hearted guy."

"Not any more?"

"I don't know what his story is, but when he came over the night of Mrs. Waters' death, he basically accused me of murdering her and then burning down the school to cover my tracks."

"Motive?" said Callie. Despite her shock that Newton was a prime suspect and that Pete was involved as a police officer, she tried to play it cool.

"Mrs. Waters and Gib Setter saw a guy they think was me at the scene of the crimes. They also spotted my truck there."

"That's it?"

"Pete believes that Theresa Waters was struck in the head at the schoolhouse by a guy wearing my blue and white jacket."

"Not good."

"I've been worrying, too, that Pete will turn up something idiotic like that attitude I had towards our art teacher."

"You were mad at her."

Newton sighed. "You have a sharp memory, Miss Ursa Major, Great Bear lady."

She smiled. "Do the police know the whole story of you and Mrs. Waters?"

"Don't know." Newton lowered his head dismissively.

"You must be terrified." Callie was looking at him in a new way.

"There's one last wrinkle. I ran into a wacky couple in the forest. It wouldn't surprise me if they mentioned my existence to the State Park."

Newton told her about the urban campers and how they were lost and had lost their senses, too. "That pair was a forest fire just waiting to happen," he grinned. "I wanted to leave them be, but when I saw ol' Bobby take a gallon of lighter fluid to that woodpile next to the dead trees, I had to do something."

Callie went for more coffee, and Newton followed, walking right into a bunch of dried spices hanging from the kitchen ceiling. "You didn't answer me about being scared. Are you?" She picked up Iris, who had emerged from the warm place behind the refrigerator. Callie stroked the calico cat under her chin.

"Maybe a little," he said, coughing as the basil and garlic invaded his nose. "Who knows if they told anyone at the park about seeing me."

"Yeah, a Sunday hiker you're not," she said, handing him a refilled mug. "You look like a permanent resident of the forest." Callie leaned towards him and picked off a burr that was on his collar. "Look, here's a twig, too. God, Newton, you really do look like you could use a shower! You are a walking bush."

"Where's a twig? These clothes are pretty clean, I just –" She was brushing off his back. He felt like a mess, but when he turned and saw her smiling so big and fondly at him, he grinned foolishly.

"Hey, when did you see Pete again?"

"Oh God, it was years ago. Not important, Newton."

He took her up on the shower, and after he was dry and clothed in a russet, maternity robe that was tight across his shoulders, they sat down and Callie told him which rangers he should watch out for, and that she was certain the urban camping couple had reported him to the State Park. "Don't worry about Sorrento. He's not one to chase after glory by catching out the odd hunter."

Newton nodded, accepting a handful of sunflower seeds from the jar Callie was eating out of. Pillows at their elbows, they stretched out opposite one another on the braided rug in front of the tall triptych windows. Callie had lit the candles on the table behind them. "What about that guy, Marsh? You skipped past him fast," Newton said, watching her closely. He hadn't missed the extra beat in her voice when she mentioned how Ranger Jack Marsh was a stickler for rules.

"Did I?" She flicked her wrist. "He likes to act as if he goes by the book. If he could, he'd have everyone paying fines for jaywalking or tossing an apple core." But Callie was thinking of how she had laughed the day Jack told her he loved her. She looked at Newton, his brows scrunched together in concern, and realized that never in her adult life had she believed that a man loved her. Not that she had given many a chance to tell her so, but still there it was, her mistrust.

Callie felt a sudden draft. She got up, rubbing her arms briskly, and drew the curtain across the windows. She turned to Newton, fingertips on her temples. "Jack Marsh did see you once. Don't forget that time you were in the bar, it was November, and Jack spotted you for a hunter."

"I never got a look at him."

"It doesn't matter." She eased down on the rug next to him. "All the same, you ought to watch yourself, you're crazy to come into town like this, not if you want to continue the gypsy life up on the mountain." She ran a hand through her hair. Her lips twitched. "Gypsy hunter." She dropped her chin. "After the bear."

She looked so sorrowful Newton didn't know what to do. Gingerly he reached over and touched her hair, his palm toying with the fine strands that looped forward under her chin. "I wish I could stop. Every day I say to myself, 'Clear out of here.'"

Callie was trying to listen but it was hard when there came without warning a warm current breaking through her. And this was not her waters, not the baby. No, this was unfamiliar.

"But then I end up staying, waiting for her, the bear." His hand slid off her hair. "Or is it you I'm waiting for? Callie, I was desperate to see you," he faltered. "All this stuff has been choking me. I had to tell you."

There it was again, a warm current down her dark passageways. Perhaps a prescience of the baby to come? Again, no. These were waves of plain happiness breaking through her as he spoke. She couldn't believe he would so carelessly trust another human being, that he risked visiting her after she knew he was camping illegally, and hunting. She looked at him in wonder. "Newton," she said boldly, "You must have wondered who the father of my baby is."

Newton rattled the jar of seeds on the rug near them. "Not much," he hedged.

"No?"

He poured himself a few seeds. "I haven't wanted to think about it," he said. "Yeah, I wondered." He squinched open a shell with his tongue. Then, turning to her, "I've wanted to kill the bastard. It hurts to think of you like this."

"I thought, I mean, you *said* –" she drew her shoulders in. "A few months ago you talked differently, told me you were glad I was happy being – even said you wanted to help me out," she trailed off in a whisper, "when the baby is born."

Newton flung his arms around her. "I meant all those things, and it's down-right peculiar, but I do feel close to your baby." He shifted his weight so that Callie's head rested on his arm. He cleared his throat. "I don't want to shoot the bastard, the father; maybe just maim him a little. You know, see him buckled at the knees, then ask him why he left you to shift for yourself."

Callie lifted the lapels on his velveteen bathrobe. "Did you ever consider that it might have been the other way around? That maybe I left him?" She laughed ruefully. "It was Jack Marsh, the eager beaver ranger I was telling you about. He's the official father." She slid a hand into the robe, and rested it on his chest. "I don't love him." She wound her fingers in the tight curling hair where the top of the robe had fallen open.

"You don't?"

She laughed nervously, and was tugging at his chest hair. Newton ignored the pin pricks. "Marsh thinks he loves me."

Newton looked resigned. "I guess a lot of guys have loved you." Then, suddenly tender. "How could they help it?"

"Not so many guys, in fact – " she stopped herself, embarrassed to tell him how few lovers she had known.

Newton felt confusion, but he yearned to touch her too, and Callie saw it all in his face. She couldn't separate what was hurting from her desire to have him, and she wanted him to take away her pain. She motioned him to get the comforter to throw down on top of her rug. She knew what to do.

Some minutes later after challenging gymnastics to get around her bel-ly, Newton had turned away from her, his narrow backside just touching the swell of her stomach. The lovemaking had happened fast, belly or no belly to contend with. Too quick, he thought. What must she think of me? *You dog*, he muttered, addressing his manhood, the wretched instrument that had fired off quicker than he had ever remembered.

"You say something?" came Callie's voice behind him. Her arms circled his waist. When she squeezed him he jumped in surprise. He had felt her baby rise up and move in a circular thrust. Newton rolled over and kissed Callie where the leg or arm of the fetus made her belly jag up like a mountain peak. Then he kissed her in other places, and soon they were engaged again, Newton consumed with the sense of Callie's round shapes, the hilly rise of her belly, the way it complemented her small chin or high curved cheekbones. And this time, as his hand closed over her buttocks, he was not in a hurry to quench the strange sensation that he was making love to two beings at once. Newton was subsumed by the soft and loud tickings of her body, by the sum of heartbeats in his head.

Chapter SIXTEEN

Later that night Callie put on a sleeveless white nightgown and went to see if Newton's clothes were dry.

"Problem?" he asked lazily.

"Your shirt and pants, they're still damp. I forgot to turn on the drier. How are you going to get out of here? I've got to get some sleep."

"Worry about the clothes later," Newton said, unmoving. "Let's go to the bedroom, we can both sleep."

"This is my bedroom," she said, pointing to the blue sofa. "It folds out into a bed." She looked at it longingly. Newton got to his feet, struggled into the too-tight bathrobe, and came over to the sofa. "You look whipped," he said, holding her by the shoulders. "Hey, you never told me, what were you up to, out in the snow just before I got here?" He thought of her wet coat, boots, and hair; that look of utter exhaustion on her face, as if she had just come out of battle.

She pursed her lips. "I wonder myself."

Newton raised a brow quizzically.

She smiled, then closed one eye and widened the other in mock puzzlement. "Let's see. Oh yes. I was talking to the bear."

"The bear!"

"That's right. On the mountain top."

"You mean same black bear we saw together?"

She snapped her fingers. "The very one."

"I see." Now he was smiling. "So, you were just out there chatting up the bear? Maybe you went for a ride on her back too?"

"No, no." She laughed. "I climbed my favorite tree and waited for her. I talked to her from there."

Newton joined her, laughing heartily. "And while you were doing that, I was down at the State Park offices, having a drink with Jack Marsh. He said he loved having a gypsy like me living up there in the forest."

Callie stopped laughing.

"Hey, come on," Newton coaxed. "I don't know what to say when you go into this kind of routine." He knew that anything he mentioned about the bear would make things tense between them. And there was something else. In the last minute or so he had felt spooked again, the way he had at the quarry tonight when that lamenting howl crossed the ravine.

He jiggled his foot. "So what is this, some part of your heritage? Did your grandmother or great-aunt talk to Brother Bear, Sister Sky?"

Callie walked into the narrow hallway. "I think your clothes are dry." She felt the damp cuff on his shirt. "Perfectly dry," she said, handing it to him.

"I can't leave."

"Excuse me?"

"My truck's broke. Meant to tell you." Newton sat down on the sofa, then asked her if he could hitch a ride in the morning to go pick up some special tape at an auto supply place to patch the gouge he figured was in the radiator hose. He could see Callie's mood had taken a nose dive. First the bear business, now the truck, and to make matters worse she couldn't go to sleep with him there. He asked her why.

"I just can't, that's all. It was different that night together up on old Grandmother. Must have been the mountain air." She shook her head. "I like to be by myself when I sleep."

Newton squared his shoulders. "I'll go outside and walk around for a while. Three or four hours and it'll be morning, stores will open and I can get the tape." He stepped out of the bathrobe and handed it to her. She watched him stroll naked across the room for his pants.

"Wait." She went up and hugged him as if he were about to disappear forever. The two of them unfolded the sofa-bed. They got the comforter from off the braided rug, and blankets and pillows out of the cedar chest. Callie was asleep in five minutes.

Newton tossed, thumped his pillow, and closed his eyes. Then he became aware of something watching him. It was Iris, sitting perfectly still on a bookcase, head cocked in his direction, her gold eyes unblinking. Newton turned away from the cat and stared down the narrow hall. He was thinking of the cry in the woods that night. He was thinking of his own cry back: Is it you?

Not able to sleep Newton searched for Callie's phone. He pulled the long extension cord into the bathroom, stood undecided for several moments, and then dialed Pete Myrick's home number.

"Hello." Pete was entirely asleep. In Littlecomb, it was pouring rain.

"It bugs the hell out of me."

"Who is this?" By the time the words were out of his mouth Pete was awake and had guessed exactly who it was.

"Sorry. But you told me I could call and talk to you."

"I meant it, Newton. Where are you?" Pete had stumbled out of bed, dimly aware that thunder was booming out his window and that he probably shouldn't be on the phone.

"It bugs the hell out of me that you think I did it."

"Tell me Newt. What were you saying about your jacket? Where is it?"

"Ask my brothers."

"Did one of them go after Mrs. Waters? Were you in any way involved?"

"What about you, Pete? Did you do something terrible, too?"

"This isn't about me," Pete said. But Newton had hung up on him. The trooper threw the phone down in despair. Should he record the conversation or go back to sleep? He set his hands down on the low bureau in his bedroom, and was startled by the showy lightening that revealed his reflection in the glass. Still me, he thought sadly, as if expecting to find the intense blue eyes faded to a pale nondescript hue, or his equally intense gold hair to have turned deservedly white.

Pete decided to write down what Newton had said. But where was his trusty notebook? No good, he remembered. Have to use the computer now. Orders from Hal. He clicked on the machine, and brought up the right file. He set to work getting down his few recorded words with Newton when a clap of thunder out the window blackened the screen, the room, and Pete's mood. All at precisely the same second. That was the power of Mother Nature.

Newton has a lot more explaining to do, he thought grimly. I meant to ask him about his pyro tendencies. Hadn't Betty Denman admitted to the time he set fire to his family's yard?

"What was he up to?" Pete had asked Betty. "Was it a party that got out of hand? Did he have a few friends over?"

"No. No party. He was alone."

"Was it at night? Maybe he wanted to build himself a campfire."

"No," said Betty. "It was a huge bonfire. And it was broad daylight. I think he wanted to burn down his treefort. He was furious about something, that boy was."

"Hungry?" Callie called, getting out the cereal. She had slept well, and had no idea Newton got up in the night to call Pete.

"Sure," Newton said, turning from one of the wall hangings, which by daylight showed a group of slender green trees bowing in different directions. Behind him, the morning light bounced off the glass candlesticks and onto the batique.

"You were right," he said, coming into the kitchen. "I just saw it, the sun shivering the batiques."

"The dancing ladies!" She sloshed a cup of milk into her cereal bowl.

"The trees, I was looking at the green trees."

"Same thing," she smiled. "Get yourself a chair. I'm starved." Callie inched backwards to the kitchen island and lifted herself up onto the counter. "I have an idea what we can do about your car." Callie dipped a spoon into her cereal.

"Fix it, that's what." Newton poured milk into his bowl.

"You won't need sugar," she pointed her spoon at him. "Are you planning to tinker with the engine right there on Main Street? Then hustle off to the store to find this radiator tape – if it is the radiator that's broken?"

"Radiator Bandage is what it's called," Newton said, crunching energetically at his cereal. "Hey what is this stuff?"

"It's not safe," she said.

He made a face.

"The cereal is fine, it's you who's not safe if you go parading around town. You could be seen by Jack, Vernon, or maybe their buddies. Small community, don't forget."

Newton half-shrugged and said, "I can't ask you and your belly to crawl under the truck."

Callie set her bowl into the sink. "There is someone I can persuade to come over and help."

Newton balked. "You won't give me away?"

"We don't have much choice," she said testily, "The mechanic I'm thinking of is trustworthy, pumps gas down at the Mobil, and works on cars after hours."

"Who is this gas jockey?"

"You'll see." Callie licked her spoon and picked up the telephone. Newton glared at his empty bowl. "That cereal was different."

"It's ringing." Callie held her hand over the mouthpiece of the phone. "Rolled oats, barley, and wheat; carrots, toasted rice, bran, and corn; dried apples, plums, dates and raisins. Fresh avocado if I have it."

"Avocado, that's what I tasted." He didn't have to ask if she made the concoction herself.

"The singing mechanic is here," Callie's cousin announced as she came in the door. Mary Cowell was wearing a white leather mini-dress with a fringe along the bottom. Attached to her back by long porcupine quills was a fanspread of feathers that stuck out above her metallic rust hair. She wore long looped quill earrings and had on a beaded belt and moccasins to match.

"Help me off with these feathers will you?"

"Mary, this is Newton," Callie said.

Newton felt her scrutiny. "Have you come to stay?" Mary said. "Need a job? My cousin says this town needs fishing guides. You any good at that? This area's famous for its fly fishing."

"Hello Mary. It's nice to meet you." Newton was a little stunned. Callie unhooked the feathers where her cousin directed. "Why are you in that costume at the crack of dawn?" She turned to Newton. "Mary is part of a dance and drum troupe."

"It's not like we have a great following, seeing as how most of the old tribe has split," Mary said. "Gone to New York."

Newton nodded dubiously. Interesting enough, but this wiry woman with dusty brown-gold skin and orange hair did not look remotely like a mechanic to him, especially in this get-up. Mary asked Callie if she had an old coat she could throw over her white dress. "Then we'll see about the truck," she said, glancing again at Newton. "I'm the lead dancer." Then, drawing herself up proudly, "The Eagle Feather Singers use five drums when we dance *The Sacred Circle of Life*."

Newton thought he should say something. "Is that what you'll be dancing today?"

"Yup, in about an hour. Usually we're a nighttime show, but the William Penn Elementary is studying Indian cultures and asked if we could come do an assembly for the kids. Say, I heard they're on the lookout for Appalachian cloggers, they're studying mountain folk culture next." She looked expectantly at Newton. He threw up his hands. "Not me. No clogging!" Newton walked into the kitchen for a second cup of coffee.

Callie carefully laid out the big bundle of linked feathers on the bed. Mary turned up the radio. "Good old song," she said.

"It's a yellow truck," Callie said to Mary, who was belting out the lyrics in unison with Linda Ronstadt. "It's so easy to fall in love," she sang, her lips reverberating over the "love." Callie laughed, then came in at the refrain. "It's so easy, it's *so easy*," Callie emphasized.

Newton strolled into the room and was looking right at her.

Callie stopped singing.

"Are we going to meet up again?" he asked.

Mary stared at the two of them, then walked over to the radio and fiddled with the speaker.

"How about a week from now?" Newton persisted, looking through the steam from his coffee mug."

"A week and a half," Callie said. "I'll call you. There's that highway phone booth you can get to. No. It probably doesn't have a number."

"But it does," said Newton. "I even wrote it down so that we could reach each other. Shoot. It's somewhere here." He was going though scraps of paper from his pocket. "Bingo." He handed her a gas receipt with a number scrawled on the back. "When will you call?"

"Ten days. That's Sunday. What time?"

"One o'clock in the afternoon."

"One o'clock," repeated Callie.

Mary clicked off the radio. "Don't mean to interrupt, but wasn't there something about a yellow truck you wanted me to see to?"

Callie turned to her cousin. "The truck! It's parked right in front of the apartment." In distress, her eyes skipped to Newton.

Mary picked up on the situation. "Not to worry, I won't ask any questions," she said, with a sidelong glance at Newton. "At least not until after he's left town." Mary danced toward the door, doing some kind of toe-hop, two-step thing. "This is the sneak-up dance," she said, over her shoulder. "It's a courting ritual." She was out the door, and then a second later she stuck her head back in. "I didn't really do those dances justice, not without the drums."

After her cousin was gone Callie began to laugh. "That's Mary."

"I don't see what's so funny. What is she, some kind of loon?"

"She's just revving up for her show." Callie looked hurt. "My cousin is not loony."

"Sorry. She makes me a little nervous, is all." They sat in silence on the blue sofa-bed.

Then Newton said, "Her hair sure is a bright orange. Did you say she's mostly Seneca?"

"A lot of people dye their hair," Callie said dryly. "It looks a hell of a lot better than when she had it platinum blonde." She sighed. "I guess it was dark brown once. A long time ago." She fixed her eyes on Iris, or rather her waving tail, which was sticking out of a paper grocery bag she had crawled into near the kitchen. "Mary, she's not exactly consistent in her beliefs. Neither am I. It's hard to follow tribal customs when you don't have a council. There's not an official tribe either, just a few of us, drifted together after the government built the dam, took our land."

"Yeah," Newton said, feeling helpless. He hated to see her so sad. "It must have been different for your ancestors in Tuscatanning, hundreds of years ago." Then, more intent, he added, "For one thing, the forest wasn't stripped regularly by the timber industry."

Callie let her head drop against his shoulder. "You know what, I was glad, really glad when you told me how you stopped those two idiots from starting that fire. You were thinking about the woods, watching out for them."

"And myself," Newton smiled, and then started talking about the mountain, how the best places on old Grandmother had no trails. He told her he had camped out in enough State Forests to know that whenever the park officials decide to bulldoze some new nature trail, the animals knew it, the trees knew it, and not plant, animal, or even the earth could adjust with grace. "There's enough trails up mountain already." Newton was animated. "Did you see the way that last one your park people carved below Holler Lookout destroyed the habitat of the fox, woodchuck, and wild turkeys? Think how hard it is on the animals in winter. Summers too, when a load of tourists charge through their territory and trash the place. Not that most of them are like that, but still…" he muttered vaguely.

Callie was surprised. He was truly concerned. "Mmmnnnn," she said, cautiously, anxious to steer the talk away from her employers' contradictory methods in preserving wildlife. "It would have been horrible if there was a fire."

"Right. A fire," said Newton, trying to keep his eyes off her face. When Mary came in, she was all business, right down to her grime-smeared face. "A busted hose, that's what it was. No wonder your radiator leaked." She held up a ripped black rubber tube. "I replaced it, had a brand new one right in my truck. I keep all kinds of parts."

Newton was grateful. "Hey thanks."

"Don't thank me yet." She scanned the apartment. "Where'd you put my feathers, Cal? I have to clear out of here." Mary reassembled her costume and joked as she straightened her feathers in the small mirror in the living room. "I've been trying to get Callie to sign on with the Eagle Feather Singers, but she won't do it. Some grand niece of Winoshca, you are."

Callie waved her hand. "You think people want to see an eight-month pregnant lady doing the sneak-up courtship dance?"

"Don't see why not," Mary countered. "You're going to dress up as a kangaroo or maybe a mongoose in a couple of weeks for The Good Shepherd Church." She raised her brows at Newton. "Callie's in this production of Noah's Ark for the church, isn't that right, Cal?"

Callie tossed her shoulders. "It's a Miracle Play, the story of Noah's ark. I was going to be the Assistant Director." She sighed. "But I gave the job to someone else. I don't go to service at The Good Shepherd any more."

Mary opened her mouth in surprise. "Why not?"

"I'm not sure."

Mary opened her mouth again, but "Oh!" was all she said. Then, "Okay, I'm out of here. How do I look? Will the students at William Penn Elementary be wowed, or what?"

"There will be thunderous applause," Newton said, following her to the door. Callie came too.

"Don't forget dinner tomorrow." Mary squeezed her cousin's hand.

After she left Callie turned to Newton. "I was thinking about your brothers back in Littlecomb."

"Those big galoots." Newton tried to smile.

"Don't joke," said Callie. "From what you've said it sounds like they might know something about the death of Theresa Waters. They wouldn't turn on you, would they? I'm afraid for you."

"No way. They're my brothers," Newton reassured her. But he had begun to wonder how far they would go to save their own necks.

With the friendliest of smiles, Superintendent Bud Mason patted a chair for Callie to sit down. He was an intelligent and reasonable administrator whose only weaknesses were Spence's rich cheese steaks and the pinball games at the Jolly Logger. He had become dependent on the cheese steaks after the death of his wife Ginette, who had been a fine cook and a great hiker. Once, right after the funeral, he confided in Callie that the only reason he stayed on at Pitch Pine all these years was Ginette. That woman had loved the mountains. It was painful, though, to have spoken of her to Callie. After that, he decided never to mention his dear wife by name. It hurt too much.

A burly man with white hair, lots of it, not just on his head but along his neck, and even feathering out of one ear, Bud did the best he could with headstrong rangers such as Jack Marsh – and as he was beginning to notice – Callie Major.

Even as he smiled at her fondly, Callie sensed Bud had not sent for her to expedite a Park snafu. Leaning forward across his desk, he took off his glasses and rubbed his eyes.

Callie waited, and tried not to listen to the sound of his eyelids clicking against the sockets. She sighed and wrapped her arms across her belly.

"There are two matters that concern me."

Callie felt a distinct prickling, a warning crawl up her back. "Yes?"

"First your pregnancy, but I'll get back to that. And second, I heard from Cameron Shawl down at police headquarters, that Jack has sighted some rough type up Grandmother Mountain."

Callie cocked her head. "Did he?"

"Probably a poacher and nothing more. I don't have many details."

Callie waited for what was coming next. She could see there was something more he did not want to reveal. Bud made an effort to change directions.

"Are things going all right for you? I'd like to know your plans for pregnancy leave."

"I haven't thought much about it," Callie said. "Figured I'd just keep working until I noticed I couldn't. Or until it's time."

Bud's eyes were large behind the glasses. "Can't get yourself rundown at this stage of the game. I've been feeling a smidgeon of guilt, you see. We need you, you know that. And I've said nothing to encourage you to put your feet up and take that leave." He paused, and then said unhappily, "You're the best we've got at Pitch Pine."

"Thank you."

"Don't forget about that poacher. He might be more than we bargained for. Promise me, what with your baby and all, that you won't try to bring him in."

"I can certainly promise that, Sir."

She and Mary had a dinner date in town. As they made their way to a booth in the Jolly Logger, Callie saw Bud Mason for the second time that day. He squeezed out from behind a pinball machine that almost no one played anymore since the arrival of two video games. "Hi there, ranger," he said to Callie. Then, turning to Mary, "I guess you're busy choosing the numbers this week."

Everyone in town knew Mary loved to bet the daily lotto. "The Jackpot rolled over big, didn't it?" he said amiably.

"I'm balancing my numbers this time," she said. "Aiming for a total between ninety and 130."

Mason nodded. "Ever since the Jackpot took off, Spence's place is hopping." His eye skipped from Mary to Callie, who was tense and tired. The late night with Newton was taking its toll. She saw Bud looking at her in concern, and had to smile. It was nice that someone cared.

He went on about the jackpot. "Come next two weeks we won't even be able to buy a loaf of bread from Spence. That place'll be swamped with people wanting numbers."

Callie laughed sympathetically. "No cheese steaks for a while?"

"Don't know how I'll survive. Did you buy a ticket?" he asked Callie.

"No way."

"I got an unbeatable angle this time," Mary broke in. "I came this close in the Pick-Six-Lotto last month." She pinched her thumb and forefinger together.

They found a place to eat near the back window of the tavern. Callie felt a headache coming on and she was glad to sit down. The booth was deep and comfortable and there was something decidedly soothing in picking out what you wanted to eat. It's the having a choice that makes it so nice, Callie thought. "I see you're wearing the earrings Winoshca gave you," she said to her cousin.

"I've been wearing them a lot lately." Mary fingered the fragile brown and white quills looped through her ears. She lit a cigarette. "It so happens that tonight is special, and I'm hoping to get lucky."

"A man or a lotto game?"

"Don't be funny. You know there's nothing going in the games tonight." She leaned over the booth. "He's real cute. Works down at the Exxon. Charlie, that's his name. My guess is he could be all of," she paused mischievously, "twenty-five."

Callie laughed. "Mary, Mary."

"Careful," her cousin narrowed her eyes warningly.

"All I said was – "

"Cut the superior act, okay? There's nothing wrong with young guys."

"I wasn't making fun."

The waitress had come up to the booth.

Mary glared at Callie.

"Ahem," said the waitress.

Callie tried another tack. "I get a kick out of your love life, that's all."

Mary did not look consoled.

"How are you today? Would you like to hear tonight's specials?" The waitress believed in politeness even when her customers did not.

The older cousin waved the cigarette to her lips. "Your problem is that it's been way too long since you got laid. Not that you can do anything now, not in your current condition."

"I'll come back, *ladies*." The waitress turned on her heels. Callie wiped her eyes with the back of her hand.

"Hey," Mary said, "You laughing or crying?"

"I don't know. Laughing, I think."

Mary handed her a napkin. "So there is something special between you and that nice, dark-eyed, what was his name again?"

"Newton Denman." She felt that headache gaining on her.

Mary hallooed the waitress to come back and get their order. "Who is he?" she demanded after she ordered a taco salad with everything on it, plus extra sour cream, and Callie had asked for a cheese sandwich and chocolate milk. "Why do I have to keep my lips buttoned about him being in town?"

"Shhhhh," Callie begged. She had just sighted a couple of rangers from the park. They greeted Bud Mason, and then walked towards the end of the bar. "Listen, I don't want to talk about it," Callie said, touching her aching head. Someone was in there blowing up a hot air balloon. It was the no choice situation that had her panicked. It was Newton filling her head. She had not chosen to be so caught up with him, and it seemed to her that she ought to do something about the way she was being sucked into him, to his touch, and most of all his voice that cried out for help. She thought about this. Why was his voice her business?

"All right. So you're not going to say anything more about this guy," Mary was saying. "But hey, Cal, who can you trust if it's not your cousin?"

Callie stared at the napkin in her lap. "I called you up to come over about the truck, didn't I?" She looked up as two plates of food descended. The waitress took her time planting each fork, knife, and spoon on their napkins.

Mary rolled her eyes at the woman as if she was a first-class intruder, and Callie jumped at the chance to change directions.

"You do look lucky these days. Maybe you'll win the Super-seven."

"Not shifting the subject on me, cousin, by any chance?"

"Damn right I am," Callie said cheerfully. She ate a bit of sandwich and handed Mary her pickle as she always did when they ordered at the Logger. "When did Bud say the big lotto day is?"

"Two weeks from today," Mary paused, her face lighting up, "and I aim to be ready. I have a sure strategy this time around. It's all logic, pure and simple. No consecutive numbers, not too many evens or odds, and you know, your personal line up of what's gonna work best."

"How many tickets you plan on getting?"

"As much of my paycheck as possible, that's how many. Already I've done a few tickets with family data. You know, lucky stuff like Winoshca's, yours, and my birth dates. She crunched on the pickle. "Did a ticket today with Charlie's license plate numbers."

"Most of your paycheck?" Callie echoed. "But you got in debt last time."

"This is different, Cal. Pure science will be at work for me when those little ping pong balls blow out of the machine this time two weeks from now. *My number's going to be there, you wait and see.*"

Callie laughed, and then swallowed too much sandwich. She coughed and was gulping water when she felt the baby knock at the walls of her stomach. She tried to think of the vibrant sash inside, the umbilical cord that stationed her and made her strong, but for the moment it failed her. It felt like the baby was striking the cord. She imagined the sash tearing, her child without its life support, Callie without her vital lifebelt.

She grabbed Mary's hand and blurted, "Do you think it was safe, my making love to Newton? With the baby and all? I've heard stories about women going into labor too early because of it."

Mary studied her cousin's face and then took her two hands. "Baloney! Double baloney and horse shit, that's what those stories are. Hey, it's like planted seeds that sit through a gorgeous spring storm. You think they're hurt by it? You're making a baby in there, not building a bomb. It won't go off, not until it's ready."

Callie felt so grateful she wanted to weep. "I hope you win this time, I really do," she said to her cousin.

"Speaking of jackpots, look what we have here," Mary said, glancing at Jack Marsh, hands in his pockets as he strolled up to their booth.

"Thought I recognized your neon-do," Jack said to Mary, who answered him with a sickly sweet smile that wouldn't fool a love starved dog.

"Callie," he nodded formally in her direction.

"Hi Jack," Callie said, not meeting his eyes.

Just as flustered, he turned to Mary. "Saw you belly down, working on a truck the other morning. It was yesterday, right there on Main Street." He smiled, more composed. "Bought yourself a new truck? A lemon?"

Mary wasn't going to give this guy an inch. "That truck wasn't lemon yellow. Definitely not lemon yellow."

"Yeah, sure. Maybe it was canary, or what say, butterfly yellow? Thing is, I noticed it was parked in front of your place," he said, lifting his eyes slowly to Callie. "Could be that truck belonged to a friend of yours? Old Mrs. Pope never has visitors. You entertaining lately?" He paused. "I don't see why I'm not invited. Especially since I could tell you a thing or two about that scumbag hunter. Callie, you have no idea what you're messing with."

Callie studied Jack a minute. She was nervous, but it was very interesting what was going on inside her. She could feel the play, the pull and release of a lightly girding cord. The secret umbilical sash seemed to encircle her womb, anchor her even as it floated and vibrated with life supplies for her infant. Gone were the currents of disorder, gone for now the loosely defined Callie.

Slowly she chewed a piece of cheese and crust, then, looking Jack squarely in his snapping blue eyes, she said, "Why are you so nosy? I hadn't heard that Bud requires us rangers to check out who owns what vehicle in town."

Jack's mouth tightened. "We've been through some things together, Callie. You know what I mean. My God you don't know what you're getting into." And more quietly, "I worry about you."

Callie felt a pang of pity for him, even compassion that she couldn't give him what he wanted. Then he spoke again, a hard edge to his voice. "That truck's been in town before. Early winter."

He searched her face, and she guessed that he must have sighted her a few months back, driving Newton's truck to him the day she got him out of town in a hurry.

He scrutinized, and she scrutinized right back.

Jack ran a hand through his short straw hair. "Just watch out for yourself, would you?"

As soon as he had turned to go to the bar, Mary said, "Imagine, I used to think he was some kinda hunk."

"You and me both," Callie said, watching his easy stride, the brown pants pulling at the seat as he slid his hands into his pockets. She turned to Mary. "I didn't know you liked Jack?"

"It was nothing. I asked him to come up one night, about a month ago. He shot me down, though. Guess he thinks he's hot shit."

"No doubt." Callie shifted uncomfortably.

Mary stared at Jack, now swinging jauntily up on the bar stool. "Seems like he wears it everywhere, he never takes it off."

"What's that?"

"His uniform." Mary plucked at the shell of her taco salad and broke off a big piece.

"I've seen it off," Callie said quietly.

Mary dropped the taco and stared at her cousin. "Hey wait a minute. Didn't Jack say he was worried about you? First I learn about Newton. Now you and Jack. Would you like to tell me anything more?"

Callie shook her head dumbly, and then feeling Mary's divining eyes, she said. "Yeah, there is more, and this part has nothing to do with a guy. The other day I went up Grandmother Mountain and climbed a tree. Wait, no judgments please. I'm pretty good at it, pregnant or not. Last few times I've gone something strange has happened. The great bear, the one I've talked about on and off, comes walking out of the forest and ambles over right below where I sit in a v wedge of branches. She and I communicate. We," Callie was embarrassed. "We talk, so to speak."

At this, Mary forgot about eating entirely. She reached for another cigarette.

Callie took a deep breath, reminding herself that if there was one person who might understand, it would be Mary. After all, she was the daughter of Winoshca.

"I ought to back up and say that a few months back, I was flipping through this book I stole, well, borrowed, from Newton about bears. It talked about bears who are pregnant during hibernation. Some really cool stuff, like about how a bear's temperature drops two degrees during hibernation, even if pregnant, and weirder still, they can go months and months without peeing. As they rest or sleep and the cub grows they are able to turn the urine into protein."

"No shit," Mary said, in spite of herself. She had decided to shelve, for the moment, Callie's communication with this bear.

Callie stared off dreamily. "Here's the odd part. My temperature has gone down by two degrees in this last month when most pregnant people are filled with heat, and odder still –" she paused, "I don't pee at all. Just don't have to," she said dismissively.

"What? That's crazy," Mary said. "Pregnant women are supposed to pee more than the average woman, and besides, Callie, that's just not safe. I don't care what you say, I do not see you turning into a bear right here in front of me. You better go to the doctor, something must be wrong."

Superintendent Mason was driving across the lot of the State Forest Offices to his usual spot near the large glass and brick offices. "Hey Marsh, what's up?" he called out his window to Jack, who was dashing towards his 1963 Land Rover.

"Morning sir, an emergency, sir!" Jack met his boss halfway between their two cars.

"What's happened? Which campsite?"

Jack's eyes were intense, the brightest flecks of blue. He cocked his head, top teeth just touching the bottom ones. "It isn't exactly a campsite problem."

"This huff you're in," said Bud, exasperated at Jack's histrionics, "is it work related?"

"Oh yes sir. Of a particular nature though." He wanted to get Bud's okay to go over to the State Police barracks. He told Mason that after checking out a few leads in town, and at the Jolly Logger last night he had strong evidence of a squatter, hunter, arsonist and murderer rolled into one. "Most likely he's hiding out up Grandmother Mountain."

"In Park jurisdiction?"

"State Forest, I think. That's our responsibility too. Primitive camping permitted just one night –"

"Don't recite the rules to me, Marsh."

But Jack was like a train. "And no hunting, except in specified areas."

Bud was amused at Jack's righteousness. He knew that a few of his own rangers hunted freely in the restricted parts of the forest, Marsh being one. "Yes, I see." He paused, deciding not to confront him just now. Time enough for that. "Well, who the hell is this poacher, or should I say – arsonist and murderer rolled into one?" Bud was not prepared to take this thing seriously. Jack's charge was too hot-headed. It sounded like there was something else going on here.

Jack handed him a copy of the wanted poster with a photo of Newton. The ranger sped through the events, beginning with his glimpse of Denman and his yellow truck in November, the witnesses, Bobby and Margaret, who had sighted him up mountain in February, and the reappearance of Newton's truck day before yesterday. Jack pointed to the write-up on Newton. "Even the Chevy pick-up is mentioned, right there in black and white. I mean, yellow. The truck is yellow."

Once again, thought Bud, Jack's zeal is getting the best of his logic. "You saw this pick-up the other day?"

Jack hesitated. "Yes sir. In town." He smiled, but the corners of his lips tucked down as he thought of what sort of connection there might be between Callie and the hunter. He looked off at the flickering trees, the wave of blue that billowed up between them. Jack tried to think back. Had Callie ever mentioned this guy, Newton, before? Hell, she never mentioned any guys. He knew she hadn't been around, at least not much. Forest sprite, off communing with trees like those, he thought, surprised at his potent image of her.

Jack Marsh was more used to another set of feelings. When he thought of Callie, he felt a huge wave clenching him in its undertow, and he was floundering, not breathing. This, he supposed was love. Jack longed for the days when he had believed himself a master at compartmentalizing women, one type of female for this situation, another for that one, was his credo. The scheme fell apart with Callie.

Bud Mason interrupted Jack's meditation on Callie as a wood nymph. "Go ahead on over to the barracks," Bud said. "Give them your report." He yawned. The buttons across his hefty chest glinted in the sun. "Like to get my coffee and apple fritter, that's what I'd like." He threw his khaki Park jacket over his shoulder and straightened his glasses, squinting hard at Marsh.

"After the report's in, you stay out of it. If this is about arson and murder, then it's not our business."

"Sir." Jack nodded perfunctorily. I'll stay out of it, he thought. In a pig's eye, I will.

Part Three

Bears will make their wishes clear with "whines, grunts, or sighs" (that) could mount to a breathy sigh of AO that resembled a foghorn... The female in particular has a tendency to pop her lips, a sound that to Schneider suggested the "effusion of unsatisfied longing."

from <u>Bears</u>, *a brief history*, Bernd Brunner

Chapter SEVENTEEN

"Doesn't seem like you're getting very far with the Waters case," Detective Rendell told Pete, as they sat having a beer after hours, in the Big Springs Lounge.

Pete was the kind of guy who did not pretend to know more than he did. "You're right. I'm stalled."

"Are you using the laptop?

"Trying to. Sort of off and on."

"No wonder you can't organize yourself," said Hal. "What about those brothers of Newton Denman? I'm not convinced they aren't part of the picture."

"I think you're right, sir. The autopsy is telling us that there may well have been more than one perpetrator."

Hal gave a tight lipped smile. "Get on those leads, boy scout. And use that laptop. Sometimes I have the feeling you don't want to get with it, up to date, if you know what I mean."

Pete winced. Not that Boy Scout stuff again, he thought. It goes to show. Never divulge one's private life to anyone.

That night his dream had a familiar setting. He was climbing a steep incline of rocks. As Pete neared the top of the mesa, the rocks turned white and gold with flashes of red from the sun. It resembled one of the three tall mesas where the Hopis Indians live, but it felt different. Here there was menace creeping towards him. Once again he had a banner in his hand. This time he was calling out for people to read and honor it.

At his feet were several rattlesnakes, and then two men approaching him.

"We've come to take them away," said Natty Denman, his eyes filmed over, the lids closing like a lizard's, from the bottom up.

"You're about to lose your family," said George Denman, whose eyes were as empty as an Arizona wash.

It was early spring in Tuscatanning. Anyone who stood on Main Street and happened to look up into the face of Grandmother Mountain would see it partitioned in swatches of darks and lights, the deep, unchanging green of the pitch pines, and then the new growth, pale as lichen, which lay in smooth planes between the evergreen forests. It was in one of these lucent planes which was also known as Great Meadow that Newton had set out to rustle up a rabbit or a woodchuck, some small makings for a stew.

He moved sluggishly, having stayed up half the night repairing the waterproofing on his tent. Part way across the meadow Newton made the sheepish discovery that he had forgotten his rifle. Exasperated at this unprecedented act, he sat down for a minute on a cushion of new green earth. He was tired, and before he knew it he was on his belly, sprawled in the short rippling blades. He fell asleep, watching at worm's eye as the wind gently parted the grass and sent a silver line zigzagging through the field.

When he stirred, the sun was at three o'clock. Newton felt refreshed, even pleased with himself. It was good taking the odd nap, relaxing this way. Forgetting his gun seemed to have had a strange effect on him.

He left Great Meadow and hiked down into the forest trail that led to his campsite. Not far from the quarry a short barking growl followed by a loud thrashing told Newton the bear must be in, or very near his camp. He had left the bait pot simmering, never thinking he'd be gone this long. He raced towards camp, regretting that he had weakened where the bait was concerned. He should have thrown it out as he had resolved last month.

Newton edged towards the cluster of pitch pines at the quarry clearing. He would feel better once he got his rifle in his hands. He knew exactly where it was, propped up against the pine tree with his food bag tied up in it.

Through the opening at the quarry he saw the bear under that same pine. She had demolished his food bag. Newton stared at the shreds of checkered cloth strewn on the ground. Oozing over his sleeping bag that was in tatters was a stream of liquid smoke and honey. So much for Newton's bait station. The bear moved moved quickly to the other side of his camp and rose on her hind legs. She clawed a sweatshirt and jacket that had been hung out to dry on the branch of a tulip tree. Now down again on all fours, she rammed his tent.

Newton slipped around the perimeter of the woods, heading for the tree under which his Remington lay. Everything Spoons had said about black bears came back to him, all the awful facts he'd dismissed lightly: that her behavior was unpredictable, how when angered she razed anything in her path; that black bears had mauled and finished off more people than people would like to remember. That although smaller than the grizzly, the black bear was the aggressor better known for following through in its attack, better known for dealing climactic deaths to hunters. Without stepping into the clearing, Newton inched towards the tree that held his gun. Newton pictured himself raising the rifle, his chin on the stock, his sighting true. He stumbled. It was only a root he had tripped on, but it was sound enough to alert the bear.

The great creature whipped around, eye on Newton almost as if she was waiting for him to try for his gun. Newton froze. He stared at her face, noticing the way her ginger colored snout curled up from her lips. The bear stood about ten yards from him. She was rolling her head from side to side, not truly looking at him, although Newton was wishing she would. When she roared, an unfamiliar feeling swam into his breast. It cut deep as pain or desire and made him long for her to capture him with her eye.

He was intensely aware of her as a mammal – not inferior to him and manageable as he had handily imagined – but one wholly different from himself. There was her vision that was different, far seeing; her hearing, intimate with the earth sounds; even her bristling coat shocked him because he saw her raised fur vibrate with messages only she understood.

Then she came at him, not charging the way a maddened animal might, but in bounds and leaps, almost graceful. Possibly she was not moving as fast as she could. Not pausing to consider why the bear came at him slowly, he turned and discharged himself through the woods, stumbling, scraping past trees, and hurling down Hairpin trail. When he realized she was no longer chasing him, he stopped running, and plunged into a thicket. Into its thorny recesses he burrowed, as though making a nest. He drew his knees up to his chest, and stayed that way a long time. Once he looked up at the sky through the vines, and saw a blue jay perched at the top of the overgrowth. Newton dropped his head to his chest.

It was absurd this sudden dread he felt towards the creature, the not knowing what she was. For several seconds he had an overwhelming desire to beg her forgiveness, to tell her he was sorry for thinking he could con her with so low a ploy as the bait station. And then, too, what a fool he'd been, imagining that he could hunt her as an animal himself, that he had earned a kind of animal status by living so long in the woods. He huddled tighter into himself. He wasn't ready to face his campsite. Not yet. He had to think. No, that was the last thing he wanted to do. He felt in his pockets. No money, but he had change in the truck, loads of it in an empty mayonnaise jar under the front seat.

Cautiously out of the thicket, and then Newton tore through the woods to his hidden truck. So he had been routed by the bear. For the first time he understood that she had not invaded his campsite so much as he had invaded hers, large though it was. The interloper tramped down mountain. He was going to make a phone call.

Newton squeezed inside the highway phone booth, pulled the door shut and dialed. Still shaking, he fumbled, and dropped his change. It was stuffy. He imagined the computerized operator waiting as he got together his quarters.

"Hell-lo."

"That you Nat? Get Ma for me, will you," Newton said, kicking open the door. He glanced out at the empty road.

"For crissake! We had all but took you for dead, it's been so long – "

"Nat, I'd like to talk to Ma."

"Well sure, Newt. Course I'll go get Ma. You still after that hyooo-mungus bear?"

"Maybe."

"Figured you were. George and me, we were talking the other day about how you really go after an animal. What you need are some dogs to run that critter down. You know George has himself a fine pack. I can't believe you've been disappeared all this time. Where'd you say it was you been living?"

"I didn't say."

"Lordy, what I'd give to get out and bag me a bear. Oh, here's Ma."

Newton wanted to know that his mother was okay, and to hear her speak, let her gravelly tones do their work: soothe him. He didn't mean to tell her about his besieged campsite but once he heard her voice all sorts of things came rushing out of him, like where he was living on Grandmother Mountain, how he was scared he might be losing the upper hand over the bear, and last, he told his ma that he wanted to marry Callie Major.

"Major? You don't mean that girl what broke your heart when you were fifteen? She's been gone for years."

"Yup, that's the one." Newton's voice cracked, and he wondered where it had come from, this admission that he wanted to marry Callie.

There was a muffled silence, hand over the mouthpiece on his mother's end, a few words to somebody, probably Natty, maybe George. Then, to Newton, "Are you all right?"

"Sure I am. Could be I'm a mite shook up over my campsite that bear tried to devour."

"Listen to me." She drew in her breath sharply. "About that Indian girl you knew twenty years back, well I think she's like a ghost to you, son. You never got over her."

"I did meet her again, Ma. It was downright peculiar too, me alone as a body can be up on the mountain. And there she was, swimming in my icy cold quarry."

His mother coughed. "You have to pull yourself together, hear? The boys, Natty and George, they've been talking about riding out there to help you finish off your business, the hunting and whatever. I could send money with them to give you so you can get clear of that place, move out of state."

"What are you saying?" Newton was slow to take her meaning.

"What about West Virginia? Get yourself a new start."

"Don't tell George and Natty where I am, Ma. It's not a good idea." He was tired, deflated.

After he hung up, Newton stepped out onto the highway. The phone rang and he swung into life, reaching it in half a ring. "Ma? Don't do this."

"Seventy-five cents please," came the operator monotone. Newton repeated, "Don't do this to me."

Pete rarely had nighttime visitors and the knock at the door at eleven hardly registered. He sat for several seconds in the leather chair that had been his father's. At the second knock, he jumped up, slipping his hand gun into his pocket before going to the door.

"So you still live here," said Wendy Waters, smiling just the way her mother did.

Pete stared unceremoniously, making sure that this really was the Wendy he remembered from high school days, the daughter of Theresa Waters. Both the deceased and her daughter had tiny half-moon mouths. Now Callie Major, she had curvy lips too, but in a heart shape face, sharp, striking, rather like a barn owl, thought Pete. Why was his mind leaping this way again? Must be Wendy's presence, the reminder of bygone school days.

"Here I am, your witness for my father's whereabouts on that night."

"Please come in," Pete said, walking ahead of her, scooping up newspapers off the floor. "I didn't expect company. Sorry for the mess." Pete waved a hand for her to sit down in his living room.

"I'm here on leave," Wendy said.

"It's been a long time." He smiled. "I met your daughter."

"Allison. I wish I didn't have to be away from her. I head back to Sarajevo in a week." Wendy sunk down into his leather armchair. "So you never sold the place." She surveyed the cluttered, comfortable room.

Pete walked over to the T.V.

"I wouldn't have figured you for a Seinfeld fan," she said.

"It's daft." He clicked off the re-run. "Yeah I like it. It's all about friends hanging out together. Just like my life here," he said with a wry smile.

Wendy took a deep breath. "I only came to tell you that I was on the phone with my father during the time my mother –" Her voice rose. "Got hit on the head."

Pete waited a respectful few moments.

"I wasn't sure you got my message. I'm glad you followed through." He looked at her. "It will help if I could see a phone bill or record, that sort of thing."

She blanched, and he changed his tack. "Is your father well?"

"Did you hear that he wasn't?"

"Yes, I'm afraid so," said Pete, having heard nothing of the kind. He had discerned a catch in her voice. "Isn't he on medication?"

"Look, he got depressed. My mother's health was bad. He worried."

"What kind of medication?"

"You have no idea how much he worried. Daddy has always been moody. Black moods, my mom used to call them." She folded her hands in her lap. "My parents lived together a long time. They were happily married. I want you to know that." She laced her fingers together and smiled at Pete. "Not that you would have any experience there, being such a staid bachelor and all."

Pete gave her a guarded smile.

"How come you never married?" She leaned towards him.

"I almost did once," he said shortly.

"Pete, if you ever need company? I'm not around a lot, but still."

He looked closer at her little half-moon smile. He had not considered the possibility that she was interested in him, and yet she had chosen to come by in the late evening when she could have made an office appointment in the morning.

He was too stunned to be flattered. "I'll let you know. Thanks."

Dejected, she stared at the blank T.V. screen. "You're not still carrying a torch for that girl in our middle school? Long time ago. Callie Major, that was her name."

"I believe you're confusing me with Newton Denman," he said evenly.

"Am I?" Her smile returned, though it was not a nice smile. "Both of you were crazy about her. Of course as I remember it, she chose Newton."

"Thanks for coming by." Pete got up. "You've been so been helpful."

"I want you to remember," said Wendy, tears gathering, "my parents had a happy marriage. They were the happiest couple I have ever seen."

After Wendy Waters left, Pete was in a panic. Had he loved Callie Major way back then? Perhaps he did, without quite realizing it. And Wendy was right. Callie always loved Newton. This was important for him to keep in mind. He walked into his dining room to fetch a letter. He went over it again. There was the drawing Callie had mailed him last week. It was the first time he had heard from her in years. He wondered if anyone at the Big Springs Lounge noticed his nervous reaction to the envelope Elijah handed him. Who was there? Just Elijah, Gib Setter, the Denman brothers, and Spoons. Darn the old man, thought Pete. He's hoarding, holding onto something he knows about that night Theresa died. I'll have to pay him another visit. Back to Callie, thought Pete grimly. He had been truly astonished when Elijah handed him her note and the attached picture. "Mail call," Elijah had said in his easy going way.

Mail call, echoed Pete. He had decided against going to Grandmother Mountain immediately, even though Callie indicated she knew where Newton was. First there was a little more probing here. But what about the picture? I should make a simple phone call to Callie and ask her directly what connection there is between this drawing of a bunch of people near a treefort and Newton's innocence, that is, if he is innocent.

He examined the sketch again, then placed it in his police files. I can't talk to her, he thought sadly. I just can't.

But there was one thing he could do. Pete went to the mildewed cardboard box he had gotten from Ralph Waters. Must have flooded something terrible in Ralph's basement, the Trooper thought.

He had sifted through the papers right after Waters gave them to the state Trooper, but so much was stuck together that he gave up on it.

This time was different. Tonight he was persistent and methodical. He sat down on the floor. Gently, so as not to rip anything, Pete eased apart each stuck paper and envelope. There were birthday cards, note cards, calendars and engagement books, medical records, cancelled checks, and stacks of old family photographs. Talk about no organization, thought Pete. This takes the cake. He spread the contents out on his dining room table, dividing up the various kinds of papers into single stacks. The stench of rotting paper filled his nostrils, but as he worked he became oblivious to it.

He put his hands on a once white, eight by eleven envelope. The gray watermarks made it impossible to read the name on the cover but inside was a stack of yellow post-it notes. Several of the sticky notes stood out, one a message of recrimination from Theresa to her husband, Ralph, and the second, his response to her.

Ralph, How could you? read one from Theresa to Ralph. And continuing on the next note, in the same hand, *How could you ruin my art. You made me cry.*

The next four post-its, a near staccato shout, were in Ralph's hand: *Forgive me. I can't explain what happened to me....I do love you so....Thank God you know that.*

Pete stared at the notes. Who would think? This is gold.

He was in a hurry now. Back to those medical records he had set aside. He held up a notice from Ralph Waters' insurance company, a paper stating that it covered Ralph's medication. Here was what Pete had been looking for. A little more research and this could explain Ralph's actions, as suggested by Theresa. Did it also explain his actions the night Theresa died?

Next, Pete went through the family photos. Nothing much there. Last of all there was a stack marked *Littlecomb Elementary. My Teaching Years.* There were pictures of Halloween parties at school, photos of the Art room, big projects that decorated the school hallways at Thanksgiving, Christmas, and Easter. There were also pictures of art students. Pete slowed down. He went backwards through the stack. He had spotted something familiar.

In a pale blue Hallmark envelope there was a black and white photo of Theresa Waters standing before a treefort. In the treefort were two people, Callie and Newton. Theresa was waving her hand, smiling, if Pete wasn't mistaken. Callie looked indifferent, but Newton Denman was waving back, positively beaming. The two of them had to be about thirteen years old. It was unusual that you could see the expressions so well in a photo. It must have been a good camera, photographer, or both. Pete raced to the kitchen counter where he had left his police files. He pulled out the drawing Callie had sent him. It was almost identical to the photo.

What could it mean, he wondered. Newton looks happy, and yet I thought he disliked Mrs. Waters. After all, there was that attitude problem Nat had told people about. He flipped the picture over in his hand. Nothing written there to give a clue. As he put it back into the pale blue envelope his eyes landed on a scrawled message on the back of the envelope: *Give copy to my dear Letty Block.*

By this time Pete recognized Theresa's handwriting. "More gold," he whispered, a smile playing on his lips. His fingers closed over the pair of real gold nuggets that he had slipped into his pocket, for luck, every morning for fifteen years.

"To Miss Block's house," he sang out loud, glancing once at the seat next to him to make sure the envelope was there. It was hard waiting for morning to go to the Dewey Day Retirement Home in search of the old lady who might help explain a thing or two about Newton's connection to Theresa Waters. After his discovery of the troubled relationship between Ralph and Theresa, Pete felt more keenly than ever that she might have been murdered by her husband. But he had to be sure. He needed to yank every cobweb from Newton's name, including this matter of the hunter's bad attitude towards the deceased.

"Newton was one of my good ones. He was quiet. Not like George," the retired first grade teacher told Pete.

Letty Block was not one of those old ladies who have forsaken all manner of fashion in favor of a loose housecoat. She even wears a bra, Pete noted. He had been in the business of interviewing long enough to have observed a number of old ladies who decided to let it all hang down.

"Really. Tell me about George." Pete slipped the blue envelope back into his pocket. Miss Block touched the corner of her lips as if to make sure her lipstick was not caked there. She wore too much make up, but her lips perfectly matched the red skirt she wore. Though it had been almost thirty years since Pete sat in Miss Block's class for first grade, he still held her faintly in awe. She was a perfectionist, very sharp, he remembered.

"One day that George Denman brought a small rubber ball to class. I guess he had it concealed in his pocket. Right in the middle of our lesson on the A and P sounds, short A's you know, cap, lap, map. I had them writing all of these words, and it was only October," she said proudly. "George threw his ball at the cloak closet. I chastised him and made him fetch it. But if you can believe it that ball escaped his hands again. This time it rolled under my skirt. That bad boy chased after it. He crawled under my skirt to get the ball. Do you know why he did that?"

Pete shook his head dumbly.

"So he could peer up me."

Pete pulled the envelope out of his pocket. Perhaps it was time to change the subject.

"I fooled him." Miss Block picked a mote off her red skirt. "You see I was wearing gauchos. He couldn't see up."

"Good, I mean, I am sorry." Pete was trying to say the right thing. He felt they had gotten badly off track.

"I had to punish him. Not that I believe in striking a child. I pinched him on the cheeks. Pinched him hard enough that he would never forget."

I guess not, thought Pete. "So George didn't like school much?"

"He hated it."

"What about Newton?"

"Oh that boy loved every aspect of school."

"Even his art teacher?"

Miss Block registered surprise. "Not only did Newton admire Theresa Waters, he considered her his friend. You see, she was his advisor."

Pete was baffled. He had expected Theresa's dear friend Letty Block to be aware of the rumors that Newton had screamed at his old advisor and refused to talk to her. "I had heard there was a terrible upset between them," Pete said to the old lady. "Newton wouldn't speak to her. He must have been twelve or thirteen. You knew Theresa well. Did she ever say anything to you?" He brought out the picture of Newton beaming down from the treefort at Theresa Waters.

"There, you see," said Miss Block, pounding her forefinger on the face of the photo. "It's all there. She helped him get the wood to expand his fort, you know. They had made up. Ask Newton's mother. She knows about this. It wasn't the boy's fault, or the teacher's. It was the parents who caused a falling out between Newton and Theresa."

Pete thanked Letty Block. He was marching out the door of the Dewey Day Retirement Home when the old teacher called out, "You forgot to give me my picture. Young men today are downright thoughtless."

It sometimes happens that family loyalties are more real to people than their allegiance to any other thing, and where family law is atrophied, other kinds of law tend to lose their importance. As Newton hiked back to his campsite after the phone call to his mother, he was thinking of one unhappy memory. He winced and then let it drop deep into his boot soles. It was a dim recollection, after all, of blood, and of his father standing over him shouting orders.

Newton chastised himself for being melodramatic. He was not one to analyze wrong doings in his family, especially the non-violent ones. For the first time he thought about Betty's petty income tax evasions, Natty's rendezvous with the bookies, the drinking debts accrued by Nat and George; all these small infractions, weighing very little or not thought of at all by his family. Even government regulations that defined where and when hunting was legal meant nothing to the Denman men. How did I get to be this way, wondered Newton. Is there no way out?

To be sure, many of their violations were small, but where Betty and her men were lax in civil law, they were stern, ironclad in their collective wills to preserve family codes, and to protect one another.

As he came into the clearing at his campsite Newton was not thinking about why it was hard for him to stand up to Nat and George, but about George and their ma. Why was George favored with her love now, and what had he, Newton, done to be shunted?

At the quarry he surveyed the damage wreaked by the bear. There was his once sturdy green tent ripped to shreds. Newton shivered. The rope that held his meat at a safe distance from hungry animals was chewed to pieces. He glanced around. Much was ruined, though he noted that his reserve sleeping bag had been spared. He spotted the rifle he had been desperate to reach. Still there, under the pitch pine.

Newton was convinced all his cooking utensils were smashed beyond repair. But then he found the frying pan and coffee pot intact. He could get by on that. Everywhere things were sticky, the spilled honey from the overturned black kettle of bait, still oozing in narrow creeks across the canvas tarp that was knocked to the ground. The honey-smoke began to glom in crusty lumps on his blankets and tools.

He found the remains of his library book on bears. Only the binding left. Worthless. Several of his paperbacks were glued together; the cover of *Tracking*

Prey was stuck to two of his detective mysteries and an issue of *Gunning Times*. This last, a dated magazine he'd picked up in town was shredded, confetti like, and recognizable only by a torn corner that read: *Magnum Breakthrough*. Newton remembered one article's boast of having the first pump-action .357 rifle. For a minute he thought of Callie, and her reaction to guns. He had tried in their teenage years to interest her in target practice, and had at last persuaded her to go with him to the local shooting range. He wasn't surprised that she did well. She had better aim than most of his pals. Not that he had told her this. Instead he acted surprised that she could shoot at all. "I can't believe it," he had said after she hit bull's-eye the third time in a row. "Pete and the guys will say it's a fluke."

Newton threw down the magazines the bear had dissolved. What was wrong with me, he thought. I should have told Callie how very good she was. Between firing she always held her rifle gingerly, sometimes touching the bolt, and then staring at the weapon with a great deal of respect. But her practice at the shooting range was short lived. Two months into her initiation as a marksman she quit.

When Newton asked her why, she said simply, "Look at the way you cradle your rifle. I don't have that need."

Newton found another pair of paperbacks in the wreck left by the bear, novels he'd had since his brief college career. *The Pioneers* and *The Last of the Mohicans* were books by Fenimore Cooper Newton had loved for their heightened descriptions and hunter-hero. It was true that Cooper had his turgid moments, but Newton overlooked the books' faults. He liked Hawkeye's frugal, thoughtful attitude towards the woods. Natty Bumppo, thought Newton, correcting himself. Hawkeye gets a new name in each book of the series. These stories are salvageable, Newton decided. He noticed a trace of saliva, as if the bear had licked the old paperbacks, and decided she would let them be.

On closer inspection of the camp, Newton saw that there were items untouched by the bear's claw and the honey spill. Maybe if he did a thorough cleaning he could see what was what. Newton went to work, lowering a dented bucket into the water. A little later, hanging over the quarry ledge to refill the bucket, it came to him that his ma's fixed loyalty to George had not happened overnight.

There was that first summer Callie came to us in Littlecomb, thought Newton, as he scrubbed his tools. George had started asking Nat and me to cover for him: 'Newt ol' buddy, best brother, if Ma asks you if you seen me at a beer or two, just say no. Would you do that for me?'

Newton put his tools away and went to work soaking his blankets to loosen the crusted honey. He remembered that summer was just plain out of kilter. First, George drinking more than before, and then Callie new in town. She changed everything for him. Life had a new rhythm, a very pleasant one. They started off working on the treefort together. Later, their play grew more intense.

Newton began to examine his various belongings. He separated them into piles of salvageable and non-salvageable. Definitely worth keeping was his large black kettle. What a challenge to clean. The layer of honey bait was more tenacious than egg left too long in a frying pan.

Breathless after playing a scene from "Sleeping Beauty," he and Callie rounded the corner of the wood shed, nearly running smack into George and his ax. He was swinging it wildly, missing each time he aimed at the wood he meant to split. Newton saw he was drunk. Callie was frightened. Nat stood doing nothing. Newton knew it would anger his oldest brother, but he went to get Ma. He was scared George would strike his own leg with the ax. Worse, he might fall on it, or it would fly from his hands and hit someone else.

Their ma lectured George bitterly. But it was no use, for George had discovered the pleasures of drink, and knew nothing of how it would turn on him in the years to come. They screamed at each other for half an hour. It had seemed to Newton that both mother and son wielded axes. And missed their targets.

Thereafter, Newton had noticed that his mother was more tired than before. She began to look the other way whenever George was drunk or irresponsible, the one state feeding the other.

Newton scrubbed and rinsed the kettle a third time. Finally, all the hideously sticky glop was out. He found a soft cloth and polished the insides of the pot with a thin layer of protective grease. He was pleased with the results.

Exhausted, several hours later, he leaned back on a flat rock at the edge of his newly arranged, much reduced campsite. He had saved a few hunting magazines but gone was the clutter of newspapers, pile of tools and gadgets he had planned one day to fix. So many things gone. It felt a little lonely. He leaned on an elbow, and stared off at the closest pitch pine. The image of his mother's voice circled back again, hovering like a great dark bird. He could see her too, not as a bird but the way she was in the early years when Newton was twelve or so. The high color in her cheeks, her sad eye as she pitched him one of those sweet smiles that said how much she loved him, and how much it had cost her to be married to his father. And what was she doing? Oh yes, the potatoes, she was showing him how to cook the red spring potatoes. "Shake that pan," she had laughed, "Cover every inch of those potatoes in flour. Roll, shake, rattle." In the years after, that voice had turned dry and loud. Newton looked up at a noisy bird in the pitch pine. It was a boss chickadee, its black cap bobbing, short skinny legs hooked tight to the branch. "Chebeche, chebeche," it squabbled. Callie would know exactly what that bird is saying, Newton speculated. One time she had explained to him that a chickadee had at least eight different songs. Wish she were here now, he thought, spreading his hand over the flat rock on which he lay. The feldspar was smooth and cool under his palm.

That night he woke up at four o'clock. Newton was thinking about the times his father, Joe Denman came in to the woodshed to watch his son at work skinning. "How's it going, Bird Dog," he would say to Newton. Usually the son looked up, smiling shyly. "Go get it Bird Dog," was a familiar refrain to Newton. He was always fetching the dead duck, or skinning and cleaning what his father and older brothers brought home.

Another familiar refrain was the music of the hounds his grandpa Spoons kept. He trained them behind the woodshed, with George as his chief assistant. There was no escaping the hunting business in the Denman household.

A tall man with a pair of scampish black eyes, Joe Denman had joined the Marines at age eighteen. In 1943 he was a flame thrower in Saipan, a job for which he had no preparation or training. His sergeant had needed a quick replacement, and Joe was it. It was after his combat days that he had time to reflect on the thirty-three minute average life expectancy of a flame thrower. Some nights Joe woke up trembling in fury at how his sergeant had him handling the deadly weapon for months before he was ordered to take a flame thrower training course. The fighting was long over by that time, and Joe didn't miss the irony.

Disillusioned with the Marines, he believed there was no reason to touch a gun again, except in hunting – which didn't count as killing, in Joe's way of thinking. But the truth was, he missed the excitement of war, and for the rest of his life supplanted it with his mania for guns and game.

He rarely spoke to his family of his career as a flame thrower. He preferred to speak longingly of his ancestors' rugged hunting days, or the mythology of such lives. "It's easy work from here on," Joe said, leaning over the worktable. Newton was skinning the animal. "But you got to take care to do it right. Pull that skin with an even movement, from foot to ears."

Newton hunched over the carcass. "I know, Daddy," he would say.

Mr. Denman sat down at the far end of the work table. "You better set those stretchers up. You want to make sure that skin dries right away."

Newton had yet to go on his first deer hunt, but he was prepared. Any boy who cleaned dead animals at the rate he did could deal with shooting a deer. At last it was arranged that he would go with his father into the mountains. Before the weekend event, his brothers spoke of nothing but how Newton had to bring down a buck.

Of that father and son outing, Newton would never forget his perfect shot, or so it had seemed. He lowered his rifle and went to the deer, believing it dead. Instead he saw a live creature in horrible pain. It was a young male, and Newton had looked into his eyes. He went for his handgun to shoot the animal in the head, put it out of misery as fast as possible, but a large arm stopped him. His father took the gun from him and commanded Newton to slit the deer's throat. Tears streaming, the boy did as he was told.

The strength of his own emotions scared him, and Newton determined that day to guard against it. What good was it, he reasoned, to permit feeling to cross your heart and cut it in two?

The sky was dark and empty. No stars. Newton sat up straight and had the sensation of being very light and in the center of things crashing all around him. He got up to shake off an odd feeling that it was his own family members falling, one by one, away from him.

Newton clicked on his flashlight and reached for one of the magazines he had turned up in the cleaning. He held the least sticky one under the beam. *The*

Tracking Heart, he read. "Must have picked this up with those maps at the rest stop." He threw it down sleepily.

Ensconced for a second time in his sleeping bag, Newton rolled over and looked up into the night. Now he didn't mind that he had no tent. In his drowsiness he wondered who or what a tracking heart was. Could it be someone like George? Not his ma, surely. What about Callie. She didn't shoot things, But Newton could picture her going after what she wanted, persistently, patiently, same as a hunter.

Newton fell asleep dreaming of a woman with a bow and arrow. She stood in a path of moonlight, no water in sight but there were fish leaping. The rainbow trout leapt over her head but the archer didn't notice. She was aiming for the moon.

Inside the Tuscatanning police station, Officer Cameron Shawl was on the phone. "You've got my emergency number," she said, talking to Callie. "It's not that far off," she warned, referring to the date Callie was due to go into labor. Cameron laughed at something the forest ranger was saying, and ran her hand through her straight brown hair that was sparse through the middle part. She had been told by one doctor that her near baldness resulted from the fact that Cameron's parents were first cousins. "You can lay blame at their feet," he had said rather insensitively. She did not promote cousinly love, but Cameron never blamed her parents for falling in love. It was her credo to listen carefully to passionate motives.

She gave full attention to Callie and laughed at what she was saying. "Oh sure, make fun of me," Cameron smiled. Callie was giving her a hard time about what office she was calling from: "Don't forget to change hats before leaving the police barracks and dashing over to the Good Shepherd."

Cameron was both police officer and Deacon at the Church of the Good Shepherd.

After the phone call, Officer Shawl thought for a minute about Callie. For the ten years she had been with the State Park she held herself apart from many people in town. Lately, she had retreated further, as if she thought herself in exile. Cameron had not asked about the father of her baby; there was something in the ranger that discouraged questions of an intimate nature. Still, Shawl wished she knew her better. Again she laughed at what Callie had said about her. To be married with children (now almost grown), work full time as a police officer, and extra hours helping out at the church; why not? Didn't all women lead multiple, disguised lives?

Her shift over, Cameron was about to lock up when into the station burst Jack Marsh. Officer Shawl eyed him cautiously for there was something about the man that was not quite right. He was lost to anger or righteous indignation, maybe both.

"Would you sit down? Makes me nervous to watch people pace up and down," Shawl said to Marsh, who had launched into an incrimination of Newton Denman. Jack took the chair opposite the officer.

"All right, slow down," Cameron said. "You mentioned him and something about some campers on the phone to me, but you didn't say much. When and where was it that you first laid eyes on this hunter? Denman, you say?"

"He was sitting at the bar in the Jolly Logger," Jack sat forward intently. "Didn't know then that Denman was wanted by the police. But I noticed how scruffy he was, kind of an outsider, and definitely a hunter. It was my duty to pay attention to him, seeing as how hunting is illegal in the state forest."

Cameron pushed a lock of thin hair behind her ear. "Did he act like he had something to hide?"

"Hell yes," he said, remembering that actually Newton had been leisurely eating a cheeseburger, sipping a beer and watching a Fliers game up at the bar.

"This was when?"

"Oh, back in November."

"And the last time you saw him?" Shawl asked kindly.

Marsh placed a stack of 'Wanted' posters of Newton on her desk. "The day before yesterday." Jack flexed his hand, then tightened it. "I didn't precisely see him, but I saw his truck. It matches this description to a T." He tapped the write-up on Newton that Cameron was studying.

"Not the man, just a truck?" Officer Shawl said doubtfully. "You get the license plate?" She dropped the poster on the desk.

Jack felt foolish. "No. But this couple I was telling you about, those campers were witnesses. Wasn't a month ago that they had their nasty run-in with Denman. He's up there on the mountain all right, and lurking in town too."

"Bring in those witnesses," Cameron said, hands folded in her ample lap. "We can go from there on this arson and possible murder."

Jack jerked his head up. "They took off, that couple did. I don't know where."

"It's looking a little thin, this whole project of yours," Cameron said. "We can't go traipsing up and down Grandmother Mountain for a guy you think resembles the man in this picture, and the person you've seen maybe once, and way back in November, at that."

"It was *him*," Marsh crackled, his forefinger covering half of Newton's face in the photograph Betty Denman had to hand over to the Littlecomb police. He was thinking how he could just about smell that man when he was up at Callie's place. The yellow truck sure didn't belong to some guy visiting old Mrs. Pope. And Mary, she was there working on his truck. She and Callie were thick as thieves. "I told you, I saw him, or rather his truck parked right outside Callie Major's place."

"Callie!" Cameron was interested. "Why do you think he was there?"

"Take three guesses." Fury contorted Jack's handsome features. He had reviewed the possibility that the owner of the truck was one of Mary's lovers. But when he saw Callie's face at the Logger the other night, he knew otherwise. She had given herself away, all right, Marsh thought grimly. The second I mentioned Denman's name her eyes blazed like fall leaves just after you set a match to them.

Marsh stood up. "Thanks for your time."

Cameron Shawl rattled the police sheet at Marsh. "Take it easy. I don't mind working together with you folks over at the Park. But we need to see this guy in the flesh, verify that he is Denman. I need more evidence. Listen," Shawl said, noticing that something hurt and cruel had crept into his blue eyes. "Maybe you're on to something. However," she searched his face, "I'm a little confused as to who it is you really want to nail. This Denman guy or Callie Major?"

Chapter EIGHTEEN

Newton

The day after Callie and her aunt Teeny moved to Littlecomb she came up our dead end street. On the way to my yard where I stood watching her, she stopped to touch the patchy bark on a large sycamore tree. Another few steps, and she was stooping to examine Miss Babb's rundown rose garden. A third time she stopped, tilting her head to the sky. I could swear I saw her narrow her eyes, and sniff at the air.

When she introduced herself to me the first thing I noticed was her shiny hair. I liked her long heart shaped face. Except for a shadow of fine down above her upper lip, her skin was translucent as a sunflower seed. Then I saw the stuffed bear she cradled in one arm. Milk white pads were sewn into the four paws. It had glass eyes with black pupils that pretty much matched Callie's eyes. She held out the bear for me to admire. Guessing she must be much younger than I was, I thought I should say something polite.

"What do you call him?"

"Bear."

"How old are you?" Forget the politeness.

"Twelve."

Just as I thought. Way too old to be carrying around toys like that. The bear's fur was worn, and shiny and smooth as if just combed. It looked old. "Where'd you get him?"

A faint wheeze escaped her throat. "I can't remember. I've always had him." She smiled at me. "Asthma," she said, brushing back a few wisping strands that sprang free of her long, loose ponytail. "It's no big deal."

I was thirteen, so don't ask what made me leap around like a little kid. I grinned back at her.

It was our first climb to the treefort that sealed the bond between Callie and me. Both of us were starved for a friend to confide in, and from the beginning I wanted to do everything right for her. I wrapped and tied heavy hemlock fronds around the boards so that Callie had a good seat. She was comfortable leaning against the plank highest up.

There wasn't much to the place those first times she came around, only a few planks of wood wedged between two broad branches of the poplar tree in my backyard. In the winter months before she and her aunt moved to Littlecomb I would go to the fort and spread my rocks along one board, identifying and cataloging until my work gloves with the fingertips ripped free went stiff in the icy wind. I had in mind that I wanted to figure out all the earth's parts, learn how it fit together, the riverbeds, valleys, and mountains. It didn't happen. I never did become a geologist. Betty and my dad, Joe, they played their part in discouraging me. But self-pity won't help me with that one. Best not think about it.

There was a storm the summer Callie and I met, one of those oddball storms with little rain and a lot of wind. It charged through my yard, snapping the poplar tree in two. The fort came down but that didn't stop Callie and me. We rebuilt it at ground level, adding walls so that it resembled an odd shaped cave. The fallen tree trunk made a solid wall and we found saplings for cross pole supports to build a second floor. We contrived to make it inaccessible to intruders by keeping the door hidden. We made shelves from the red clay of the creek and a roof of brushy hemlock boughs. Every month or so Callie and I devised a new feature or moved the door. We could not seem to stop fiddling with it. We could never get our fort quite right.

"Let's do something else," Callie said, after we had toiled at putting the entrance way in the roof. That same summer my older brother George took to drinking out behind the woodshed. He was skipping out of his work at the skinning table and he often cajoled me into covering for him: "If Ma asks, tell her you saw me sweating bullets out back."

Then laughing, he swept his eyes over Callie. "Tell her, I'm drinking chocolate milk with the Indian kid."

We tried to avoid him. Usually Callie and I were up to one game or another. I welcomed the chance to be kidlike in ways I never had, and with a few other kids we played freeze tag or sardines. We climbed trees too, Callie scooting to the tippy tops of the maples and tulips. Or maybe it was one of her play acting games. Those started when Miss Babbs' little kids charged over to play in the woods behind our fort. At first they begged Callie to read them something out of her storybook on *Ali Baba and the Forty Thieves* that she had in her lap. Instead she directed them, Sue, Billy, and Lonnie in a version of Aladdin and the Magic Lamp, using a coca cola bottle for the lamp.

She wanted me to join in. "I don't know," I said. "It doesn't look good. Suppose Pete stops by to see Nat or me."

She dropped the pink veil she was handing to little Sue, and spun around. "But I want you to play. We don't have to keep going with Aladdin. We can do another game."

I shrugged.

"How about Artemis," she said. "The Greek goddess, the lady I told you about? You'd like acting out that story. You could be my brother, Apollo." She waved a hand. "See these golden arrows?" She kept her eyes on me while reaching over her shoulder for the invisible arrows. "We're going to hunt the hunters. Look, they've hurt one of our hounds." She crouched over a log, and stroked it. "Poor hound."

Then up she leapt, with a fierce look on her face. My chest prickled in excitement. Call it dreamy nonsense, but if she wanted me to bay with her hounds, I would do it. Callie could talk me into anything.

Callie didn't care for the sport of hunting and for a long time I did not talk about how George, Natty, Grandpa Spoons, and my dad, Joe, were all avid hunters. But bit by bit it leaked out. There was no helping it when she came over as often as she did. I told myself that she'd get used to the idea that the other members of my family trapped and hunted. Sometimes I couldn't help but be bursting with pride at what they brought home. I recounted the size and weight of a recent kill on the hood of our dodge pick-up when it rolled into the drive. It was my family's habit to show off the carcass for several days, especially if it was something big. When a bear was hung from the Denman front porch for all the townspeople to see, Callie was among the few who never came around. It was as if she had vanished from the neighborhood.

One of those times I caught sight of her slipping through the backyard of Miss Babbs, our postmaster. I followed. She was racing through all the backyards of our neighbors, Mr. Childress, the taxidermist, Sally and Ed Bahn, the nice man and lady with horses, and next, the place with all the chickens owned by Elijah Jones. I caught up with her there.

"Hey, what happened to your hand?" My eye traveled from the grass stain on her forehead to the limp fingers that she cradled with her right hand.

She winced. "I did something dumb. I fell out of the treefort." She tried to smile. "It was just a game."

"Are you okay?" I was alarmed.

"Sure. Good as gold. Hey, want to play the backyard game?"

"I don't know," I said, uneasily. I was worried about her purpling fingers.

"Here's how it goes," she said. "We run through everyone's backyard and don't let anyone see us. We spy, we hide –" she broke off, dropping her chin. "I was so sad about the dead animals that came home on your daddy's truck. I went to the treefort, and then I fell."

"Maybe you should go to the doctor."

"One of the boards broke." She made a face. "Newton, I don't mean to be a baby, but it's beginning to hurt. And I feel so awful about the fort."

"We can rebuild. Come on," I grabbed her good hand. "Let's go find Ma."

She came out of the kitchen at once, and after a quick examination of Callie's hand she called the Steel Mill where Teeny Wick worked. The supervisor answered and I heard Ma say, "This is Betty Denman, let me speak to Teeny Wick." They put her on the phone and Callie's aunt told Ma that she'd rather not leave work right then. It wouldn't look good, so then Ma drove Callie to the doctor. Two of her fingers were broken. The doctor set her up with two finger splints, and she said she was fine. I guess you could say I never did understand exactly what happened to her that day. I don't think I got a straight answer out of her.

I may have garnered a reputation as a decent hunter in these last few years, or maybe ever since Callie left town, but it wasn't always so. Quite the opposite.

The fall after Callie broke her fingers, Nat came home from a hunting trip with a buck laid out on the hood of his car. After boasting about the kill, he turned to me: "You're up soon, Newt. We Denman men start serious hunting at exactly your age. You better be thinking about what day you're going to take your rifle in the woods with Spoons or Daddy." He kept at it, wheedling me about when I was going out to bag a deer.

"I'm beginning to think you're getting to be a sissy boy."

"You're crazy," I retorted.

"Yeah, then why are you dragging your feet on wanting to go out with Daddy?"

"I'm not in a hurry, that's all." What I was really thinking of was how Callie said she hurt all over when the kills were brought home on the pick up. That conversation with Nat rankled worse than I could have imagined. After our five o'clock supper, I headed out back, nearly smacking into the deer hanging up on the porch. I thought about how soon it would be cleaned and dried, and then only the skin left, flapping off a line until its real smell was all but gone.

At the treefort I couldn't get comfortable. I huddled under a shabby wool blanket in a corner and leafed through a pamphlet on chemistry experiments. I tossed that aside and picked up Callie's book on Greek myths. I flipped through it idly and was reading about nymphs in some far off place called Arcadia when the oversized camper's flashlight that served as a lamp fell off the shelf, knocking over her old stuffed bear that sat cattycorner from me. I brushed the dirt off its nose. It no longer had the creamy white pads that marked its paws. Callie shouldn't have left it here, I decided. I jumped up, bear in my hands, as if this was a crucial mission.

At Callie's house no one answered my knock. I didn't expect Aunt Teeny to be home from her clerking job for another hour, same time half the folks over there at the steel mill got off. I knocked again and shouted hello. Nothing. I tried the door knob and walked in. There was Callie sitting in the den next to the wood stove with her back to me. A fire poker was in her hand, same hand that was broken when she fell off the fort. It was healed, except for her bent pinky.

When I came in, Callie did not look up but nodded, having recognized my step. I went over to the hearth. There were tears streaming down her face and the poker poised in the air as if she was ready to do battle with the burning logs.

"What's wrong?" I sat down beside her.

"I hate this stove." Callie wept in halts and jerks.

I chewed on my lip. I could feel my brow contort into a thousand wrinkles. "I was at the fort and suddenly I had to come find you, tell you something important, only I can't think of it now." I hadn't noticed that I dropped the stuffed bear. It was at my feet. "Callie, tell me. What is it that's so bad?"

She shivered. The tears were gone and she looked at me with those eyes that, I swear, could darken from buff brown to blackest night. "Something's going to be different soon," she said, waving the poker. "We won't like it."

I tried to take it from her, but she held on, and stared at the flames and the small logs shifting as one piece burnt through and collapsed on top of another. A middle log shot forward towards the hearth. Callie caught it with her poker.

I jumped as the log shot out. "I'm going home," I said.

In bed that night, I closed my eyes and went right into a dream where I was on a mountain ridge. It was unfamiliar to me, and yet I behaved as if I'd been there all my life. It seemed to be my home, and I was going about my business, checking my trap lines. Then I spotted a girl, and it was clear that she was the one Callie became in our plays. She was Artemis.

I was hunting for you, the girl said, coming up to me. A golden bow was slung over her left shoulder. She bent over to tie on her sandals. *Follow me.* She ducked into a thicket. I hurried after her, fighting my way into the tangle of vines. She was gone, and in her place was a growling bear with a glossy coat of brown and reddish hues. Stunned, I fell back.

I am the lady of beasts, she said.

I saw that she was beautiful and would not hurt me.

The rain woke me up, or maybe it was the shouting downstairs. Betty was having it out with George. Sour voices chastising. Recriminations, and George's promise to be good. Thank God for the wind at my window. The pane rattled. It needed putty, some kind of sealing. The glass shook and drowned out the voices. I was glad of that. The wind blew the shutters and tapped the ivy. Soon I fell asleep again, ears open to the thick rain, slicking down the ivy. Ears open to the sounds of the thicket near the treefort.

Callie

I haven't learned yet that sensitivity comes with a price. Here is what I see. I am hardly more than a child: Their furry bodies arrive in truckloads. Newton races over and his brother George gives him a hand up into the back of the first truck where most of the dead bodies lie. There is Newton climbing to the top of the heap. There he stands, arms folded as if he thinks he's playing King of the Mountain. "I'm the king of the mountain and you're the dirty rascal." He can roll me easy down the tall compost pile near his house. I always end up being the crumpled, composted, get myself together again, rascal.

I am watching from the nurse tree that runs up alongside the treefort in the thicket behind where the Denmans are pulling in. I am snugged down in a nice elbow joint watching as Newton flies off the side of the pickup and races ahead of the others to set things up for the skinning in the woodshed. As usual, he's ahead of himself. Nat and George will make sure they hang a few of the animals out on the porch for show. They won't get to the skinning for a good while.

Spoons and Newton's daddy stroll on in the house, leaving all those dead folks on the truck. Not that they're people, mind you, but they had feelings same as we do. And some of them with colors as soft as yellow root and rat's bane, so many furs, tawny reds, old soot browns, heaps and heaps of colorful creatures hugged together, not knowing how all the men will come back outside with drinks and sandwiches, and they'll size up the kills and place bets on whose shot will bring in the best price, maybe a possum pelt or more likely a soft rabbit fur or a muskrat.

I think about how I was in the Denman kitchen one morning a few days before this, fixing my special mullein and jewel root tea for Spoons' bad throat. His throat gets raw on account of the terrible amount of chaw he thrashes around his mouth. Newton was talking about the hunting weekend up ahead for his brothers, Joe and Spoons. He seemed to have forgotten how much I hated to hear about those dripping bodies they bring home.

"Next time they bring home all those animals," I said, "I'd like to set them up outside, each one leaning against a tree to dry out and let them sit up and get the air one last time before you take their skin off."

Spoons sucked hard on the wad in his lower lip, and said nothing.

"I'd set those animals up, each one under those hazel trees that form a circle in your yard."

"That's dumb, Callie. Dead animals can't feel anything," Newton said with a patronizing swagger.

I set the mug of jewel root tea down on the counter for Spoons. "You can't say what the dead feel or don't feel. Not for sure, you can't."

Things that hurt the most I have a habit of stashing. They mutter at me, they stick together like a rival gang, and finally they muster an attack. There was a day that Nat came back from a hunting trip, boasting about the year old bear he'd shot. When I saw that poor animal on the front of the truck I was more upset than ever before. Even through his fur I could see his hungry look, as if he hadn't found enough to eat that spring. Spindly, that one, but such soft fur and skin. I ran off to the treefort. Why did they have to kill a thin creature like that? Tears sprang from my eyes. Tears of fury.

I ran past Betty Denman's clothesline with ten legs of blue jeans belonging to the men, a tan skirt, an undershirt, and a loose and flowery housecoat I wanted to reach out and touch. I climbed to the top of the treefort which we had built up high again, and got right into my Artemis game. It worked better when Newton was there, being Apollo, but I didn't care right then. I swung out on the rope ladder with my imaginary arrows on my back.

Hunt the hunters, I whispered. *The waiting is over. Take up your arrows. Empty your quiver.* I jumped over the side, but didn't jump wide. Going down I hit a board sticking out, the one we were always going to nail on better. I clamped my lips tight so as not to scream.

I broke my fall with my left hand, and the rest of me landed cheek first on a mound of scrappy grass. At first I felt nothing at all, and that was nice, having no feelings to hurt. Then the pain came after me, singing in my finger bones. I got up and started running. I ran through a few backyards near where I lived. That's when Newton spotted me.

"Callie, what are you doing?"

"Playing the backyard game, want to play?"

"Hey, your hand is hurt," he said, coming over beside Elijah Jones's chicken coop.

I held my hand aloft. "Why does your family do that carcass hanging? I can't stand to see the flies eat their meals off those poor dead animals."

"Let me see your hand."

"Newton, I don't think I can stand it if I see another bear your family kills."

He got me to go home and let his ma look at it. Betty was good in accidents. Blood was nothing to her, what with all the boys in her family. She said she couldn't get hold of Aunt Teeny, but she blushed when she said it and I knew she was lying and didn't want to say that Teeny wouldn't come for me. Betty was the one who took me to the clinic in Littlecomb. It turned out I had two mashed fingers, chipped bones in my thumb and pinky. The doctor fitted my hand with a pair of matching splints.

That night Aunt Teeny did not even glance at my fingers.

"So you got yourself in trouble," she said. She began to sort through her magazines. "Always up to no good. Go to bed, I don't want to see you."

I shrunk up the stairs to the landing. All I wanted from her was a gentle word or touch, but Teeny never hugged or touched me. There is something about skin on skin that is comforting, and vital. I remember how I used to melt into Winoshca's arthritic, stiff-boned, skin warm embraces: "Callie and Mary, come here you two. Give an old woman a hug."

Her voice as much as her arms were a comfort, and never more than that night after my fall from the treefort. I was in the window seat on the landing half way up to the second floor. I pressed my hurt fingers against the pane. It felt icy, a pleasant numbing. Then I pressed my cheeks and lips, too. I wiped off the smoky mark my breath left on the glass. From downstairs I could hear Teeny mumbling to herself, all the usual complaints. Aunt Teeny, she had maladies from head to foot, ears that buzzed at her, grinding teeth, and toes that had curled, hammertoes, she called them. I pictured what would happen to Teeny Wick if her toes, along with each part of her started to curl in on itself. Soon she'd be ball shaped, and maybe one day I'd go downstairs and she'd be balled up so tight she couldn't undo herself. She'd roll down the kitchen steps, roll far away. I'd be on my own, and left to my own devices I would find my way back to Grandmother Mountain.

Aunt Teeny droned on, and then an odd thing happened. It was no longer Teeny, but the voice of Winoshca that surged up the stairs, Winoshca slipping up over each worn step and into my soul. She was telling me something and it seemed to be about Artemis, except that wasn't it at all. She was saying that I had gotten the wrong story. Greek myths about Artemis were well and good, but I had forgotten the old stories, the ones in my own family, the ones Winoshca used to tell. I had to listen closely, and then I would know how things were going to change for Newton and me, I would see the thing that was going to come between us and wreck everything.

I was a small child when Winoshca told me about the society of women planters in the Seneca tribe. She sat me down next to her. We were side by side on a wooden bench, my short legs straining towards the flame in our stone fireplace. I looked out the cabin window at the snowy camber of our yard.

"Long ago there were three sisters, squash sister, bean sister, and corn sister." Winoshca smiled, and then became solemn. If you didn't know her better you might think she was glaring into the fire grate. I knew better. Winoshca had heavy, straight brows that held laughter and sadness, and I felt, held us all together.

"There is a story our people have about the sisters sitting one day with the Great Bear, also known as Talking God. Suddenly Great Bear motioned the others to be quiet. She listened, and then sent corn sister to go see what was outside their cave. She walked towards the edge of their cave, her green stalks swishing as she moved. Great Bear and the sisters heard a mewling in the rain outside. Sister Corn went out and found a lost, drenched boy. In a voice not unlike a rumbling volcano Great Bear called to him, inviting him into the cave for shelter.

The boy hung back, frightened. But then Great Bear said something else and the boy followed her voice into the cave. At the sight of her great shaggy face he was frightened again. The vegetable sisters at her side calmed him down. They patted the warm hearth stones and he crept closer. He warmed himself at the fire. Great Bear took pity on him. She gave him the path home to his family, and she gave him one thing more.

"This is a present that will bring sustenance, and take away the fear of starvation for the rest of your life," she said. "You may take Sister Corn home with you and she will feed you and her family. When the dawn comes each day, your family members may pull one ear of corn off her back. Gently take it, shuck the corn, it is yours. But each of you is to take one piece a day, and no more. You must not squander this gift."

The boy gave his promise and off he went with Sister Corn. When he got home that boy was faithful to his promise. He told his parents and sisters and brothers what transpired, but the family paid no heed to his instructions and warning. They pulled the ears off Sister Corn's back willy-nilly, they yanked them greedily, and with each act of taking too much, the bear in the far away cave winced and writhed in pain. She had so wanted to trust the human family. Over time her trust shrank. She began to grow angry.

"What happened?" I had asked, alarmed at the fear in Winoshca's voice.

"I don't know." She folded my hand in her larger one. "We will see."

Chapter NINETEEN

"The lightening!" said the white haired midwife to Callie during her visit to the Birthing Center. "You'll know it when it comes."

Several days after her checkup, Callie had the sensation of being in an elevator that drops ten floors at once. So this was it, her belly descending to its new position. She remembered the midwife saying that she could expect to feel off balance. For Callie, the reverse was true. Gone was her sway-back. She was not at all off kilter, and the fetus no longer crowded her lungs. Though she had a number of chances to tell the midwife that she hardly ever peed, Callie's instincts told her not to bring it up. If she had some unusual identification with the bear, it was her business. She felt healthy, and that was enough for her.

With the baby tilted forward, Callie now walked at a slant, forward moving and leaning towards the earth. On Sunday, driving back from the State Park, Callie was surprised that she could not find a single parking place in town. Rather than go straight home she had planned to grab a cheese steak at Spence's and then make her one o'clock call to Newton. She was nervous and excited at the thought of hearing his voice. Never mind her other difficulties.

The streets were double-parked. She circled the Grill and Grocery a second time, wondering at the crowd lined on the sidewalk. Finally, she parked behind the Good Shepherd Church, some four blocks from Spence's. As she hurried past the high arched doors of the church, someone caught her arm. She wheeled around to see Deacon Cameron Shawl, or rather, at the moment she was a split identity. A police hat in her hand, she wore blue uniform trousers and the black shirt of the clergy, replete with high white collar.

"Hi, just locking up the church," Cameron said. She had once shared with Callie the ups and downs of her former life. As she described it to Callie, she used to be a nervous woman whose husband had energetically deposited six seeds in her womb, despite Cameron's protestations. Callie admired how Cameron had weathered six children, and then carved a life for herself. Her brood nearly grown, she had joined the ranks of the state police some five years ago, and just last year gained a hard earned title of Deacon at the church.

With hat in hand Deacon Shawl pleaded with Callie to reconsider helping out with the Noah's Art production at church. "Our director has resigned. I've taken over best I could. But we could use your know-how. We have a whole month to work on it, and you'd be a natural at directing our amateur actors from the congregation, and the children too. I remember all your good help when we did 'Amahl and the Night Visitors.'"

"In six days my baby is due," Callie said pointedly. "I'm sure motherhood will take up all my time. I can't possibly commit myself to outside activities."

"Of course," Deacon Shawl empathized. "You'll be glad to know, there is a life after pregnancy, dear. You'll see."

"We'll talk soon," Callie said abruptly. She walked at a good clip until she hit the block before Spence's place. The area was mobbed and she was knocked off the sidewalk by a thin man waving a bunch of unstamped Numbers Game tickets.

"I've filled in ten this time," the reedy man said to no one in particular. "Don't care how much it set me back."

The Jackpot! Winners to be announced early this evening, Callie realized. Poor Spence, swamped with people mad for last chance Lotto tickets. She fought her way back to the sidewalk. It's Sunday, she calculated. Spence's is the only joint open. Got to get to a phone. No time to go home. Newton is probably hiking down the highway right now. She was checking her watch (it was a quarter to one) when she gasped. She had been stabbed in the back.

In a moment she knew better. She was in labor. The pain moved from her back to legs to stomach. "Oh God!" she moaned. Then thinking, this can't be, it's too early. She leaned against a lamp post. People pushed past her. Strangers everywhere. The town had never looked so populated. Maybe it's not labor, she thought. Just more of those early Braxton Hicks contractions. Don't make a big deal of this. Concentrate on talking to Newton. That'll be nice, she nodded single-mindedly. Her face was damp. She unzipped the top of her jacket, and pressed forward towards the store.

"You stole my ticket!" a woman screamed, not a yard from Callie. "I saw you grab it!"

The accused man, young, possibly twenty-one or so, shouted back. "Lady, you dropped it. I was picking it up for you."

"Where is it? Give it to me," she shrieked. "I saw you cram it in your pocket!"

Close to the store, the line had dissolved into a huddle, a tight ball of those who meant to buy tickets or to have their already purchased cards stamped. Callie saw Cameron (now transformed into Officer Shawl) as she ordered a guy to move his car off the sidewalk. What is this mania? Callie wondered. Then came another stabbing pain in her back. Not so bad, she convinced herself, trembling as she timed the contraction. Fifty seconds before it peaked. She was disoriented after it passed, and thought only of getting to a chair in the back of Spence's Grill and Grocery. Someone shoved her and she would have hit the sidewalk but for the throng she fell against.

Why couldn't Spence have a back door like most stores, she raged dismally. Then, halfway up the block, she saw a familiar – and at this moment – beloved face. There was Mary, blue-jeaned, hair color as dazzling and unreal as the sudden red of a Japanese maple in the fall. She was sweeping her arms to keep back the line cutters.

"Mary!" Callie cried out, elbowing towards her cousin.

Though she held her own in that mob with the strength of a linebacker, Mary seemed to be in a trance, not entirely comprehending what Callie was saying.

"Got to call Newton. I promised. And there's this pain, it comes and goes. I need to get to a chair."

"What?" Mary yelled out. "You want to cut your hair?" She waved five tickets in her hand. "One of these is the big winner. I know it. Go on home, Cal. Call Newton when you get there. Isn't this wild? Two major fights, already!"

"I can't. It'll be too late to call. I'm starting to feel funny again." Callie gripped her sides, rocked forward, and although she wasn't going to fall Mary reached out instinctively and caught her around the shoulders. Aghast, she said slowly, "Are you? Oh Jesus Christ, you are."

Mary's eyes came clear and she shouted, "Move over. My cousin's having her baby! Move your butts!" No one paid attention, so Mary, who had a heavy hand when she needed it, sheltered Callie and directed her forward, knocking bodies aside on their way up to Spence's store front.

Newton burst out of a hedgerow and onto the highway. He walked defiantly near the middle of the road, the afternoon sun beating down on his wool checkered hunting cap. His head itched under the hat, but he would not remove it. Newton was in a mood to be punished by heat and anger.

Gone was his brief elation after the run-in with the bear. It had been hard getting used to the newly reduced campsite, and then, too, the brief conversation with his ma had left him depressed. Now, here he was at the phone booth again, this time to hear from Callie as they had arranged. He scuffed at rocks and sticks, and tried to settle his nerves. He would be talking to Callie, to Callie, to Callie, he repeated like a mantra. It did no good.

Got to tell her about George and Natty, he reminded himself. Callie will keep an eye out, she'll let me know if those stinking skunks show in Tusca. They won't get the bear. She's mine, he thought with sudden vengeance. Then he paused. What was happening to him? Only the night before he had believed he was set free of twisted family loyalties. Here was the emptiness that came with the freedom – the awful prospect of being alone, betrayed by his brothers and mother. He reached wildly for connections. Old rivalries with his brothers or the family code of hunting, these were things he could hold on to. The fierce longing to do something acceptable in their eyes – such as bringing down a huge bear, his father's will to gain the quarry at all costs – these family credos rose up in him and kept at bay his briefly glimpsed respect for the bear, and respect for himself too.

The door to the phone booth was crusted in dirt blown up from the last rain. Newton tugged at the door, his boots slipping backwards in the mound of earth.

"Can't even get into a fucking phone booth," he said angrily. Once enclosed in the narrow phone box, he sat down and breathed deeply. It was one o'clock. He looked up at the telephone expectantly.

A half hour later, Newton was still sitting, eyes closed, waiting for her call.

Even in the storage room at the back of Spence's Grill and Grocery, Callie could hear the lottery crowd outside. Collapsed in a chair, she imagined them now with knives in their hands, all one voice: Callie Major cut in line, we'll *cut her*!

"You're in second stage labor," Jessie, Spence's wife was saying to her. Then to Mary, "How fast can you get to the Birth Center?"

"Fifteen minutes," Mary said.

Callie did a double take. The Birth Center was thirty miles away.

Heading out of the faintly mildewy storage room, Mary grabbed something off a shelf. "Here, I want to buy this," she said to Jessie, slapping a hot water bottle down on the front counter near Spence, who was dealing with Lotto tickets. "It's for Callie. I read somewhere that it helps labor pain." She searched her pockets for money.

"Pay later," Jessie said. "I'll fill it for you. Good hot water for the ride."

She returned with two items, the hot water bottle wrapped in a towel, and a rolling pin. "Take this too." She brandished the rolling pin. "My mother rolled one across my back the night I gave birth to my first boy." She directed Mary, "When she's hurting, roll it good and hard. That way she won't think of the other pain."

"No rolling pin," Callie begged, edging along the counter towards the door.

"In a half hour I close down," Spence was telling the crowd. Callie and Mary plunged through the howls of dismay and the voices wheedling Spence to keep the Numbers Game open longer.

At the Birth Center Mary was right at Callie's side. "Here. Ice chips," she said. "You're supposed to suck on them. Those midwives, they've been teaching me all kinds of stuff." She smiled in surprise, "Hey, can you believe it, I'm going to be your coach."

Callie was lying on her side, trying to remember the exercises she had practiced to breathe through the pain, but it came harder and longer now. Once she raked her nails across Mary's hand and wondered if she had been knifed. Now the hand was doing something, maybe rubbing her lacerated back.

"Counter pressure," she heard Mary say. "That's what you need." Callie felt the rolling pin on her vertebrae. She groped with the back of her hand, touching where the pain came hardest to prove to herself she wasn't wounded. Then, clutching Mary's arm, "I want to quit, I'm losing it. And I'm sleepy, so sleepy. Don't want to do this anymore." Out of the corner of her eye, she saw the midwife standing near.

"I'm not doing the breathing right. I'm tired. Can't breathe at all,"

"Do you think she needs oxygen?" Mary said to the midwife.

"We have oxygen," Brenda was saying, and then Callie blotted out her voice. If only she could sleep, then the pain might go away. But it felt like something or someone was keeping her awake. Maybe it was simply the pain. She began talking to it. Get off my back, you creep, mole, bug, smaller than a bug. Nothing but a scrap, flyspeck, mite, mote. And Callie, fomenting her stronger self, spoke to that age old enemy that brings life, the *suffering*, and in her mind she rambled on as if there was nothing left, really, beyond this agony except her voice. When her words dropped into a rhythmic chant, she began to notice that she was on top of the pain, and that it was actually shrinking. Gone. Less than a mote.

She opened her eyes and sang out, "I've got the breathing!"

"That's my cousin," Mary said, wielding the rolling pin in long steady strokes. "She's one of the warriors, all right."

"Oh sure," Callie smiled faintly. "Off to do battle."

Newton was at the creek that ran along the base of the Great Meadow. Why hadn't Callie called? Maybe she was hurt. Something could have gone wrong with her pregnancy. She wasn't due for how many days? Seven or eight, he was pretty sure. Then again, maybe she had lost his phone number. Don't get carried away, he told himself. Best to take your mind off this.

Go fishing. It came to him naturally, even though he hadn't been at it in a long time.

By the end of March there was always trout to be had at Black Run Creek. The trouble was he had no rod. He thought of cutting one from an aspen, but he was impatient, not to mention a perfectionist when it came to his fishing rods. He had taken such care in the ones he used to make.

Newton put on his insulated hip boots and slipped into the water.

It was too bad that his fishing had taken a back seat to the hunting. But that was the way it was. That was his family's main deal when he was growing up. The closest thing to a purpose he had ever known was the year he tried every kind of angling. Fly fishing with a sunk fly was best. He knew all the places where it was the only fishing permitted, and the ones too, where you had to release your catch. Newton figured that if he couldn't do the very best thing, then why not be entirely insane, and go hand fishing. He loved fishing in a very personal way, even this which was certainly beyond the bounds of reason. He waded upstream until he found the right looking bank to go to work. Spoons had called hand fishing the direct method, and it required speed, silence, and disguise. He lay on his belly and plunged his arm under the mossy overhang and into the ice cold current. He crooked his fingers, stayed dead still and in perfect jeopardy of attack by an unseen muskrat whose home might be hidden under the bank. Newton was intent. This was a better challenge than the aspen rod. The stakes were higher.

He looked at his arm under water. It wobbled and rippled as though part of the current, though he knew it was perfectly still. He was beginning to feel still all over. It was a good feeling, this being steady, quiet, and yet supremely alert. Then, so quick Newton himself couldn't see the action, his hand shot out to where it had sensed the motion of a fish. His fingers closed over a fin, then the head.

Nice breakfast fish, Newton thought cheerfully, plunking the small sized Rainbow into his bucket on the bank side. Once he started, he sometimes went three, four miles around twists and bends in the creek bed before he quit. He was thinking how he loved the different choices you had in finding game, he loved that Spoons had taught him well how to turn the hand into a trajectory. He was standing at a shady bend, hand underwater, and staring at a dark wavering pool when overhead there was a sharp "Kya–Kya!" Newton looked up, shading his eyes with his fishing hand. A Golden Eagle coasted in front of a line of cirrus. It dove slowly a long ways down, then sailed above the creek, not twenty feet from Newton. He rocked back on his heels to get a better look. Coasting again, perhaps waiting for a thermal to give its wings a lift, the eagle, now gold and sienna in the sun, shrieked again. "Kya-Kya!"

Newton's hand came to his mouth. Callie! He thought suddenly.

"Trust me," Callie said softly to the child in her warm grotto within. She flexed her muscles and tightened to bear down again.

Some of the pushing came naturally to Callie, but not all of it, not the way people told you it did. She was exhausted and shaking, she wished it was over, she wished the baby had learned to swim; find its own way out.

Into her head came all manner of people pushing and thrusting. She saw beautiful men applying pressure on their dance partners' middle backs, leading them, launching them through the thirty-eight step Samba. She saw women refusing to follow the lead of their men. She saw women's naked thighs thrusting up to take the men they loved, and the men in pleasure, thrusting down. She saw Sisyphus grunting and groaning the huge boulder uphill. She saw Jack Marsh pushing a knot of men up Grandmother Mountain in search of Newton. She saw people pushing and shoving to get in the door at Spence's Grill and Grocery to get rich at the lottery. She saw someone, was it Newton, tumbling down the mountain? And then came something different. She felt something else nudging her forward; Callie imagined the bear breathing at her side, nudging her out of a forest. Callie sighed, and felt her own power.

The baby's head crowned. Callie bent over and caught the child with her hands.

Chapter TWENTY

The phone rang, and for once Pete was awake for an important call.

"Hi, I'm back in town. Three days this time."

"Wendy Waters?"

"I knew you'd guess. I had this idea. Why don't we have dinner one of these nights?"

"Wendy, I am so glad you called," Pete said, corralling his thoughts.

"Really? I'm glad we're on the same wave length."

"Listen, I'm trying to solve a little puzzle. Do you, by chance, remember a photograph of your mother looking up at Newton Denman and Callie Major, in their treefort?"

There was a pause, then Wendy laughed. "I took the picture. My dad had given me my first camera. I was over at the Denmans that day with my mother."

"It looks like a happy scene. Newton wasn't mad at your mother any more?"

"My mother got my dad's help, and together they made a sturdy rope ladder for Newton's treefort. He had just put it up. No, even though she was no longer his advisor, they were friends, Newton and my mom. Say, how about if we meet in town right now. Forget about those ancient days. Let's go for a bite to eat."

"One more question," said Pete. "We need to talk about your father. You told me he was a little depressed."

"So what."

"You never said anything about him being on antipsychotic medication and his sociopath history, or that he stopped taking the medicine that helped his delusions and violent temper. Sorry to have bring all this up, but your father gave me a box of old papers to look through. I found his medical records."

"Pete?"

"Yes, I'm here."

"Dinner's off."

The dial tone sounded in Pete's ear.

The next day at the barracks, the State Trooper told his superior officer that he had a suspect high on the list, but still could not entirely rule out Newton, or possibly his brothers.

"So Ralph Waters is the new suspect," said the wiry Hal who was sitting with his knees crossed and one foot wrapped behind the other ankle. "This is the first I've heard you come down hard against the man. What have you got?"

"I have the updated autopsy from the expert in Pittsburgh. Turns out Theresa was assaulted on the head in several places. In the front and in the back, as we knew before, and in the front there is a serious indentation and bruise, along with evidence that she was struck."

"A wooden implement, right?"

"Yes sir. Two different ones. But here's the kicker. That head wound I had sighted, well, turns out she was shot, grazed by a .22 caliber. No bullet of course, but the coroner says it had to be old. Hell, gun and bullets could have been picked up at a yard sale thirty years ago, if I know Ralph."

"Did you find the gun? Does he have a motive?"

Pete watched his boss twisting one foot behind the other. There was something hopelessly nerdish about old Hal. "No clue about the gun, and I'm still trying to unscramble what could be a motive."

"Anything on Newton? We need to sort out if it was him in his own jacket. You haven't turned up anything to disprove that, I presume. Also, the truth on his pyromaniac tendencies, and what gives on his anger towards the deceased?"

Pete was silent, thinking about what could have caused Newton to be angry or upset enough to burn down his treefort. Surely one incident didn't qualify him as a pyro. The trooper decided against revealing his meeting with Miss

Block to Hal. It was a good start but he needed to talk to Betty or Spoons to get the lowdown on Newton's relationship with Theresa Waters.

"O.K. boy scout. I see you're determined to be carefully vague." He shrugged. "Keep tracking."

"Sir. I have a favor to ask of you. Please don't ever call me boy scout again."

A mild wind blew into Callie's apartment, scattering a pile of State Park student exams on the coffee table and batting the silk screens against the wall. Baby in one arm, Callie got up to shut the windows. Mary leapt out of the rocker and gathered up the loose papers.

Both women turned to the windows where the sun was just a nubble of carnelian flickering across the mountain peak. Callie held the sleepy infant up to the window. "There she is. That's Grandmother Mountain. You might think she's going to sleep just like you – don't let her fool you," she said, watching the spark of carnelian shrink to nothing and the old Grandmother go dim.

"Sit down." Mary waved at the rocker. "A new mother needs her rest."

"Do I look tired?" Callie struggled to hide her real emotions. She was still getting used to the fact that her baby was a boy, not a girl. She went over those moments on that snowy day when she was sitting in the pitch pine and the great bear was staring up at her. Like the other times, the bear entered that circle of pitch pines and walked majestically, calmly over to where Callie sat above on the branch. But that afternoon the bear had looked up deliberately. It was her deliberate gaze that held Callie in her thrall. Every inch of Callie's skin had been on fire and she knew that the bear, too, was sending off messages through that massive furry coat. Callie had the distinct impression that she was being told, no, might as well be honest about it – the bear was prophesying the birth of a girl with bear components. Of course it was nuts, made no sense and yet Callie had felt in every fiber of her, that it was so.

She was disappointed, no girl had been born, and no bearlike qualities, or special powers whatsoever. So ridiculous of me to have counted on that, Callie thought. But I was different when pregnant, my temperature weirdly low, and no sign of the egg attaching itself to the uterus until I was four months along. How can I not wonder what was going on with me?

"You look, well, sort of weary," Mary said frankly. Everyone they knew worried that Callie was doing too much. On the other hand, Mary figured that she might be the only person who understood the unusual strength of her cousin.

He doesn't weigh much," Callie said, cradling the five week-old infant. She stared dubiously at the rocker that had once been Winoshca's. "I don't usually sit there."

"It's a nice chair." Mary ran her fingers across the thick hollowed arms and curved back. "I used to love to see Winoshca in it."

Callie nodded, noticing the curlicue weave across its back. She lowered herself carefully into the broad seat, trying not to wake Will whose miniature fist was pressed against his mouth. She glanced down at him, wondering at his new growth of hair after being bald for weeks. This hair sure beats the first lot of it, she thought. That fine, downy lanugo, it had covered his shoulders and back, making him look soft and faintly fuzzy.

Then, remembering Mary, she lifted the baby up, and asked her cousin a second time if she wanted to hold him.

"No thanks. My motto is: never hold a baby or else next thing you know I'll be crazy to have one of my own." She leaned back on the sofa, lifting one leg and resting an ankle across her knee. She was wearing a tight skirt and her rust hair was teased into wings on either side of her face. Except for their short waists and similar curve at the base of their backs, the two cousins did not look as if they shared the same blood. Callie dressed differently – tonight in a green t-shirt and a pair of leggings the same color as her loosely pulled back hair – and her nose was higher than Mary's, her legs longer, the hips more narrow. There was something bold and wonderful, though, in Mary's full hipped stance, especially when she stood with her arms akimbo, sizing up a car's troubled engine, or when she stepped out front of the Eagle Feather Singers and sang and swayed to the drums.

For having given birth so recently, Callie was full of energy, but all the vigor in the world could not confer peace of mind. For several days she had met each morning with forced cheerfulness. She was overwhelmed by the prospect of raising a child, she worried over her leave of absence from the Park, and she was depressed about Newton. It seemed to her that their connection grew more tenuous each day they were apart. Today, incited by her cousin's visit, she tried to put aside these worries. "Hey, you weren't bad in the delivery room," she said to Mary. "What a coach. I mean it."

"You trying to thank me?"

Callie nodded, and rocked back in the chair. "What I really want to know is how you're doing after this lottery business. Are you still upset?"

"I got over it," Mary said unconvincingly. "I'm glad your labor pains got me out of that line at Spence's. The big Jackpot," she added bitterly. "What a scam. Did you know that the winner was some out-of-state jerk? Some guy just passing through. He hadn't even heard about the Big One. He bought one ticket. Do you hear me? Just one, and he cleans up." She stood at the window, tapping her lighter against the pane.

"Yeah. That's lousy," Callie said, rocking forward so that her feet came flat on the floor.

"You know what," Mary laughed. "It seems like a bad dream to me now, the way I went so crazy over the lotto."

Callie pulled Will's blanket off his neck. "Look how he sweats in his sleep. Twitching too," she said.

"Betting on something, wanting it so bad. Then you lose, and it's like coming out of a dream. I can't see it happening to you, Cal."

"Can't you?" Her eyes skimmed the broad seat of the rocker. Will woke up fussing. Callie walked him up and down in front of the windows. The sky had turned blustery. Callie felt a damp draft in the room. Grandmother Mountain was the color of slag, and going darker by the minute. "Want to hear something?" she said, sinking down again into the rocker. "When I was straining to get this baby out into the world, I had the weirdest sense that the big bear, the very one we've talked about, was there with me keeping me awake. I was so sleepy for a while, even with the pain."

"Yeah? Then what happened?"

"Nothing. Will was born."

Mary looked at her sharply, then shook her head and stood up, yanking at her tight skirt that had hiked more than half way up her thighs. "You were hallucinating. Having a baby probably makes everybody think weird shit."

"You think?"

"Definitely."

"They didn't give me any drugs."

Mary shrugged. "My most fantastic dreams jump me from behind. I can be having the most normal day, and suddenly it happens. They grab me by the heels, flip me over, and flatten me. That's what a steamroller dream does. Doesn't matter what state I'm in when *it* wants to take over." Then, stretching her arms and wiggling her skirt down, "If you ask me though, it's a waste of time analyzing them. I think guys like Freud were full of it, thinking they could weed a body's mind like it was an overgrown vegetable plot. I mean, I'm sure not about to tear apart that lottery business. It was a dream I got sucked into, and now it's done with. Kaput. Plain and simple....Can't believe the money I blew."

"How much?"

"Fourteen thousand."

Callie was stunned. She sat down again. "Are you kidding?"

Mary shook her head. "All my savings." She dropped the lighter. "I might have to get rid of the Corvette."

Callie's eyes widened. "I am so sorry." The two women were silent. Then, after a bit, "Mary, what happens if that dream comes back to haunt, what happens if it tries to take you again?" Callie stared down at the cross-hatching on the seat of the rocker. It blurred for a second, with the motion of going to and fro. "What do you do then?"

Mary smoothed out her skirt. "Oh to be as wise as Ursa Major," she murmured, staring out the large windows at the night sky.

Callie blinked. The brown wicker crosshatching looked exactly like a harrowed field. "Something's gone wrong with Spring this year," she said vaguely. "A few teasingly bright days, then overcast again. I was so sure it would be blue and clear after Will was born."

Despite her six-week maternity leave, Callie had promised Bud she would stop by the State Park. She searched for her uniform. Now Will was crying. Hungry again? She sat down with him in the rocker.

She didn't want to go to the Park today, even though it was only a two hour stint she had promised Bud. It wasn't any one duty at work that had her feeling this way, she thought, shifting Will for a sip or two at her other breast. She was vaguely uneasy, and it wasn't just that Will was a boy and not a girl. Or that he had no special powers. For one thing, she was relieved – she now realized – that her child did not have disturbing or unusual strengths. Plain and simple, she loved him, and she was determined not to *wonder* at her strange connection with the bear. Her uneasiness had to do with other demons; it had to do with the men in her life, the ones she had loved, and loved still.

The old shape shifting sponge had crept back into her bones. She felt as though her body was loosely put together, vulnerable to chaotic matter, disorderly waves of it passing through her. These days she couldn't concentrate for long on any one thing. Sometimes she thought of Newton, of how she wished she had a chance to tell him why she hadn't called, and of the birth itself, the whole event.

Dressed and ready to pick up Will and fly out the door, she caught sight of herself in the mirror. She stared in disbelief. Where was her round solid belly, that fullness and semblance of a whole earth girded by the secret sash within? She looked again, and this time Callie laughed out loud.

She had put on the oversized uniform she wore in the last months carrying Will. She had put on a baggy, shapeless self.

Stepping outside, now in the khaki uniform she wore in her early months of pregnancy, Callie still felt not quite right, as though her old figure was an acquaintance she hadn't seen for years and perhaps no longer got along with. She was hard on the old friend, and was certain she had gone soft. There would have been argument from anyone who saw her in the crisp green uniform and shining pony tail swinging side to side as she carried Will down the street to her Jeep. In truth, she had bounced back quickly, not unlike so many creatures of the forest.

With one eye on Will in the seat beside her, she drove slowly to Spence's house where Jessie was to watch the baby until Callie got back from the State Park. As she walked to the offices at Pitch Pine, her mind was on Will and how she hated leaving him for the first time, even with so reliable a sitter as Jessie.

Then she heard her name. "Callie! Over here!"

Bud Mason was standing by a half dozen chicken wire cages near the employee entrance to the Diorama Center. She greeted him and he in turn dropped his hand around her shoulders. Bud asked about the baby, and how she was getting along. She answered briefly, amidst the soft, full noise of doves flapping inside the pens.

"What's all this?" she jerked a thumb.

"Bird antics," Bud said dryly. "They went amok, and we had to do something."

"How amok?" She looked at the cooing birds, and smiled fully for the first time that day.

"They've decided that the campsites are their new feeding grounds." Bud shook his head, his chin wobbled. "Pestering the hell out of campers, is what they're doing. Bird-droppings everywhere up at South Bend campsite. They perch on the tents or clotheslines and swoop down any time there's a whiff of food."

"It probably started with one camper throwing hamburger buns to a few doves," Callie said.

"Word gets around quick in the pigeon community. Next thing you know – hundreds." Bud gestured at the cages. "We took the truck over to South Bend and caged some of them, as you can see. It's an experiment," Bud sighed. "Now we don't know what to do with them."

He took off his glasses. "Wish you'd been here, Callie. A couple of the rangers weren't thinking, didn't handle the situation right, to my mind." Bud clicked his tongue and grumbled something inarticulate. "It was mostly Marsh. Those we hadn't caught, Jack decided to scare with gunshot. Didn't aim at them of course." Bud closed his eyes, placing a middle finger at each eye socket. "He scared three doves, and at least thirty campers."

Callie knelt at the nearest cage, her eye skimming the dozen or so gray and brown birds that filled the air with a soft guttural B-d-d–d-d-d.

"Marsh wanted to try firecrackers next," Bud said, watching as she sat down and spread her arms to the doves.

"Great," Callie shook her head. "Nothing like a firecracker to help the wildlife." With her face flush against the wire opening of the cage, she pursed her lips, imitating the bird voices. In a few minutes they were purring back at her, gathering close to her face. She reached into the cage and gently plucked up the most motley dove.

"Set the birds loose way up mountain," Callie said, examining the dove in her hand.

Bud gave a low whistle of admiration. "Those birds act mighty tame around you."

"This one's just a little thing," Callie said.

"Yeah, I think it'll work," Bud nodded. "Put these cages in a truck and let 'em go up in the Pitch Pine Forest."

"Hey, there's blood on your neck," Callie said to the small dove, her fingers working through the ruff of feathers under its beak. "A bad scratch. Grazed him right here on the throat." She looked angrily at Bud.

Bud was surprised, then shame-faced. "Damn that Marsh." Callie stood up, unbuttoned the top of her shirt and tucked the bird inside. "He looks weak, wasn't eating the birdseed. I think he's starving."

She went to the staff kitchen and was looking in the refrigerator for a loaf of bread.

"Excuse me, can I get in there too?"

As Callie turned the dove inside her shirt fluttered up.

Jack Marsh reached around her and pulled out a sandwich. "Callie, I thought it was you, but I couldn't be sure. You look different." He was shaken at the sight of her. Yes, she was different, he decided. Not quite like she was before she got pregnant. More fiery. Still beautiful, he thought morosely.

Callie stiffened. Then resolutely, she turned back to the fridge, got out a loaf of bread and took it to the round kitchen table. Jack followed.

She said to him, "The baby's name is Will."

"Why didn't you call me?" His insides were churning. "You should have let me know." He dropped his sandwich on the table.

She untwined the plastic coated wire from the bag that held the bread. Jack picked it up, twisting it around his forefinger.

Callie tore off a heel of bread and lifted the dove out from her chest. "First you told me to get rid of the baby. When I refused you said you hated kids. Besides, you could have called me," she said. "You, of all people, could figure out when our baby was due." She offered a bit of bread to the dove. It turned its head away and squeezed out of her hand and on to the table.

Jack glanced at the bird, now sitting absolutely still. "Pigeons!"

"They're Rock Doves," Callie said.

He yanked nervously at the wire twine in his fingers. "They were pests," he said. "Had to try something. Godammit Callie, I don't want to talk about birds."

His eyes sparked. The voice softened. "I would have called you. Only you've acted so cold. I've been thinking about us. Your place isn't big enough for you and the baby. You could move in with me, we could live like a family."

"It's too late. I don't want to live with you." She offered the bread again. The bird refused. Callie closed her eyes, "I'm sorry, Jack, I don't love you." She hated to hurt him, even now.

The dove seemed to come alert. It hopped in odd diagonals across the table, first near Callie, then towards Marsh, and back to Callie. She mashed the bread in her hand and offered it again. The bird hopped away.

"I did try, Jack." She was shocked that she could say the truth so plain and clear.

Jack had twisted the plastic wire as tight as a cork screw. "I know who got in between us," he said. "It's that asshole hunter isn't it? Newton Denman. Tell me you know him!"

"I know him. Okay?"

"Easy enough for you to melt for him. Ice maiden, my ass." Callie winced. She lowered her chin level to the table top, and called to the bird. "Eat, you have to eat." Her chin trembled. Jack's eyes followed her hand slipping up behind the Rock Dove.

"I'll tell you something else about your lover. He wants to kill that big black bear we have in the forest. Don't forget I was your lover too. You told me about the bear, how you think it's so special. Well, I have news for you; Newton Denman is a murderer and an arsonist. And I have this straight from the police. The man is ruthless. His next illegal act will be what he does to that bear. He's been waiting for her to come out of hibernation. First chance, he'll take her down."

"Don't tell me about illegal hunting," Callie flashed back at him. "I've seen you in the woods at night, spotlighting deer, blinding them so you can shoot them, pick them right off the road. You didn't figure I knew that about you, but I go up to the mountain myself. Plenty of nights." Slowly she turned her eyes on him, and smiled.

Jack looked at her in wonder. It was a brilliant smile this wild woman had, and she had to be wild or nuts to go up mountain at night, alone, probably without a gun.

"I'm sick of your holier than thou accusations." She held the dove up in her hand so he could see the stain of blood on its neck. Then, putting the bird down, "You're the lowest kind of hunter."

Jack shuddered. Palms spread out across the table, forearms shaking, he leaned across the dove between them. He was livid. "Newton Denman is hiding out, Callie, can't you see that? Using you for a little sympathy. Using you."

The table reverberated as he let go. He stared at her and the dove and his uneaten sandwich, then walked out of the room.

Feed the bird, Callie thought mechanically. Feed the Rock Dove some bread. She placed the corner heel in her mouth. Once softened, she held the bird close to her lips. The dove looked at her with its perfect pea shaped black eye, then ducked its beak into her mouth. She tore off another nugget of bread and let the bird feed again, then another piece, and one more. Her eyes watered and then spilled over. The Rock Dove cooed and tapped against her teeth. It was oddly comforting to Callie that its beak was in her mouth. She felt the soft ruffle of head feathers. She felt the hard cool tongue eat her bread and drink her salt water.

Chapter TWENTY-ONE

Newton was the same height as Callie at the beginning of that long ago summer in Littlecomb, but by September he towered over her. She was changing too. Her heart-shaped face was fuller now, and her arms had grown round and solid, almost womanly. Several times when her wrist crossed his in reaching for an after school snack, Newton found himself wondering what it would feel like to have the weight of her arm on top of his, or better, around his waist.

They were half-way to school one morning when he asked her if she would come with him tomorrow in his early morning rounds, checking the traps laid in the woods by his father and brothers. She was silent.

"Come on Cal. Don't think I'm big on the idea, okay? I have to do it, my daddy says so. I've been at it for a few weeks now. Not every day, or anything."

"But almost every day."

"How would you know?"

"The mornings you come from trapping, you smell like balsam and rotting leaves and creek water, and animal lure, and today you must have walked right through a pile of hazel nuts." She laughed.

Newton was slow to respond. True he hadn't showered afterwards; but it was strange how she could scent these details so accurately.

She grew serious. "I don't see why you're asking me to go with you, I told you before, I can't stand the thought of an animal in the teeth of metal jaws." She walked faster than usual. Despite his long legs, Newton had to run a few steps to keep up.

"I'm not crazy about that part of it either. That's why I want your company. It won't be like my regular days out, not like real trapping. You gotta say yes!" He leapt in the air and landed in front of her, his eyes sharp with excitement. "It's not all the way dark at four thirty in the morning, it's different, you'll see. I found a new way to get to Comb's creek. First I pick my way through that big old cornfield, then –"

"Okay, I'll go. So long as you know I might go home when you get close to the traps."

They met the next morning in the black predawn hours. Newton carried his trapping tools and two pairs of yellow hip boots for when they got to the creek. Callie brought a thermos of tea. The two left Littlecomb behind them and walked fast until they reached a cornfield that rose before them.

"That's where –" Newton began.

"Why are you whispering?"

Newton cleared his voice. "That's where we have to go, up the field, then loop over to the pine forest, cut straight through it and down to the creek."

They stood at the edge of the field, Newton feeling excited and solemn. The corn was dark yellow, like burnt and broken wedges of cornbread. There was a low wind that broke the stillness. The husks rattled gently. Newton turned to Callie. She was dressed in dark colors, but her eyes and hair stood out from her pale face, illumined by the planets overhead, whole paddocks of them.

"When I come out here alone," Newton said, "I always tell myself that morning's coming soon." He jerked his head around once. "If I thought it was midnight right now it might be creepy."

"If it was midnight, you'd be scared stiff."

"I didn't say that."

"That's what you meant." Callie threw open her rounded arms in sudden exaltation. "There's nothing to be scared of here." Then she took off, running in zigzags between the cornstalks, missing near collisions with each one.

Newton followed, and the two of them ran all the way to the end. Gasping for breath they collapsed in the grass along the edge of the cornfield. "I wish there was a place so high you could see the whole world from the top," Newton said, stretching out his gangling legs.

They tramped through the stand of pines at the hilltop and then down toward the water where the traps were set. The two were lively now, running the last stretch to the creek, exclaiming at a pair of Screech owls that flew up out of nowhere, and screeching back at them when they called. Soon they were in the creek bed, hip-length boots slapping and making squishing noises as they walked.

"There aren't any traps for another quarter mile or so," Newton assured Callie. I'll let you know in plenty of time.

A little ways farther, and Callie's right foot got stuck in the mud at creek bottom. Newton sloshed over to help. He yanked on her arm to pull her free and the two of them fell into the shallow water. He started to laugh until he saw Callie's face.

"I don't like wearing these boots," she said. "I can't move right."

They walked on, Newton some yards ahead of her.

"Stop Newton. Stop!"

Newton turned slowly in his awkward boots. He heard an unusual cry. A scratchy whimper, and now a woofing that came from behind. For a split second he thought this was Callie being funny, making animal noises. Then he realized he had overshot his estimation of where the first trap was; something was caught and he had walked right by it.

There was Callie at the bank side kneeling before a black bear cub, its back leg clamped and bleeding in the mouth of the trap. He rushed over.

"That wasn't supposed to happen," he said slowly, gesturing helplessly with his arms. "It's a number eight. That size trap is not meant for bears."

Callie was stroking its furred back. "This baby doesn't know your trapping rules." The bear raised its eyes to Callie. She put her hand over its short clawed paw. The cub began to hum. Newton looked around him. The humming grew, it vibrated and seemed to pervade the woods.

"That's his nursing noise." Callie was barely audible. "He's doing it to soothe himself. Or maybe, he's hoping he'll be rescued and fed." She turned to Newton, her voice cracking. "I don't think it's right that you have to set traps. This is the worst – " she broke off. "I'm going to try to help him, I see how he's stuck." She stood up, and in that moment Newton felt his spine tingle in rage.

He was beside himself for not knowing how to act, what to do. He wanted desperately to control the situation, to use what skills had been taught him to handle the trap and attend to this indelicate mistake.

"I have a handkerchief in the pack," Callie was saying. "He needs to have that wound wrapped right now. The jaws tore his leg up. Snapped the bone, too."

Newton was barely listening. "You don't know how the traps work," he said to Callie. "I'll spring him free. You just watch."

"We have to be very careful. Please let me try?"

"You've never done this before." He elbowed her aside.

She dropped back. "He's weak. And bleeding more, right there above the break."

"Callie, I've seen more mangled animals than you can count. You stay back," Newton commanded. He turned once and saw Callie staring at the cub, her head motionless, her eyes filling with tears. No emotional contortions, just an ashen face slipping out of sight as she stepped backwards into the woods.

"Don't go. Everything will be fine," Newton said feeling for his gloves. "Do you hear me?" He bent over the cub who was whining in a strange high staccato.

"I'll fix this, you little mongrel." Newton was all business. He felt his mechanical abilities soar. No problem here. Hadn't he worked the spring free from some ten or twelve slightly mangled possums, fox, and muskrat? A thought struck him. Each of those times the ensnared animal had died, not an uncommon thing in trapping. In most instances the skin was what he was after. This time it was different.

He rubbed his fingers nervously across the tops of his yellow boots, leaving long muddy smears. He would save this bear for Callie's sake. Together his will and his know-how would rescue it.

Mechanically, he worked at the spring which refused to budge at his first and second try. He went to the teeth thinking that if he could pry open the metal mouth a little ways the spring would give. This didn't work. He stared down at the bloodied fur enmeshed in the snare.

"Damn. It's worse than I thought. Bad break. The cub's in a bad way."

The cub snuffled and whimpered. Once, the soft fur of its shoulder brushed against Newton's face, giving the boy a jolt. He looked up and saw through the trees on the other side of the creek the first streaks of gray layered on the horizon line, the same spot where he and Callie had stood an hour earlier.

"Hey Callie, it's getting light out." His back was stiff from hunching over. He craned his head to see her response, but there was no one there. She was gone, and he hadn't even heard her boots in the leaves. A twig fell into the brown, slow eddying water. He listened for the mourning doves whose voices come with the first light. Newton felt a pang of fear he could not place. "Too quiet," he said aloud. In a flash he realized that the cub, too, was quiet. He spun back to the trap and saw the black furred animal slumped over.

He stood transfixed before the stiffening bear cub. "I didn't do anything wrong, I didn't." His face did not confirm this, his eyebrows formed stricken question marks. He squatted down in a mound of half damp, fall-turned leaves. Newton inhaled the composting leaves, forearms on thighs, hands clasping and unclasping.

Part FOUR

Finally the bears were untied and led from house to house....
The train lurched along to the angry roaring of the bear that was
being pulled back and forth. Bear Festival in Tebach.

from <u>Bears</u>, *a brief history*, Bernd Brunner

Chapter TWENTY-TWO

After her meeting with Jack, Callie did exactly what she had not planned. She collapsed in pure exhaustion. For days, she slept whenever Will did, put her feet up each chance she got, and did nothing other than baby tending activities. Her body told her she needed to shore up her energy.

She had extended her pregnancy leave one week. Callie may have slept more than the baby in those two weeks. So much was upsetting in her life. There was the incident with Jack, and worse, she had not seen Newton. Why hadn't he come? She got out of bed to answer Will's cry. All day she had napped on and off, and now it was getting dark outside. Was it so easy for Newton to forget about her, and was it possible, as Jack said, that he had been using her?

Callie moved Will's face to her rock hard breast, the one leaking the most, and as the milk let down she felt the tug at her breast reverberate like a small seismic shake. It came in waves, from breast to toes to womb.

Soon she was buttoning up, and in a near slumbering state Callie gathered Will and went outside. Carrying him in a knapsack that held the baby against her chest, she walked six blocks to the church yard of The Good Shepherd. It seemed natural enough that she would come here, a place in town with a few trees, some open space.

Callie spotted a familiar dogwood. She looked under the tree for the violets that sprang up every year, but she was too late. They were gone, had fled with the month of April.

Will began to whimper for the rest of his meal, which had been interrupted after one breast, and Callie's desire to go outside. She unbuttoned her shirt a second time, and sank down under the tree. If it were still April, she thought, I would bring my rocker here, and set it down in a lap of violets.

As she rocked slightly with the baby at her breast, she saw herself in her family rocker, and for a split second felt herself being held, though she couldn't have said who or what held her.

Callie raised her head, and saw the moon through the treetop branches; so far away it looked no larger than the cuticle on her forefinger. It was glowing and white. Callie felt more awake than she had in weeks. She thought of the moon moving around the earth with no fixed place, its hard orbiting body steadily turning through waves of dark and light. As she stared it seemed to grow larger. How solid and real that arc of moon, hard and round as a font, rock hard and round as a breast before giving milk. From font to faith, was hers the only leaky vessel? It was so easy when she was pregnant, faith connecting the baby and her, faith siphoned through their shared cord.

Callie pictured herself, big with life, the child, the cord, and now that form of life gone, expelled into something new. It scared her to think that she could not keep and arrange her feelings, or anything that she loved passionately; not baby, or bear, not even faith or fear, not true love – faith here, or old love – there fear.

The next morning Bud called again. "I hate to keep busting up your maternity leave like this," he said. "I know, you have three more days at home." He told her that he was short one lecturer in the Park education classes, and was hoping she could come in and do a class on fire prevention. "Callie, you there?"

"I have four days left, not three," she said, in a panic. "Bud, I am a new mother. Does that mean anything to you? I can't leave Will." Callie heard herself; exasperated, frazzled. She hated the tone of her voice.

Bud was silent, then apologized again for bothering her and said good bye.

Callie sat up in bed, holding the dead receiver. I should go to work, she thought. No, I shouldn't go to work. What am I supposed to be doing here, caring for Will, for doves, for the fire safety of the Pitch Pine forest? Everything at once?

The phone rang. Better not be Bud, Callie prayed.

It was Deacon Cameron Shawl. "Yes, everything's fine," she said to Cameron. "What's going on with the Noah's Ark production? What? All right, I am not fine. No, please keep talking. Tell me about the ark, how are you going to build a ship up front in the church? Will you move the Eucharist table? Tell me the news."

Newton's arms were around the bear cub that he had finally freed from the steel trap at the creek. Callie had tried to save the baby, said she knew how, only he hadn't let her. Why not? He would have done almost anything for her. With the dead cub in his arms, he hoped to slip into the work shed unnoticed, but George and Nat were there when he arrived.

"Will you cipher this!" George said. "Looks like you trapped yourself a little cub, a bee-u-tee, I might add."

Nat, smiling, saw-toothed – same as his father – strode over to see what his youngest brother had snared. "Way to go, Newt. It's got a nice coat, too. A shame it's so puny. Won't make much of a rug," he cracked. "What're you going to do with it?"

"I don't know," Newton said lamely. He put the carcass down on the wood-shed table. Then, because he had to talk about what had happened to some-body, he said, "Callie went with me this morning trapping. She saw the cub while it was still alive." He flicked his eyes over the black and blood-stained fur. "I think it broke her heart."

Nat and George exchanged glances. Nat looked uncomfortable, George stroked his soft beard, his most successful one to date. He was twenty now, and Nat, eighteen. Newton was sitting, rigid in the work chair, his neck so tight he thought it would crack.

"Well hell," said George at last, "Why don't you make it up to her. Do that bear up nice and give her the fur. Any girl would love to get something like that shiny black bear fur."

"I'm not sure Callie wants a bear skin."

George placed a hard hand on Newton's shoulder. "Didn't you just tell us how much she loved that bear baby when it was alive?" He elbowed Nat, and winked. "Well think, you'll be giving her something to always remember it by. Besides, she'll love you, and she'll love you good, then."

"It's not like that." Newton stood up, twisting the tail of his shirt.

"All us Denmans like girls, no shame in it,"

"He's got it bad for her," Nat snickered.

George turned to Nat. "He's a Denman through and through."

There was a noise, the woodshed door scraping open, and who was it but Pete Myrick. "You guys picking on Newt again?"

Tall for his age, Pete was bigger than Newton who had not yet hit his major growth spurt. They had been one year apart in school, until last year when Newt was pushed up a grade.

"We're giving him some advice on love, his truest love," said George. "You know Callie Major, don't you?"

Pete nodded seriously. "She has B lunch same as me, and she sits one table down from mine. Come on guys, let up on him," he said, taking in Newton's distress.

George went over to his youngest brother. "Hey, what's this? Hey Newt, we didn't mean anything by it."

Newton was sobbing, nose crushed against his hands. After Pete left, his brothers soothed him, or tried to with more talk of giving Callie the cub skin. The boy rubbed his face with his shirttail. "All right, I'll give her the bear, but not just a regular pelt. She wouldn't want a bear rug. I'll think of something so special she'll know that –" He stopped. His brothers were grinning. Nat pointed to his lips and silently mouthed *Lover boy*. Newton ignored him. "I'll clean this cub up good. It'll smell as nice as a brand new car carpet, and then I'll make something of it."

Newton ran to the house, splashed cold water on his face and changed clothes for school. He went out to meet Callie but she wasn't where they always met, at the rose bushes. She didn't show up at school, either. He thought about her all day. He thought about the bear cub too. He couldn't get free of it. Somehow there was a connection between Callie and that bear, or was it all bears? It made his head ache to try and figure it out.

Right after school he went to the work shed and began to prepare the bear for skinning. He examined it thoroughly for scars and tears and he cleaned the fur until it was glossy. Methodically he made his cuts, sharp and clean, from hind foot to tailbone. He pretended he was addressing his brothers, all of them, and his father and mother, too: I love Callie. I can't love anyone else. I'm not like the men of this family. I'm different. She's different.

He had pulled the fur up to the jaw line.

Now he recited an imaginary response to his declaration of love. This was Nat: Sure you love her, sure you do. That's right, she's a pretty girl.

The job was almost done. He separated the head and skin from the body. One more step. Newton looked down at the skinning knife between index finger and thumb. The blade shook.

She's a pretty girl. All us Denmans like pretty girls; you're just like us. When are you coming with us on a real bear hunt, hunhh Newt? That was Nat, or was it his daddy, or maybe Spoons; it was all the same. Newton felt suddenly tired. He was tired of arching his brows into questions that begged an understanding of his family's ways, and Callie's ways, too. He felt himself harden against all the difficult questions. He would just cut, he would do the job as he knew how. He looked again at the blade, now stilled, poised above the bear's shaggy head. It would be a beautiful muff. He moved the knife downward. Careful incisions around the snout, under the eye sockets. He removed the eyes.

Pete made a face as he swallowed the tepid coffee at the Big Springs Lounge. "Elijah," he called to the proprietor. "I'm sorry for it, but I have to voice an objection."

Elijah Jones was distracted, but he had to smile at Pete's manner. He swept a frayed bar towel over his shoulder and walked over to where the state trooper sat.

"Weren't you going to get rid of this tin dispenser that keeps nothing hot?"

"It's on my list." Elijah ran his fingers along the pine wood bar top. "I need to buy some polish, new sponges, towels, and I swear to you, Pete, a thermos to serve that coffee in."

Myrick tipped his hand in acknowledgement, noting that he had heard this before, and that Elijah Jones was tense. Otherwise, the man looked the same as always, bald, and gray complected with the odd mole here and there. Some said he resembled a tough old potato. Pete watched Elijah scan the room. He might have been doing a head count of customers, or taking an inventory of the bar stools.

Jones turned to Pete. "I have something."

"Did you want to come over to my office?" Pete kept his voice down.

Elijah smiled at Mrs. Osborne, who had come in to fetch her husband who would not leave the Lounge for anyone but her. He spotted her and he was up in a shot. Now there were just seven folks at the bar. "I can't leave the place for long. The Denman boys come in every day near this time. He glanced at the clock. "In about ten minutes, I'd say."

Pete took his meaning. "We can sit in my vehicle. It's parked in front. Over by the trees. Nat and George will park in the back."

Elijah was surprised at the comfortable seats in the police officer's old car.

"It's about the night Mrs. Waters got killed."

"I figured," said Pete.

"You know how I was convinced Nat and George left town right from the Lounge at nine pm?"

"I remember," Pete said, trying to recall Elijah's exact words. "Several men in the parking lot saw them leave. The Denmans were genuinely excited about their hunting trip. Nothing faked, you and the others believe."

"There was not a question in my mind. You know when a hunter is hell bent to head out. But Pete, I might not have mentioned what the boys said just before leaving my Lounge." Elijah was agitated. His brow wrinkled half the distance over his bare head.

"Nat was at the door, checking with George. 'Do we have all our gear?' he said. And George, who was pretty well snockered, said, 'Sure we do. Besides, I'm not going back home, now.' Then Nat gave him a look."

"What kind of look?"

"One of those, 'George, you-have-it-all-wrong looks.'"

"What else do you remember, Elijah?"

"That's all. I'm sorry this is coming out now." He tapped his forehead. "More forgetful than I'd like to admit. The night was rolling along. It did seem clear they left town way before the trouble started. Everybody thought so. But I've had time to cogitate," he paused, looking straight at Pete. "It could have happened different."

"It could have been that the brothers did go home," Pete said quietly. Never mind that their mother and old Mr. Denman had denied it.

"Thing is," said Elijah, "Those guys had no reason to go to Littlecomb Elementary School."

"No more reason than Newton, I expect," said Pete.

"There's one more thing about that night. The Denmans forgot the case of beer they bought. I kinda expected they'd be back for it. Not like them, even when they're out of it, to leave the buds behind. Makes me wonder if maybe they were preoccupied."

"Seven minutes," Pete smiled, so that the watch face glinted. "You can get them their beer now."

He thanked Elijah, who returned to his patronage. Sure, plenty of time, thought Pete. The key was in the ignition. Pete glanced up once at the lacy green and brilliant white of the birch trees that lined the parking lot. The Denmans very well could have gone home for the gear, he thought. Just as Newton said.

And the road beers? Suppose George and Nat did go back for them? After picking up the missing gear at the Denman home, one would think they'd go the shortest way to the Lounge for that beer. But if George was thoroughly drunk, he could have made a sloppy decision and taken the other route on High Street. That was the road he took every morning to work at the steel mill. In this case, they would drive right by Littlecomb Elementary School. If they had spent ten to fifteen minutes at home, that would put them at the school very close to ten o'clock.

It was a pretty day. Pete did like the Alleghenies in the springtime. As he pulled out of the green rimmed parking lot he began to whistle a tune he and Newton used to sing in music class at Littlecomb Elementary. When the trooper first came home from Arizona it was always on his lips. It was a song about a cowboy in the month of May. Then what? The cowboy roams along, sings a song. He's looking for something. Damn. Elijah wasn't the only one who could not remember.

Chapter TWENTY-THREE

As Newton drove into Tuscatanning his fingers went gingerly to his chin. He stroked it as if he were touching something brand new. This morning he had shaved off his three-month beard and in his gray painters pants and the pitch pine green, pullover sweater his ma had given him last Christmas, he looked almost reputable. His dark hair was clean and combed, and except for the parts his beard had covered, his face had a wind burnt glow. But Newton did not feel respectable, and had noticed that his hiking boots were dirty, the sweater a little tight, his arms, his whole damn body, he thought, was too tall, and rough and hard from living outdoors. He had come into town to see Callie, only she didn't know it yet.

Newton wanted to show her, prove to her he didn't mind a bit that she had not bothered to call him as they planned. Then bleakly, he had to ask himself where had it gotten him, this proving he was without feelings? No stinking place at all, except on the pity pot, that's what. If he owned up to how he felt right now it had to be that he loved Callie. This much he could finally admit to himself.

It was hard to believe that it had been over a month since last he saw her. But Newton had decided that either she did not call on purpose because she had changed her mind about him, or, she could have had the baby, and needed recovery time. Newton wasn't sure Callie wanted to see her woodsman who knew nothing about infants. He needed to remind her that he was eager to learn.

But he didn't know where to look next. Not at her apartment. He had just checked there. At the hospital? No, he remembered she was going to deliver at a Birth Center, wherever that might be. Was the baby really born? Christ, where was Callie, how was she? He drove slowly past Spence's Grill. It was Sunday morning, no one out on the streets. It was a good time to move about town unseen. He felt a strong compulsion to see her in the daylight. Not another surprise night visit, he thought. We need to be together when the light is clear.

At the stop sign across from the Good Shepherd Church, Newton spotted Mary Cowell. He pulled over to the curb and leaned out the passenger window. "Hey Mary!"

Mary grinned when she saw who it was. "Well, well, look what the sandman brought. A handsome stranger in a dusty yellow truck."

"I'm looking for Callie. You seen her around?"

"Got a match?"

"I think so."

"Are you sure she wants to see you? Callie doesn't mention you much. She acts like you're not to be trusted."

"Where is she, Mary?"

Mary took her time. She studied him through a puff of smoke. "In there, that's where she is," she said, waving a cigarette at the church. "I think she's practically running the show. In fact I'm on my way now to watch."

"Not the Noah's Ark thing? April Fools, right?"

Mary let that one slide. After all, today was May first. "Yup, Callie is in the chapel getting ready to go on." She glanced at her watch. "Morality plays are not my idea of fun, but this is Tuscatanning. Not much happening on a Sunday. Besides, my cuz would kill me if I missed it."

"I thought she didn't want any part of it." Newton was only vaguely aware of what he was saying. "You know, left the church, she told us." He thumbed the steering wheel, then tapped it nervously. It was hard not to be distracted now that he had discovered Callie's whereabouts.

"Beats me what her reasons are. It amazes me that she's there at all. You should have seen her last week. She was dead on her feet."

Newton worried. "What time is the show?"

"Begins at ten. It's taking the place of the regular service."

"Thanks. See you inside." Newton started up his truck.

"Hey, just one darned moment," Mary shouted. But the truck was barreling towards the church parking lot. Mary finished her question, sotto voce. "Aren't you hiding out, Mr. Newton Denman? You're a fool to chase after Callie right now. Practically everyone in town will be seated in those pews, praying to be entertained."

Newton searched for a back door, and easing inside found himself in the children's chapel that connected to the main body of the church. He swung around in panic. Surrounded. There were strange animals closing in on him. A boy with tiger stripes on his face asked, "Are you playing God?"

Newton stared at him a second. The child's nose was painted black. He had whiskers and there were skinny orange triangles pointing in towards his mouth.

"Mr. Engle plays God," corrected a gangly giraffe whose sex was ambiguous. Then Newton heard Callie's voice. He followed it to the other side of the room. There she was, facing a host of animals. "Okay gang, check to be sure you have your humps, tails, and feathers. It's almost show time." A yellow billed, black feathered bird tugged at her shirt. Newton smiled, watching her show the plump seven or eight year old girl how to waddle like a duck.

Callie caught another child around the waist. "Hey, no running. What animal are you?" She squinted at the gray creature with pointed ears and a straggly tail.

"I'm Wile E. Coyote."

"Of course. Easy to see." She laughed and turned her attention to a well-padded boy sitting in a chair, waiting patiently for her to paint his face. She bent over him, paintbrush in hand. "Hold your trunk up for me. That's a good elephant."

Callie was finishing up his rosy cheeks when a thought pounded home. "I'm in church again," she whispered, as if noticing for the first time. Palm to her forehead she stood up, turning slowly as if to take in every detail of the play production. On spotting Newton, who stuck out like a sore thumb among the quilted and corduroy costumed beasts, she grabbed a chair to steady herself. "Oh Newton." She stared in dismay.

He was at her side, his elbow under her sagging arm.

"You're all right!" He squeezed her around her shoulders. For the briefest second Callie sank against his chest, then pulling herself upright she stepped back.

As she drew back, he came forward. "I know this isn't the best timing. Callie? Hey, what's wrong? I came to see you, to hear about your baby. She must be born," he said, tenderly surveying her figure. "Are you okay?"

"*His* name is Will," she said, carefully distancing herself. Callie did not want to believe there were still crimes he was withholding from her, but once again Jack's charge filled her brain.

Newton admired the baby who was in a day crib in the corner of the room. Will slept placidly, as if the noise of children was no big deal. "You said your baby would arrive the same day as spring. It must have been a great day," he said lightheartedly.

"I miscalculated about the day. I was off by a long shot. And it's not as if it was a great day trout fishing," Callie said, knowing nothing of his recent foray into the cold, fish filled Black Creek.

No wonder she didn't call me that day, Newton realized. He tried to focus on what she was saying. "You're right," he said. "It must have been hard. My god, you've been through a lot, Callie."

"I hope the church is filling up," said Cameron Shawl coming up behind Callie. She noticed Newton. Callie looked nervously from one to the other. Deacon Shawl turned to him. "Are you a new recruit?" And to Callie, "I thought we had all our animals."

"Watch out. Coming through!" Callie and Newton leapt out of the way as three big teenagers and a man who looked dazed set down a huge wooden siding. They leaned the heavy lumber flush against the door where Newton had come in.

"Extra prop," the boy who was Playing Noah's son, Ham, informed them. The other two boys were also Noah's sons. The man who was wearing a brown hooded robe, was going to play Noah. "More stuff coming," he said pointedly to Deacon Cameron.

Ham deciphered for his father, Noah. "What with all the animals and other players, there's not room out by the altar for this much ark. We overestimated," he shrugged.

"Oh dear. We're not terribly organized," Cameron said to Newton, eyeing him curiously. "Did I miss your name?"

He and Callie exchanged wary glances. The child who was a duck waddled over to Cameron. "Deacon Shawl, I peeked out the stage door. There's lots of people."

Cameron grabbed Callie's hand, "If I didn't see with my own eyes how fit you were in pregnancy, I would not let you do this."

"Am I wan? Drooping?"

"You look fine. Come on, let's check out this crowd." The deacon went with Callie to the other side of the room. Newton exhaled heavily. "Do you have a handkerchief on you?" he asked the kid who thought Newton was playing God.

The boy shook his striped face, no. "You're kinda sweaty, aren't you?"

"I'm about ready to get out of here," he said, realizing that he couldn't leave quite yet, not until he had made arrangements to meet with Callie later. "Hot, isn't it?" He smiled at the boy in the tiger suit.

The young tiger reached behind him. "Here. You can use this."

Newton took the tip of the tiger tail offered him and caught the sweat off his brow. All around him was commotion, more extra lumber coming in, other characters, Mrs. Noah, two young women in white leotards with streamers attached to their arms, and children everywhere, rioting. A knot of them got hold of a bowl of fruit and were tossing bananas and apples and tomatoes up in the air.

At the door to the altar, now transformed into the Noah's ark stage, Deacon Shawl and Callie peered out to see if they had a full house. "It's a good turnout," Shawl said. Callie nodded, recognizing Mayor Kennedy in the front row. And there was Mrs. Neet and her brood, Dr. Ur and his twins; in the second row she spotted Spence and Jessie. Hurrah, Callie thought, smiling at Will who was up now, and sitting in Jessie's lap. And Mrs. P. who never left her apartment was there! Next to her sat Ranger Sorrento. That was nice, his wife and new baby, too. And beside the Sorrentos, going towards the center of the third row was Vernon Vale. On his right, sitting tall in his seat she saw Jack Marsh.

"Ouch!" the Deacon cried.

Callie had shut the door in her face. "Cameron, are you all right? I was looking at someone in the audience." She was too rattled to explain.

"I'm okay," the Deacon said, rubbing her chafed nose. "What someone?"

"Not important. We better make sure the children are ready," Callie said, her eyes searching for Newton. There he was, near those rascally kids into the stage fruit.

A child who had been juggling the fruit picked up an overripe tomato and threw it straight at Newton's head. "Catch!"

Newton caught it. "I should have known. Nothing artificial about your props," he said to Callie, wiping the runny tomato juice on his pant leg. Behind them, Deacon Shawl was directing some thirty children to sit down together until their cue to go out on stage.

"The other moose isn't here! There's only one of me," a stricken teenager said to Cameron Shawl. She tugged at her huge Styrofoam antlers. "What will I do?"

"Let's see, you can't go out alone," Shawl said methodically. "Two of every creature. I'd help dear, but I'm the narrator. Callie, can you help out?"

"I can't be a moose," Callie shouted. "I've got that other part. Got to get into my costume. They're starting the music." She turned to Newton. "You had better get out of here. Marsh, Vale, and Sorrento are out front in the audience."

Newton's heart jumped. What could be worse than a team of big game hunters come to visit this jungle of animals? "I'm leaving," he said in a low voice to Callie. Both of them looked toward the outside exit. It was blocked, ten feet of lumber stacked against the door. In front of the lumber sat the thirty children, now quietly listening to last minute instructions by Mrs. Noah. "Don't take off your mask, Karen. Remember children, you must act like animals the whole time you're on stage."

"Couldn't your friend be the moose," Deacon Shawl said suddenly, studying Newton. "It's a big costume."

"Very kind of you to offer, but I'm afraid I have to go." Newton said quickly.

"Oh but you can't," said Shawl brightly. "You see how it is," she waved an arm at the blocked exit. Newton sized up the lumber and tried to think if he could lift what it had taken four men to do.

"We're desperate. Please be our moose. The costume's got to be right here –" Shawl looked under the table. "Aha! The only one not filled!" She held out a furry robe and a pair of unwieldy Styrofoam antlers. "Here's the nose," the female, teenager moose said, crawling out from under the table.

"No, I won't do this." Newton caught Callie's eye and she moved close to him. She tipped her head in a slight nod towards the stage door, and whispered fiercely, "The only way out is through the front door. Do you think you can walk out the way you look now? Be the moose."

"I don't see how –" His eyebrows danced in consternation.

Callie's eyes traveled to the stage door, then back to him.

"Curtain time in three minutes!" Noah called out.

The narrative, a flamboyant Chester libretto, signaled the first act of the play. Noah and his family marched on stage. The crowd of actors offstage heard the hammers sing out as Noah and his sons built the mock ark erected in front of the altar. Cameron Shawl lined up the children to go in.

Newton yanked at the hem of the chocolate colored moose robe. "It's too short," he said to Callie, who was looking at his hiking boots, and the long hairy legs sticking out from under the robe.

"Well, at least it comes down to your thighs," she said.

"Hold still so I can attach these antlers."

He bent forward. "When I'm on stage I'll pretend it's you and me play acting, like when we were kids."

"Too much play acting," she said shortly.

Newton watched nervously as the animals rowed up in twos to go on stage. Got to stay calm, he thought. He studied Callie's lips and felt better. "Remember our Beauty and the Beast game? God I was a bungling beast."

At this she half-smiled. "Close your mouth. We have to tie your nose on."

Then, barely moving his lips. "Beauty. You were her."

Callie dropped her eyes to his chest, now wrapped in the brownish-red robe. "I wish you could tell me something." Her fingers brushed his cheek. "Why am I helping you?"

He looked up at her, about to answer when a shimmering blue and white heap of material tickled his face. It was Deacon Shawl waving a costume. She handed it to Callie. "This is yours," and to Newton, "Hurry. You're going on."

He looked at Callie a last time. "What am I supposed to do out there? Is there a script?"

"All your part calls for is a hard head."

"Right," he said. "You're so sure you have me all figured out."

Newton was herded out in front of the audience. Taller than any of the other animals, even the rangy adolescents who were giraffes, he filed on to the make-believe ark, stooping and bending his knees in a slow clumsy gait beside his sister moose. As the animals trooped in, two by two, a trembling voice sounded from the balcony of the church telling Noah that it would rain for forty days and forty nights and the flood of waters would cover the face of the earth. Newton scanned the balcony where the God actor, the pianist, and various spotlights were stationed. Then he noticed that all the animals had their palms upturned and were looking towards the ceiling. "It's raining," his moose mate whispered. Newton nodded and copied her example.

"The boat is rocking," she added, now tipping back and forth on her heels. As he leaned forward and back, Newton held on to his yard of antlers and listened to the narrator, Deacon Shawl, read, "The fountains of the great deep were broken up, and the windows of heaven were opened." Everyone rocked furiously and the deacon read on, "The ark went up on the face of the waters.... The breath of life, of all that was in the dry land died."

The church grew dark, and Newton didn't pay much attention when three female figures flitted in from the wings, waving their arms in slow undulations. They were wearing white leotards with colorful banners attached to their arms. The women whipped around, revolving faster and faster, like crazed Maenads.

Newton's nose itched and the costume pulled at his chest. Why is it, he wondered, that when I see Callie I end up in a bathrobe? He looked out across the audience and spotted a latecomer just entering the church. He recognized Mary's bright red hair. She sat down in one of the last pews. The front door, Newton thought. I can make my escape while the lights are out. Sneak down a side aisle. He pushed forward between a pair of donkeys and elephants crouched with their eyes closed. Newton headed for the steps down to the aisle. A lion with feathers forming a ruff around his head, hissed at him, "It's the dark, stormy night. All us animals are supposed to be sleeping."

It was also a short night. The lights came on as Newton's foot touched the bottom step of the altar. Jack Marsh, who had dozed off during the night storm, opened his eyes and stared sleepily at the huge moose frozen on the step, some distance from the rest of Noah's animals.

Newton slunk backwards up the stairs and stood behind the stone font that remained on stage because none of the cast had been able to lift it. He bent his knees, trying to appear shorter. Marsh, though close to dozing, found himself following the movements of the awkward moose. Didn't that guy know where he was supposed to stand? It wasn't as if this musical was some kind of mental challenge. Just a simple story, he thought. His eyes fluttered shut when a beautiful dove stepped up to the front of the stage. This was a slim teenager with feathers sewn to her breast and silk wings sprouting from her shoulders. Noah spoke to the dove, and then it danced offstage in search of dry land.

Newton's knees ached from standing with bent legs behind the baptismal font. It didn't hide him in the least. Again, the shy voice of God spoke from the balcony, telling Noah that there would be a great wind, and the waters assuaged. Newton looked down in front of the ark at the three swaying women with banners. They haven't let up once, he marveled. It sunk in that they were dressed as waves. He looked closer. The center wave was Callie. Why hadn't he noticed before, had she been there all this time making the storm?

She wore a white leotard. Some sparkles too, Newton noted. Her legs and arms were covered with dark blue streamers. Newton watched her do a turn and revolve on her toes. Now she and the two other women leapt in the air and came down, bowing their heads. He strained to catch sight of her face. Newton held his breath, he saw in her smile something utterly self contained and rapturous.

The dove returned with an olive branch. The lady-waves were dying down, sinking to their feet. Noah sent the dove out a third time. The lady-waves rolled back slowly on their shoulders and lifted their legs in a bicycling motion. The blue streamers fluttered against their calves. Their toes pointed skyward.

He forced himself to pay attention to Deacon Shawl who was reading: "The dove returned not again to him anymore." When Newton next looked at Callie she was nearly still, her back curled round like an oyster. Her long hair falling forward over her face made him think of a dark sea plant, and to him she was life giving, she was like the sea. Newton drifted to a place of nothing but white-capped waves. It was a lovely place and he wanted to stay there, but the voice of God interrupted. Softly, it instructed Noah to leave the ark, to take his family and "every creeping thing that creepeth upon the earth." It promised Noah there would be no more flood to destroy the earth.

What with the waves, and the voice of God, less timid than before, the tall moose had to fight off an odd feeling that he *was* a creeping thing living aboard the ark. Newton touched his smooth shaven chin, passed a hand across his face, as if to make sure he was indeed a man, not a moose. But in that quick motion the rubber moose nose that covered half his face, loosened and dropped to the floor.

In the audience, Vernon Vale was laughing at the moose antics. "Am I missing something?" Jack wanted to know. So far he hadn't seen one funny thing.

"Just Bullwinkle, up there," Vernon whispered. "He's a sketch."

Jack scanned the animals. He smiled. There was that tall moose with the crooked antlers on his hands and knees. What was he doing, anyway?

Newton snatched the large rubbery nose out from under someone's foot. He stood up shakily and tried to get the thing back on his face. It slipped out of his fingers and he was on his knees a second time.

"Best part of the show," Vernon whispered. "Didn't I tell you?"

"Like you said, a real sketch." But Jack wasn't laughing. He was staring at the moose. Then, turning to Vernon, "That's no member of the Good Shepherd Church. That's our arsonist and murderer."

Deacon Shawl was narrating the covenant of the ark, God's benediction to every living creature. Newton, with his moose nose attached sideways on his face, squinted in the sudden light beaming down from the balcony. At God's benediction one giraffe held up a bright paper sun, and her mate a pale yellow moon. Noah's sons, Shem and Ham unfurled a rainbow that glowed with iridescent stripes.

What next? Newton wondered. Four or five animals scurried down the nave with armfuls of white stars attached to long skinny sticks. They handed them out to Mayor Kennedy, Dr. Ur, Mary in the back of the church, Ranger Sorrento in the third pew, and Jack Marsh in the middle of the third pew. They gave out two dozen stars and then reconvened on the ark. Newton shook his head at the phenomena. The chorale was rising to glorious heights. Up in the balcony, a trumpet accompanied Miss Lee's piano. As the animals filed out of the ark the audience swayed and twirled their stars. The paired creatures began their procession down the center aisle. Someone had opened the front doors of the church. The afternoon light streamed in.

"That's my sign from heaven," Newton said to his moose mate. Then he bolted.

Jack saw the shaggy moose in his antlers and hiking boots galloping towards the front entrance. The ranger threw down the five-pointed, sparkling star in his hand. He struggled through the people in his pew, and then ran into Noah and his family moving benignly behind the animals in the parade out of the church. Jack pushed through only to get caught in the feisty mass of children who knew they could be kids again. They were tearing off their tails and humps, whooping and stomping. They behaved as animals might, after being freed from the ark.

Despite the congestion, Jack was certain he could catch Newton and get the police to check the wanted poster that verified him as a man on the run.

As Marsh raced past the last pew a barrier smacked him at the knees. He tripped and hit the rug runner hard on his chin. Jack massaged his jaw to make sure nothing was broken. Whose leg, what oaf had gotten in his way?

There was Mary Cowell sitting at the edge of the pew, one long leg in black stockings swinging over the other. She smiled at him.

"What the fuck? Why you – " Jack could think of no words adequate to describe his fury. He scrambled to his feet.

"Exciting show, wasn't it?" Mary grinned wider.

Once out of the church, he scanned the parking lot for Denman. Nothing. Not a sign of him or his yellow truck.

Bud Mason came up behind Jack, standing tensely in the center of the parking lot. "You okay, Marsh?"

"Denman. He was here, not five minutes ago." Jack was caught between rage and exhilaration. "I have to go after him, Bud, I mean, *Sir*. I'm going to talk to the police, round up some people if I can."

Bud's eyes grew big and piercing behind his thick glasses. "You're too wound up. It takes a reflective state of mind to go after justice."

Jack's foot jigged up and down. "You be reflective for the both of us, sir. Let me make my move."

Chapter TWENTY-FOUR

On this visit to Betty Denman's house she eyed Pete as if he were her worst relative descending, uninvited. She could not pretend to smile, and from his view the freckles dusting Betty's snub nose were her most persistent sign of life. He told her that he had been to see Miss Block.

Betty flinched. That old bat had made her son George repeat the first grade.

Pete asked Mrs. Denman to tell him again about Newton's relationship with his former academic advisor, Theresa Waters. "Didn't she encourage him to think about going to college?"

"He had the grades, it's true. But you don't know the half of it," Betty said.

"What do you mean?" Pete wondered if George and Nat were living at home again. There was a clothes basket heaped high with men's t-shirts, underwear, and jeans.

"Theresa Waters whipped him into a frenzy over that college idea. He thought of nothing else."

"Was that bad?"

"His father and I argued over it. He was against the idea. I wasn't. At least not at first." Pinpoints of color came into her face. Bright, childlike marks. Sheer pink. She lit a cigarette. Betty's marriage had been a disappointment. Her Joe had cozened her into the engagement, she felt, led her to believe he would love her fully, when the only two things that claimed his full commitment were the pack of dogs he and Spoons owned, and the going after game. Still, that man did make her laugh. He told some good stories, and there were years when she couldn't wait to slip off her nightgown for him. Not so nice were the times he sunk into strange rants about his war experience. His was a bitterness she couldn't touch. On thinking back, she wouldn't have married him had she understood his limitations, but then again wasn't she desperate for love, and anxious to get away from her father whose life made her own miserable?

He never struck a soul, but with his sodden ways, he had as good as chased her own mother away. Yes, he had beaten her down, and then one night she did leave, taking her infant son with her. Betty was hiding in a closet, waiting for her parents to stop yelling. Then she fell asleep. When she opened the closet door some hours later, there was no one to comfort her. Her mother was gone. So was her baby brother.

At least Joe didn't drink, she thought. Betty exhaled and looked at Pete. "The fighting between Joe and me over that college business had to stop. It was bad between us. Finally, Joe, that's Newton's father, persuaded me that we could never afford to send him away for school."

Pete mentioned that he learned from the former principal of Littlecomb Elementary that Mrs. Waters had spent months researching scholarships for Newton.

"I wouldn't know about that," said Betty sharply. "Look, all I can tell you is that soon after Newton's thirteenth birthday he got so upset that he asked for a new advisor. He never spoke to that woman again."

Pete brought forward the photograph that Theresa Waters had earmarked for her friend, Miss Block. It had taken some doing to convince the old lady he would return her picture.

"This looks pretty friendly to me," said Pete. "Do you know what's going on?"

"Oh my." Betty studied the photo.

"Newton would be about fourteen here?" said Pete.

"Thirteen and a half."

"That's less than a year after he was never going to speak to Mrs. Waters again."

Betty stared at the picture of Newton beaming down at Mrs. Waters from the treefort. "Maybe they had made up by then." She was thinking about how her own mother had tried to make up with her, had gotten in touch seven months after leaving her own daughter at home with her inebriated father.

Pete handed Betty the drawing of the same scene, this one signed by Newton. "So they weren't mortal enemies. Newton did not have an ax to grind against this woman?"

Betty put out her cigarette. "No they weren't enemies, and it's true, they made up. But I never did like the woman. Now are you going to start suspecting me of murder?"

"Murder, Mrs. Denman? No. Confusing Newton's chances for getting his name cleared? Yes."

"How dare you. I love all my sons."

"I am sure you do. By the way, would the older ones happen to be lurking upstairs? I need to speak to them, too. Nothing new. Don't be concerned." The state trooper did not want to repeat his mistake with Newton. Give them a warning, and they are gone, he thought.

"The boys aren't home."

"What about Spoons?"

"Not here."

"I'm sick of being not here," came a voice from the downstairs bedroom in Betty Denman's house. Spoons emerged pursing his shriveled daisy petal lips, and trying to smooth his hair that stuck up like a shout.

"How are you sir?" Pete was all smiles when he saw the old gentleman.

"Master Sergeant." Spoons signaled with a hand to his brow.

"Pete will do," said the state trooper. "Is it okay if we go over that night your grandson disappeared, night of the school burning?"

"I'm going back to bed." Spoons wheeled his stiff torso around.

"What about the fire in your yard that Newton set off at some point after the fallout with his advisor. Why a fire at all? And why at the treefort?" As Pete spoke he noticed that Spoons had begun to shake. First his head, then the broomstick straight back began to vibrate full throttle.

"What's wrong? Let me help," said Pete, rushing over to the old man.

"Let him be," said Betty. "He needs to say something."

The old man spoke with quiet urgency. "Newton is a hunter gone wrong. Sergeant, you have to stop the madness."

Pete stared. He hardly guessed that soon enough Spoons would say this again. And that he should have paid attention the first time.

After Pete left and Spoons had quieted down, Betty thought about the drawing of Newton, Callie Major, and Mrs. Waters at the treefort. Newton never did that drawing, she realized. Those curlicues were not his style.

When George and Nat came in later that evening Betty told them about Pete's call. "He wants to question the two of you again."

The men looked at each other, and then at their mother for guidance.

"What you boys have to do is leave town at once."

She held up a hand to quell them. "You must go find Newton."

"Go *get* him?" asked Nat, with undisguised pleasure in his voice.

Betty turned to the kitchen window. She straightened a curtain, then pulled it aside so that she could see her clothesline. "Newton can't come home again." Her voice quavered as she tried to make sense of her decision to save the two boys at home, and her prayer that the one already gone was smart enough to save his own life. In a moment she had composed herself. "Nat, I have money for you to give to Newton. You've got to persuade him to leave the state. Pete won't follow him, I feel sure of it. Here's how it'll work. Both Pete and that new detective chief, Rendell, will figure Newton did those crimes because he's run out of state. Looks guilty, doesn't it? Then, they'll be off your backs."

Betty handed Nat a brown envelope. "Here's the money. Six thousand dollars. It's all my savings."

"But, we don't know where Newton is," George said.

"Oh yes we do. He let it slip last time I had him on the phone."

In the dream Pete could not keep his footing. It was a summer night in the high desert. Cool enough for all the snakes to come out. Pete was slipping down a steep grade on the north side of the mesa. He dropped the banner and there was dust everywhere as he slid into the huge lowered arm of a Saguaro cactus. He became aware of the diamond back rattlers forming a circle around him. At the same time a high pitched cry rent the desert air. It has to be a desert fox, Pete thought. He remembered what the old hunters said: a fox screaming at night sounds like a human baby being strangled.

Pete knew he was lost.

He woke up in terror at four in the morning. *I'm in Littlecomb, and it's over, done with. No, it's not. Who am I kidding?*

In his boxers and bare feet he went to the back room with the cement floor where he kept things he had not looked at in years. Except for the vial of gold nuggets, there was nothing from his past he cared to keep close at hand.

Pete walked over to a bill collector desk. He didn't notice the cold floor, so intent was he on retrieving and then holding to the light a repugnant object. It was a rattlesnake head, its mouth open, showing retractable hollow fangs. You could even see the venom pouches behind the teeth. A glob of amber colored poison skillfully prepared by a taxidermist hung frozen from the fangs.

Pete shuddered, and put the snake head away.

He raced upstairs and got dressed, made a thermos of coffee and fed Pandora, who was startled at her master's nocturnal turn. Through a half-hearted rain Pete drove six blocks to the street where the Denmans lived. He did not stop there, but drove the route from the house to the elementary school very slowly, sipping coffee and considering how even in one's deep malaise this hot elixir, this first coffee of the day still worked its magic.

He glanced once at the passenger side where his beautiful Panasonic computer sat on the floor in darkness. Pete angled the coffee thermos (also on the floor) away from the computer.

He turned off his wipers. The rain had died to a trickle.

At the school Pete opened his car door, but did not get out right away. He inhaled more coffee and waited for the world to dry off a little. At the first hint of light he got out to survey the schoolyard. He didn't expect to find a .22 or any other weapon lying about, but he meant to give it another try. Twice he circled the remains of the charred building. When he went to sit under the old oak planted by one of the founding fathers of Pennsylvania, Pete was surprised to find he was sitting on a yardstick ground into the dirt. It was a cracked yardstick after Pete sat on it. Nonetheless, he held it up as if it were a divining rod. He touched the squared off end. Paint. Just what was found embedded at the back of Theresa's scalp. Who exactly was on the premises that night?

"I'm taking it to the lab to check for fingerprints," Pete said, speaking to Hal from his car phone. "Whoever whacked Theresa on the head acted out of impulse or fear. A yardstick is not the weapon you choose to do serious pre-meditated damage."

"Good work," said Hal. "What about Mrs. Waters' gunshot wound?"

"Either the guy wasn't much of a shot or he was of two minds about killing her."

Hal was excited. "Could be we're talking about someone with ambivalent rage. Did you consider that angle?"

"Yes, Sir. You know what, I am not going directly to the lab. Got to make a house call first. I'll check in later."

"Wait. Can I ask you something?" said the detective. "Why are you so offended by me calling you the B word?"

Pete laughed. "Oh that. Boy scout. It has nothing to do with being offended. It has everything to do with how I see myself. My Eagle Scout days are long gone."

Hal was perplexed. "Okay Myrick. Whatever. Now, when you go in for your house call, don't forget to take the laptop. Good for fast interviewing."

"Sir, it's a lot of bother worrying about this machine. Think of the jelly donut quotient, the spilled soda or coffee. You can't guess at the messes we officers in the field make."

After the Noah's Ark performance, Callie and Mary met at the Jolly Logger. "Newton and I, we used to live on the same street," she told Mary. "Newton had a treefort. We spent a lot of time fixing it up, rebuilding parts of it. Before my first visit he had wrapped pine boughs around the boards he knew I'd be sitting on. He was so thoughtful that way." Callie felt unaccountably sad. "We liked being together, we couldn't stop talking to each other."

Mary flicked her cigarette on the saucer at her elbow. "Hey Cal, don't. Not if it makes you feel lousy."

"You asked me about Newton –" Callie was silent. The day he trapped the bear cub and she saw it die slowly she did not go to school. She sequestered herself in the treefort until nightfall, when it began to rain. She took the shortcut home through Newton's backyard, stopping once at the Denmans' clothesline. All that laundry getting soaked, she thought. Newton's ma must have forgotten to bring it in. There's Nat's and Newt's shirts, his ma's dresses, his pa's things, and George – he's the tallest – his long pants are dancing like there's no tomorrow.

Callie had hurt so much she wanted to feel nothing but the cold rain on her lips and eyes. At home she leaned out her bedroom window and shook her shoulders, not thinking anything in particular, not of the bear cub, or of the Denmans and the way their very souls seemed to hang from a clothesline. That night the Denman family clothes were bandied about, the dark blues, off-whites, peach yellows, and corals; gorgeous, blowing upward and downward. They clung to the line, to that which pinched and pinned them, all in a row. Gorgeous, when the rain cleared and they whipped dry in the dark wind.

"You can tell me about Newton another time," Mary was saying. She leaned out of the booth. "What about an ashtray over here!" The waitress brought two clean ashtrays and a cheese sandwich with chips and pickles for Callie. Mary had not ordered yet.

The forest ranger tapped her water glass. "I'm going to forget about him." She handed Will over to Mary so that she could eat. Finishing half her sandwich, she said, "I'll tell you what I've decided. I don't want to leave Will again, not for a long time. Don't know what made me go help Cameron out with the Noah's Ark show."

"It couldn't have been that it was important to you," Mary said with obvious sarcasm. Then, in earnest, "They needed your help. You used to love that church."

Callie was evasive. "What happened to my cup of juice? Do you have to smoke when you're holding my baby?"

Mary put out the cigarette, but not before one last puff, carefully blowing away from Will, hunched in her arms and staring up at the blue-gray swirl that came out of his aunt's mouth. "We're getting jolly now," Mary said, meaning that the Inn was filling up. She had her eye on two tall men hustling in the door. "Haven't seen those two before," she murmured.

"Where's our waitress?" Callie said. "I'm going up to the bar to get my drink." Mary nodded.

Callie called to the bartender she knew. "Hello-o-o Junior. Can you get me a cup of tea?"

"I'm swamped. Ask Malcolm, he's the new guy." Callie sat down to yell her order at Malcolm. One of the men sitting to her left was getting rowdy. "All we gotta do is ask, Nat boy," he said to the person next to him. "Somebody'll know how to get to Blue Quarry."

"What I can get you?" Malcolm, the new bartender smiled at Callie. But she hadn't heard him. Who were those two guys, and why did they want to know how to get to Blue Quarry?

She thought of Newton's campsite.

"Hell, nobody goes up that way," volunteered a guy sitting next to the two strangers. Callie recognized Vernon Vale's voice. "The Quarry is clear up over Lookout Holler. Pretty place, the Lookout. I haven't been up that way in an awful long time," Vernon said, a little wistfully. "You can see straight down into the saddle where we folks sit now. Our town here, I mean."

"What'll it be?" the new bartender repeated to Callie.

"Cup of tea, please." She strained to hear what the two men were saying about Blue Quarry.

"I don't think we have tea. How about a coke? A beer?"

"I believe you do have tea."

"Get the lady what she wants," called Junior from half way down the bar. At this, one of the two men at Callie's left, the slightly shorter one, turned to look at her. She revolved her bar stool so that he couldn't see her face. Could it be Natty Denman? She had gotten a quick glimpse. Same nose and bumpy teeth that she remembered. Then again, she hadn't seen him in probably twenty years. Maybe it wasn't Nat.

"I'm sure that Lookout Pass is mighty nice," Nat said politely to Vernon. "But what my brother and I were wondering is how do you get to Blue Quarry?"

"Like I said, nobody goes up there much. People say there's peculiar voices what live in the woods up there. Some bear spirit. Kind of haunted, you could say. I myself don't believe it. Just the wind bouncing off the quarry walls, I expect." Vernon looked for a reaction in the two men. "Course if you're determined, what you gotta do is find Hairpin, that's the old switchback trail socked up in the pine stand above the Lookout. Leads right to the quarry, but it's grown over in parts. Been my experience you can lose that trail easy."

"If Newt's up there, we'll find him," the larger man said. Callie saw Nat slide a foot over and smash down on his brother's boot. But it was too late for secret signals. Callie knew who this pair was.

Natty Denman glowered at George, and then at the two empty shot glasses at his big brother's elbow.

Suddenly Callie remembered Vernon. Had he heard, too, where Newton was hiding out? She leaned out from her barstool to check his face. Damn it, he was already gone.

"I never saw Vernon leave a drink before," Junior said, picking up the full beer. "Didn't even take a sip."

"I'll take it," George offered. Callie looked hard at him, as if trying to remember something. Then she left the bar. Nat picked up Callie's untouched tea, and set it down in front of George. "This is all you get."

At the booth, Callie said to Mary, "I'm going home." She held out her arms for Will.

"It seems like we just got here," Mary said grudgingly. "I didn't even get to tell you how I tripped Jack Marsh after the show. He was tearing after your Newton," she said with perverse emphasis. "Sorry. Not your Newton anymore, right?"

Callie turned on her heels. Mary frowned after her. A minute later and she had nabbed a waitress. Mary wanted tacos with hot sauce, and almost every condiment in the kitchen of the Jolly Logger. She gave her order: "Don't hold back, give me the works."

Chapter TWENTY-FIVE

Forget you saw those Denman boys, Callie told herself, walking very fast towards her apartment. Mind your own business and let Newton take care of himself. Speaking of business, what about diapers for Will, now there's a practical thought.

Into Spence's Grill and Grocery she went, marching straight for where the Pampers lived. Coming out of the last aisle with Will and two big boxes of paper diapers in her arms, she saw Jack and Vernon at the counter. Automatically she hugged Will closer and closed her eyes. Callie wished she could close her ears, as well. Jack was talking bullets, making sure Spence got down the right ones to fit his Ruger.

Callie wrapped Will's blanket high around his head so that he was nearly concealed. Perhaps if they stood like statues, Jack would never notice them. And better, she wouldn't have the slightest idea why he had bought the bullets. She wouldn't have this clammy throb in her breast.

"Eavesdropping again?"

She opened her eyes.

"I remember the last time." Jack fixed his gaze above the bundle in her arms. "November, I think. You raced out of here and drove your friend Denman to some safe hole in the woods. Is that about right?" Will squirmed in her arms.

She loosened her tight grip on him. "All right, no more eavesdropping. But I want to know what you're doing. Tell me you're not going after Newton."

"Sorry, you lose." He turned to go.

"No!" she grabbed his hand, dropping the boxes with pictures of the perfect baby on the cover panels. Will started to cry.

Jack's gaze slid down and met the baby's face. Shock – and then regret – overtook him.

Timidly, Callie held out Will. She caught the change in Jack's countenance. She softened. As for Will, he peered up at the strange man and wailed. Jack directed his attention to Callie. "I'm going to find Denman. Make sure he learns that he can't get away with what he's done."

Vernon added solemnly, "Kind of a posse, we got us, Callie." He turned to Marsh. "Tell her to quit. Can't stand it when a woman looks at me like I'm low dog."

"Don't flatter yourself," Callie said. She rocked the still wailing Will.

Vernon perked up. "Here she is, part of the team."

Officer Shawl had come into the store. She waved at Jack. "I've gotten the go ahead," she said, referring to her clearance to find and arrest Newton.

"Hey Callie. Didn't see you at first. How's that sweet baby?" Cameron twiddled Will's toe and ignored his screams. "Jack tells me you know this Denman guy."

Callie nodded dumbly. She picked up her boxes and walked slowly to the counter.

Cameron Shawl watched the ranger's shoulders slump. She had a strong urge to apologize for her own involvement in this posse, though she had no good reason for doing so. "I'm not thrilled about this wild goose chase, but Jack, he made quite an appeal to the Lieutenant, so I'll go for a look at the mug shots we've got, and then find this guy, see if his face matches up."

"Callie knows the mountain inside out," Jack said nonchalantly. "Maybe she'll help us."

"I won't be a part of your manhunt," Callie hissed, as she put down a twenty dollar bill on the counter for the diapers. Cameron looked at her oddly and the ranger found she couldn't meet her eye. Instead, she walked casually out the door. Then, with Will and boxes banging at her chest, she raced the three blocks to the Jolly Logger.

Cameron turned to Jack. "I didn't get a chance to mention, we've got one more on board for this outing. He wants to take his own car, though. He'll bring up the rear."

"Who do you mean?"

"State trooper by the name of Pete Myrick. He called us this morning to say that Denman was his man. Accused of the crimes in Littlecomb, as you know. That's Myrick's jurisdiction. He should be in Tuscatanning any time now."

In Littlecomb, Pete was on his way to Ralph Water's house. The all-night rainstorm had made the world preternaturally bright, and Water's fieldstone house with the swing set and jungle gym out front looked as if it had been polished by a gem specialist. Pete stepped out of the car and onto the gravelly drive. Computer in hand and gazing for a second at the intense blue sky, Pete lost his footing. He did not go all the way down, but the laptop shot forward into a watery and oil-skimmed pot hole. The machine gurgled pathetically.

The state trooper retrieved the computer and as quick as he could got out his manual. He read aloud: "*Water resistant, not waterproof.* Sorry, Hal man, I tried to tell you."

"Tell you what?" came a small voice from down the drive.

"Well hello Allison." Pete was happy to see the child. He promptly forgot his computer woes.

"Nobody's here, not even my granddad." She headed for the house. "He went to the gym with Honey."

"Your dog."

"Granddad takes her everywhere he goes. Do you think Honey runs in place on the walk master?" She giggled.

"Should you be here alone?"

Allison shrugged. "I have his number and my mommy's, even though she's very far away. Can you come in? I never got to show you how I can read."

"I'd like that." Pete set the computer down on the picnic table. He put away his search warrant and followed her inside. They went upstairs and into a small sitting room. He was surprised when she kept going, opening double glass doors at the far side of the room. "I keep all my books in here."

Pete had noticed this extension one day when he stood in the yard below, and considered whether it might be a conservatory. The room was all windows, a place designed to let in maximum light.

"My granddad is a builder and he put this extra room on himself. It's my playroom." She went to the bookcase and lifted down a heavy edition of Mother Goose Rhymes. Arranging herself and several stuffed animals on pillows in the colors of a sunrise, she began to read.

"Four and twenty blackbirds baked in a pie."

Pete noticed a stack of painted canvasses against the wall.

"When the pie was opened the birds began to sing." Allison glanced at Pete mischievously. Then she was on her feet, jumping up and down, flapping her wings.

Hanging above the canvasses was a photograph of Theresa painting outdoors, a box of watercolors at her side. The picture was in a cheap frame. No glass.

"Was this always a playroom?" Pete asked.

"Don't interrupt," said the little girl, who had returned to her pillow and was finishing up the rhyme. "I'm sorry." While listening he walked over to a large flat bed set of drawers. He glanced at some unused paper in the middle drawer. A stamp on the paper read: Finest Cold Press Paper, made in Paris. Theresa's watercolors filled every other drawer. No surprises there. He toyed with the idea of pulling out some of the watercolors, but got distracted by Allison.

"Grandma told me –" She looked sad.

"You must miss her," said Pete kindly. "She loved you very much, and you should be proud of her. She was a fine painter."

"I know that! This was her studio." The excitable Allison was again jumping up and down. "Jack be nimble. Jack be quick. Jack jump over the candlestick." As both feet landed hard, the photograph of Theresa fell to the floor.

Pete stared incredulously. Maybe he was mistaken. It was, after all, only a dull hole in the wall. He went over for a closer look. He was not mistaken. It was a bullet hole made by a .22 caliber handgun, the same kind of weapon that had grazed Theresa's head. He smoothed his finger over the depression. Ralph had to have fired from across the room. There was residue, but no huge powder blast.

The state trooper hung the photograph back on the wall, covering the bullet hole. He turned to the canvasses, picking up one after another. Over half in the stack had been slashed by a knife.

Pete remembered the 'post-it' he'd found: *How could you ruin my art. You made me cry.*

Allison sat still, much subdued by the sight of the paintings. She turned to Pete. "All of them are stabbed in the heart."

Pete patted the little girl's head, unsure what to say.

She leapt up and clung to him. "I miss my grandma. I miss my mommy." Pete crouched beside her. "You know what, I think you should be with her. Listen, Allie, we can drive out to the Police Barracks and call your mommy at once."

"I want my mommy."

"I know." Pete stroked her head as she clutched his other arm. "Hey, would you like to see something very neat? "

She looked doubtful.

"This is probably the most special thing I own. I've had it a long time."

She was interested.

He felt in his pocket. Pete hung on to the object for a split second, and then he released it into her small palm. It was his glass vial with two gold nuggets.

"For me?"

"Sure, keep it. Solid gold, for you."

Allison was radiant as Pete walked her to the stairs.

"Are you in a hurry?" she whispered. "Because if you are, we can jump down two steps at a time."

Pete smiled. "We are in a very big hurry."

Returning to the Jolly Logger, Callie found her cousin with sour cream on her face.

"What's this, you here again?" Mary took a last bite of her messy taco. Callie looked past her to the bar. Natty and George were still there. Good, she thought, sliding into the booth across from her cousin. "I have to warn Newton."

"I guess you haven't sworn him off, after all."

"There's a posse forming. They mean to find him."

Mary's eyes widened. "Now?"

"Would you watch Will for me so I can go up mountain? I want to take Newton's brothers with me. They're sitting over there at the bar. Those two, in the red checkered caps." She lifted her hair, twirling it into a loose knot. "Newton, he's been charged with two terrible crimes. Let's see, how do I begin?"

"Save it for later," Mary said. "Just hand me that intelligent baby, and get moving."

Callie smiled. "Be back in a sec," she said, forgetting to hand over Will. She went to the bar where Nat and George were curled around their stools. There was no one else, really, for her to turn to. Not a soul in Tuscatanning knew about Newton and the strange trail he had followed to Grandmother Mountain. And hadn't Newton made a point of proclaiming the brothers' loyalty to him when she timidly suggested otherwise? Surely he knew these two better than she. Big galoots, he had called them, fondly. Straight off she told Natty and George that Jack Marsh and some officers were after their youngest brother. That part seemed easy. The two reacted in a strange, almost hypnotized manner, staring at their feet, nodding at whatever she said. It took her longer to explain her connection to Newton. They had a hard time seeing that she was Callie Major from their childhood days in Littlecomb and that she had a vested interest in Newton as a friend. Then George remembered the tea she had ordered at the bar.

"Didn't you drink tea with a lot of milk in it when you were a kid?"

Callie smiled. "That would have been calico tea."

"Yup, that's what you liked to have when you were at our house." He looked at Natty for verification.

"I thought it was chocolate milk," Natty said distrustfully. "Is that Newt's baby?" He looked Callie and Will over as if they were vagrant gypsies.

"Listen," Callie pleaded. "I can't give you my life history now. Do you want to help your brother?"

George stood up valiantly. "Damn right. He's our Newt. Come on, Natty, do you hear what she's saying?"

"I heard," Nat said evenly.

The brothers glanced at one another, then followed Callie over to her booth. She nodded at her cousin, signaling that the two Denmans had agreed to help. So far so good. But when Mary stood up and opened her arms to take Will, Callie blanched. She found that she could not detach her fingers from his small form.

She saw the Denman brothers peering at her. "I've changed my mind," she said to Mary. "Something could happen to me on that mountain. Something could happen to Will."

Mary put a hand on Callie's shoulder and shook her gently. "For the next fifteen years do you plan to stay locked inside your apartment, keeping Will safe?"

"My mother didn't stay home with me," Callie said, her voice breaking. "She fell from a scaffold when I was two weeks old. She was on a job. She wasn't careful."

"How do you know that?" said Mary warmly. "You've had to invent her. What happened was an accident. Winoshca told me that as a house painter your mother took all precautions. She was careful. Maybe she had to go to work, to take care of you the best way she knew. Maybe she had no choice."

Callie buried her face on Mary's shoulder. She held on to Will. Mary spoke in a low and fierce voice. "Are you your mother? People do not, categorically, turn into their own mothers. Look at me. Winoshca and I couldn't be more different," she said wistfully.

"Are they screwy, or what?" whispered Natty to his brother. But George was transfixed. He had followed the conversation, shaking his head yes, then no. He stared at Callie, as if seeing her for the first time.

The forest ranger handed Will over to Mary. "This is harder than you think," she said to her cousin.

Callie made a move towards the door, then hesitated. Mary was talking to Will. "I wonder if your mother has told you about porcupines yet. Your great aunt used to make beautiful necklaces and earrings from their quills. Thing is, she never killed one to do her work. She used road-kill porcupines, the ones smushed by cars going too fast. And guess what I thought a porcupine was called when I was little? Oooooooshy-Gooooooshy. Yeah, that's exactly what they looked like, too. Poor old road-kills. Poor old Oooooooshy-Gooooooshy. Here's part of him, right here." She fingered one of her delicate white and brown quill earrings.

Callie shook her head to disguise a smile. "These are gruesome stories you're telling my son."

"Get out of here. Go do what you have to for Newton. Tell him I'm rooting for the sandman with the dusty truck."

But Mary's cousin had something else to say. "I guess I have no right to judge my mother. No right at all, given my own history." Callie stood with head tilted and her chin cradled in the palm of her hand. "Remember that other man I mentioned? My connection with him all but ruined my life. For my mistake, my beloved child got killed. It was bizarre. It was horrible."

Mary looked at the baby in her arms. "What are you saying? *This* is your first child." She was astounded.

"No. Will is my second chance."

"Jack knows my Jeep. What about we take your car?" Callie said to the Denman brothers when they were out in the parking lot.

"Sure, no problem," George said. "I have a truck. It's over there, back of the bar.

Natty shrugged. "We got our hounds with us so we have to take George's truck. Hey, you all hear about the fugitive hiding in the hills of Somerset? The police got out all their gadgetry. They had motion detectors, heat sensors, special night vision glasses. Those gadgets didn't help for nothing."

"What do you mean?" George lit a cigarette.

"Take that motion detector; it can't tell a cow from a man from a fox. Yeah, that guy's probably clear to Ohio by now. Too bad they didn't use a few snitches and some hounds. They would have caught him by now."

"Forget that guy. It's your brother we have to worry about," Callie said. She could see and hear the dogs as they went towards the truck. She wondered what kind of hunting they had in mind.

The three of them started off, Nat driving. Right away, George said, "Pit stop!"

Nat sighed. "Too many fucking beers. Didn't I tell you?"

"There's nothing open at this end of town," Callie said.

"What about in there? Looks good enough," George pointed at the Good Shepherd Church coming up on their right. Natty pulled into the parking lot, and George jumped out.

Nat closed his eyes, and Callie, feeling tense, got out of the truck. In the churchyard she walked over to the dogwood. Sitting there under her favorite tree, Callie forgot to worry about what could happen up on the mountain tonight. She was watching the stars and thinking about the beginning of things. From her own tribe she knew the Seneca story of Sky Woman. She had read others, too, and was especially drawn to the Navajo view of the creation. The thing was, there were so many stories afoot in the world, all of them saying approximately the same thing. Take what happened to Adam and Eve. Their adventures might not seem to have anything in common with the Navajo legend of First Woman, but look again.

First Woman was assigned the job of placing the stars in the sky in a particular order. This order gave direction to the people on Earth. All they had to do to live in harmony was to read the laws spelled across the sky. Placing the stars was a long, hard job. But along came Coyote, who insisted on helping First Woman. Soon he grew impatient with the work. He grabbed the sack of stars and emptied them willy-nilly in the sky. Afterwards chaos reigned. Of course. People knew these things. It was deeper than any one religion. Out of the garden and into explosive, disorderly life. Callie preferred to read about First Woman. She was uncomfortable reading about Adam and Eve because this story involved an evil snake. Callie hated snakes. She could not stand to see one, even on the written page.

Chapter TWENTY-SIX

The earth eased up under his boot and Newton felt the month of May in every step he took. The change in ground had brought something else too. Good tracks for him to follow. This was important for he had seen where the bear was feeding that morning, and then lost valuable time by going into Tuscatanning to find Callie. A lot of good that did, Newton thought bitterly. That trip had turned out all wrong. Himself as an animal on the ark – had he done the right thing by going aboard as Callie instructed? And that awful moment at the play's close with the forest cop chasing after him. Newton leaned against a thick understory of brush. He felt humiliated, running, hiding in a moose costume, and Callie, he knew she didn't trust him. But why? It didn't seem fair, what had he done after all? Then, wiping his nose, he realized he was sniffling like a child.

Shocked at the tears, afraid of them, he stopped in his own tracks beside a thorny wall of vine and leaf. He stood fuming at his weakness. Newton turned to the brush, and punched his fist into the wiry vines. He looked at the clean dark tunnel his fist had made, and then at his hand where the knuckles were dotted with pinpoints of blood.

Wasn't the bear close by? And tiring too; he'd known this for a month. Seen the signs in the way she no longer came to the same feeding places from five different directions, just to baffle him. No, the tracks had shown she was coming directly to the animal scraps lately. He decided she was growing weary and careless.

Newton checked his cartridges, cleaned the Leupold scope on his Remington, readjusted its shoulder strap and set off following the tracks up mountain. This was better than waiting in the tree or ground stand, he thought. This was the best kind of hunting. No bait stations. Just your own slow sedulous stalking, your cautious step through the spring glades. Newton knew that the ground he walked – no leaf crackle or ice crunch as in fall and winter – was now his silent friend.

In Jack Marsh's old Land Rover, three diligent officers, two from the State Park, and one Vernon Vale drove up the mountain. Following at a comfortable distance was Pete Myrick in his unmarked Crown Victoria.

Vernon was chattering, pleased that he was the one who remembered best how to get to Blue Quarry. "You have to trust Jack and me on this one," he said to Bud, who sat in the back next to Officer Cameron Shawl. "It was Denman we saw in that Noah Play. I myself am Jack's witness for the fact."

Bud pulled out a handkerchief and rubbed each thick lens on his glasses without taking them off. "Why would this woodsman, this foul hunter of yours, decide to go high-stepping in a church play?"

Jack touched his chin where he had fallen near the exit of The Good Shepherd. "I can't say what devious plan he had."

His eyes were a stony blue as he thought of Callie, how maybe she had invited Denman to come be in the Noah play, and then afterwards, meet with her privately.

"Dressed as a moose!" Jack squawked involuntarily. He glanced at Bud nervously, then dropped his eyes to the double white line shivering up the highway.

"You could tell he was crazy," Vernon said. "Planning to do something awful. Shoot people at the church, probably. Only then he got an eyeful of me and Jack there in the audience, and chickened out."

Bud sighed, lifted his binoculars off his chest and began cleaning these lenses.

"You could tell he was a mad man?" Officer Shawl asked skeptically.

"Oh yeah," Vernon said. "Mason, you were there at the church. Did you get a load of his disguise? Antlers crooked on his head, nose upside down, costume hiked up to his hips. Gawd, it looked like he was wearing the remains of some real moose someone forgot to salt."

"Pretty offal," Bud chuckled.

"That's what I said," Vernon nodded. "Awful crazy."

Cameron yanked her cramped elbow out from under a back pack between Bud and herself. "How much farther to the cart road?" she asked with deliberate patience.

"Three quarters of a mile," Vernon said, glancing back at Bud Mason as he returned the lens caps to his field glasses. "What kind of gun you bring?" he asked the superintendent.

"Don't own one," Bud said. "All I need is to see clearly." The park superintendent patted his night vision binoculars that he liked to think were up to date, state of the art. In fact, they were army surplus, a special buy he and his wife Ginette got. They had been avid birders who often went out for nocturnal sightings.

Vernon laughed. "You are something else! Whoaaa Jack-buddy, what's that climbing the next hill?" Vernon leaned forward over the front seat, pointing towards a pickup truck that had just come into view.

"Something is jumping like hell in the back of that vehicle," Marsh said, squinting to make out the truck clearly."

Bud lifted his binoculars. "Hounds. Better than a half-dozen of them."

"I guess someone else besides us is planning on a hunt today," Jack said.

Bud kept his eyes on the hounds. "No hunting on our part. We are going to go talk to this man, and hand him over to Trooper Myrick if it turns out he is who Marsh thinks he is. That's all. Just talk. Am I right, Deacon?"

"That's *Officer*, if you don't mind." Then, softening, "You're right. No violence. Marsh understands," she said, just so Jack would hear it again. "We want to bring him in on probable cause." She craned her neck to make sure Pete's car was still behind them. Cameron was thinking about her brief meeting with the state trooper before they set out for Grandmother Mountain.

"So your main interest is finding your murderer and arsonist up on the mountain?" she had asked him.

"Finding my suspect," said Pete "is one of the main objectives." Then he paused, as if, Cameron felt, he was deciding whether to trust her. "It might also turn out," he had said quickly, "that I am going up the mountain to prevent my suspect from being murdered."

Jack stepped on the accelerator. "Let's see if I can't catch that pickup. I got a funny feeling about it, want to see where it's headed."

"Hey, not so fast," yelled Shawl, sighting the speedometer. The Land Rover crested the hill at eighty miles an hour. Jack expected to see the pick-up directly in front of him.

"What the hell?" Jack craned his head.

Everyone screened the road but there was no truck in sight. "Got to be over the next hill," Jack said. "I didn't think a truck full of hounds could fly like that." He hit the gas pedal harder. "We'll find out in a minute. You didn't catch anything with those glasses, did you?" He caught Bud in the mirror lowering his binoculars.

"Just some springtime color," Bud answered.

Through the blind of new growth in a roadside thicket, Callie watched the Land Rover and Crown Victoria tear up the highway. "It's Jack's Rover, all right," she said. "But who's in that other car?"

George stepped out from behind a beech tree. "We fooled them. Got to hand it to you, lady. Must be your Indian blood that knew to turn off into this track of vines."

"Get down," Callie ordered. "Wait until the Rover's over the next hill."

They had pulled off the road in such haste that the key was still in the ignition, the radio blaring. Some guy on a talk show was ranting about the millennium even though it was four years away.

"Listen to that," said George. "When it comes, the whole world is going get sucked into one of them black holes of the universe."

"Let me turn it off for you," said Callie, walking over to the truck. "Pay attention to the things close by. Pay attention to nature." She was thinking about the bear. "She'll tell you more than that garbage."

No one said a word for a few minutes, except the hounds who were surprised by the jolt into the bushes. They whined softly, wondering whether to leap out of the truck, even though they'd been given no order to do so.

Natty checked on the animals. "Good boys," he said. Then, in a surly voice: "Look at your truck, George." Nat hopped around to the hood. "All scratched up, and half buried too."

"Oh God, that's nasty looking," George moaned. He lit a cigarette.

"No time for your smokes," Callie said, plunging into the woods beside the thicket. "We've got to move if we want to get Newton out of here before Jack and his crew show up at the Quarry."

"Where you taking us? This is not a trail," Nat called, running at the heels of his dogs, George mixed in with them, and Callie in the lead.

Several minutes later she stopped to catch her breath, and to search her pockets for a rubber band to keep her hair from catching in the branches. "Jack will be at the cart road by now. They'll have to park in the small lot there for hikers. Then they'll head towards Lookout Pass. If we're lucky it'll take them over an hour. As for us, we'll just cut through the woods and get to the quarry first. But it's a hike. About three and a half miles," she said, estimating wildly because she had not come from this direction before. She was still panting some. Clearly she was not back to pre-baby fitness.

Two of the hounds who had been sniffing the ground, waiting for George or Natty to give them the go ahead, suddenly yelped into action. Callie swung around following their point. A rusty colored fox dove into a bank burrow off to her right.

"Nice vixen," George smiled. "Wouldn't I like to give her chase." He winked at Nat, who said, "Wait'll our dogs get scent of this walloping bear Newt's been after all these months."

Callie did a double take. So Newton had said something to them about his hunting these last months. What else had he shared with his brothers, but not with her?

"There won't be any bear," she said coolly.

"Not the way we've been cracking through the brush," George said sadly.

Nat smiled. "I'll wager there *will* be a bear, and I aim to get him."

Callie, keeping her eye on a cedar waxwing in a tree above the bank burrow, spoke gently. "It's a her. Now let's get going." She glanced over her shoulder and saw the bird eating rose hips, some of them spilling down the breeze to the forest floor. She tried to remember where the wild roses lived.

Nat kept up an annoying banter as they hiked. "Didn't we tell you, me and George are going to help Newton bring down that bear."

"Does he know this?"

Nat looked straight ahead.

"Why are you here?" The sight of the fox had brought back an unmerciful memory. "I know it has to do with Newton."

"We just want to catch him, same as you." Nat smiled.

"Catch him? It's a rescue that we're up to," Callie said, panicking. What pranksters and bullies they were when she was young. There was the day Nat threw a bloody, skinned fox in her face. George had laughed, and Newton, where was he but weakly watching, distraught but too small to defend her.

Could the arson at Littlecomb Elementary have been a prank set up by these two? What about Mrs. Waters. Maybe she was simply taking a walk in the wrong area. There by mistake.

Tired of shouting and walking fast, Callie sat down on a log covered with ice blue lichen. One of the hounds, the smallest of the pack, slunk over to Callie. It sniffed at the log she sat on, then ran to George.

Point blank, Callie asked the two men, "Did you guys see Newton the night Theresa Waters died?"

Natty was silent, standoffish as he'd been since first seeing her at the Jolly Logger. George was pushing his fingers through the dog's coat, making it stand up at the back of his neck.

"What about Newton that night?" she asked again.

George had brushed the coat up in a short ruff around the runt's neck. "Hey Natty. Don't he look like a lion? He does look fierce now."

"Newt must have driven himself over to that crummy old school when we were at the Lounge, don't you think, George?"

"Oh yeah," said the older brother. "He was at the school. Lot of people at the school that night. Wish I hadn't been one of them."

Callie stood up, then wished she hadn't. She felt dizzy. "George, you just said you were at the school that night."

Denman stammered. "You heard wrong. I hate that place. Wouldn't go near it with a ten foot pole."

In that instant Callie knew that George and Nat were involved in the crimes. "Gather your dogs," she said to the brothers. "We'll go this way."

Callie walked slowly. She was thinking about what to do. Best not to take these traitors to Newton's home in the woods, but how to get out of it now? They had been useful in giving her cover to ride out here, but there the helpfulness ended. How easily time blots out the bad things in favor of a rosier view. It had been years since she had seen these men, and foolishly, Callie now realized, she expected them to have improved.

She considered out-running George and Nat. She entertained the thought of suddenly ducking into a dense part of the forest, and disappearing on them.

"If you're thinking about ditching us, think again," called out George.

She could practically feel their trained hunting eyes cutting up and down her form as she led the way.

"And don't try leading us some place else," said Nat. "Isn't that right, George? Don't forget, we're the ones with the rifles."

Callie reasoned that if she kept up her slow pace Jack and his group would surely get to Newton's campsite first, and if things worked right their noisy advance would warn him off. He would be gone by the time she and the brothers arrived at his camp. They couldn't do any harm then, and it would give her a chance to find signs of Newton's whereabouts, and get her hands on one of his guns.

Near six o'clock, they stumbled out at the top of Hairpin trail. There before them was Newton's campsite.

George stated the obvious. "He's not here."

"So this is where our little brother's been living," said Nat. "I never would've guessed it. It's way too clean and orderly."

Callie had to agree. She was astonished at how Newton had cut down on his belongings, much of the paraphernalia – extra pots, pans, manuals, papers, junk tools he meant to fix – gone. No tent even, but there was his sleeping bag and the bright red blanket rolled up under a pitch pine, and next to that the old brown pack he sometimes used for bait. She looked out across the deep pool that was exchanging silver and green lights. "There's Blue Quarry," she said.

"Don't look blue to me," George mumbled, speaking for the first time since the confrontation a few miles down the mountain. Callie scanned the campground again. No gun in sight, but her eye picked up something else. There at the foot of the tarpulin pole Newton had rigged to hang clothes out was a plastic lens cap.

"From Bud's camera." She twirled the gray cap in her fingers. "So he came with Jack." It was understandable that he might go with Marsh and yet she felt betrayed. She wondered if Bud knew of her friendship with Newton. God knows what Jack had told him.

"If the posse beat us here," she murmured, "I wonder if they already have Newton," and to herself, – Bud wouldn't let Jack or Vernon take a pot shot at him, would he?

Nat was unimpressed with the discovery of the lens cap. He kicked over Newton's one remaining bucket, and examined his kerosene lantern. Then he picked up the old brown pack Callie saw earlier. "What do you know. This belonged to our daddy," he said waving the trapbag. "I didn't know Newt had it."

"It's his bait bag," Callie said.

"Not any more it ain't." He went through it, tossing out a couple of paperbacks. "What's this?" He pulled out a shiny, black fur, sewn with extraordinary care into a muff with deep hand pockets at either end.

"My lord, I can't scarcely believe it." He grinned irascibly at Callie. "So, he kept it." Nat ran the flat of his hand over the fur, his expression hardening. Then looking straight at Callie, he spat on the muff. "That's what I think of you, and what you done to my brother."

Callie shrank backward a step. Bewildered, she stared at the old token of apology.

"Want it now?" Natty said, stepping near her, holding the muff out under her nose. "Sorry." He jerked it away. "You're too good for it, wasn't that right? Too superior to take the present my brother gave you."

"Hey, let up on her," said the older brother.

"Why should I? She's out to get us, George. Think about it, she don't need us." Nat stepped up to Callie and whisked the muff across her cheek. She stood strong, trying to quash the panic in her chest.

"You used our truck for cover," said Nat. "And now what? You're wanting us out of the way, I bet. Just so you can sneak off with our brother, tear his heart up again."

"Cut it out," she yelled, determined not to break into tears. The sun was dimming and the quarry had turned black. She thought of that swim she had the fall before, the evening Newton spotted her splashing in this pool. She closed her eyes and tried to imagine diving in that cool, wide awake water.

Chapter TWENTY-SEVEN

Callie stood at the bank that rimmed Blue Quarry. She had not expected the brothers to suspect her motives, and now she wondered at theirs.

"Come here quick Nat," George shouted. "Some goliath bear! Yessir, ol' Newt wasn't exaggerating." Kneeling where he had been scuffing with his boots, he took out his buck knife and placed it flat alongside the bear track. "I figure this paw for twelve, thirteen inches. What do you reckon, maybe close to nine hundred pounds?"

"Never heard of a black bear that big," Natty said, bending over his brother for a look. George called to his dogs. "Cooooooom on," he cried musically. "Coooooomere Sneaker, Hardpoint, Fang, Growler. You too, Wag and Whine." He had a name for all the hounds but the runt.

George found a second print in the damp ground, then two more where the bear's hind feet had overstepped the front. The dogs snuffled at the tracks. One or two began to moan softly, their tails straight up. George flashed a grin at his brother. "They got it all right."

"Let's go," Natty said, pitching the furred muff on the ground.

"Hey!" Callie cried. "Is it the bear or Newton you're after?" she asked.

"Cooooooom-on boys, that's it," George crooned to his dogs. He trotted after them into the woods. Natty turned to Callie. "You are a fool, Callie Major. You don't get it. Wherever the bear is, that's where we'll find Newton."

Nat charged after his brother. Callie trudged over to where he had thrown down the muff. She eyed it skeptically, then stared at it and kept on staring until the fur began to swim before her eyes. A few minutes later, and she was running after Natty and George and the hounds, all of them racing up the peak, towards Great Meadow.

Newton walked around the shallow depression, then got down on his hands and knees and pinched a few of the long, fine hairs from the hollow marked with claw scrapes. Mid-way up the Great Meadow and behind a wild rose bush, the bear had dug herself a day bed. Not in use any more, Newton noted. But it was a pretty spot and the bed beckoned. As Newton had no one to answer to in his life on the mountain, he took quick naps whenever he felt like it. He had left the bear tracks in the woods, she wasn't near, so why shouldn't he borrow her habitat?

He didn't sleep. Newton was thinking about the saddest time in his life. It was those nightmarish weeks after the bear cub died. Newton had spent every spare second working on the transformation of the bear skin. Finally came the day it was finished, tanned so perfectly that the leather was soft and pliable. That night Newton went to Callie's house. He was waiting downstairs in her aunt's parlor, a tidy room with dark, secondhand furniture. A tall, gold-painted cross hung on one wall, and on the mantel there was a statue of the Virgin Mary holding an infant Christ. It was a wan Virgin Mary, wearing a washed-out blue robe. Newton thought she looked like a tired angel.

He fidgeted on the sofa. The pillows made him sneeze. Ten or more of them adorned the straight back chairs and the stiff sofa he sat on. Each pillow had an embroidered edging, little flowers that were the work of Aunt Teeny, Callie had told Newton. It was decent work. She couldn't be all that bad. Still, Newton never saw her pay Callie the slightest attention.

He was anxious and excited. Callie had barely spoken to him since the morning the bear was caught in the trap. Newton looked down at the special present he had labored over. The cub had been the perfect size for a muff that would keep Callie's fingers and wrists warm. Newton was proud of his decision to keep the ears intact. They formed a decorative, scalloped border on one side of the muff. Another interesting feature were the bear claws that he sewed on in between the ears. It's a good design; he nodded, looking down at the soft fur in his lap. He smoothed it with his fingertips so that Callie would see its full beauty.

See this token of apology.

This was not the way she saw it. When she came into the room her eyes went directly to the bear cub muff he held out to her, almost as if she had known or smelled it in the house before she came downstairs. Callie's hair was brushed back from her face.

"Callie!" He leapt up with the present in his hands. For a moment her face revealed nothing. Then it registered, and what Newton saw made him shrink inside. He saw that her love for him was gone, clean as if he had with all his skill taken a knife to her face and severed the way she used to hold him with her eyes.

"You don't want this, do you?" The fur drooped in his hand.

She turned away, but Newton could see the profile of her heart shaped face. The small chin quivered and she closed her eyes. It was not a beautiful present at all, he thought. The claws, why did I put them on? The whole thing is hideous. He opened his fingers and the muff slid to the floor.

Callie stared at the black fur humped on the rug. She scooped up the muff. It quivered in her hands and then she tossed it at Newton. He caught it before it hit the rug. "You killed him," she cried. "Assassin!" She covered her mouth with her hands.

When he left her house Newton was wild with remorse. At home he went straight upstairs, speaking to no one. He sat at the edge of his bed and gazed morosely at the handiwork that dangled from his fingers. Then he got up and stuffed the muff in the small brown army pack his father had given him. Newton stored it on a high shelf in the closet.

A few weeks later his puzzlement and dejection had turned to anger and he thought himself made a fool of by this girl who had been his friend, but was certainly no real friend or true love if she could cast him aside so lightly. One day he went to the treefort he and Callie had rebuilt together. The sight of it made him sad. On the ground floor and first landing were some of their things. There was a hacky sack, a deck of cards, a book of matches for their marshmallow and hot dog roasts, a book on the Greeks in the Golden Age, pad of paper, two pencils, four miniature metal race cars, Callie's collection of fairy tales, and a red ribbon he had seen in her hair when she wore a French braid.

He missed her more than he could have imagined. He had to do something concrete, anything to stop the pain.

Newton bagged the articles on the ground floor of the fort and climbed up the rope ladder to the first level. Stacking the belongings together he lit a match and dropped it on the book of matches he had placed on top of the pile. Quickly, the boy swung out on the rope ladder and leapt to the ground. In a daze Newton watched the fort burn. He thought he saw the red ribbon flutter out into the wind, but then again it was hard to see through the smoke. It could have been a scarlet spark.

He hardly noticed as the fire spread. His father and brother George came outside. Even a neighbor showed up, everyone yelling, hauling water, buckets, and a hose. They put the fire out just before it reached the wood shed.

Newton remembered Nat having a field day with the business, saying to their daddy later that night, "Look at how Newt almost burnt down our yard."

He didn't see Callie after that, except in school. Every time Newton got a glimpse of her in the hall his chest constricted and he had to take deep breaths and clear his throat before he could move. She would look at him too, but not for long, not as she had before.

Newton leapt out of the big bear's day bed. A scattered peal of hounds filled the air. They weren't in sight, but seemed to be coming up the ridge and thickets that framed the meadow east of where he stood. Ducking low through the grasses, Newton ran half the length of the meadow to the bottom land. There, he clutched his pounding chest and crouched behind a nurse tree and a fat-girthed oak.

Newton noticed how quick the sun had disappeared. Overhead, the night colors congregated, the sky turning a deep blue that went dark only above the moon. The hounds were still climbing the ridge. *But who is running these dogs and why do they sound so familiar? Not after me, are they? Not unless, stop, don't give your mind a field day.*

It had to be the bear; someone's going after her. No one has a right to get in on her trail now, he thought. She's mine. Since that first marking on the bear tree I've chased her over forty miles. It's me who closed her in on this peak.

Grandmother Mountain was shifting into that time of night when all sounds become particular and sharp. Newton paid little attention to the shudder of wings, maybe an owl leaving a branch high over his head. What the hunter noticed was that the hounds were yelping infrequently, as though they had lost what they were after. Newton stirred from his position at the oak tree, and as he shifted so he heard something else shift footing. He raised his rifle and again something mimicked his move, a kind of swishing in the air, very near. A chill sweat erupted on Newton's back. Before him a tangle of pitch pines distended. Newton saw a silhouette profiled against the trees. The bear. How to be sure? Too dark in these woods. He steadied his rifle, lining it up with the profile of the trees that had moved. Then came a deep rasping growl. Taken by surprise, he swung the Remington to the left. The trees seemed to shrink back into themselves. He waited. Five minutes passed. The only noise was the pack of hounds giving confused cries. They must be going in circles. Newton thought to switch on his flashlight. Then his hand began to shake. There, where no grass grew next to a gnarl of roots the flashlight targeted a fresh bear print.

He hiked a little ways up the ridge and found bear droppings, a still warm, mess of colonial ants and termites. Newton was sure he could her find before the other hunters did. Hadn't she stood right there with him? As this realization sunk in, a cold streak of fear jagged across his chest. Why had she come so near?

The little dog was lagging behind. "Can't you keep up," shouted Ralph Waters. "Look at that full moon. If Theresa were here she would put her hands on her hips and smile at it, probably going on about how beauty was its own truth, or was it the other way around? It was something she got from a poem."

At the turn off to the Elementary School in Littlecomb where he, and Theresa before him, took Honey on evening outings, Ralph stopped. The leash went slack in his hand and he gazed again at the heavens.

"She admired poems by Keats and people like that, but it was nursery rhymes she loved best. Hey Diddle-diddle, the cat and the fiddle, the cow jumped over the moon."

Honey sat back on her haunches, head quirked at her master who had tears in his eyes. Ralph missed Theresa dreadfully, even her idiotic artistic take on the world. Perhaps he had envied her spontaneity. Certainly her capacity for joy rankled. Why did he always feel left out of her world? Why couldn't she have loved him enough?

Ralph Waters scooped Honey up in his arms and held her skyward. "The little dog laughed to see such sport," he recited brightly.

Once home, he went directly upstairs, through the sitting room and into his wife's former art studio. Ralph went directly to the flat bed drawers where his wife stored her pastels, paper, and watercolor paintings. He opened the middle drawer in the file and ran his hand across the textured watercolor paper. He groped deep at the back and pulled out a .22 caliber handgun.

"Here Honey, come to your master," he called out. But the dog had refused to follow Ralph upstairs, and was hiding under a skirted armchair in the den. Ralph stood in the doorway of the former studio. He checked the gun cartridges and closed up the slideback. He wasn't especially knowledgeable about firearms and wanted to be sure he had enough bullets.

"Honey? Honey come at once." He waited another minute. "Be that way," said Ralph, gun in hand as he walked over to the stack of canvasses painted by Theresa. He had thought about this a long time, and began to make plans soon after Theresa was gone. It was important that Allison was not home – he wasn't insensitive, for God's sake – and wasn't it nice happenstance that the moon was full tonight? Perfect for his plan to enter her art.

Chapter TWENTY-EIGHT

Sighting Jack's Rover, Pete parked at the edge of the cart road and had just gotten out when his car phone went off. Pete dove for the call. It was Detective Hal Rendell. "I think we've found the weapon fired at Theresa Waters."

"The .22?" Pete knew there was more. It was Hal's style to leak the big news second.

"It belonged to Ralph Waters, and we found the same kind of bullet that grazed Theresa's head. We found the gun inches from his fingers, and him dead on the floor in his own house. Looks like he put a bullet into his left temple. We found him in the second floor of his home, in what looks like a kid's playroom."

"Allison!" Pete regretted that he had returned the child to her grandfather after taking her to the police station.

"The granddaughter was spared this nastiness. Your attempts at connecting with Wendy Waters paid off, though I noticed she had nothing good to say about you. Anyway, Allison's mother came to get her, and with no protest from Ralph. That was yesterday, right after you left for Tuscatanning."

"Suicide," Pete said. He sat back down heavily in the driver's seat, and stuck one leg out the door. Outside it looked like a circus. There was that loud fellow, Jack Marsh. He was lecturing Vernon Vale. Superintendent Bud Mason, while tightening his boot laces, upbraided Jack for lecturing Vernon. Only Officer

Shawl was quiet, although Pete could see her lips moving. She had a prayer book in her hands, and perhaps she was reciting from it.

"It was weird," Hal said. "Waters seems to have laid out six canvasses on the floor of that play room. They were contiguous to one another and when you walked in the room it looked like one giant picture. Good size paintings, probably three feet tall each, but half of them had been slashed by a bowie knife."

"That would be Ralph's doing, Sir."

"When I got to the house today," the detective said, "there was his six foot frame stretched out on top of those canvasses. Lying flat on his back, can you believe it? As if he was the foreground."

"And the paintings were his background," supplied Pete. "I wonder if one canvas was left intact. It's an oil of a cow jumping over the moon. Used to hang in the living room."

"How did you know?" asked Rendell.

"Theresa wanted to make a book of nursery rhymes. That was her only completed painting for the group. Ralph told me that," mused Pete. "Mr. Waters was actually quite tender when he spoke of it."

Rendell coughed. "This last act of his is a most unusual demonstration of affection."

"That's love for you," said Pete.

The state trooper's conversation was interrupted by shouts from Jack and Vernon. "Come on Myrick. We want to get moving, not much light left."

Pete looked out at the deeply rutted cart road. There was Officer Shawl advancing to his car. "Hal, hang on a minute."

Cameron Shawl stuck her head into the driver seat window. "I've been trying to get a word with you," she said, oblivious to the intrusion of her face, six inches from his. "You need to keep an eye on Jack Marsh. I don't think he's planning on bringing Denman in amicably. Maybe you already know."

"Jack, you say?" It was the Denman brothers he was most worried about. The state trooper covered the phone with his hand. Pete had wormed it out of Betty Denman that Nat and George were on their way to find Newton. But this dope on Jack was news. "What's his stake?"

Shawl turned to see Marsh coming towards the police car. "I'll catch you later."

Pete spoke to Hal. "Sir, I have to go."

"Didn't you hear me," said the detective. "We have the murder weapon, the gun."

"Yes sir, but is that what killed her? Hal, I have to find Newton Denman. We need his help."

Led by Vernon Vale and Jack Marsh, the small band hiked several miles and found Blue Quarry, but no Newton. After trudging behind Jack and Vern another twenty minutes, Bud Mason stated flatly, "What's the plan, Jack, you do have one?"

Vernon added, "It's getting hard to see."

The ranger quickened his pace. "He's got to be up this way."

Into the crown of pines at the top of the mountain he took the group. "Not so dark here," Jack said. And he was right. Where it had been nearly black in the bottomland trees, the mountain peak was bright with moonlight. Blue ropes of light slanted down between the forest pines.

Bud was uneasy. "I don't know how I let you talk me into this expedition. Feels like I was dragooned, me, your boss."

Jack's breath came in stitches. He had heard the hounds and their voices exhilarated him. He laughed softly and said to Bud, "Remember the time you said, 'whatever you do, cover your ass, son.' Guess that's why I worked like the devil to persuade you to come."

Bud frowned. "This wasn't the kind of situation I had in mind."

"Listen to them," said Pete, trying to mark the keening of the hounds.

Officer Shawl was listening. "I say they came from the pickup truck that disappeared off the road."

Vernon caught sight of one of the dogs swinging his head out of a pine stand. It was the one George favored, the black and white runt. "Watch out. Skunk!" shouted Vern.

Everyone laughed, except Jack who was not looking at the runt, but across the woods at a man wearing brown fatigues and a red checkered hunting cap. It was a tall figure with wavy hair. The man leapt between trees, and there was just enough light that Jack caught sight of his face. Instantly he recognized the features he'd seen in the mug shot, in the bar, and in the church play. Jack shook his head. I'll be damned. Didn't figure Denman to show so easy. Maybe he's in with these other hunters.

The police ranger let the others walk on ahead, then slipped into the woods after the hunter. Soon Cameron noticed Jack was gone. She checked for Pete's reaction, but saw that he was otherwise occupied, heading over to Bud in a purposeful way. Officer Shawl decided she would double back and find Jack.

Pete had not seen the mysterious hunter, but he had a good idea who the hounds belonged to. Nat and George Denman have found Blue Quarry, he thought. He listened again. They must be near.

Pete figured it was time to fill Bud in. The park superintendent listened to a short version of the night of the crimes, and of the possible motive George and Nat had for coming to Grandmother Mountain.

"I hope I'm wrong, but rancor runs deep in this family, and these brothers are desperate. They want Newton out of the way." Not that they would admit to themselves that they might take a potshot at Newton, thought Pete. They're too cowardly and dishonest for that.

"That switches the picture around," Bud said. "Do we go after this Nat and George instead?"

Pete did not answer right away. He was thinking about his last visit with Betty, how she had confirmed George's resentment towards Littlecomb Elementary School. She admitted it had been brewing for years, beginning with his antipathy for his first grade teacher, Miss Block. The meeting with Elijah had unlocked a door for Pete. The old proprietor was a witness to the brothers' debate on returning home for their gear, which in turn supplied Pete with the reason – the forgotten road beers – that would send Nat and George back towards the Lounge, passing the schoolhouse near ten thirty, just fifteen minutes before the building burst into flame. Pete smiled at the thought of Elijah's cogitations. As for his trip to see Betty Denman, the best part of that ordeal was the appearance of Spoons.

Pete had been grilling Mrs. Denman for the umpteenth time. "So you are pretty sure your sons, George and Nat did not return home after they left the house at seven p.m. on the night Theresa died."

"I was at Bingo, told you that. When I got home there was not one sign those boys had been in this house. And a mother will notice these things, right down to a stray sock on the stairs, or the juice glass that George favors and will leave out. I tell you, there was nothing."

It was then that Spoons entered the conversation. Betty had married his son Joe and was the only woman left in the family so he called her daughter. "Daughter, I have tried not to interfere, but when you talk of signs I just can't stand it. The sign is that Newton needs help. The signs were all over the house that George and Natty did come home that night. Course they did. They was roaring drunk. I expect they don't remember talking to their old grandpa. That's why I never pushed the point with them or anybody else. Figured they plain didn't remember where they were or how they told me just what to do with Newt's jacket."

"The blue and white jacket?" Pete was animated. "Where is it, man?"

"I tell you those boys was in a blackout. They don't know that night happened. Me too. No liquor in me, though. I just start forgetting." Spoons began to work his mouth and soon it closed up like a bloom at nighttime. No amount of prying would get old Mr. Denman to speak again that day.

But no matter. For Pete, the case was beginning to come clear. He felt confident on his journey out to Tuscatanning, though anxious to warn Newton. Nat and George had a motive to keep their brother quiet. Now on the mountain, it was different. The uncertainties loomed.

Pete turned to Bud. "No switch arounds. We'll follow the original plan. Just be on the lookout for the older brothers." He examined the fancy motion detector he was carrying. Courtesy of Detective Hal Rendell. "This gadget isn't going to do me any good."

"Sure it will. I'll tell you what." Bud touched the big pocket on his khaki vest. "I've got the upgrade on a dandy pair of night vision goggles here. You won't see me throwing them away."

Pete wore a bemused smile. "Did you read about the fugitive north of here? The police had every new electronic gimmick in the book. Nothing worked. They finally caught him with basic detective work and good bloodhounds." Pete held out the motion detecting device. "See, it doesn't even have a nose."

Bud laughed. "You mean you aren't going to put all your eggs in the basket of advanced technology?" He walked on ahead. "I'm going to follow Cameron's track. I think she's gone after Marsh."

"I don't want to trust that basket," Pete shouted after him, surprised at his strong feelings. "The old and the new, I'm stuck between them." His voice dropped. "I don't see which way to go."

Chapter TWENTY-NINE

Looking like Lady Liberty, Callie stood sentinel on the knobby terrain at the brow of Grandmother Mountain. She had never been to see that noble Mother America, the Statue of Liberty in New York Harbor, and certainly her resemblance to her was not on her mind as she faced Great Meadow, its steep expanse open but for a wild rose bush a third of the way downhill.

Callie was watching for Newton, or for the bear. Both needed protecting tonight. She was feeling calm and smooth inside, the way people do after walking a long distance. Newton, my heart is listening to yours, she thought. I am not Artemis. Please believe that. I was as guilty as other hunters when I was a child at the treefort pretending to hunt the hunters. It was a false game. I wish I could tell you that I've thrown down my arrows.

She found her second wind. The ranger was preternaturally alert.

It was in this state that Callie saw her loping gracefully up the outer edge of the wood. It was odd how quiet she had come out of the forest. Under the moonlight, her back shimmered like coffee with cream. The ranger caught her breath but was not surprised to see that the bear had outsmarted the hounds. A short distance from Callie a man burst from the woods. It was Vernon Vale and he was standing some twenty yards from the bear. He raised his shotgun. Callie could scarcely believe that the mighty creature who could hear better than a whole flock of men paid the hunter no heed. The bear bounded a few steps out onto the brow of the meadow, her nose lifted to the night air. Callie had a momentary flash that the big animal did not give a hoot that Vernon was there. She was enjoying her passage through the short, plaited grass. She luxuriated in the scent of wafting roses.

Callie screamed just before the gun went off. The bear slumped. But no sooner had the ranger recovered her wits than the animal heaved to her feet. She growled in pain and cantered for the woods. Before Vernon had her in line for a second shot, she had turned into the crown of pines.

Callie swung around, panicked. The pitch pines seemed to sway, she heard their branches knocking. No wind, though. Was it the old Grandmother herself shaking her head, bent on repelling this nightmare from her woods? Callie ran down a path to an old day bed the bear had once made for herself.

There was no bear nursing her wound at the shallow bed, though someone had lain there recently. Perplexed, Callie traced the imprint of an arm and shoulder in the dust. There was no time to think, she decided, whereupon immediately she thought of Newton. Would he be the next to get shot? Callie closed her eyes. There was the crack of Vernon's shotgun, and there was the great animal's massy fur rippling in distress. Stay with me, she prayed to the bear. Stay with me, she prayed to the Great Spirit.

Perhaps the bear was not badly hurt. Where else might the wounded creature go? One hot day Callie had spotted her stretched out comfortably next to a feldspar mine, her long nose inching under the shade of a wooden overhang at the side of the pit.

She looped in and out of trees, feet flying. I must find her, she thought bleakly. As for Newton, if he came out of this okay she would not press him to explain all his actions. She was through with that. With new ferocity she pounded towards the mine shaft.

Callie noticed that her breathing had changed. She was panting heavily enough for three people. "Clear out of the way!" she heard behind her. Then, "Nuts!" She recognized Jack's voice. But when she turned it was George she saw, nearly in her face. He thundered past, followed by Jack, ten yards behind. Farther down the trail she saw Officer Shawl, and then Bud Mason chugging uphill. He caught up to her. "What are you doing here?" he said, grabbing her hands. Directly ahead a gunshot startled them out of their meeting.

Bud dropped her wrists. Cameron Shawl felt for her gun.

The shot came from the mine shaft, Callie realized. Suppose the bear had gone there? The three ran forward, following the shot. There was Jack straight ahead, almost at the pit opening. From inside the pit came a low moan.

"Good God," said Bud.

"It's Denman, I got him," Jack crowed, staring down the shaft opening.

Bud came over. "Did you have to put a bullet in him?"

"I didn't. I put a scare in him." Jack spun his shotgun in the air. His fingers missed, and the weapon landed at his feet. Jack glanced at it casually. "With a guy like Denman, you don't even need a gun. I was chasing him and the fool fell down the mine."

Jack hung over the shaft opening. "You aren't dead, are you?" In his smugness he did not notice Callie picking up his .44 Desert Eagle Magnum off the ground and slipping it into her jacket.

Officer Shawl pushed forward. "Hello down there. Talk to us. Are you all right?"

Jack turned to her. "He might be bruised, could have busted a bone."

Bud beamed his flashlight into the pit, and saw a big man whimpering and hanging onto a ladder about six feet from the top of the shaft.

Jack kicked some gravel and sticks down the pit. Then he checked for Callie's reaction. Now she would see Newton Denman sniveling, and in a pit where he belonged.

"She ran off," Bud said mildly.

Jack was surprised.

Bud shook his head. "I don't know what's going on here." He straightened his glasses. He turned to go. Marsh grabbed his arm. "You should've stopped her. She's probably aiding and abetting this whole gang in the woods. Hey, she stole my gun!"

Bud looked straight at Jack. "I'd rather see her with a gun, than you. It's safer."

"You don't understand. She took my magnum."

Bud narrowed his eyes at Jack. "You had no business with that kind of weapon. You're a Protective Ranger, not a U.S. Marshall. Where's your standard issue?" he said, referring to the .40 caliber most rangers carried.

Jack pulled it from his jacket pocket.

Bud held his hand out. "I'll take it."

"But I'm guarding Denman."

"You'll get it back." Bud took the gun and handed it to Cameron Shawl. "Keep an eye on the excitable boy."

Cameron understood, and Bud went off in search of Callie. Despite his defense of her ability to carry a gun, he was worried about her.

"I ain't Newton," howled the voice down the pit.

"What!?" This time Jack spoke in disbelief. "You have to be him. I saw you."

"I wish I was Newt," George said forlornly.

Walking swiftly at night lends itself to sober thought. As Pete went in search of the brothers, he considered the other party suspected of causing the death of Mrs. Waters. Ralph was capable of madness and rash action, I knew that. Why didn't I keep a better eye on him?

Ralph Waters had posed as a practical man, a builder of houses, a good provider for his family, but in the end he was the ultimate non-rationalist. Perhaps he had longed to be part of what Theresa loved. He wanted to be a figure in her paintings, and had opted for art tipped over the edge, art gone beyond the creative into dangerous territory. Pete thought about what he had said to Wendy Waters about her father's medical records and Ralph's severe depression and violent tendencies. Still, it was hard to fathom the depth of his hostility towards his wife. Was it envy, or love and obsession? What sort of delusions, Pete worried, could drive a man to his death?

He was not unhappy to have his contemplations interrupted by Cameron Shawl, who had run faster than she had in years to catch up with him. "Marsh got away. I was seeing to George who fell down a mine pit, and then Jack took off. He's got a gun, too. Don't worry about George. Only his ego is bruised."

"Let's slow down," Pete said, forcing himself into a reasonable walking gait. "So George is all right. Do you have a clue as to where he and Marsh are right now?"

"That's what I want to talk about. Jack Marsh," said Cameron. "If you want to see Newton Denman alive at the end of this night, then you and I ought to work together."

Pete preferred to work alone, but he did not say so. Instead he asked Cameron, "Why is Marsh so determined to get Newton?"

A chesty little owl whistled and chuckled over their heads. "Marsh is in love with a woman named Callie Major. She's a ranger at the park who's involved with this Newton guy."

Pete stopped in his tracks, and Cameron, judging his face, said, "Oh right, you and Callie are both from Littlecomb. I bet you know her."

Pete said yes, he knew her.

Cameron gazed up into a tree from which came a hilarious whistling shriek. "Those screech owls," she said. The officer grew serious. "I think Jack may be the father of Callie's child."

Pete's eyes widened. He worked to keep control of his feelings. "Callie has a child?"

"The problem is that she's taken a fancy to the hunter, as my colleagues refer to him. Newton Denman. It's making Jack crazy."

"How old is the child?" asked Pete.

"Just a baby. It is a cute baby, that little Will is."

"Did you say Will? That can't be right."

The wind was unpredictable tonight and vagrant breezes ran wild on the mountaintop. They threw the bear's scent off, keeping the hounds in a state of confusion. Along the lower ridge Newton waited patiently for a down-wind blow. Then he could move, the bear would get no scent of him, and he would catch her out. Scrunched low in some faintly slimy marshmallow and tall arbor vitae, he was surprised when a shriek rang out across the hillside. Then came a loud crack of gunshot. The shriek was familiar to Newton and it reverberated in his head long after the shot died away. Scrambling to his feet, he peered out of the underbrush into the meadow. Not a thing in sight.

He knew the gun blast had come from the peak. Newton had the audacity to think that he alone might guess the bear's maneuvers on Grandmother Mountain. There was no one who had lived for months up here waiting the beast out, as he had, no one so intimate with her ways.

He guessed she would duck out of the woods on the east side and come down the ridge to this end of Black Run Creek with its safety net of dense thickets. Newton smoothed a hand down his pale deerskin vest, feeling for extra cartridges. He spat on a finger and tested the wind.

Nervously he listened for the hounds. Yes, there they were yapping in excitement, but here was something new. Their voices had moved downward, out of the mountaintop wood. They had to be coming along the ridge again. His eyebrows shot up in consternation. Had they got her track? Newton pushed through the vines, ducking, running low and soft to the open hillside. He stared in surprise at the meadow. It was never this bright so late. The sky had begun to crowd with stars and the moon, high up, was circled in a bluish-green corona.

A night to see things good and clear, he thought uneasily.

The dogs were so loud that Newton automatically crouched and raised his Remington. The hounds, now in the thicket from where he had come, bayed in conviction and near triumph. Newton too, grew excited. He began to feel as if these dogs might as well be his own. Yes, they would chase the bear right down the gully, she would go that way, straight for the cover near the creek, and there he'd be, waiting.

As he hurried back to Black Run Creek the peal of hounds seemed to swell into a single chord, and Newton trembled, felt himself part of the chord. For that moment his desire to bring down the bear was the truest thing in him. His adrenaline was up, he could hardly contain this surge of excitement. The cry of the hounds told him that hunting as he had been taught by his father and his grandfather was what made him sound and real.

The leviathan seemed never to tire. Newton didn't see how she could give the hounds such chase. All right then, he conceded, she must be faster than any quarry they'd known. Twice in the last ten minutes he'd sighted a hound, and heard the footsteps of men, too. But he was safe, no man or dog would scent Newton crouched in this blackberry bush at the creek edge. "Come on," he whispered. "Come on bear, right through here. I'm waiting for you."

Three hounds sprang yelping and snarling from the trees across the creek. "What the hell? Don't lose it, dogs," Newton said through his teeth. "Stay on her, bring her out in the open." He waited, and was surprised. Nat emerged from the opening of the woods. Newton's brother was running fast, and caught the figure with the raised rifle in his peripheral vision. "Oh no you don't." Nat whirled and fired. Perhaps the careless brother hadn't seen who he hit, but Newton's cry did not stop him from running away, down to the creek bed.

Newton was struck, and it felt like boiling oil was coursing through his leg. For a moment he thought his head might explode. There was plenty of blood but he told himself that it wasn't so bad. At least it was only his leg that Nat hit.

Two men were approaching. The one in front saw Newton sink to his knees. Ranger Jack Marsh stared as if he couldn't believe this was the real Newton. He did not make a move to help the wounded man.

A step from behind jounced him out of his consideration of Newton Denman's fate.

Pete rushed past Jack. The police officer knelt beside Newton. "Let me see your leg."

"What the hell?"

"Sorry to surprise you like this."

"Pete, my God."

Myrick knew how to stop the blood and to temporarily bind the wound. "Okay, raise your legs above your head," he told Newton. "You're cold, you'll be in shock." Pete took off his long-sleeved blue uniform shirt and wrapped it around Newton. Then he walked over to where the ranger stood awkwardly.

"Marsh." Pete looked at him. So this was the guy. Jack barely acknowledged the police officer. "You were thinking maybe you could just let Newton bleed to death?" Pete said. "And hey, wild thought, then Callie would be yours."

Jack shot Pete a look of surprise. He closed his mouth tight.

"That about right?" Pete persisted.

"How would you know?"

The state trooper felt his defenses caving. He glanced at Newton, who was resting on his elbows. Without turning his head to Jack, Pete said quietly, "I loved her, too." Then with a shade of pride, "Once we talked about getting married."

Soon Pete was giving Jack instructions on making a chair with their arms on which they would carry Newton. But when the two men came out of their huddle, Newton was gone.

Chapter THIRTY

A hobbled but determined Newton headed in the direction of the baying dogs. His leg hurt like hell, but it looked like Nat had just creased him. He waited at a bend in the creek, expecting the hounds to drive out the bear a second time. The pack bayed in fury, then abruptly there was no sound at all. In a minute Newton saw half the dogs hurry past him, tails low and their hind quarters scuttling as though they were being pursued.

Newton was astonished. More evidence of the bear's intelligence at work. Had she so confounded the dogs that they lost all direction? The hunter shoved though the unripe berry bush, and stood up uncertainly. He had a sense that though the dogs were gone, the bear was not. He felt her presence just as he had in early evening. There it was, a slow crunching step, a distinctly heavy tread up a ways on his side of the creek. He turned once. Something rising like black mist. He was afraid.

Newton's leg throbbed. He rubbed it, but couldn't quite get the feel of skin on skin. He squinted at the creek and it blurred before him. Hiding, I've been hiding too long, he thought desperately. Hiding from brother, mother, criminal charges, even Callie. Haven't I hidden what's been going on from her? Oh God, somebody help me.

Stumbling forward to the creek, he collapsed on his knees. He dunked his face in the water.

When the stars moved to their highest orbit Newton left the creek. At the same moment he reached the meadow, the bear emerged from the pines half way up the ridge. She walked slowly, almost purposefully it seemed to him, not stopping until she got to a tall bush with slender, thorned branches. The wild roses, Newton thought. His fear subsided. Now that's strange. She's going for a meal out in the open.

Newton glanced up at the peak, half-expecting to see the other half of the hound pack pour out of the wood. But no, he heard them singing out in despair and confusion at the far side of the mountain top.

He edged uphill, working in to a better range. Although Newton was thinking distances and where to position himself for a good shot, his Remington hung across his back. He had no desire to hurry. It was that cry he was thinking of, and it swept over him now, a sadness and longing that spread from his heart to foot to earth. He stood still. The leaves rustled in the thicket behind him. In the meadow before him, the crickets sang. Newton walked forward until he was fifty yards or so from the bush, which stood out in silhouette against the field. He saw the bear half enveloped in the bush of night-blackened roses. As he went for his rifle a jet of pain surged through his leg. It will pass, he thought. She won't move. She doesn't seem to know I'm here.

Then she turned her head, and in that moment's turning he felt her strength before him. He had an uncanny sense that she had lured him out here. That she sought him. Not in any small measure, no mild plea that he respect the earth she tended. With a moan, or possibly a growl she spoke to him, asking that he come in full submission of that which must be if there will be the green-making, the earth.

Newton did not think so much as sense her will, and he fought mightily against it. He crunched towards the bear through the mix of tall grasses. He was conscious of each step, and the nearer he got the more he tried to call up his old howling voice, the one that centuries had trained man to hunt and kill.

He squinted at her. She was grand and terrifying. She was utterly tranquil at her post in front of the thorned rose bush. Newton sucked in his breath sharply. Something quivered across the broad field beyond the curling rose petals. He strained to see, but it was too far off, and besides what did it matter who was there? No, he thought, creeping persistently forward, it doesn't matter. She's mine now.

Soon he was twenty yards adjacent to the bush and to the bear, whose flat articulated lips, long curved nose and black eye he could see as clear as if he were standing next to her. She made no move to escape. He eased his rifle around his chest, felt the barrel cool against his moist fingers.

Newton raised his rifle. Suppose I can't. Just suppose. He felt lighter at the thought, but his brows rose in the old question marks. His head hurt. Hadn't she tormented him? He saw the stars rushing overhead. She tormented him because he would not submit to her rule over the woods, her right to be there. Why had she a right any more than he? And that was not all. He owed himself this shot; it was the sum of killing the bear cub, the answer to Callie who had hated him for killing something she loved and he could not love. It made him angry to think of it. He would prove to her and to himself that he had nothing to repent. Newton paused. Nothing to repent except my fear, he thought suddenly. What I am afraid of most is that I won't shoot her. He dropped his eyes to the sweet timothy grass at his feet.

At the bush, the great creature stripped the rose hips with her tongue. She ate the seeds meticulously, even delicately, this bear whose ingress was the deepest kind of green-making, born perhaps from her death-sleep in the moss and bark lined den where this winter on Grandmother Mountain she had lain on and off for months. Without water or food or waste letting, she slept until spring's turning ground brought her back to life.

Newton was watching the bear at the roses. Suddenly she pivoted, front legs off the ground. She was slowly rising, shaggy, heavy limbed, growing tall against the sky. She was so tall he stared in wonder and could not separate her shape out from the heaving, rounded forms of the bushes. Then she was as tall as a poplar. Furred, leaf-feathered she was growing to the size of an ancient hemlock, as massive as the Seneca pines Callie loved.

High on the peak, unseen by Newton who could not take his eyes from the bear there were others, witnesses drawn to the locus of a singular event. Out from under Grandmother Mountain's crown of pines, under her hoodwinking brow, came a group of people. Officers Myrick and Shawl, Vernon Vale, Jack Marsh, Nat and George Denman, and a step or two out front, Bud Mason advanced downhill in a wavering horizontal line. They were moving towards one object – not Callie, standing midway down the hill, not Newton, a mere stick figure coming up the hilly meadow – but towards the bear standing on her hind feet at the wild rose bush in the center of the meadow.

Each person in this straggling line felt more tired than he or she had ever known before.

Cameron Shawl was thinking, I'll go home soon, get out of this collar and robe. Then she touched her hat realizing that she wasn't in her church vestments. She ran her fingers over the badge on her navy blue shirt. Robe or badge, what's the difference? Time to change out of these clothes, see to the family. I'll slip into my comfy stretch pants. No clerical collar until tomorrow. I'm sick of my costumes.

Deacon Shawl looked down the hill and recognized Callie standing a short distance down the hill from the rose bush. She saw how close Callie was to the bear. "My Lord," she gasped. "The book of Isaiah." The deacon's hands folded in a prayer: "We roar all like bears, and mourn like doves."

Walking beside Cameron was Vernon, his eye on the bear he had shot in the chest. God, I figured I kilt it. That creature's acting like I clipped her shoulder. A wounded bear is an animal gone mad, he was analyzing. That giant critter, it hardly seems like a normal bear, and it don't seem right, standing there calmly. But maybe it ain't so calm as it looks. I'll watch my step. Don't think I want to be the one to bring it down, anyways.

Close to Vernon was Jack, walking as if the discs in his back had fused together. He was ramrod straight and his fury was draining him. He could not believe the way this night had gone. He had a duty to carry out, and yet it had been thwarted, foiled at every step.

George and Nat were there, too. Soon after the fiasco at the old feldspar mine, when George was presumed to be Newton, Cameron pointed out to George that he could climb up and out of the pit on the very ladder he was clinging to. Cameron had put down her gun while she guided George. But Jack spotted it and shouldering her weapon he raced off. Minutes later, Nat had appeared, looking for his brother. Now together, George and Nat Denman came down off the mountain top with the others until Natty motioned to his older brother, who was startled out of his own reverie. George was thinking he ought to do something about the arson mess. Maybe he should go right up to that Bud Mason, he seemed like an easy going guy, and make a clean sweep of everything. *Tell him how I was out of it and don't know exactly what happened.*

George pondered. He needed to screw up some courage. Why not get the hell off this mountain and go visit the Jolly Logger first? Then he'd see how matters stood. He was slow to notice his brother yanking at his jacket.

Nat was having the same idea of escape. Without a word, he guided George to the edge of the group and then led his brother who was happy to comply, out of the meadow and into the woods. Got to get out of here, Nat thought in a daze. Take that trail, what was it, Knife Edge, or did she call it Hatpin trail. Doesn't matter, it leads us back to the road. I remember where our truck is. This is too much. That bear, she is not normal. She's gone huge. She's here for a haunting. I'd say Newt's done for. That monster will get him.

Bud Mason had not noticed Nat and George slinking away. Field glasses glued to his eyes, his focus was on the bear. Ursus Americanus, he whispered softly. He gaped at her size. His eyes had to be deceiving him, his eyes were worse than he had realized. But oh she was a beauty. His lousy job was almost worth it, at least when you could nab a sight like this. He shifted the binoculars downward, then in a hurry, he tracked upwards, above the bear. That hunter in the lower field, was he going to fire? And Callie! Yes, she still had that heavy automatic. Unsure how to deter the hunter without harming Callie, Bud stood stock still. Except for Pete, the others followed suit, and were soon standing close behind Bud.

Pete Myrick felt as though he was being dragged feet first down the hill. Against his will, dragged into a new and forbidding dream, or even that most frightening dream, the moment of birth.

He was fighting all the way.

Then he saw a reason to acquiesce. Pete could hardly believe he was seeing Callie again. He had figured he would run into her over in Tuscatanning, Cameron had prepared him, but he was not calm and analytic as befitting many years away from an old love, he felt not a trace of time's dulling balm. Instead, Pete's head was feather light, his whole being charged with happiness.

He was content just to look at her again. For once he felt unburdened by the guilt of his past. Birthed at last into a good clear daydream, he thought. Only it was night, and there was a bold nightblue sky, riddled with stars.

Newton tried to concentrate on his quarry. Line her up, he told himself. Just move her into the notch, that's all I have to do. The bear's great head was bent, lowered into the bush. Newton lifted his rifle, and as he raised it so she raised her head. Then he was lost. The bear held him with her eye. There was some distance between them but it was as if he were standing so close she might strike him. For a second he saw himself in one of his father's or Spoons' stories. He expected the bear to bellow in fury and pitch headlong at him.

Her front paw went out and Newton was convinced that the full weight of her shaggy limb was coming down on his arm. Newton felt a deep longing and cried inwardly for the weight of that arm to secure him, and as he gave in to this desire the face of the earth seemed to change. Under his feet was a green and brown particled hill, not grassland but something stark as coriander. There was a leaf green dust that blew into his eyes and there was wind and in the wind an awful roar.

The bear turned away, her muzzle to the bush. Now Newton saw her black-red fur. Why was it so red? Maybe the roses against her chest? The rifle faltered in his hand. She was good and beautiful and terrifying. Newton's eyes swam upward to the sky, he marveled at the royal blue, and then he fired.

Callie

It is deep night. We are, all of us, in the Great Meadow.

I am trying to see what's going on. There is Newton racing towards the bear slumped at the foot of the rose bush. I lower the gun in my hand and watch as Newton forgets what every hunter is taught. Incautiously he approaches his quarry before making sure she is dead.

She's not dead but she's in great pain. I'm a ranger and I ought to know. How strange that she stands up again. The crickets are roaring. The noise is almost deafening.

She is standing tall, her coat so many fine colors all at once. Her fur is suffused with earthen pieces, black siennas, reds as deep as Indian Paintbrush, soft limes from the earth, sharp bright bits of feldspar, and there are blazes too, white ones at her throat. She is feeding. She is speaking to me. What is it, fine old bear? *Oh no, that is not what I want to hear. Please do not tell me that I am not done, that I have been confused. Wait, be patient, she says. The child will be. What child are you speaking of, bear? You are bleeding, and I feel as if I am bleeding too.*

She is feeding, and there is blood. How is that possible? The bear is feeding. She is at an altar eating roses.

Chapter THIRTY-ONE

The shot Newton fired exploded not once but several times over. His ears had to be playing tricks on him. Newton heard a shriek, and there was no mistaking it now. It came to him that it was like the shriek he had heard on that snowy night, the time he got so spooked out at the quarry. It was the same cry he had heard in winter, in spring an hour ago. It was Callie's cry.

Then he saw the bear fall, he saw her shadow cross his heart.

Directly above the bush stood the ranger, her arm herky-jerky lowering the shotgun. Callie had fired when she saw Newton shoot into the sky. *The bear is wounded*, Callie thought. *Not by Newton but by someone else. Oh my dear one, you are in immense pain.*

As she fired the cry on Callie's lips rang out across the meadow. It blotted out all sound except the pack music, the dogs' disparate voices, tinny and factious as if they were lost and had no mistress or master.

In the next moment when all were shocked into sudden quiet, Jack Marsh crept downhill.

At the sight of Callie with her head buried in the coat of the bear, Pete Myrick, ahead of Jack, came forward towards the rose bush. Ten years it was since he had met Callie. No time to consider this new setting and how to get her attention. He watched as she, some distance above on the hill, gave her all to the bear. Out of the corner of his eye he saw Marsh raise his gun at Newton who was approaching the rose bush from below.

His hand was steady. At last, he had the object of his manhunt. Not sixty feet from Denman, Jack aimed his weapon and shouted. "Put the gun down, Newton, or I'll shoot."

Newton's back was turned away from Marsh. But Pete saw what was happening. He ran towards the bush. Pete leapt forward.

"Duck!" Inserting himself between Newton and the line of fire, Pete tackled the hunter. He wanted to push him out of the way, but pandemonium followed. Marsh fired and struck Pete.

Newton spun around, horrified to see the effect of the .45-caliber bullet that hit Pete's chest. The hunter cried out and went to him. Newton tried to mop up the blood with his shirt.

"You'll be okay." He was cradling Pete's head.

"That's what I told you a half hour ago," said Pete. There was a crushing pressure in his chest.

"See, you were right." Newton pointed to his wounded leg.

"Between friends," Pete said, a slow iciness creeping up his limbs, "Tell me the truth."

Newton exhaled. "I was lying. I don't think you're okay."

"My ribs, I think they're caving in."

"I'm going for help." Newton leapt up.

"No," Pete said ferociously. Thirty minutes, he told himself. That's my grace period before the thought destroying pain comes on. He closed his eyes. "Newton, you are one of the two people I wanted to see."

The hunter was so surprised that he blurted out what had been on his mind. "Will you tell me something?" Then more gently, "I heard you tell Marsh you loved Callie. Is that what you've been running from?"

"Ask her." Pete's eyes were turning glassy.

Newton lowered his brow.

"Wait," Pete grabbed the hunter's arm. "Not finished. Hear me out. It's about the death of Theresa Waters."

A few minutes later Pete was spitting up blood. "I'm having a little trouble breathing," he whispered. "Everything compressed."

"Hang in there, please Pete, hang on." Newton ran off to find Officer Shawl. She was so talented, maybe along with everything else she was trained as a medic.

Lying there on Grandmother Mountain, Pete saw himself with Callie a long time ago in Arizona. The ball of his foot was in a stirrup, he was up and onto his horse, riding away from her into the forbidden territory, into the land of red walls, those majestic upthrown sandstone canyons. It was Canyon de Chelly in Navajo country. They had been together then, Callie, himself, and the baby. All his life he had striven to do things carefully and thoughtfully. How did he get off course?

"Pete, do you hear me? It's Callie." She had been lost in her grief over the bear, and in shock she had moved downhill to where she found Pete.

"Callie." He felt the pressure of her hand on his. He was gasping for air.

"I'm here with you in the Great Meadow." She had never been sure what she would say to him if they met again. Pete, bad off as he was, knew what he needed to say but could hardly get the words out.

Callie took up the lull. "We never meant to hurt each other, or anyone else."

"Yes." He tried to smile.

"Pete, are you there?" She cupped his face.

"Yes, Callie. I am." It was as good as the land of milk and honey. Her fine long hair was falling over his face. They spoke together, just a few words. Then he was happy, even though the walls were closing in on him. The steep sided canyon was marked with ancient petroglyphs, the dust gently whorling upward. The red fortress was shaking. But what was this? On the canyon floor there were long tailed sheep with bells, the flock that belonged to the Navajos. They were grazing under the cottonwood trees that rattled in the wind and light. He remembered the light out west. Pete was so happy he thought he might burst.

Chapter THIRTY-TWO

Bud Mason winced at the thought of Pete Myrick's death at the hands of Bud's own senior Protective Ranger. Jack Marsh was in jail waiting to be tried. His defense was that he had fired in the line of duty. Newton was armed and had refused to lower his gun. "I gave him warning," Marsh had told Officer Shawl who arrested him. "It looked to me like he was going to shoot both the bear and my colleague who was lying on top of the animal. I had to fire. I was protecting Callie Major."

Pete had died from the gunshot wound in the Great Meadow. What an awful way to go, Bud thought. The cause of death was a flail heart syndrome. Myrick's ribs, the whole wall of them, had caved in and caused cardiac rupture. His heart had split open.

It was pouring rain, two streams gushing down the downspout outside Bud Mason's office window. He riffled through a stack of papers. According to Callie, the bear was fatally wounded before she fired. He remembered that the creature was standing at an overgrown bush, eating and bleeding to death. That was close to the moment Callie chose to free her from pain.

The dizzying part was that there had been three shots fired one after another in Great Meadow. The way Bud saw it Newton was aiming at the bear, about to shoot it, and for some unknown reason changed his mind and fired into the air. But that shot was the catalyst. Callie imagined the hunter was firing at the bear. She made a snap decision and followed suit, to make sure the creature was put out of her misery. Last, there was the report of Jack Marsh's pistol, the one that killed the state trooper.

Bud's binoculars revealed, too, a moment of reckoning in those few moments when the bear stood at the rose bush. He had the distinct notion that all of them had been gathered at the center of the hill, but why exactly he could not say. The Park Superintendent had been subsumed by a sweet aching exhaustion, as if the work at hand was nearly complete.

But not quite. Bud was swamped in the last week with calls from reporters who were certain that the Park Superintendent understood the connection between the manhunt, bear hunt, and the murder for which Newton was a suspect. But he had nothing helpful to offer, not even to Officer Cameron Shawl who was putting her head together with Detective Rendell from Littlecomb. Hal Rendell had taken over Pete's responsibilities in the arson and murder case.

Twice now, Cameron had stopped by Bud's office to interview him about his knowledge of Callie and the Denman brothers. The second time he told her frankly: "The only one of the bunch I know at all is Callie."

"What are they saying at the Logger?" Cameron asked, trying to put the sermon she was writing out of mind. She had driven over to see Bud during her lunch hour at church. She knew that he spent considerable time at the Logger. Since his wife Ginette's death, Bud often played the pinball machine and ate his dinner there. "People have been talking," she said. "I heard that on the day we went after Newton, the others, meaning Callie, George and Nat Denman were seen at the bar in some kind of powwow."

"Sorry, no dope there," Bud said. "The main talk at the Logger is whether Jack Marsh is guilty or not. The town is divided. Half the folk say that my former ranger fired at Newton strictly as a matter of duty. Others say it was a crime of passion, that he was claiming his territory, meaning Callie, for his own."

"Jack never could sort himself out," Officer Shawl said sadly. "His ego and his passions, all bundled up together."

The rain came steadily down. Bud got up from his desk. As he went to pull the blinds on the dark sky outside he noticed a Jeep roll into the back end of the lot. Bud was pleased to see Callie leap out and walk purposefully towards the penned up doves. That's nice, he thought. She's going to help us get that mess of birds out of here. It really is handy, he thought idly, to have someone like Callie. I can count on her to finish a job. Then Bud saw the infant saddled to her chest like a marsupial. He felt badly. There was no daycare in Tuscatanning, and he had forgotten how difficult it was for Callie to find someone to watch her baby.

He left the window and sat down in front of the report he was filing to the Game Commission concerning the bear. Maybe he was being weak, letting his soft spot for Callie get in the way of his duty as Superintendent. When it came to her odd request that he not hand the bear carcass over to the Game Commission, he had said he would think about it. Then she went into action just like she had the go ahead. Yup, tended to that animal like it was a relative of hers just died.

Callie took the dead bear and buried it in a hollow where she said it had last hibernated. Irrational, that's what it was, especially the trouble she went to, getting those friends of Mary Cowell's to help her haul the heavy carcass. But didn't he know what it was like to be a little irrational – so what if Callie had loved that bear? And she did, he could tell by the shakes in her voice when she had asked permission to keep the animal on the mountain. He had proof that in this instance she hadn't cared one whit about her impropriety of the rules. She didn't care if she was fired for shooting the bear, or fined for burying it herself. No, what she wanted was to keep the bear from being skinned.

The superintendent closed his eyes and leaned back in his chair. He had to ask himself: how rational was I when Ginette died?

Then Bud said her name out loud. "Ginette." He repeated it. "Ginette!" He called her name in anger. He called her name in anguish. "Ginette." He called to her lovingly, making her name sweet on his tongue.

"Ginette, I wish you were here."

Bud gazed at the ranger outside. Why did he stay on at the Park? Just habit? He stared harder at Callie in the rain. Then he smiled. Bud Mason understood in a flash that his chief value was to make sure this park had a decent steward of the forest.

He knew, too, why Callie drove herself like this, staying late every night, and taking on extra shifts. This was how she was dealing with her shock and sadness. But which earthly creatures was she mourning, the bear, Pete Myrick, or Newton who seemed to have abandoned her?

Bud's chair squeaked as he rolled it around his desk. Without getting up, he reached out and slammed the office door shut. He picked up his pencil. That spooky huge bear. Appearing out of nowhere, he mused. I suppose Callie had to do what she did. She knew it was dying after Vale blasted it in the chest. Too bad he had those wonderful binoculars. Perhaps the Park Super had seen too much. There was the truck hidden in the thicket when Jack Marsh was zooming up mountain. Bud had protected Callie's whereabouts then. He didn't know why, but he had done it. And then later. He really wished he hadn't glimpsed Callie's face when she aimed at the bear.

He bounced the eraser end of his pencil on the desk, stared at the Game Commission paper in front of him. He had filled it out, kind of exciting to do, too, considering the information he had on the bear. The animal was too big not to measure. Before he let Callie and her cousin and friends haul it off he had gotten some men to help him weigh the beast. Nine hundred and forty pounds. Next day, he'd poked around the game records, double checked his findings. Callie had shot the largest black bear to be recorded on this continent.

Bud took off his glasses and rubbed the bridge of his nose. He wondered exactly what the Game Commission would do once they got this report. Naturally they'd want proof of such a spectacular specimen. Would they make a trip up mountain, and dig up that old bear from its grave in the hollow? Of course they would. Then what? Probably get the skin of it, split its lips, do all those things to garner some statistics, and walk away with a mighty big fur to boast. Bud's fingers moved to his eyes. He squished his fingers across them.

He went to the window. Callie was still at it. He could see her lips pursed, probably cooing to that last lot of pigeons. No, they were doves. Callie had said so. Only one more cageful to go, it looked like. Already full were two large dog carriers she had borrowed from Cameron Shawl. Callie's pant legs were mud covered and her poncho flapped in the wind. Out of the woods two last doves appeared and lighted on her shoulders. With the birds perched close to her neck, she walked carefully as an aerialist.

Bud sat down again. He rapped his knuckles once on the Game Commission report, then closed his hand over the paper and dropped it into the can under his desk.

A week and a half later, Newton had returned to his mother's house. George and Nat were there, too. Neither had been charged with a single crime, and they had resumed their old lives. Soon it was common knowledge in Littlecomb - courtesy of Natty and George - that Newton Denman refused to step outside the house. Word was that he sat all day at his mother's kitchen table in silent cogitation. It would be more accurate to say he was silent when George and Nat were in the house. This morning Newton stared out the kitchen window at the tall nodding thickets at the end of the yard. He hummed anxiously to himself. His mother's fuss over him was irritating.

"You better eat your sandwich. It's good ham," Betty Denman set down a basket of laundry near the table. She lit a cigarette. Newton glanced at the plate. He had already eaten one of the two sandwiches she fixed for him.

"Wish you'd stop that humming." She tried to clear her voice, an impossible challenge given the emphysema that was stealing her breath. "It's no tune I ever heard of."

Newton paused, curious himself at the high strained hum on his lips. He had picked it up a long time back, he knew that. Perhaps in the woods. He didn't permit himself to push it any further. Had he dared, he might realize that it was a call to be nurtured. It was a nursing call once made by a bear cub who lay in the grips of a steel trap.

Betty surveyed the clothes in the basket. "I've got to get this load out on the line, else George and Nat won't have a thing to wear." Arms akimbo, she looked at Newton critically. "You didn't give me your dirty clothes."

"I washed them myself. Yesterday."

Newton watched his ma move to the sink. As she scraped the burnt oatmeal from a pan George used late that morning, the sun caught the bright flowers on her quilted apron. Her slender hands, still beautiful even with their patina of golden nicotine, went to work scrubbing the pot. She wiped her fingers on the apron skirt, and seized Nat's coffee mug.

Newton drummed his fingers on the checkered tablecloth. He needed to talk. "My father would have gone after a bear like that, same as me. She had her chance. That bear could have run, why didn't she run?"

Betty turned from the sink. "You said it yourself. Your daddy would have done the same thing. You killed a bear. All right then. No one even caught you for doing it in park land. Count yourself lucky."

"I told you I didn't shoot her, though it was my fault more than Callie's." Newton faltered, his brows reared up. "The bear was terrifying. My Lord, she was a terrifying beauty. And I didn't see that she was hit already. In pain she was, that's why Callie took the shot."

Betty took a seat at the table. Her snapping blue eyes traveled from son to cigarette smoke, then back to her son. "You're dreaming up that girl again."

Newton looked closely at his ma. He was tracking her face, marking the signs she made. His months in the woods had taught him to look at things carefully, watch for what gives away an animal's behavior.

"Callie was there on the mountain," Newton said evenly.

Betty reached for her ashtray. "You think maybe she's going to come to Littlecomb and rescue you, your Callie Major?

Newton started to hum.

"Don't start up," his mother flashed. "It's better if she stays where she is."

"Callie would never come here," Newton said. He was confused. Did his ma want him to live at home forever, was that it?

An alarm went off in Newton's head. "What do I need rescuing for?"

"From the police when they sort this thing out." Her face twitched in worry and she turned so that Newton couldn't see her. Betty picked up the clothes basket. She was leaving the room. Despite his wounded leg, Newton leapt up from the table and was at the screen door, his rangy frame towering over Betty. Deftly, he closed his fingers down on the door handle so that she couldn't go outside.

"You know I didn't kill Theresa Waters or burn down that school. Tell me you know it, Ma." Newton released the door handle. His hand hovered rigid as a steel wedge above his mother's gray head. "I guess you're going to keep covering for George and Nat, same as I was doing all these months."

Betty's face was locked. But Newton could see her struggle to unlock, and in that moment he realized that she never meant to hurt her sons. Newton had always been astonished at her ability to love, given the dearth of it in her own upbringing. It came to him now, how she had used her children to fill her up, and keep filling her with the love she had missed in her own parents. She had not, as he had supposed, deliberately manipulated one brother against another, but rather begged the love of one, and then the other at different phases in her life.

This understanding had to be enough.

The flat of his hand touched his mother's hair gently. "I have to go out now, Ma."

It was not for Newton or Betty to examine how she had willingly sacrificed the one son for the two others. Leaving her clothes basket inside, Betty ran into the yard calling after Newton. It hurt her throat to shout: "Wait. Newton I know you didn't hurt the school teacher." Her face crumpled. "Where are you going?"

"Down to the Lounge. I've arranged to meet with Detective Rendell."

Betty looked frightened. "To the Lounge," she repeated. "That's where your brothers are now."

"Yup. I'm counting on it."

Betty's face hardened. She was thinking about the money she had given her two older sons to give to Newton, and how they had never given it back. She closed her eyes for a long minute. "Wait there. I have to find something." She turned and went back into the house. Newton waited at the rose bushes where he used to meet Callie in the mornings to walk to school.

Instead of his ma, Spoons came out the door. "Your mother says you're going to speak to Hal Rendell. Here, you should wear this. Don't you feel the chill?" He handed Newton a rumpled bundle.

Newton stared hard at the long missing, blue and white striped jacket.

"I've been meaning to give it to you." The old man scratched his elbow. "Had it stuffed down that hole in the floorboards under my bed. It was keeping out the rats and weasels."

"Grandpa, you know weasels don't get into the house."

"Stranger things have happened," Spoons said, smiling. "I was just on my way to the Lounge. You coming? How's that hobbled leg of yours? If it's like my back you'll be feeling ornery, downright wrathy."

"You go on ahead," Newton said. "I'll meet you there." He had noticed that his mother was waving him inside the house. She held out a grocery bag.

They sat down together. Newton looked into her great blue eyes and sagging shoulders. Most animal tracks were easy to read, he was thinking. Animals follow patterns, they fall into set ways of doing things, same as people do. Some habits are probably passed on for fifty generations. I bet my mother doesn't think about how her tracks run, how they got formed when her own mother left her. I remember though. She used to tell me the stories. And it's a good thing, too. They have a powerful kick. They remind me that I can't afford to keep in Ma's tracks.

Betty was subdued. She opened the paper bag. "Take this to the Lounge, too. Not that it will be much help," she said. "Another thing. You might want to look in the pocket of that jacket Spoons gave you."

"Thank you, thank you very much," said Newton in an almost courtly fashion as he took the bag from her and glanced inside. "These wouldn't belong to George, by any chance, now would they?"

Chapter THIRTY-THREE

The Saturday afternoon bunch had gathered at the bar in the Big Springs Lounge. George Denman, with four or five beers under his belt began to notice that he had drunk down his earlier glow. He was uncomfortably hot.

Elijah Jones was thinking that the room was reasonably cool as he made a pot of coffee. When it had brewed he poured the pot into one of his new thermoses that would take the place of the old tin dispensers.

"Why the change?" Gib Setter demanded.

"Someone complained that the coffee got cold in those old dispensers. I should have done this a long time ago," said Elijah.

"Denman boys! That's us," George crowed. "We're a wonderful bunch."

Nat shot him a hard look. "Sometimes I think you're a little twisted, George."

"Twisty, you say?" Spoons, the latest arrival to the bar, was already on the brink of snoozing with his face in the palm of his hand. Now he woke up. "You talking about those buck horns up on the wall? Them antlers are perfect. I should know," he whispered sadly.

Rendell asked the bartender for a ginger ale. The detective was on edge waiting for Newton Denman to appear. It rankled Hal that up in Tuscatanning they were moving their end of the case right along. Officer Cameron Shawl and Bud Mason were eye witnesses at the fatal shooting of Pete Myrick.

No such luck here. Everything was on hold regarding the death of Theresa Waters, especially with Newton being so secretive. He said it was Pete's dying wish that they meet at the bar like this, and expose the real killers.

The detective thanked Elijah for the soda.

"Give me another one, too," George said, signaling his empty beer glass. He was staring at a small pointed fox head over the bar.

Nat eased off his bar stool and walked over to the fireplace mantel where Elijah kept a box of toothpicks for his customers. "I'm ready to cut out of here. Grandpa? How about you, George?" Nat said nervously.

"Is it time?" Spoons sat up ramrod straight.

"Going home to see to your little brother?" Gib asked solicitously. "Poor old Newton. I never did figure him for murdering a school teacher and burning down a school."

Nat flipped a toothpick in the air, catching it in his front teeth. Then, with a jittery laugh: "Let's go George, we've been here long enough."

"Did I hear you say to these folks that our brother is sitting home at the kitchen table," George said belligerently. "Probably still in his boxers, you said?"

"Just kiddin' about Newt, George. Besides, you're slowing down. I was talking about underwear a long while back." His eyes darted to the men sitting at the bar. Nat couldn't resist checking for an audience response. A bare chuckle would do.

"That wasn't a nice thing to say about our brother." George trained his gaze on the fox again, wondering why its face was suddenly prickly. Nat looked at George, then unconsciously followed suit. His eye scooted past the fox and landed on the scavenger dog head over the mantel. He noticed the dark cavities where the eyes used to be.

"It wasn't nice at all." The voice belonged to Newton, who stood in the doorway. He was wearing his blue and white jacket. "As you can see, I finally got it back," he said, running his hands down over the zipper in front.

George swung around. Nat's face stiffened.

"Hello brothers. Grandpa. Hal." Newton nodded at the officer who was doing Pete's job, even though everyone knew that Myrick did it better. Rendell was an overly confident bureaucrat, short on people skills, and apt to arrive at a decision too quickly.

Hardly favoring his bad leg at all Newton walked inside, and then he hesitated. He wasn't sure where he needed to go. He went up to the bar and waited for Hal Rendell to take the lead. They had rehearsed up to a point.

Looking pointedly away from George and Nat, Hal spoke: "Newton is here to clear up a few matters small and large, regarding the crimes this town has accused him of. No, don't get up, people. Stay and listen."

Elijah rubbed his eyes, and he was not the only one. The inmates were squinting because Newton left the door wide open. The blue and white striped jacket on Newton sparkled like a lake with whitecaps. The sunlight cut into the Lounge and scattered at the far wall. The splayed light played off the trophies. George slid off his stool and stared uncertainly from brother to brother. He joined Nat at the fireplace.

Newton's throat constricted. This was not so easy. Not his style, at all. Since when was the kind of guy who takes charge?

In a blink Nat was at his side. "Hey Newt. Everything okay with you?"

The hunter turned to his brother. Nat was smiling at him in a familiar way. Newton saw what was behind his voice: 'Never mind little Newt, little less than a Newt, don't speak up and hurt your own brothers. Don't you never mind what this police fellow wants you to say – let George and me take care of you.'

The jacket on his back felt heavy. Newton was in a fever to get it off. "Take it!" He threw it at his brothers. George caught up the jacket before it grazed the floor.

"It belongs to you, Newt," said Nat smoothly. "I don't see what we would want with your jacket."

"Oh but George has been looking for it, haven't you? Ma says you should check the pockets."

George gave Newton an odd look. Shrugging his shoulders, he pulled out his own wallet. "I don't know how it got there."

"Yeah, it's peculiar, especially since you lost it the night of the fire and Theresa Waters' death. Double peculiar, since I saw you wearing it out of the house that night. And Spoons remembers you, George, in my jacket as you scrounged outside the house for my car key. That about right, Grandpa?"

"Yessir. People always think I'm asleep."

George looked alarmed.

"I'd like to take credit," said Newton, "but it was Pete who got this information. I guess he knew how to talk to Ma, after all. And to Spoons."

Nat stared at Spoons, who shrunk not one whit under the scrutiny. "Yessir," said the old man. "I been keeping ahold of that jacket in my room since last August."

An astonished George turned to Spoons. "Don't you remember me asking you for it?"

"It wasn't mine to give you. The jacket belonged to Newton."

"I have something else," said Newton. All eyes were on him as he held a paper grocery bag in one hand, and with the other pulled out a pair of badly singed jeans. "Worn the night of the fire, I wager. These will fit no one but you, George."

"No way," The brother said unconvincingly.

"Your name tag's inside, on the waist band. You know how Ma still sews 'em on if she gets the chance."

Gib Setter whispered to Spoons, "Just look at those jeans. Talk about being worse for the wear. Or should I say, a turn for the burn?"

Newton tossed the pants at his brother.

Hal was on his feet. He intercepted the pass. "Sorry George. I'll take those." To Newton he said, "Good job. This is evidence Pete would have loved to see."

Newton felt sad. If only he had been more helpful to Pete in those phone calls they shared about his missing jacket. "He was so close to figuring everything out," said the hunter, scarcely aware that he was ruminating out loud.

"I didn't want him to get shot neither," George said. He'd had it with trying to be bluff and defiant. His heart was sodden. He wanted to cry.

"It's because of me that Pete died. He never would have gone off to look for Newton if I hadn't did what I done that night at the school." George searched the room for sympathetic eyes.

"It was all a mistake! Just a bad drunk, and some meanness in me towards an old teacher who crowned me when I was a kid." George's voice shook. "I never meant to kill Theresa Waters. I was so mixed up and I hated that Bitchety Miss Block…. I didn't mean to, but I don't know. I don't remember," he repeated, his voice rising in horror.

Nat spoke up. "You didn't do it, you chucklehead. I'm sick of this whole thing."

"What do you mean?"

"You heard me."

"I didn't hurt her?"

"Nope. I saw everything, well, almost."

George stared at his brother who was leaning casually against the wall near the mantel. "You've known all this time that I didn't do it?"

"Sure," said Nat coolly, and then attempting a joke, "Kept you in line didn't it?"

George was inflamed. He jumped on his brother's back, and Nat buckled at once under his weight. The older brother yanked a shank of Nat's hair, forcing the thin man's head back.

"You tell us what happened."

"Let go my hair. Come on Georgie, don't hurt me."

George dropped Nat's head. "Talk then."

Rendell, who had rushed forward when George attacked his brother, now chose to stand back and see what transpired. Nat was on his knees, and George still on top of him.

"Mrs. Waters saw me at the school," said Nat. "She called out Newton's name because I was wearing his jacket. Remember? You had it first, then threw it on the ground. That's when I put it on. Mrs. Waters waved at me and started across the street, and I knew I had to get out of there. I didn't want her to see you either. Can't you get off my back, George? I can't breathe."

George climbed off of his brother.

Nat hunched forward, rubbing his forehead. "I was standing in front of the window. You were inside the classroom going crazy, throwing school things every which way. Chairs, tables, you name it. A yardstick came out the window, and I picked it up off the ground when I saw Mrs. Waters coming over. I didn't want to hurt her or nothing. I just felt better having something like that in my hand.

"I ducked around the corner of the building, thinking she'd take herself and her dog back home. But no, she had to nose around. I hardly thought about what came next. I only wanted to slow her down. George and I needed to get out of there."

"So you whacked her on the head?" Newton looked away in disgust, and Hal wondered how a blow from a yardstick could possibly cause the lethal damage the coroner reported.

"Course I didn't. No, I tripped her with the stick as she came around the corner. The yardstick flew out of my hands. I think she landed on it. Her head might of hit it as she came down."

Newton and Hal exchanged glances. It sounded like one of Nat's weasly confections.

"That blow hardly made a dent in her," said Nat, anxious to move ahead. "It just bought me time to hide behind that large oak tree in the school yard."

Newton nodded. It had a huge circumference, that tree. It was reputed to have been planted by William Penn, himself. Newton and Pete had talked about this very oak, for the state trooper found the yardstick there, and had learned soon after that Nat's prints were all over it.

Nat was talking faster. "Mrs. Waters got to her feet, kinda dazed I guess from where she ran into my yardstick. She hadn't gotten far when Mr. Waters, he came out of nowhere, and he scared even me. He must have followed her over, and was trying to find her, calling out 'Sweetheart, Sweetheart,' in a sickly mean voice. He wanted to get her."

"What do you mean?" Newton asked.

"He pulled out a gun, she yelled out: No Ralph, no. But he fired. I don't know the damage done there, but it looked all surface to me. Mrs. Waters must have panicked because instead of going out to the street, she wobbles over to the open window. She sticks her head in and yells, 'Help! Help me, Newton.' Then her voice goes shrill: 'Ralph?'

"That's when that old window shuddered like it did earlier. I had seen it come down on George's foot, but I'll tell you it wasn't a sticky sash this time. I saw Ralph's hand at the window. He slammed it down on her head. I figured her for dead right then, but Mrs. Waters' yanked her head out and the window hit down with a boom. I guess Mr. Waters took off. The fire started right after that.

"That explains the assaults to the head," Newton said, turning to Hal. "According to those notes Pete left, the wood chips with black paint embedded in her skull came from the yardstick. We know about the bullet graze from Ralph's gun. As for Ralph slamming the window down on her head, that's the freak bit that caused the internal bleeding. Put it all together and she'd have to be made of cement to have survived."

Everyone in the Lounge stared at Nat, and then George.

George, looking stunned, turned to Nat. "You son of a bitch. You could have told me. We've been together all this time." His eyes registered disbelief and injury.

"You might have run to the police to say it wasn't you who killed Theresa outright," Nat said, "but what with you starting the fire and all, it didn't look good for us. Don't you see, Georgie, I was protecting you."

Chapter THIRTY-FOUR

After the rains of May, Grandmother Mountain turned velvet green and her waters began to flow. At Black Run Creek the water line was high. Callie sat on a rock near the creek, and Will lay underneath at the side nearest the woods. Twelve days had passed since the tragedy in the Great Meadow. This was Callie's first time up mountain since the day she buried the bear. She and her cousin had come for a picnic, and Mary was putting away the last of the tuna salad and shortbread cookies that Callie had brought.

"Have a banana?" she asked Callie.

"No thanks." She blew a bug off Will's light hair. He sucked on his hand and watched her face. She stroked his face. "Why did Pete have to die? And the bear." Callie slumped. "And me the one to put her out of her misery. I always figured nature was the one thing you could count on."

Her shoulders shook. "But look at how it really is. The bear is gone. And what about Will? I was so sure *he* would be a *she*. I thought *she* would be born in a warm and glorious spring. But no, what do I get –"

Mary broke in. "The coldest spring in years."

"Even his hair," Callie went on. "Another trick of nature. I figured it would be like mine. Look at it! So pale this kid will have sunburned scalp all his life."

"A calamity." Mary feigned horror, and then got serious. "Hey, I'm sorry Cal, I know, too, that you were thinking this was going to be a special baby...." She trailed off.

Callie shrugged. "Nothing reliable to go by," she said, watching her son reach for the silver lichen growing out from under the rock where he lay. His fingers went for the loose crumbles on the ground.

"Who says the seasons, or bears for that matter, have to do things your way?" Mary blurted. "I've had to listen to your bear talk for years, and I have to tell you Cal, I was plain sick of the way you hoarded her spirit like it was a pot of gold."

Callie bent forward and snatched a tuft of silvery lichen from Will's mouth. "I thought I knew her," she said, hunching over her son.

Mary ran her fingers lightly across the rich leafmold on the bank. She watched a rush of water break over a log. "That's dangerous thinking. Nature is one wild lady." She tapped the earth, her fingers playing out a beat she sometimes danced to with the Eagle Feather Singers. "Things work out best for me when I follow her lead." She nodded at Callie. "No matter how crazy the dance, she'll do right by you."

This made sense to Callie, but it rankled that Mary should be the one dispensing wisdom. A touch churlish, she said, "So who's in the lead when you blow all your money on the lotto games?"

"Yup," Mary rolled her eyes. "It's only humans who act vindictive."

"Sorry."

Mary sighed. "When I go for broke in the lotto, It's me trying some fancy footwork that never comes off. The only thing I pay attention to is my own obsession. Find me a cure for that one."

"Get a new obsession. But find a good one this time."

They both laughed.

"I'm half serious," said Callie.

Before they started down the long slope to the Jeep, Callie insisted on a short detour.

"What now?" her cousin asked, as they stepped out into the nearly knee high, sweet timothy in the Great Meadow.

"Nothing. Just want to look around."

Mary sank into the grass. Callie put Will down next to her cousin. The baby studied the bluets, and his aunt sprawled on her back, eyes closed. She was thinking that since the night chase and shootings here in the meadow, Callie had not once mentioned Newton's name. What had become of him, she wondered. Mary sensed that he and Callie had not been in touch.

"What made you rescue Newton?" Mary opened her eyes and looked at the sky. "After the baby was born, I got the feeling you didn't trust him. Then came the day of the manhunt. The way you tore out of the Logger to find him, that was something."

"I did it because –" Callie broke off. There was no sense in talking about the bear again. She scanned the hill where Pete had died. "You're right. I can't blame nature. Or myself," she added, scarcely audible.

Mary lifted her head. "Are you still on the bear?"

"Right this second I'm thinking about Pete and me losing our baby."

Mary sat bolt upright. "Not Pete Myrick, the police officer who died? He was the guy?"

Callie dug into the picnic lunch. Maybe a piece of fruit would help. "He was the guy." She found a pear, and sat down beside her cousin.

"Twelve years ago I was graduated from the ranger training program at Pitch Pine State Park. As I sifted through positions in state forests throughout the country I came across an opening for a park ranger in Canyon de Chelly, Arizona. I read about it and knew I wanted to try for the job. It was described as a smaller, elegant version of the Grand Canyon, a place filled with Anasazi ruins. I was half way through the application before I thought of Pete at all. But then I remembered that he had gone west and ended up in Arizona.

"He and I knew each other slightly from Littlecomb Elementary." Callie sat in the grass cross-legged. She raised her eyes to Mary. "He used to look out for Newton, especially when he was being bullied by Nat and George.

"Pete had nothing to do with my decision to go to Arizona. It's a big state, and Canyon de Chelly is in Navajo land. I wanted to explore, get out of the east. But when I landed the job I got in touch with Pete's parents. They told me he was pretty happy working on a ranch out there. Wrangling cattle was what he mostly did. I asked for his address, and found out he was outside Tsaile, which is on high ground, beautiful country. Best of all it was near where I had my ranger duties for the Canyon.

Callie smiled. "Pete and I had fun together. After his cattle busting duties he used to borrow a couple of horses from the ranch where he worked and we would ride out in the early evenings. I showed him Spider Rock and the ruins of the ancient peoples in Canyon de Chelly. He said he wanted to climb up into those hidden apartments. Find some clues as to why the Anasazi disappeared so mysteriously. But I wouldn't let him go. I told him that the cave dwellings are strictly prohibited to Anglos.

"When we were first together Pete and I talked about Newton and how I had been his childhood sweetheart. As time passed, his name came up less.

"Because you and Pete fell in love?" Mary asked.

Callie ate the last juicy bite of pear. "He was good company, and so knowledgeable. He was a little reserved, but terribly solicitous; he wooed me liked no other man had."

She dropped the peach pit into a paper napkin. "It was too much like what happened to me with Jack. I wasn't really sure I was in love, but I went ahead anyway. Why have I done these things?" She thought for a minute. "Pete was a kind man. I looked up to him."

She took Will from Mary and pressed him to her chest. "But I was cocky and foolish. We both were. I got pregnant, and when the baby was born Pete moved in with me."

Callie cradled Will, who was gurgling and waving his tiny arms. "There, there," she said, more to herself than to the child.

Callie

It didn't work out between us. Pete's position at the ranch changed, and he was gone much of the time. Mostly on roundups. I was worn out. There's a look women get after giving birth. Have you seen it? Their eyes suddenly lie deep in their sockets. Vision moves close to the bone.

I could see that Pete and I were miserably young and unprepared for the task at hand. We had started to argue. I look back and see that I had high expectations and feelings I didn't know how to talk about, let alone, recognize them. It got harder for us to get along. We weren't ready for marriage.

Finally, I asked him to move out. After that we still shared duties with the baby, me having little Will – yes that was his name, too. I took care of him most of the time. But when Pete had the baby he was good with him. I trusted him completely.

That's why what happened is so hard to imagine, even now.

It was early morning and Pete surprised me. He was knocking hard at my door. Still in my nightgown, I let him in. I've told you that he was a somewhat reserved man. Well, on this day he wasn't, and it didn't fit him. It scared me. He was talking crazy, his voice was damp and heavy. Scary. Insistent.

He was more affected by our separation than I had realized. He kept telling me that I had grown so as a woman, and that we had to get back together. He told me that no one would ever love me as he did. I drew back. It was stultifying.

He looked at me a moment, and then went over to the bassinet which our baby had just about outgrown. Before I knew it, he had tiny Will in his arms, saying that he was taking him out for a while.

"But it's my day," I told him, referring to the arrangement we had made for shared childcare.

"According to your schedule," Pete flashed back. "There's not one good reason I shouldn't take Will today. I don't have to work this morning, and you do. Why should he have to go to a sitter?"

He had scoped out the place and concluded that I had not planned to spend the day with Will. Evidence of Pete's early detective skills, I guess. And true enough, I had arranged for a babysitter. I had no choice. My ranger duties dictated that I take a group of hikers into the canyon, all the way from the north rim down to Antelope house, one of the Anasazi ruins.

I looked at Pete. He was wildly needy. Our son was curled comfortably in his arms.

"I thought I'd take him on a ride," Pete said. "I have to exercise one of the ranch horses."

Ordinarily this would not have disturbed me. Pete had held Will on the saddle in front of him several times. He always used a chest baby carrier, and chose an elderly palomino who was generally quiet. But that day I asked cautiously, "Where will you go?"

"I'm going to show our baby the White House Ruins."

"What? You know it's forbidden. You can't go there without a ranger or a Navajo guide."

He focused on Will and said nothing.

"Forget it," I said emphatically. Then, I saw him start for the apartment door.

"No!" I reached for Will, but Pete shoved me out of the way. I was so surprised I came forward again, and this time he pushed so hard I fell to the floor. People assume women lose their innocence when they lose their virginity. Not so for me. I had been struck by a man. This was where I lost my innocence.

I hit down on my shoulder. Bruised, nothing broken. His eyes met mine, and I knew he was sorry. It seemed to me that he was gasping, he had lost his breath, lost his way. It was a weird moment. I was aging as it happened.

I thought he would talk to me, but no. Pete was moving out the door. I was stunned. Then scrambling after them, trying to reach Will, I went in a daze out to the hallway of my apartment building. They were gone. What does a person do in such a situation? I was convinced that it must be my fault this had happened. We are taught to think this crooked way. Even if it is not humanly possible to hold hearth and home together, we blame ourselves.

I cancelled the babysitter and rationalized that everything would be fine. I pulled on my khaki pants and shirt and tried to focus on getting myself to work. The Antelope Rock hike is an all morning expedition. During my break (I was showing the tourists where they could take pictures of the petro glyphs) I thought about Pete and Will, and wondered if they were in the canyon.

I walked across some grassland and watched two Navajo children head their flock of belled sheep into a pasture that ran up against a wall of sandstone.

This face of rock had brilliant black stripes. It was a hot morning. Cloudy overhead, but the sun was creeping around.

Then I noticed the sand eddying near the canyon walls. One minute the air was lambent, and the next my group and I were choking in a dust storm. Everywhere, whorls of minutia, stick, sandstone, and white rock shivers. I got the tourists under the protection of a cave, but all the while I was worrying about Will and Pete.

Later, he told me in full detail what had happened.

That morning Pete did ride up to the White House Ruins where the ghosts of the Anasazi are said to roam.

He was on horseback climbing a trail near one of the ancient apartments when that awful whirring sounded. Loud as a generator, and unmistakable. It was a Diamondback rattler on the trail in front of them.

Pete's palomino spooked. He said that the old horse must have jumped a foot. Then it backed into a cactus. People seldom realize there are cactus that far north, but there they are growing in the crevices of the canyon. With cactus barbs in her rear quarters, the mare was crazy with pain. When she lurched into the air a second time, Pete and Will got thrown.

Pete landed first, breaking the baby's fall, but he had landed right next to the snake. That's when the creature bit his hand.

The venom won't affect you right away, and Pete took advantage of this. He picked up a rock and stoned the rattler. Then he took his hunting knife and cut off the head. Some cowboys will keep a rattler head as a trophy, put it on their belt buckles or on top of their ten gallon hats. Pete had no interest in sporting such a thing on his hat, but he figured he could sell it.

He began to feel the effects of the bite, faint dizziness and his fingers and arms began to throb. He stuck the head and body into a plastic bag that held Will's bottle. But instead of returning it to his saddle bag, he threw it on top of the saddle so that he could go right to work tying a tourniquet with his bandanna, just above his bite. Tough to manage with only one good hand, and it was too bad he didn't know that in a few years doctors would recommend that you touch nothing until they see the bite.

Pete was back on his horse, carrying little Will against his chest in the carrier. By then he was in such pain it's likely he didn't much attention to that plastic bag looped over the pommel. He set off, his whole being intent on getting out of the canyon and to a medical center to treat his snake bite. He got there all right, but not as he intended. Pete had grown up in Littlecomb, Pennsylvania, far from Diamondback rattler country and he had no idea that a rattlesnake is capable of using his fangs lethally, even after its head is severed. Even without a body, their nervous systems are still alive, their poison pernicious. Pete's palomino stumbled on a rock and the bag flew up against our tiny blond infant in the lightweight carrier. Dead as that snake was, it reacted to the sudden contact with Will. The rattler fangs sank into our child's plump leg.

Pete did not see what had happened, and he says he never heard a cry. Did our baby cry out, I wonder? After riding a ways he sensed that something was wrong, that Will was not merely sleeping. Pete found the multiple fang marks and the swelling. Already, Will had lost consciousness. Soon enough he'd go into shock, followed by kidney failure. But Pete tried to save him. He stopped and got off the horse, this time to find his knife. He made an incision over each fang bite and then put his mouth like a suction over the wound. He was terrified that it was too late, that the poison in Will had already spread through his little body.

By the time he got our baby to where he could be helped, Will was dead. As for Pete's bite, he lost most of the forefinger on his left hand.

Afterwards, we could hardly speak to each other for our grief. One day it had been raining and I had my windows open. The desert air was full of the resinous creosote bushes. Odd that Pete had always loved its fragrance. The smell disturbed me, too spicy and I don't like the oil it gives off in the rain. That day he came by one last time. He came over to me where I was lying on the bed. My eyes were fixed on the window, watching the rain send darts into the mesquite and creosote when I felt Pete's fingers along my back. Just two fingers in a familiar way.

"No one knows your curves like I do," he said.

I turned to him, amazed at his brashness after the death of our child. Perhaps he was in shock, but I wouldn't have known, not then.

"I'll never forget how much I loved you when I was sixteen. But you were Newton's girl."

I spoke mockingly, "Are you going to tell me again how I've grown into a woman?"

"We need each other," he begged. I could see the despair in his eyes. He hugged me but my own sorrow and rage at him were so great that I couldn't respond.

He let go of me. He was bitter. "If only you had loved me enough," he said. "This never would have happened."

Mary consoled her cousin. She could not tell Callie how much the story had shaken her.

"That was ten years ago," said the forest ranger. "I had lost my first Will, and every day afterwards I hated the smell of the desert. I left that job and came back east. As for Pete, I didn't want to know what he was doing. Less painful that way."

Callie smiled wryly. "A few months ago I learned from Newton that Pete had returned to Littlecomb and become a policeman."

"So it was after Arizona that you took the job at Pitch Pine? I remember you were around, but I hardly ever saw you." Mary stretched her torso. She wanted to get up off the damp ground.

"Mostly, I sequestered myself like a hermit. Went to work and that was about it." More minutes passed before Callie took her cousin's arm. "Come on."

Both women stood up. Callie looked out over the Great Meadow.

"Things have changed," said Mary simply.

Callie nuzzled the child in her arms, her own ample head of hair rubbing against his. "It wasn't until I was with him, there," she gestured up the hill where Pete had lain dying, "that I understood the torment he had lived with all these years."

"Go on," Mary pressed, taking the baby from her arms. Her cousin's body was quaking like an aspen tree.

Callie wrapped her arms around her shoulders. "When I saw that Jack had really shot Pete, I went to his side. He began to talk about what happened, how we lost our son, and then he said: 'Despite all of it, I wanted you to love me.'

'Pete, I did love you as much as I knew how, but oh God, how little I knew.'

'You think I blame you for what happened to us, to our son?' he said. 'I can't do that anymore. I'm sick of my own arrogance. Don't you see? You trusted me that day, and even in my rage you believed I would take care of our child. Cut yourself a break. It was me who took your Will into the desert.'"

Callie turned away from Mary, flushing deeply. She thought her face might crack in two for the sorrow and the relief she felt. She shaded her eyes and gazed at the mountain top, surprised at its strength and the way it suddenly entered her.

The rose bushes had spread into a large crooked U at the center. Beyond it, up along the peak, the brown folds of earth lay inert under a hazy sky. Things were still, not even a hawk buzzing the ground for small game. "I can't sleep through the night. I never had that trouble before."

Mary looked at her cousin. "Will you tell Newton about Pete and the baby?"

"Newton again!"

"Yes, your hunter."

"Not mine by any means. He's gone. Newton's gone home to Littlecomb."

Mary started to say something, then changed her mind. Instead, "Sky looks like one big warm bowl, doesn't it?"

"I haven't paid it much attention lately. The sky circle."

Mary nodded. The two women stared off at something beyond the range of Grandmother Mountain, intent, waiting for the circle to bring them home, make them for a minute, as round and finished as the world.

Chapter THIRTY-FIVE

Her hands were full when the phone rang. Towel over one shoulder Callie snapped up the top button on Will's sleeper. She put him down on an indigo blanket next to his favorite fuzzy stuffed rabbit and picked up the portable receiver on the fifth ring.

It was Newton. Callie sucked in her breath and sank to the floor cross-legged. "Where are you?"

"I have to talk to you. I'm calling from my mom's."

"You're still in Littlecomb?" She was let down.

"I did it, Cal. I told Nat and George off. Some other things came out and the detective, that Hal Rendell, he knows I didn't hurt Mrs. Waters. Turns out it was everyone but me. Nat, George, and Ralph Waters. Even the school seemed to conspire against her. A window fell on her head."

"Now wait," protested Callie. "Our old school house did not want Mrs. Waters dead. Who did it to her?"

"Okay, I'm getting carried away. It didn't just fall. I'll tell you more when I see you."

"Where were you when you found out?" Callie cupped the phone in both hands. She had to picture this. It was important.

"At the Lounge. Just a few hours ago George blubbered about the fire. And Natty, he stood there in a stew until finally he started talking, too. They got in a fight, the two of them. George jumped on Nat's back."

Not a little bewildered at what had transpired, Newton shifted his weight off his wounded leg. Standing barefoot at the screen door in the kitchen of the house in Littlecomb, he noticed the morning glories that climbed the wire fence on his ma's vegetable garden. Closing up before his very eyes, the blue flowers hung limp and dark in the twilight. "It was hard seeing George like that," he told Callie. "Him sobbing about how he never meant for all this to happen. I felt badly for him."

Callie pressed a palm to her forehead. Thank you, thank you, she prayed silently.

"Callie?"

"I'm here."

Newton stared through the screen door past the clothesline and the vegetable garden. The thicket was dusky. Only the loose round tangle of honeysuckle caught the light. "I want to be here, I mean *there*," he laughed, flustered. "On the mountain with you. I want to propose to you, properly, that is."

"Oh!" For a moment Callie was entirely happy. Then, more uncertainly she asked, "What would you do up here?"

"Find work. Be alive with you. See what it's like not to live outdoors?"

Callie worried. Newton had told her he didn't want to go back to Barnes Utility Plant, but he had no other prospects she could think of. Callie moved away from the crib and walked over to the large windows in her apartment. She made a point of speaking lightly.

"What, no camping? No tent?"

"Tent's gone. The bear took it." Newton closed his eyes. "The bear took me for all I was worth. Go ahead and say it."

"What?"

"That I had no right to hunt her like I did. I don't understand exactly what she is but I know that I trespassed." Newton looked up into the coming darkness.

There was quiet on both ends of the wire, after which Callie asked, "Is it a clear night in Littlecomb? What kind of sky?"

Newton was listening for a second to the floorboards creak overhead. It was Betty on her way down to the kitchen. He threw open the screen door and stepped outside, dragging the long phone cord with him.

"It's clear."

"And there's a breeze?"

"More like a wind. Stirring up good."

"I like to picture that," Callie said. "The wind blowing your mother's bright clothes up on the line."

"You'd be surprised," said Newton evenly. "Ma's line is empty."

As soon as she hung up Callie felt anxious. She puttered for several hours and was glad when it was bedtime. She couldn't find a nightgown that hadn't been burped on or milk spilled by the baby. Callie settled on her red long johns. She yanked out her ponytail holder and let her hair fall down her back. She cranked her windows open, then closed them again. She checked on Will several times. He was sleeping soundly. Callie was so tired she didn't bother with the foldout sofa bed so she got herself a blanket and slept on top of the couch.

Two hours and very little sleep later, she sat up. Her apartment door had creaked open. Was it the wind? In a fogged state she heard a deep swishing voice, and it was hardly the wind.

"Callie, I'm here."

She smiled slowly.

The rangy figure with the curly hair and restive brows stood at the edge of the living room ten seconds before flying to her.

"It is you!" She was in a daze.

"I'm sorry."

"For what?"

"I couldn't stay away. I had the key you gave me."

I need to make sure this is right, Callie thought. One more minute of hugging him and she knew. "Come sit with me," she said. Callie went over to the sofa. Newton limped over and eased down with her. Right now he felt no pain whatsoever.

"You asked me what I would do if I came here to live."

At that moment Callie did not care, so long as he was there with her.

"Remember when Mary told us this town needs fishing guides? Well, that's part of my plan. I could be a fishing guide. And that's not all. I'm going to take my bank savings and set up a sporting goods store here. Callie, I want to do it right. We'll have handmade fishing rods."

"Yours! You were really good, Newton."

"I'll do a whole line of specialty fly rods, you know, composite strips of bamboo put together."

"They'll be collectors' items." Callie was matter-of-fact.

"Wait until you see the fishing tackle in this store. Every kind, the best possible."

"Did you forget to say hunting gear?" She had to ask.

"Maybe I don't need that kind of gear any more," he said slowly. "I don't know though. Been a hunter so long."

"You make it sound like a thousand years."

"That's right." He smiled at her.

Chapter THIRTY-SIX

Spoons was in his element. He was telling stories at the Big Springs Lounge, and tonight there was no George or Natty to take him home early. He glanced out the one window of the Lounge at a spangled dogwood outside. He looked closer and saw a basket of spindly branches. A ripe old moon hung in its balance.

Until their court dates, Nat and George were restricted to home, or attendance at the A.A. meetings the court had ordered. Spoons had noticed that the older brother was taking to it better than Nat, but then George was always the more honest of the two.

"It's a fact!" Spoons rasped. "It's a fact our Newt is the sharpest hunter up and down this county." The old man raised his chin, and puckered. "Folks here is plain forgetting that my grandson went after the biggest black bear in America."

"How come we just hear these rumors," Gib said dubiously. "How come it isn't reported in the hunting pamphlets?"

"You got to take my word for it," Spoons said, shaking his head at the very idea that Gib Setter, his long time buddy with whom he played checkers every Wednesday night, had doubts about Newton's bear hunt.

"I believe what folks are saying about Newt's bear," Elijah chimed in.

"The way I see it," Spoons leaned across Gib Setter, and narrowed his eyes thoughtfully at Elijah and Hal Rendell sitting next to him, "that bear was gallopin', roaring, and laffin' – "

"Laughing?" Gib curled his lip in disbelief.

"That's what I said. Laffin' and gallopin' straight through the brush, straight for Newton. Crackin' and slammin' down bushes. Laffin' and *roaring* until the second Newt took hold of the ole shooter." The old man sighed heavily. Everyone's eyes were on him. "Newton, he done the kind of trackin' that haunts an old hunter's dreams."

Will demanded to be fed at midnight. Afterwards, Callie eased the sleep sodden baby off her breast. Her baby book said she should make him fall asleep in his own bed, but Callie saw no wrong in letting him slip off, happy and sated with milk. She settled him in the crib. His eyes were closed in contented half moons, his upper lip gently throbbing from nursing. Newton and Callie looked down at him for a few moments and then tiptoed backwards out of that corner of the room.

The two of them had been up talking most of the night and they were deep into the final events leading to Theresa's death. Newton was in a living room chair and Callie sat on the floor with her legs under her, a pillow at one side. "Those sad people," she said.

"Who?"

"Ralph Waters. George and Nat. Jack. All of them except Ralph, waiting to stand trial."

Neither Callie or Newton wanted to talk about the punishment that would be meted out to Jack. It wasn't easy to speak of the person who had killed their friend, Pete. Of course he was also the father of Callie's first child, and she knew there would be that to deal with, in time.

"They won't get off easy," said Newton. "Not even slippery Nat. He swears he didn't know it was me that night." Newton touched the place on his leg where Nat shot him. "He uses a similar lame argument for having struck Theresa Waters at the school, although the first time around he said differently. We'll see. Nat's not the only one. George has plenty to answer to, but it looks like he's trying to come clean about what he's done.

"That's good to hear," Callie said, "but about Nat, what do you suppose Mrs. Waters thought when she ran into him coming around the corner of the school?"

"I'm sure she never imagined he would bang her on the head with a yardstick. And that was nothing compared with what happened next, her own mad husband ramming the window down on her head. Ralph admitted it in a scrawled note Pete found in the man's house. Funny how Detective Rendell refused to believe it of Mr. Waters. But Pete never gave up the scent."

Callie crouched forward, lynx-like on her feet. "All right, Ralph dealt the final blow, but I say all three guys chased that lady to her death, even though they weren't in on it, together. The odds were against her that night." Callie sighed. "Theresa's heart was crushed a long time ago, back when Ralph destroyed so many of her paintings."

"Is it possible she forgave him his transgressions?" His voice was anxious.

Callie looked at him, thinking that she had no idea what this woman felt in the end. She did know, on the other hand, exactly what Newton was waiting for. She breathed deeply. "I forgive you, Newton."

"All my cover ups, the secrets I kept from you?"

"The world is full of secrets," she waved a hand.

When he winced she was surprised. "Tell me," she said.

"I can hide nothing from you," he moaned.

She curled a strand of hair around her forefinger. "It's not hard to see. Your brows are flexing like biceps."

"It's my brothers," he frowned, "and the way they hate me."

"They don't," Callie said quickly. "Confused by you, that's what they are. Always have been. All your questions about how the Denmans have been raised are threatening to them. You have more resources than Natty and George ever will, you must know that."

"How could they betray me?"

"Expect less of people, Newton. Then they do something nice or loving, and you're surprised."

"And then there's you," he laughed, bemused. Newton leaned against Callie, his arm against hers. "You I love so easily it's spooky. You promise no more hibernating?"

She waffled. "Well, maybe only one more time."

He looked at her. "And just what does that mean?"

Now it was her turn to be embarrassed. She struggled for a moment with her feelings. Everything that had happened with her own body during this last pregnancy made sense after she and the bear had communed that one last time. Winoshca had been right. Callie was different. She was no bear, to be sure, but she had been given unusual features by the Great Spirit.

Speaking of secrets," she said to Newton, and then rephrasing, "in a way it never was a secret, but all this time I wasn't seeing clearly. Newton, remember how the bear and I connected in the clearing in the woods? I can't reveal everything right now, but I do know that one day I will be the parent of a girl with unusual powers, part bear, part human. I hadn't understood when I first used to go climb the tree and speak to the bear, I wasn't listening properly, not with all my animal instincts. I thought that my pregnancy with Jack would bring a powerful girl infant, but no. It was about you and me, and one day in the future.

"What on earth?" Newton laughed nervously. He should tune out this wild talk of hers. It made no sense, and yet every time he had resisted her or the bear, he'd been off the mark. He relented and listened to her words about how their future child would change the face of the earth. Something about her conviction gave him courage.

"But how? What powers? Tell me more about this baby girl?" he begged to know.

"I wish I could say, but we need her here," Callie ended simply.

The two had moved outside to the lawn chairs purchased by Callie at Tusca Drugs. They sat on her balcony facing the stand of pitch pines across the street. Behind the trees rose Grandmother Mountain. Each minute the shadows in the steep canyon saddle shifted. I lived in that shadow, thought Newton.

Quick shudders, strong blue lighted mountain, thought Callie. Watching the first glimmer of day, she felt a pang of relief, and then sudden compassion for Ralph and Theresa Waters. "If Ralph had lived, he'd be going to jail or pleading insanity. As for our old art teacher, I feel a little guilty. Until the news of her death I hardly gave her a thought."

"I did," said Newton. "I remember us painting up a storm in her art classes." He stood up. "You did a great sketch of our treefort, and me waving down at Mrs. Waters. Can you believe it? I found that same drawing in Pete's notebook."

Callie nodded, thinking of how Pete in his last moments had directed Newton to go through his desk papers and unearth the notebook on Theresa's death.

"There are two weird things about that drawing," said Newton. "I mean, how did Pete get hold of it?"

"I mailed it to him." Callie enjoyed his look of surprise.

"But you signed it *Newton Denman*, as if I had drawn it."

"I wanted Pete to understand that you and Miss Waters had made up, become friends again."

"Hmmmnnn."

"I had never signed my original drawing, so it was easy enough to make a box of vines with your signature in it. You see, I was certain you didn't have the nasty attitude towards her that your brothers insinuated. I remember how they built it up way back when."

She smiled broadly.

"You are a tampering lady, Miss Major."

"Sorry. You needed the help."

"You can keep the drawing of the treefort." He shifted his eyes away from her. "The real fort is gone."

After a while she reached for his hand, and he said, "It was right after getting the picture you sent him that Pete got ready to go to Grandmother Mountain." He glanced at Callie rising to her feet. "By then Pete knew for sure that you didn't do it. He came up here to help you." She was thinking about how or when she'd be ready to tell Newton about her long ago first child.

"He was okay, Pete was," Newton said.

"Yes, he was." She did not add that she had thought about Pete over the years even when she told herself not to, and Callie would not easily forget their anguish together in that union out west. And now his being gone signaled to her a whole way of life fading away. In many respects Pete was an old fashioned fellow. Newton, too. It was part of what attracted her to him, but he had more resilience than Pete. Newton had plenty of give, while Pete had used himself up dwelling on what his actions had wrought, and moping about the disturbing changes he perceived being wrought in the world. Had he, in the end, given himself credit for having saved Newton's life and tenaciously figuring out what happened to Theresa Waters? Callie liked to think that yes, it had brought him some measure of peace.

She stepped up to the railing, placed her hands there and leaned out. She was looking at the line of trees across the road. "I could swear those pitch pines have grown taller than most of them do."

Newton smiled. "Maybe it's all the rainfall in global warming? There you see, hope for us all." Newton saw a far away look in her eye, and wondered if she had heard him.

Callie watched the trees tilt in the wind. "I did read somewhere that what forests we have left are growing taller. I'd say they're trying to remind us how much they need to be here.

In the Big Springs Lounge, Spoons looked up at the remarkable, twisting antlers of the buck on the wall. Once, a newcomer to the bar had exclaimed that surely an artist must have carved those antlers from wood.

"A deer like that," Spoons said to anyone who would listen, "is such a beauty it makes me mournful. And I should know. I brought the critture down."

Elijah Jones and Gib Setter turned in surprise. "I never thought you were a trophy hunter," said Elijah.

"I'm ashamed of it," the old man whispered.

"I thought you loved a good deer track," said Gib.

"It's the hoof of the critture, what makes me sad. Ever looked at one after you brought the deer down? Each hoofprint is a split heart."

Gib Setter coughed. Someone called for another pitcher of beer. The door swung open, disturbing the near darkness of the Lounge. There was commotion, and Spoons felt a hand on his shoulder. It was Betty Denman.

"Daughter!" Spoons checked his watch and saw that it was nine o'clock. "I never thought I'd see you come for me here."

"It's time, Pa."

"Well, I don't mind. Always did like being escorted by a pretty lady."

Gib Setter called out as the old man and his daughter-in-law moved towards the door. "Don't let it slip your mind that we're set for checkers on Wednesday."

"Have I ever forgotten?" He left the bar on Betty's arm.

They drove home in George's truck, it being the vehicle that worked best these days. As they went up the walk together Spoons said to Betty, "I enjoy playing checkers with Gib Setter. Did you know that he's been cheatin' me at the game right in my own living room these past forty-two years."

"That's terrible."

"I end up winning anyhow. Gib is a lousy cheat."

Betty smiled. Lately, and in a small way, she was introspective. This was new to her. There were moments when she wondered if she had wronged her sons. It didn't seem possible. She loved them so.

As she opened the door and waited for the old man to catch up, an odd image crossed her mind. It was of her son, Newton, walking out from under a pine tree in the snow, smiling at her, as if he had a secret to share. As if he might trust her again.

Spoons took his time coming up the walk, stopping once or twice until he felt the wind soft and white, nudging him along.

Moving to the thicket outside the home of the Denmans, the wind teased the brambles and whipped up the honeysuckle where the old treefort once stood. Launched, she blew through the cornstalks, whistling uphill to where the scavenger dogs passed through on their way to the creek. Tonight the spring blow missed nothing, brushing upright the coats of the howling dogs, snapping through Littlecomb and west towards the Alleghenies where it flitted in the cow pastures outside Tuscatanning, powered through the low mmmm-mmmmm of the Black Angus herd, and swung into town.

Newton and Callie were still talking as if their lives depended on it. He had joined Callie at the railing, one hand resting lightly on hers.

"I read a funny phrase a while back. It was the title on a hunting magazine: The Tracking Heart."

"Just that?"

Newton took her hand and traced the lines on her palm. "Who or what is a tracking heart?"

"That's easy. It's the bear. She came after both of us."

"It's you, really," said Newton with undisguised appreciation. "I feel as if you've followed my tracks forever."

They looked at each other, and Newton said, "Let's go inside."

He turned the sofa into a double bed, and the ranger opened the casements on either side of the triptych windows. "To let in the mountain air," she said to Newton. Then she went to her cedar chest and pulled out a present that he had given her. She placed a furred cub muff, black and gleaming on the pillows. Outside, all was still, and then as if returned to her rightful place, an old familiar voice rose up, and there was no mistaking whose it was, and what sweet roaring sounded through the pitch pines.

Melissa Croghan lived in Pennsylvania for twenty-three years, and currently divides her time between Connecticut and Mackinac Island. Her award winning work is published in nationally distributed magazines, and she holds an M.A. and Ph.D. in American Literature from the University of Pennsylvania. She lives with her family and animals at the edge of the woods and is always on the lookout for the bear.

CPSIA information can be obtained at www.ICGtesting.com
Printed in the USA
LVOW081853051212

310235LV00007B/785/P